# Praise for
# *Songs of Shadow, Words of Woe*

"A fucking beauty of a book, every story brilliant. I loved this collection. Matthew R. Davis makes fiction seem real. These characters, these places, live on the page, so that it hurts like hell to read about them." —Kaaron Warren, award-winning author of *The Underhistory*

"*Songs of Shadow, Words of Woe* is testament to Davis's ability to write insidious horror stories that ooze into your subconscious and catalyse insecurities and fears you didn't even know you had. On more than one occasion, I found myself wondering if a particular story was written about me and my doubts, discomforts, and neuroses. Basically, he's really fucking good at writing horror stories, and you should read this." —Zachary Ashford, author of *Polyphemus*

"Unafraid to bleed onto the page, Davis peels back the skin of diverse Aussie countercultures, cracking open the ribcage to expose the raw beating heart within. A dead-set banger of a collection, these shadow songs are monstrous, melancholy, and metal as all get-out." —J. Ashley-Smith, Shirley Jackson Award-winning author of *The Measure of Sorrow*

"Davis skilfully shifts from classic ghost story to eldritch horror to modern thriller, showcasing a deep understanding of the genre. Finding a story that can genuinely frighten a reader is a rare treat, and this collection offers that experience in spades." —Belinda McDonald, *Aurealis Magazine*

"*Songs of Shadow, Words of Woe* is yet another example of Davis's ability to subvert expectations and turn the horror genre inside out. Stories that make your flesh crawl, but executed so beautifully in the writing that you're left with a feeling of admiration, as well as a bitter taste in your mouth. A superb collection worthy of any horror collector's bookshelves." —Kayleigh Dobbs, Imadjinn-nominated author of *The End*

"Elegant, frightening, and so delightfully strange, this isn't just a collection – it's a cabal. Matthew R. Davis confidently takes your hand and guides you into the dark with stories that range from the uncanny to the moving. Come to *Songs of Shadow, Words of Woe* to be disturbed. Come for its regionality. Come and read, then grin your nastiest grin. Davis reminds us that there are many shades of delight to be found in quality horror fiction... but he knows the best are inky and reflect little to no light." —Aaron Dries, author of *Dirty Heads* and *A Place for Sinners*

"*Songs of Shadow, Words of Woe* by Matthew R. Davis is a powerhouse collection filled with rock and roll, the uncanny, the unsettling, and the all-out terrifying. A few stories had me looking over my shoulder to see what was lurking in the dark corners of my room. Fans of horror and the weird will be riveted as they are pulled into a reality where songs bring about revenge, mysterious figures haunt you from memories and photographs, and films are more than what they seem..." —Jo Kaplan, Shirley Jackson Award-nominated author of *When the Night Bells Ring*

"Davis's characters are washed up on the lee shores of myth, both ancient or modern, or music, or film production, or the treacheries of language. "I Do Thee Woe" unfolds with a darkly meta chortle, "Vision Thing" with an urgent intimacy, "Andromeda Ascends" stutters with a guilty conscience. Terrifying and humane, spanning eons and fathoms, each story in this new collection is spellbinding, wise, and courageously turns the cracked mirror on the most breakable character of all—the creator." —J.S. Breukelaar, award-winning author of *Collision: Stories* and *Remedy*

# Songs of Shadow, Words of Woe

## Matthew R. Davis

**JOURNALSTONE**
YOUR LINK TO ARTIST TALENT

ISBN: 978-1-68510-154-1 (sc)
ISBN: 978-1-68510-155-8 (ebook)
Library of Congress Catalog Number: 2025947138

First printing edition: September 19, 2025
Published by JournalStone Publishing in the United States of America.
Cover Design: Don Noble
Edited by Sean Leonard
Proofreading and Cover/Interior Layout by Scarlett R. Algee
Author Photo by Meg Wright/Red Wallflower

JournalStone Publishing
1400 North Wood Rd.
Murphysboro, IL 62966


JournalStone books may be ordered through booksellers or by contacting:
JournalStone | www.journalstone.com

# Contents

"Adelaide seems more eerie by the minute...Adelaide is an ideal setting for a Stephen King novel, or horror film. You know why those films and books are always set in sleepy, conservative towns? Because sleepy, conservative towns are where those things happen. Exorcisms, omens, shinings, poltergeists. Adelaide is Amityville, or Salem, and things here go bump in the night." —Salman Rushdie, Adelaide Writers' Week, 1984

"What we want now in Adelaide are writers and artists who work from the heart of those commonplace suburban streets, who recognise the weirdness of the ordinary, who record it before the version of it we have now is swept away. We want passion and intensity, an art that comes from places like Port Adelaide and Thebarton and Holden Hill; that stays unofficially weird." —Barbara Hanrahan, "Weird Adelaide", *Adelaide Review*, March 1988

# Songs of Shadow, Words of Woe

# Andromeda Ascends

MY SISTER ALWAYS DID have a flair for the dramatic. Day in and day out, she's kicking back against a world of bullshit that she refuses to accept, every conversation a confrontation—I've learned to turn the constant heavy metal and slammed doors and screamed accusations into background ambience, retreating inwards as she acts out her own personal apocalypse. She's always felt she was intended for something more, something better, and all her life she's been looking for a sign that she's right.

So I guess it makes perfect sense that Andy, of all people, should have been down on the beach at half-past four this morning when the night tide threw three tons of decomposing giant up onto the shore.

\* \* \*

I remember now:

Once again, Andy finds it impossible to sleep with all those demons at war inside her head, so she slides out of bed, grabs some things, slips out of our seaside home. She wraiths barefoot across the road, along the esplanade where steel sculptures throw intricate shapes at the tide, and follows the nearest set of cement steps down to the beach. No-one will see her at this hour—it's too early for even the keenest of morning joggers, and any pre-dawn fishermen will be setting up on the jetty a kilometre or so away. Swaddled in one of Dad's old jumpers that she sometimes uses as an oversized nightie or smock, she sits down a few metres back from the incoming high tide—right at the line of demarcation where the dry sand turns moist—and smokes herself a plump doobie. The sea is angry this morning as it hurls itself onto the shore, trying to reach the wall of rocks that keeps it from the esplanade, but Andy is unconcerned by its rage. She has always found the crash of waves calming, and the more violent the better.

The sweet scent of good pot laces the sea-salt that thickens the air, and Andy starts to relax as she sits back with a lit Stuyvesant. The screeches and barks of her personal demons are muted, made harmless by the haze of the dope and the repetitive thrash of the aggressive tide. She toys with the idea of shucking off the too-big jumper and the knickers beneath to lie naked under the stars, spread out like a sacrifice to the pinpoints that glint in the dark sky like unblinking eyes. That sometimes titillates, but not tonight.

Soon, the sand is starting to feel a little *too* comfortable. Andy hates the idea of sleeping here, unconscious and vulnerable to attack, and she doesn't want to wake up in a few hours' time with some old coot's dog sniffing her face. She rises on numb legs and prepares to walk the short distance back to her bed, glancing out over the frothing teeth of the waves one last time, and that's when she sees the giant.

The dark colossus is riding the high tide in toward her, its long, blunt nose making her think of a bomb falling across the world and into her lap. Andy realises this behemoth is going to hit the beach directly in front of her and stumbles backwards, conflicting thoughts rasping in her mind like duelling swords: *this is what you wanted/not like this.* She yelps and falls back onto her rump into a clot of seaweed, defenceless, as that inscrutable missile of matter washes up onto the wet sand like a ship run aground and comes to a halt not ten feet away.

Andy stares between her splayed legs at the huge and uncomfortably phallic mass, wondering if her unwitting sacrifice has been averted—if some unseen Perseus has struck the beast dead before it can take her. The tide tugs at the dark heap but cannot convince it to return to the deeps, and she soon understands it will move no farther.

Curiosity overcomes unease. Andy clambers to her feet and approaches the giant, grasping for words to help her process this development, and the best she can come up with is *fuuuuuuck.*

The newcomer is around twenty feet long and eight feet tall, and its colour is hard to define in the dark—it looks black as a frostbitten foot, but it may be another shade of gangrene such as rot-brown or bruise-violet. Its rubbery hide is slick and slack to the touch, as though it might slide right off like a loose jacket if pulled firmly enough. Its body is roughly analogous to that of a whale, which Andy first assumes it to be, but there are no visible flukes or flippers and no sign of a face—she cannot find its eyes, and if it has a mouth, it must be on the underside of its blunt end, hidden by the sand. The mass reeks of fresh salt and nauseating putrefaction, with a hint of something else she finds familiar but cannot name.

Andy is not frightened of the strange beast now, merely awed and deeply curious. She sits in the wet sand beside what she assumes is its head, letting the tips of the tide wash up her bare legs, and she starts to talk. If a passer-by happens upon the scene, they will rightly assume her to be high, and put the ramblings down to no more than teenage indulgence. But only I understand that it's more than just joint-induced gibberish. She's spoken to me of the dreams, too—dreams that have swallowed her sleep for years on end, that have kept her searching further and further afield for her purpose. Dreams that she now believes have been preparing her for one long-awaited transcendental moment.

This visitation isn't it—just a harbinger. But she knows now that she's on the right track, and pulling closer.

Of course, Andy never told me this story in such detail. While she was out on the beach experiencing this strange epiphany, I was tucked up tight in bed, fast asleep—but I *dreamed* everything that happened, as if she were streaming it live to my mind. I forgot most of it at the time, could grab only tenebrous tendrils of what I'd seen, but it's very clear to me now. That's how I know, because she wasn't the only one born with an intense capacity for night visions. I've always had them too, and sometimes, when the dreaming is strong, I can share them.

My sister saw this encounter as a revelation. I should have taken it for a warning. But mythology has never been my strong point, so I had no idea what would come of that meeting: my sister Andromeda, and the monster from the sea.

\*\*\*

I've been having the water dreams for the past three nights. They used to be my sister's thing, her ongoing quest for meaning. I appear to be growing into them at last.

I go deeper and deeper in these dreams, hundreds and hundreds of metres beneath the waves—so far that I can't even see the surface, if ever I look for it, and yet somehow there is light by which to see.

The pressure at this depth ought to crush me into a horrific mass of compressed flesh and bone and organs, but I resist its brutality with ease.

Tonight, I've reached the vast sandy plain of the sea floor, chasing a flash of electric blue. I'm swimming with strong, easy strokes and breathing the water as though it were air, though I don't seem to have grown gills or any other appropriate apparatus. I'm naked, but I always am in these reveries, and none of my co-stars ever seem to notice.

There's only one other person in these dreams. It's just she and me, dancing apart in the depths of the sea, and I can never quite seem to catch up to her. Like me, she is nude; unlike me, she has a flickering fish's tail in place of legs, and shoulder-length blue locks dart about her face as she moves. Sometimes she will stop and allow me to draw near, as she is doing now, and the dream is so vivid that up close I can see the dark regrowth coming in at the roots of her hair, the glimmer of fish-scale nipples atop her small breasts, the punky touch of the rusted ring that pierces one fluke of her tail. We hover in place and I see she has a cigarette in one hand, impossibly alight, on which she drags before blowing a stream of tiny bubbles my way; each little bauble contains a shifting curlicue of grey smoke, is a miniature crystal ball that speaks of a murky future. And I know her—her face is very familiar to me, easily sketched in by my sleeping brain—but I do not know her name.

I think of her as Blue.

She's smiling, but I couldn't tell you why, or what that smile portends. Is she leading me somewhere, deeper by the night, or am I driving her there without knowing it? Will she let me catch her in the end, and if so, will I then prove to be the one who is caught?

I look past her and see we're about to enter a forest of kelp, ragged streamers of nauseous chartreuse and umber that stretch hundreds of feet up toward the unseen surface. As if to answer an unspoken question, Blue turns and propels herself into the forest with a single powerful stroke of her tail.

I follow. The sickly fronds grow close enough together that their blades sweep across our bare skin like sweaty fingers as I trail Blue deeper into the watery woods, and I cannot help but think of fairy tales. Is there some sleeping beauty at the heart of this, some castle or casket that waits to be opened once more?

We soon reach the other side of the algae forest, where the seabed drops off sharply and shades into a much deeper darkness—a crater at the centre of the world. A ring of fishbelly-pale anemones fringes this underwater valley, waving their whorls of blood-red tentacles to either tempt me in or warn me off. Puzzled, I swim over the gaping mouths of the anemones in a few short strokes and peer into the abyss, curiously ignorant of the Nietzschean echo in the back of my mind that reminds me the abyss might choose to peer back.

Is this what Andy sought all those years? Is this what Blue has been leading me to, or what I've been flushing her toward? I turn to read an answer on her face and find only a disturbance of silt and water behind me, as if something has swept through and collected her in its jaws. A thin russet cloud spreads from where she hovered and slowly settles toward the edge of the abyss, where the anemones greedily reach for it with their crimson tendrils.

I turn back to the gaping darkness below me, and a beam of bright but murky green erupts from the centre of the pit. It roves around the walls and rim of the crater like a watchman's torch, emanating from a fixed point directly ahead and below. In the minimal backwash of this light, I see it is projected from a tall black finger that thrusts up from the sludge at the heart of the abyss. I recognise it as the corrupted conception of a lighthouse—and furthermore, a lighthouse I know from many years ago. The original tower used to stand at the farthest point of the coast nearby, painted a bold white rather than the silt-and-shit shade of its shadow below, and as a child, I'd felt comforted by its constant vigilance as its bright eye roved the sea in slow sweeping curves.

But this ray of sour light is not moving slowly now, nor is it restricted to a basic revolution. That febrile green shaft shoots about the abyss with intent—it is looking for something, or perhaps someone. My sense of unease triples, and I turn back to the kelp forest to be sure no wolves of the sea have slunk through it to creep up on me, and when I return my gaze to the abyss—

My world blazes a thick and sordid green as the beam finds me and fixes me in place like a butterfly to a board, piercing me, holding me. Knowing me.

I am found.

* * *

Like everyone else, I am fascinated by the rotting giant that appeared on the beach three days ago.

The object has caused quite a stir, in part because no-one can be quite sure what the thing is, or was. Word got around after that strange mass beached itself before my sister, lending her a brief celebrity she wore like a shirt of thorns; everyone within driving distance got a selfie and a story to tell, and then the enigmatic corpus just washed back out to sea the next night while no-one was looking. There followed much discussion about the taxonomy of this mysterious visitor, and how it came to be on our beach, but I have a question that no-one else seems to be asking: what was my seventeen-year-old sister doing on the shore at half-past four in the morning? I have an odd feeling that I should know the answer, but only shadowy impressions surface when I think on it: hands tucked into too-long sleeves, smoky scents both sweet and acrid, a wet bomb dropping.

Andy is sitting on the balcony of our family home that overlooks the esplanade, her dark head crowned by the white caps breaking on the beach below. Dusk is fast approaching and everything looks unreal in the low light, like a dream. She's plopped herself down on a padded seat in one of those curious contortions of which only teenage girls seem capable, smoking a cigarette—Mum and Dad have long since given up trying to plead or punish her out of the habit—and frowning at a hardcover book propped open on her stomach. She seems even more distracted since encountering the thing on the shore, trying to work out what it means for her dreams and her future, and she doesn't look up when I speak.

"So...what exactly *were* you doing down by the shore at four-thirty in the morning?"

"Selling sea shells," she replies, without tearing her eyes from the pages. "Did you know that rhyme was about a girl called Mary Anning, who collected and sold fossils to support her family? She actually discovered the plesiosaur, but never mind all that. You know much about Greek mythology?"

That's surely a rhetorical question. I'm the quiet and well-behaved sibling and yet I've never been much for reading, whereas she, the fire-breathing tearaway, is rarely to be found without a book within arm's reach. A memory within a memory: fourteen-year-old Andy is caught drinking on the foreshore with a group of university guys, and when the cops drag her home to face my parents, she has her canvas satchel slung over one rebellious shoulder, a corner of Ovid's *Metamorphoses* peering out from beneath the loose flap like an impassive witness to the chaos.

I sit down on the other padded seat, resigned to a lecture, and Andy carries on.

"Poseidon wants to punish Cassiopeia for being a stuck-up bitch and trash-talking the Nereids, right, so he demands her daughter. I get that she was vain about her girl's looks and all, so sure—have the poor slut chained up and sacrificed to a sea monster. Sins of the mothers, Cassie gets her comeuppance, yadda yadda yadda. But why do the myths assume said monster wants to *eat* the girl? If she's so beautiful that her own mum claims she's hotter than the sea nymphs, wouldn't Poseidon want to get in on some of that action? Those Greek gods were a bunch of horny, rapey bastards, and Poseidon was no different—so you'd think that Cetus, the great beast from below, would be the P-man himself, come to whisk the gorgeous sacrifice away to a life of scrubbing the sea floor and popping out the odd demigod. But no, because Perseus comes swooping along with Medusa's head—you've at least heard of Medusa, right? —and turns old Cetus into stone. Not Poseidon, then. So, was Cetus himself just looking for a snack, or was he after a bride? A friend, even? It must get real lonely down there in the darkest depths."

Andy takes on a pensive cast, drawing thoughtfully on her cigarette, and even though I have no idea what she's talking about, I know what she's thinking—all those deep-dreaming nights she's gone below the waves, beyond the reach of the sun, searching, searching. That far down, she's told me, the darkness is as vast and unknowable as the space that stretches out to infinity above us. You could travel through that freezing, inhospitable murk for years and not see another living thing, or any other kind of thing at all. Which is not to say that something isn't there, unseen in the black just ahead of your every stroke, reaching out in return.

\* \* \*

I'm thinking how odd it is to be back by the water. I haven't been so close since I graduated high school and ran away into the heart of the city as if I blamed the sea for what happened. Now, on a whim I can scarcely afford, I've leased a townhouse overlooking the esplanade, not two kilometres from where I grew up.

I don't go to visit—Mum and Dad are both gone, and the house only outlasted them by a few months. Every plank and beam and board of my former home, every stitch and stroke and seam, has been torn away and replaced. My childhood memories are now transient, and maybe that's why they've returned to roost in me.

Andy's weighed heavily on my mind of late, and it seems to me that I've returned to where I last saw her in a belated attempt to deal with her ghost. Not that she's any such thing, of course, but I've been haunted by her absence for seventeen years. She's been gone as long as she was here in the first place. She might still be alive somewhere, somehow—I've idly imagined her living in Cuba under an assumed name, smoking Cohibas and drinking mojitos as she pens gritty intellectual novels—but in my heart, I know Andromeda is long dead.

I sit in the open lounge of my temporary home and try to distract myself from my sister by wondering at the disparity between this place and the house where I grew up. My childhood home was old when we moved in, cracks in its pale green walls covered over by the tasteful watercolour nudes my father liked, the lounge stuffed with brown couches and rainbow antimacassars as if my parents' sense of aesthetics had been frozen in time for twenty years. In direct contrast, this townhouse is a modernist's wet dream, sleek and functional without an ounce of soul showing in its spotless surfaces and abundant right-angles; the colour-coded furnishings are square and soft, squat and ugly. There are no curtains in the lounge and the three walls that face the sea are almost entirely glass. From here, I can look out over the shifting plain of water to the horizon, and above that, the windows are filled with sky. It's like staring into a colossal open mouth that is swallowing the world.

Sick of inertia, I throw on a jacket and brave the outside world. The front yard is a brief cement ramp that slopes sharply down to the road; across those two narrow lanes is the esplanade, its winding paved path frequently breaking open into stone staircases that march down to the beach along diagonal handrails. I carefully descend the sand-dusted steps and make my way across that pale plain, hands in pockets, staring idly out over the water. The ambience of the sea should be comforting, but it sounds to me too much like a storm building.

Late on this dreary afternoon, the beach appears almost deserted. As I stumble nearer the spot where the sand is eaten entirely by stone, where the café that used to be a leisure centre sits atop the outcropping, I see still figures gathered on the rough fingers of rock that point out to sea. The waves are lapping at the feet of a tall, slender model who appears naked until I see she's wearing a flesh-coloured shift; she stands elevated above the photographer and the assistant who's holding up a light deflector, her hands reaching out in invitation as she's worshipped by a single adoring eye.

This is my first time in the Mohka Café and my eyes follow the walls around, noting where changes have been made to the leisure centre of old. The short bar that used to serve free water and lemonade has been extended into a bohemian service counter covered in handwritten signs and pieces of old nautical debris, the table tennis arena replaced by a seating area where patrons may recline in cushioned wicker chairs to drink their coffees and flick through thick lifestyle magazines that are more advertisements than content. I wander toward the counter, resolving to buy something since I've gone to the trouble of walking here.

My order for a hot chocolate is taken by the only employee in sight, a young woman with slender wrists and sea-green eyes. As she prepares my drink, her willowy figure slips into a casually cool pose the model outside could never have pulled off, and we chat while I wait. Beneath her cinnamon body spray, I detect a hint of cigarette smoke. Her limbs are slim and symmetrical, gently freckled, alluring. The front of her short-sleeved work shirt drapes discreet, upright peaks. Her shoulder-length hair is dyed electric blue, and I can see a few weeks of dark regrowth at the roots. I already know I'll be thinking of her again later.

Walking back along the beach, I let the ocean breeze blow across the mouth of my drink to cool its ardour. I hadn't even realised how much I've missed the salted scent of the sea. Ahead of me, I can see the centipedal pose of the local jetty, still walking out into the water after all these years like an ageing surfer. A few kilometres beyond that lies the jut where the old white lighthouse used to stand, and somewhere between those two points is the place where my sister gave herself up to the sea.

I haven't gone back there since. But why else am I here now? My hot chocolate lives up to only half its name by the time I've trudged along the sand, past the jetty, to that fateful patch of beach.

It hasn't changed at all, but what was there to change? It's just sand meeting sea. Sister meeting fate. But it's also end meeting end, like a circle is closing between two memories, creating a ring right here at the water's edge.

Seventeen years ago, Andromeda didn't come home. That wasn't unusual, since she was prone to stay out as long as she liked in whatever company she preferred, so we didn't worry at first. When she made no contact by the end of the next night, my parents called the police, who were familiar with my sister and assumed teenage thoughtlessness to be behind the lack of contact. No-one really became concerned until a beach stroller reported a strange find: the clothes Andromeda had been wearing the last time anyone had seen her, half-buried in the sand at this very spot, a few feet back from the creeping wash.

That's when shit got real. That's when the search began in earnest, police and volunteers combing the beach and the foreshore, Coast Guard boats bobbing out on the endless waves. But no trace of my sister was ever found, from that day to this.

And I believe that's the way she intended it.

\* \* \*

As bereaved as my parents were, I never could shake the insidious impression that they harboured a dark and shameful relief at my sister's disappearance. Andy had always been a problem child, precocious and brimful of piss and vinegar. I think Mum and Dad would have minded a lot less had she directed her towering energies into something productive, like becoming a cello prodigy or a top-level programmer. But Andy was always more interested in bucking authority, getting fucked up, burning everything she touched like she couldn't control the fury within. They loved her dearly, don't get me wrong, but her departure would have felt like the removal of an unstable radioactive element from their lives. It would be insulting to compare Andromeda to a raging cancer in our home, but less so to say she was like a peritonitic appendix that could explode in a shower of acidic poison at any moment.

Sorry, sis. They did love you. And I'll always love you, too.

I'm thinking of one time Andy was grounded—one of many—that saw her confined to her room without supper, fifteen and furious. I'm sneaking her a slice of pavlova from the dinner she's been denied, late at night when our folks have gone to bed to stare at the ceiling and wonder how they'd come to be burdened with such a wilful and chaotic child. Since I'd had no part in her latest bollocking, and since I've brought sweets, she begrudgingly lets me into her room and allows me to sit on the floor as she curls up into the corner of her bed and picks at the pavlova.

Andy's private space is a mass of contradictions, just like her, and I can't begin to fathom half of it. On one wall she's stuck a reproduction of an inscrutable Turner seascape—*Sunrise with Sea Monsters*—beside a chilly blue poster advertising the new American remake of *The Ring*. A copy of Machiavelli's *The Prince* lies face-down on the carpet with its guts splayed open, an issue of *Metal Hammer* spread-eagled atop it with Slipknot leering from the cover. A motley row of plastic figurines stares down from the top of her wardrobe: Snoopy and Skeletor, Animal and Ariel, Princess Leia and Pinhead. Two packets sit side by side on her black-painted dresser, one I recognise as Stuyvesant cigarettes and the other a flowery plastic purse that I suspect holds Period Things. I focus on watching her eat, lest I see anything else that confuses and flusters me.

"They just don't fucking get it," Andy mutters, piercing the pavlova's shell with a deft stab of her spork. "They think this is all just hormonal teenage shit, that I'll settle down and be a good little girl one of these days. It's not that at all! I'm never going to slide into some convenient slot on life's circuit board, because I'm a faulty logic gate, you see? Whenever I'm supposed to say *yes*, I say *no*, and vice versa. They want me to be one and I'm a zero, and when they want me to be a zero, I'm like, *Fuck you, I'm one*. But there *is* something out there for me—I can *feel* it. Every night, I'm searching. But it's hopeless at this level. I have to go deeper, and then deeper still."

I don't quite follow, but then her eyes flick up to mine, and I see something that's almost alien to Andy's emotional make-up: desperation.

"You dream like me too, don't you? Tell me you understand. Surely *you* do. Come on, man. *Please*."

I don't know what she wants from me, but I do know I don't want to get tangled any further in Andy's mess, so I lie. I shake my head and roll sheepish eyes, wondering if she'll swallow the act, trying not to panic. I don't talk about the dreams, ever, to anyone. How could she suspect?

"Should've fucking known," Andy says, her voice as dark as her eyes, and I cringe a little in anticipation of a pavlova facemask. But she just drops the plate onto her doona, stares blankly at the trident-tines of the spork. "It's just me, *always* just me. Alone. There's no-one else. Not even my own *blood—*"

On that word, she stabs the spork into the bare flesh above her knee. The thrust is so sudden and savage that I'm staring at the utensil sticking out of her leg before I know what I'm seeing. She takes her hand away and it stands there upright, reflecting light from her bedside lamp in pulses like a tiny steel lighthouse. I gasp in shock and lift one hand as if to help, and she fixes me with her burning black gaze. Nothing less than catastrophe has ever accompanied that look.

"*Don't,*" she whispers, and the syllable hits hard, like she's pulled the spork out and stabbed it into my heart. "You can go now. Thanks for listening. Thanks for the *pav*, man."

I scramble across the floor and find my feet, tripping over her boots on the way to the door, and I turn to throw one last look back as I leave the room. Andy is flicking the spork with her middle finger like it's a tuning fork, watching it judder in her flesh as it sends unheard vibrations down to her bones.

"When I need your kind of help, brother, I'll let you know," she says.

\* \* \*

She's calling me, but I dare not answer and give myself away. Andy's in the grip of her terrible temper, and if she finds me, I'm in for a world of hurt.

"*You little shit!*"

Why did I think it would be funny to steal her favourite pen, wait for her to look for it, and then walk casually past with the thing stuck up my nostril? It didn't make my nose bleed, but there's a very real possibility that Andy will. I should know better than this by now. It's been hard to get her to pay me any attention since she started writing *Period Things* on the weekly shopping list, sure, but this is tantamount to suicide by sister.

"*You can't hide forever!*"

I held her back for precious seconds by knocking Dad's coat rack over to block the hallway. She couldn't have seen me crawling up on top of the laundry cupboards. I'm lying flat, wishing myself invisible even as I peek as close to the edge as I dare.

Andy stalks into the laundry, her eyes stabbing left and right, searching. She checks the metal doors under the old laundry trough, because I'm small enough to have sought sanctuary in there before. Then she stands back, taking in every detail of the room, her eyes dark and relentless. How can an eleven-year-old girl look so...*dangerous*? Times like this, she doesn't even seem to be herself.

Don't look up. Don't look up. Don't look up.

In a movement that's as inevitable as it is sudden, Andromeda's head swivels my way and her eyes shoot up to the peak of the cupboard, where they meet mine. I'm transfixed, a mouse trapped by a feral cat. She smiles, bleakly certain of the torments to come, and her all-consuming black-eyed stare is piercing me, holding me. Knowing me.

I am found.

\* \* \*

Sweating in my broad townhouse bed, I close my eyes and focus on the sensation thrumming up from the very root of me. She's riding me like an erotic jockey, panting and bucking and clutching at her stiff-tipped little peaks with restless fingers, a strand of blue hair slipping into her open mouth. I lean into my work and feel the crest of the wave rising, rising, and then it crashes down and crushes me into the salty ecstasy of the raging sea.

I get my breath back. The room is silent apart from my own subsiding pants of release. Then I peel myself off the silk sheets and head to the bathroom, where the square sink gargles clear water as I rinse the sea-spray from my stomach. The fluorescent light is sterile and bright and makes everything look as artificial as itself. I can't tell if I'm dreaming I'm awake, or imagining that I'm dreaming, or something else entirely.

Towelling off, I leave the bathroom light on and pad out across the lounge, making my way around the featureless blocks of furniture until I'm standing naked at the front window. It's late, well after midnight, and there are no signs of life down on the esplanade or the beach beyond. Even if anyone were around to look up at my window, chances are all they'd see is a pale smear, a hint of ghost. The waves rippling in to meet the shore are much more subdued than the one I just summoned by my own hand. The moon gives the sea shimmering highlights, but these only serve to contrast with the black and immeasurable bulk that stretches out to the horizon.

My window-wide view of the sea is marred only by the reflection of the bathroom light spilling out into the hallway, a rectangle of light cast upon the glass from behind me. Since the rest of the room is dark, it looks like a pale doorway on the waves off to my right. I'm just looking away from it when someone steps into the frame.

No detail in that reflection, only a silhouette, a hole in the world. The outline is female, as naked as me, motionless and silent—watching me. Dream or not, it strikes me cold all through.

Because Blue was in my head, not in my bed, and I came home alone.

I don't want to turn around and see her any more clearly, and yet I can't pull my eyes from that backlit reflection upon the glass—standing at the edge of my lounge, and also on the restless surface of the sea. I know who it is, of course. You don't need a face or a voice or a scent to recognise family.

The silence drags on, and somehow, I feel just a little safer if I'm the one to break it.

"Were you trying to kill yourself that night?" I ask, looking away from the reflection in case I've provoked some dread response. "Or was it a sacrifice to some monster, like your namesake?"

I hear the patter of bare feet fading on the townhouse floor, and I expect the silhouette to be gone when I glance back at the lounge window. But it's still there, still motionless, inscrutable. Just staring and waiting for the perfect moment to pounce, like she always did.

"You never told me," she says now, quiet and low, and that voice sounds just like it used to. "All those years, and you never told me you had the dreams too."

I shake my head, emphatic.

"Not like mine, then, but so strong. *Stronger.* And you were even more lonely than me."

I shake my head again, the rest of my body following suit. This reeks of me talking to myself. I'm the only one who knows my secrets, and she's dead—ergo, I'm imposing some kind of phantasmal sleepy-time psychology on myself. But now she moves, padding slowly into the lounge like a shadow-clad panther, until only half of her body remains backlit by the bathroom light. I see that half duck down for a moment as if to retrieve something, and then I hear a familiar metallic rasp. There's a point of orange light floating in the black of that silhouette now, and I catch a fresh tang of nicotine.

I don't smoke. There are no cigarettes on the coffee table. Ergo, phantasmal sleepy-time psychology—*please.*

"Let me show you," she whispers. "There's nothing left for you here. I understand exactly how that feels."

It seems all I can do now is shake my head.

"Come below the waves," and now her voice has taken on a tone of seduction, as if that will help her with her own flesh and blood, and never mind that certain voyeuristic memories flare briefly to life, I was a child and merely curious. "Come, and be *known.*"

She ducks out of the lit doorway once more, and now the cigarette's orange eye is gone, too. I'm watching the darkness and waiting to see it move, waiting to hear the stealthy fall of her feet as she crosses the floor toward me. I reach out and place the palm of one hand upon the chill glass of the lounge window.

"I don't think I ever really knew you at all," I'm saying, and I'm still waiting for the end. But there is no silhouette in the hallway door or any closer, and I can feel that her presence is no longer here, just like I could feel it missing when I woke seventeen years ago to find she hadn't come home.

Dreaming again, then. But the window is cool and hard against the soft flesh of my palm. It feels very real.

I drop my arm and walk back across the lounge, wary of being jumped by a shadow at any moment. I'm still trying to shrug that fear off when I smell smoke, and I look down at the coffee table to see the ugly ashtray I made for my poppa twenty-odd years ago. I ended up with it after he died of emphysema and I've lugged it around with me all this time, another piece of useless history, a blunt reminder of the price life demands for its enjoyment. Three butts lie curled up and lifeless to one side of the clay bowl; on the other side is a single cigarette, half-smoked, burning down to the filter as I watch in mute confusion.

I fall into the indifferent arms of the square couch behind me, and I sit and stare as that little flame grows weaker and weaker, and when it winks out of existence, I do, too.

Now I'm waking fast, what feels like a moment later, with the echo of a familiar gunshot in the back of my mind. The front door? I turn to squint in that direction and see it's closed, giving away nothing. I look down at myself. Naked, wrinkled and kinked from sleeping upright on the lounge, all of this clear in the bright morning light that pours in through the uncurtained windows.

So—I walked out here after my internal Blue movie had come to its inevitable conclusion, slipped barefoot into a lucid dream, and then dropped all the way back into sleep here on the couch...right?

I scratch my head, woozy, a little uncertain of reality, and yawn wide enough that my mouth could have fit Poppa's old ashtray inside with room to spare. There it is now, placid and patient on the coffee table, waiting for me to see it. The misshapen clay bowl holds four cigarette butts, three curled and lifeless against one side, another burned out to a fallen column of ash on the other.

I don't smoke. There are no cigarettes on the coffee table.

*Then who—*

I'm stumbling to the bathroom, I'm pissing, I'm washing my face. I notice the light is on and turn it off. Then I'm heading back into my bedroom, looking down at the messy sprawl of silken sheets. I always was a violent sleeper, though I've never admitted the reason to anyone. I sit down on the mattress, considering a further nap to smooth out the creases in my brain, and then I notice a couple of things that will make sleep impossible for some time to come.

The sheets smell of sweat and salt and cinnamon.

A single strand of long hair is curled into a question mark on the pillow, electric blue.

* * *

The cement skin of the jetty is smooth beneath my bare feet. It's night again and the eyes of the lamp-posts that crane over me at regular intervals are dark, blind and useless. The sea washes against the sturdy legs of the jetty in an urgent, hungry rhythm. The moon is a pale doorway in the sky.

I can tell I'm dreaming because I'm naked. I'm cold, too, enough to make me wish for the thousandth time that my sleeping visions weren't so tactile. Why am I here? My subconscious has been led to believe there's a reason, so I might as well play it out and see. I walk farther along the jetty, feeling oddly like I'm being made to, that it's a long thick plank and a shark waits for me at the end of it.

I know the kind of climax these dreams often have, and the thought of it is enough to stop me a few metres from the end of the jetty. This is bullshit. I should conjure up a few pleasant details, weave myself into a happier slumber attended by wishes fulfilled. I am in charge here, am I not?

*Pssst.*

From farther ahead. Over the edge of the jetty's end. Waiting for me in the water.

My feet walk me the rest of the way, a foregone conclusion. I grasp the cool tube of the steel railing and peer over it.

She's down there, looking up at me. Her face is as pale as the skin of a drowned man amongst the black waves that eddy her hair around her head like snakes. Her eyes hold me like the gaze of a gorgon.

"You deserve more than this," she's saying now. "I always thought I did, too—and I was *right*. I always knew it was down there, waiting for me."

I don't have to voice the question.

"The dark star at the bottom of the world."

Seeing her face again, even like this, even in a dream, causes a hollow split to open up in my heart. I feared my sister, sometimes hated her, but I was always in awe of her. And over the last seventeen years, I've missed her in so many ways.

"I love you, brother," she's saying, raising one hand above the surface to clutch beseechingly at me. "Let me show you what love means. So few have ever known the truth that lies in the heart of the sea. But you can change that."

"The truth that lies," I echo. "Lies in the heart of the sea."

"You dream like no-one else," she whispers, her voice as susurrant as the waves that lap around it, break through it. "I could touch the bottom, but *you*—you can touch the world. You've seen the effects your whole life, haven't you? Even here, you've seen them. Your thoughts touched hers, and now she dreams of the deeps too."

That makes some insidious kind of sense I don't want to admit to myself.

"Come below."

I open my mouth to say something, I don't know what—a denial, or prevarication, or maybe even pure dream nonsense about the consistency of whipped cream or something—and her other arm flashes out of the water, up toward me like white lightning. I flinch back from the railing and something long and thin flickers around it, curls tight and flexes for a moment before returning to the sea—something long enough to reach from where she waits, fifteen feet below.

I stay back from the railing. I don't want to see her face now. I don't want to see the truth of her.

*"You little shit! I'm offering you everything! You're the only one who'll do!"*

That pitch sounds a lot less tempting than the one she was working a moment ago. She's shown her hand. And what I just saw flashing upward to pull me down wasn't a hand at all.

*"You can't hide forever!"*

And just like that, I'm snapping awake. It feels like bursting out of slumber as your alarm screams bloody murder. It feels like a slap in the face.

I'm awake. And I'm standing at the end of the jetty, and it's the dead of the night, and I'm naked.

I don't dare crane over the edge to see if my sister's face is still down there, peering up at me from the lazy waves. I'm cold and exposed and I need to get home, *now*. I turn and flee down the jetty, so wildly that I stumble and crash down on the cement, skinning my knees, before I'm up and moving again. I'm sickly certain I'll spot early-morning fishermen staring at me in disgusted disbelief, or flashing police lights approaching along the esplanade, but I'm alone.

So why doesn't it feel that way?

I'm running and running, and the night is blurring into a haze around me like a cheap transition in an old movie, and I'm wondering if I'm awake after all.

\* \* \*

I'm back on the beach again, on my way to find some answers.

Not here, though—the sand stretches out like a desolate plain to where the water waits, biding its time, and no-one else seems to be braving the dreary afternoon skies. I stumble on toward the place where the sand ends and the rocks bite out into the sea, where the leisure centre once occupied hours of my time with video games and Disney films and table tennis. On my way to the café, I glance out at the teeth of the rocks where the waves are breaking into spray. A slender young woman is standing above the worshipful eye of a photographer, and next to that supplicant, another man is holding up a light deflector. The wind whips his square sheet around toward me and the collected sunlight flashes into my eyes. I hold my arm up over my face as if spotted and hurry on by.

I'm walking into Mohka Café, looking for some truth, some certainty to which I can hold hard. I approach the counter, and the only service staff in sight is the young woman I know as Blue. But just how well am I supposed to know her? If she feels a jolt of anything when she spots me—excitement, embarrassment, anger—it doesn't show.

Her poise is muted today. Her general malaise and the shadows under her eyes imply she hasn't been sleeping well. Have I anything to do with that? She gives no indication that my fantasy of picking her up and taking her home was something that actually happened, so neither do I. After paying for my drink, I linger a moment as I try to think of a perfect remark to crack open the silence and clear the air, and she listlessly wishes me a good afternoon. I leave the café with no more idea of what's happened between us than when I entered.

Did I perhaps hear *her* feet padding away that night in the lounge? Was it *her* silhouette I asked about suicide, sacrifice? I shudder to think so, for I may not have imagined old scar tissue on one of those slender wrists. Such a thing would be awkward, insurmountable—but would it be worse if she'd walked out and found me talking to the silhouette of another naked woman? What might she have thought of that? In either case—if she was at my townhouse that night, then little wonder she'd choose not to know me now. If she wasn't, if we are complete strangers, then my fantasies are getting well out of hand.

I'm walking back home, not that you'd call it that. The only house I ever considered home is long gone, and I have none of the comforts associated with such a place—happiness, love, security, company, money. Always alone, I tread this earth like a shiftless ghost. I don't even know why I bother anymore, other than lifelong habit.

It occurs to me that this directionless ennui is what Andy knew, what drove her to distraction and destruction. Finally, I understand something of substance about my sister.

I can't even trust my perception of reality now. If I go back to the café again, will an unfamiliar barista tell me no blue-haired girl has ever worked there? I can't go on like this, living out an endless bad trip that melts the boundaries between real and unreal. I need firm facts—a certainty I can cling to like a barnacle to the leg of the jetty that waits farther down the beach, pointing out to sea as if directing me to my final destination.

\* \* \*

I was running away from my sister and the sea and I tripped and sprawled on the cement of the jetty and now I'm bawling, unable to stop the hot rain from falling down my cheeks. My knees blaze from the impact, but they don't hurt much, not really—the tears are more a reaction to the shock of injury, the sudden blood oozing through my torn skin. My sobs are less a cry for help than a call for solace.

While Dad chastises Andy for being mean, my mother swoops down around me and coos soothing syllables to ease the shock and quiet my cries—loving little nothings like *there there, baby* and *who's my brave little man* and worst of all, the great lie that is *it's okay*. I'm only five, but already I know things are very often Not Okay. Still, the near-religious enormity of her embrace and motherly attentions is enough to start the process of winding down the crying machine. It's the best comfort I know, even better than my *Muppets* blanket, and it never fails to set things right for me. But it makes me wonder why Andy's torments never seem soothed by Mum's consolations, why her sobs are so deep and relentless.

The sun is high in the cornflower-blue sky, circled by seagulls that flap around its circumference like moths courting the ultimate light. The waves sound friendly because we're here to have fun, and other kids are dashing across the sand as they laugh in innocent delight, and I know everything is Okay after all.

I don't know why I see a sudden flash of a black coffin, emblazoned with a crude, childish drawing of skull and crossbones that I know is supposed to represent my mother. And the next words I speak feel wrong somehow, like this memory is being revisited and revised at a later date.

"I miss you," I say.

The seagulls multiply into a swirling storm as they flock in front of the sun, a vortex of furious feathers blocking out the light, and the pale blue shades into a dark, mottled bruise-purple as the children's laughter abruptly cuts off. The day has died, all life leaving it in a flash. The beach is empty, ash-grey, and the water lies very still.

The arms around me grow firmer in their grip, harder, colder.

"I miss you, too," she says. "We should be together, you and I. We've got so much to catch up on. Tell me everything. Every moment, every memory, every single feeling and thought and dream. Share them with me, brother."

I don't dare look up to see what's holding me so close and tight. I struggle a little to test her grip, and find that my body is locked in. There's no escape from this.

"Where did you go?" I whisper.

"Down and down and down, little one. Into the deepest dark you can find on this teeming ball of shit. I found what I was looking for, and let it know me. For seventeen years, everything I'd ever been or seen or known or felt was pored over, explored, relived. The whole of my sad, confused little life was savoured like the finest meal as each infinitesimal detail was thoroughly digested. Imagine that! Even piss must be a fine wine for one who has lacked so long."

"You're scaring me," I whimper, and the grip around me tightens a little as if in reassurance. I am not comforted in the least. Where did Mum go? Skull and crossbones... am I still five?

"Hush now. Be known. You have forever to understand."

The last word opens up as if the mouth speaking it has split wide, and I'm seeing flashes of my sister in old family photographs, and in every one her lips are spreading apart into an abyss that swallows her entire face, and everything in the world is blotted black as something cold and wet and soft closes gently but firmly around the whole of my head.

\* \* \*

Yet another water dream tonight, but this time it skips blue-haired nymphs and lighthouses and jetties—or at least I don't recall any of that—and it cuts right to the chase.

I'm plunged feet-first into achingly cold water, stunned, flying fast and down into the deep like an arrow shot into the heart of the sea. I struggle to open my stinging eyes against the brutal salty assault of the water, barely managing it. There's no point anyway. It's night-time and everything is so dark as to be black, the only things flickering past my eyes the bubbles of my remaining air escaping to the surface far above. And far below, I sense something watching, waiting, eager to accept me into its embrace.

Just a dream! I know it, but it doesn't help. My dreams have always been more intense than waking life, and they don't always stay inside my head. I never told Andy about them, because I was scared—at first that she'd make fun and reject me for being different, later that she'd consider me to be the same as her and rope me into her headlong crash-dive. It never occurred to me that my dreams could be used, directed with purpose. I always respected the boundaries. But there were times when those limits *were* transgressed, and I quickly moved on. I should never have let the foghorn of the past draw me back here.

Blue's eyes, shadowed and sunken like deep-sea wrecks.

This is why I have kept to myself for so long.

My air is running out. Time to end this, to kick free and return to the silk sheets of my townhouse bed. But the grip of the dream is so tenacious that all this might as well be real. It can't be—the freezing embrace of the sea would have woken me at once. I push hard and feel the surface of the dream rushing toward me as fast as the abyss in the seabed below. I focus my thoughts and break free.

My eyes shoot open. I'm still staring into liquid darkness, still thrashing my naked limbs as I plunge lower and lower, still in the deep and drowning.

Still dreaming!

No. I know the sensation of breaking out of a dream by now, and there's no further surface to reach. This is real.

*Oh fuck oh god no!*

How many seconds left? *No.* I claw at the water in desperation and fail to slow my descent at all. *No.* How did this happen? How did she pull me down so far before I even knew it?

Doesn't matter now. Too late.

Above the screams in my head, a whisper.

*"I can save you."*

Exactly what I need to hear. And that's the whole point, isn't it?

*"I will be your life preserver."*

No choice. It's die hard or dive deep, be carrion or carry on.

*"Come below, brother. Be known."*

In the extremity of this moment, I discover the lengths I'll go to in order to be remembered. Without even thinking the word, I send it. I don't so much give my consent as beg for it to be taken from me.

A shaft of feverish green light pierces the murk below, finds me, pierces me too. An indistinct pale figure can be seen at the end of it, growing rapidly clearer as it approaches at speed. It is as though my sister's body has been superimposed upon the briny dark as she rises, rises through the sour light to meet me. I see her as I last saw her, young forever, her limbs firm and sure. She's naked and her black hair streams behind her as she swoops inexorably toward my feet. She's smiling.

I see that smile, so hungry and unfamiliar, and know at once that I have made a terrible mistake.

How could I ever have thought this was my sister? Family sees itself in every little detail, and so many are missing here. That grinning mouth told the truth, but it was a truth taken from one who gave it over willingly, as I have now done. Andromeda has long since been devoured, digested, assimilated. She's gone, but everything that was her remains to be worn and used. A skin, a skein—a disguise.

My sister's hands are no longer hands and they curl around me as that beloved face looms into mine, the eyes cold and hungry and strange, the mouth wider than the world, and I know this final mistake is one I will have all of eternity to regret.

\* \* \*

Andy is being unusually patient with my childish antics today. She's lying on her stomach across her bed, flipping through a second-hand university biology textbook like it's a *Dick and Jane* primer, one hand turning the pages as the other fishes in a bag of jelly babies for her next victim. I'm standing in the doorway, and I must be bored, because I'm intentionally trying to provoke her into chasing me. That might be because I can see she's in a reasonable mood, and the conclusion to such a chase is more likely to be tickles and giggles than swearing and punching.

"Andromeda," I'm saying, over and over again, stressing different syllables so that her name starts to feel alien in my mouth, like it belongs to someone else. "An-*drom*-ed-a. An-drom-*ed*-a. An-drom-ed-*ah*. Andro-*meeda*."

"Try all you like, you won't wear it out," she says, and then pauses at a page that seems to catch her interest. "That's the thing about the classics, little one. They outlast entire ages, whole civilisations. They live forever."

"*And*! Ro. M'da."

"Did I ever tell you what my name means, in the original Greek?" Andy looks up from the textbook and digs into the bag of lollies, drawing out a single hapless jelly to suck on and savour. "Andromeda means *ruler of men*. I can totally see that, can't you? One day."

My sister looks at me, throws me that devil's grin I'd recognise anywhere, on anyone.

"I like that, brother. I like that a lot."

She pops the jelly baby into her waiting mouth.

# Steadfast Shadowsong

RELIGION TAKES HARD WHEN you're young, when it can wind its roots deep in your heart and grow along with you...and as a boy, I gave my soul over to the Church of Rock 'n' Roll. I picked up a cheap guitar, learned the hymns and hosannas, took to the fleapit pulpits myself to spread the gospel. Never really made the grade, but it was enough to add my humble voice to that hallowed choir.

Now, fast forward four decades. The dream of Making It had long since waned, and I scratched the itch by jamming with my old lady. I played a mean acoustic blues, and Minnie, she had a voice just the right shade of rough to make suffering sound like fun. Never wrote many of our own songs, but we'd do everything from the Stones, Cohen, and Bowie to Joni and Nina Simone. Called ourselves She n' Me, and yeah, I know, but we were never after making a big deal of the thing. My youthful ambition was years behind me. With a few beers under my belt, Minnie at my side, and some appreciative folks to play to, I wanted for nothing else.

Our usual gig was Come As You Are, an open mic night held the first Friday of every month at the Steadfast Hotel. The Steadfast had been standing on a quiet city corner for eighty years or so, a cosy little pub with the gracefully grubby air that musicians find so attractive. The interior was a mash-up of styles from every decade— Art Deco chandeliers cast dim light on a modern bar, the cosy DJ booth was as likely to spin classic vinyl as spit out a digital playlist, and stickers from bands both long-defunct and brand new patched everything from the cash register to the toilet walls. Minnie and I loved the place, and we never missed Come As You Are. We were there when it began, and we were there when the sins of the past came barrelling home to end it.

Minnie and I were on the bill that evening, and a cold and bitter winter night it was, too. The fireplace in the front bar crackled to keep the chill away, aided in that endeavour by the body heat of a good fifty people. The first Friday of the month always pulled a decent crowd, and each one brought with it new acts—neo-hippies with djembes and didgeridoos, folky hipsters who were walking homages to Waits or Dylan, little ladies singing acoustic confessionals about the boys and girls who'd broken their porcelain hearts. We signed up with BJ, leader of the Steadfast's house band Billy-Joe & The Brown Bottles. Scoring the second-to-last slot, we headed to the bar to warm our throats. Another new barmaid was on, but it was the boss man himself who served us.

Alex Palmer had been running the Steadfast for five years and had proven popular with the punters—always quick with a laugh, a pat on the back, a free drink for a too-sober soul chafing at their composure. He was no musician but reckoned himself connoisseur enough to be the sole judge for Come As You Are, handing out a sweet fifty to whoever most tickled his fancy and plying all performers with free booze just for keeping him entertained. Generous to a fault, was Alex, though which fault in particular we were not to know at that juncture.

"How's our lady of the blues?" he asked, heading to the taps to pour our usual. "You going to make me shiver tonight, Minnie?"

Maybe it was just me, but I always heard a flirtatious undertone in Alex's patter. The dude was on the downhill side of forty but clung to his fading youth with a death grip, an ageing hipster trying to fight his oncoming winter to a standstill. I'd long since noted that the Steadfast had a high turnover of young female bar staff, with whom Alex was casually affectionate but never quite in the way reserved for women who could be one's daughter. I wondered if a string of short-term relationships was playing out after hours in back rooms, unbalanced dalliances that ended fast and left discarded hearts feeling too awkward to stay on.

Whatever the case, Minnie only ever met his attentions with a friendly smile—and he was lucky to get even that, because jam night's position in the month ensured that it always fell during her time. Minnie used to say it made her performance more real, that it was easier to sing the blues when the red was running. It sure added a poignant touch to her voice, and I used to joke that we'd be famous if only she bled all year round. She'd laugh and shudder at the thought, but I knew she dreaded an end to the blood more, as if that might steal away her fire and desire.

Duly equipped with drinks, we sat down to watch the Brown Bottles setting up on the mid-sized stage, and the last entrant for the open mic approached Billy-Joe to sign on. They got all sorts at Come As You Are, but this young woman was something else—pale face peering from beneath curtains of long bottle-black hair like a sliver of moon through winter-night clouds, slim white fingers protruding from long jacket sleeves, too-thin body wrapped in a Sunn O))) shirt over an ankle-length skirt and everything black, black, black. A goth songstress, then. I didn't imagine her moaning dirges would go down well after the breezy fare the rest of us had to offer—but then, my imagination has often proved to be lacking.

Conversation over, this young shadow retreated to the corner farthest from the fire. Minnie and I exchanged tolerant shrugs, then returned our attention to the stage as the Brown Bottles did a quick line check and dove into an instrumental jam to get the night started.

Billy-Joe was approaching fifty faster than me, a slouch hat perennially nailed to his grizzled head, and he sported a tobacco-burst Telecaster that he played like he'd been born with it in his hands. Marque was half that age, a long-haired bear who made his Les Paul sing with fingers far nimbler than their girth would suggest; loose-limbed bass man Percy was tight as a crab's sphincter on his Fender Stingray, so tall that his shaved black head almost blocked the stage lights; and Royce played drums like his heart was a metronome, long white beard bobbing against the front of his shirt like a jazz brush. Always beat the hell out of me why they weren't out on the road rocking halls every night of the week.

But as much as I dug their country-fried blues rock, my attention kept wandering over to the corner table where that dark young creature slouched and stared at her phone. When the Brown Bottles finished and a fiddle/acoustic duo got up to replace them, I followed BJ to the bar in order to appease my curiosity.

"So, who's the little raven?" I asked, and he knew who I meant right off.

"Calls herself Nyx, N-Y-X." BJ shrugged at the foibles of youth; she couldn't have been any older than twenty-one. "Wants the band to back her tonight. Reckon that's gonna go down like a cream cheese and dogshit sandwich, but okay."

I'd heard the Brown Bottles rock pretty much everything short of heavy metal, but BJ had a point. If Nyx started wailing and thrashing like the goth-grrrl she appeared to be, the band would be hard pressed to match her style.

"What's weird, though? I swear I've met that chick before, but I can't for the life of me work out where."

"Another open mic?" I suggested.

BJ shrugged whiskery lips, sipped his bitter. "Maybe? This joint's a bit rootsy for the goths, though. Maybe my son knows her—he's into alternative chicks, piercings and shaved heads and all sorts. Still, whatever floats your boat, right?"

I returned to my seat with our drinks, and BJ's words stayed with me. The more I thought about it, the more I felt that I should recognise Nyx too. I mentioned this to Minnie and wasn't overly surprised when she admitted that she'd been trying to place the girl ever since laying eyes on her.

"She must have been to a jam night," I ventured, "if all three of us find her familiar."

"Probably, honey." Minnie saw my stare tracking back to that shadow amongst shadows, my brow furrowing, and gave me a nudge. "Eyes this way, you old dog. She's young enough to be your daughter."

We laughed and headed outside for a cigarette, and soon old Charlie Mac stepped up to the mic with his accordion and collection of vaudeville numbers, and we drank and we smoked and clapped each act until BJ announced our turn. We kicked off with an original we'd been working on, turned to the classics with our take on "Hallelujah", then closed with a well-received cover of "To Bring You My Love". We gave the boisterous crowd a modest bow and headed to the bar—little knowing that our music career, such as it was, had just come to an abrupt end.

Alex was deep in conversation with his new barmaid, standing a little too close to pass off as casual, and the way she looked up at him could have been anxious or enthralled. He touched her wrist for a moment before she nodded and hurried away to attend to her duties, and he watched her go with the speculative eyes of a butcher sizing up the choicest cuts. Then he noticed us, and swiftly threw on that nice-guy smile.

"Top work!" he enthused, pouring us a couple on the house. "That voice! Minnie, when are you going to ditch this bloke and hit the big time?"

Either that sounded like a subtle proposition, or I was projecting my insecurity again. Minnie just laughed and accepted the praise as her due. We took the beers back to our seats and watched as Nyx stepped out of the shadows like darkness becoming flesh.

She'd paid no attention to any of the other performers, either retouching her make-up or flexing her fingers like she longed to wrap them around someone's neck. Seeing the case that dangled from her hand now, I assumed the neck in question belonged to her guitar—and seeing her face, I realised it hadn't been mascara she'd been applying. She'd drawn a third eye on her pale forehead, a simple but oddly eerie closed eye marked out in black.

Nyx pulled her axe free from its case. A Fender Jazzmaster, though I'd not seen one in this condition before. The guitar had been sprayed pitch-black from scratchplate to headstock and beaten all to shit—metal gleamed dully where paint had been worn from the steel bridge, the strings and frets were dark as if tarnished by neglect, and one of the single-coil pickups had been torn out with a humbucker crudely shoved in its place. Then Nyx tilted her guitar to jack in a lead, and I spotted a long scratch along the bottom curve of the body where the black paint had come away to reveal the instrument's original colour. At some point, the Jazzmaster had been turquoise.

Revelation slapped me in the face like I'd propositioned its mother. I *had* seen this girl before—and on this very stage.

The name seemed obvious in retrospect. She might be Nyx now, but when that Jazzmaster had been factory-standard—perhaps a year ago—she'd been Nicky. Nicky Newton, or Little Nicky as Alex had called her, his face twisting into a grotesque Adam Sandler leer. Come As You Are had been her first performance, and she'd come alone, no support group to cheer her on. Nervous as she was, she'd killed it up there, and Alex had chosen her for the prize. Yes, I remembered that shy young thing now—her voice high and clear and pure as a choirboy's solo, her cheeks flushed pink with self-conscious pride, her hair half its current length and *blonde.*

"Jesus, you're right!" Minnie exclaimed when I told her. "What the hell *happened* to the girl?"

Despite assurances of an encore performance, little Nicky Newton never returned after that impressive debut. I kept an ear out for her name on the local grapevine, figuring she'd outgrown us and moved on to more prestigious shows, but heard nothing—for all I knew, she'd never even played another gig. The last I'd seen of her, she'd been sitting alone at the bar after the Steadfast had closed, accepting yet another celebratory free drink from Alex as Minnie and I made our farewells. She'd fairly blazed then, lit up with success and promise...and now she seemed to suck the shadows into herself, wearing their skins to hide her own decay.

I know life can be hard for a girl; Minnie's own past, the parts she'd been willing to share with me, was enough to make my heart scream in helpless, furious sympathy. So I was disinclined to attribute Nicky's appearance to a mere youthful phase, and wondered—what outrages had been stoking the black flames in her dank little heart?

Nyx switched on the house amp, tested her battered Boss distortion pedal. Her guitar tone was dark and sonorous, tuned a step below regular. She muttered something through that curtain of hair to BJ, who mouthed a key to the band and began drop-tuning his E string. Percy and Marque followed suit as Nyx turned back to the room, shot us a doleful look, regarded the neck of her guitar like a task she'd put off as long as she could. Then she drifted up to the microphone, adjusted the stand to her height, cast a glance at the sound guy, and addressed us at last.

"One song, and the debt is paid. There will be no encore."

Then long white fingers appeared on the fretboard, and Nyx began to play.

I could feel the mood in the room change as she set up a descending pattern over the open low string, the drone note ringing hollow and deep beneath the haunting progression. Conversations petered out as punters turned to watch the skinny scarecrow on stage, and I wondered if any of them recognised her—this was a far cry from the upbeat open-chord ballads she'd purveyed as Nicky Newton. She played the riff over and over, taking her time to set the mood as the guitarists behind her nodded along to the plodding progression and Royce added a soft pedal hat to the two and four. I was wondering how long this was going to go on, if the audience was going to shake off their interest before she even got to a verse, when Nyx crept forward to the mic.

"*There was a time when everything was golden,*" she sang, her eyes fixed to some point on the ceiling, and her voice had changed, too— still high, but weighted now with gravitas and experience, somehow distant as if wet with its own reverb. "*The sun shone through the night, dancing in my hair. The birds all sang in major-key harmony. Bees only stung when asked, and knew that fair was fair.*"

I smiled at the way she placed that major reference over a minor chord. Nyx cast a glance at BJ, who unwound a subtle string of bended notes that blended perfectly with her part. Royce began gently bouncing the beater off the bass drum, lending the music a pulse.

"*Wide fields in green eyes,*" Nyx crooned, shifting the root note up a minor third, "*that never saw the truth of it all.*"

And back now to the main riff, with Marque adding in some octave chords and Percy plucking a low open note to fill out the drone. I watched Nyx's pale fingers shift spider-swift across the Jazzmaster's neck, and she picked the notes with a kind of resigned despondence. There was no other sound in the Steadfast's front bar now, and I noticed that even Alex had stilled, watching the band with one hand resting absently on the frosted beer taps as if he couldn't feel their chill.

"No way we're getting that fifty tonight," I whispered to Minnie, and she shushed me without turning her attention from the stage. My own eyes seemed both fascinated and repulsed by that occulted one drawn on Nyx's forehead. The room seemed darker than before, as if Nyx was drawing the light into herself, feeding on it.

"*I learned that time runs through us all like cancer. Black holes yawn in the white, staining every page. The blades all sing in dissonant mimicry. Wasps sting without regard for innocence or age.*

"*Scales fall from green eyes, and now I see the truth of it all.*"

Nyx jerked her guitar neck up and hit the one hard. The band followed her lead, Royce bringing in the snare as Percy pumped out steady eighths on the root. Nyx stepped back and eyed Marque, who dropped his gaze as if suddenly too nervous to solo. Billy-Joe filled the gap, kicking his overdrive switch and hitting a series of abrupt unison bends quite unlike anything I'd heard him play before. The sharp notes from his Telecaster jabbed into my mind like stings from the wasps Nyx had mentioned, and in a moment of rare perception, I realised that this was the intended effect. A breath of admiration escaped me, lost in the din.

Nyx turned to the band as BJ's solo reached its climax, swinging her Jazzmaster down in a gesture of cancellation, and to a man they slammed the one and fell silent, leaving her to introduce a spidery low-string riff that echoed the first and took it a step further. Sighing at the near-telepathic transition and hearing it echoed by a dozen other mouths, I looked and saw friendly faces becoming strange, losing definition in the deepening gloom. Minnie licked her lips, her eyes fixed on Nyx, but didn't touch her drink. No-one else seemed to need one either, as the bar was bare of custom. Alex was leaning on it like he needed the support, like he'd just had his legs kicked out from under him.

Royce and Percy brought in the beat. BJ turned and locked eyes with Marque, who still looked as queasy as a teenager playing his first gig. That was strange, but even stranger was the way he and BJ then started playing a harmonised octave figure in perfect unison. For a moment, I thought I had them rumbled—they'd rehearsed this! But Marque looked almost scared now, and BJ appeared startled at their synchronicity. A good musician can tell what his fellows are thinking, and I knew that no-one was more surprised by the band's preternatural tightness tonight than the players themselves.

Nyx stepped up to the mic again, closed her eyes as she waited for the right moment, then snapped all three of them open. I blinked, because that couldn't be right—that disquieting third eye must have been drawn open, and I'd simply mistaken it for closed all along. Gone was her sense of bruised melancholy, of resigned detachment. Now her gaze blazed through the murk like someone had set the woman's soul on fire.

"*The night I died, I went down into the city. There windows burned like hope and smiles were all abound. I sang my heart out and it hung there in the room. Then both emptied out and left me to be found...by you.*"

The barely controlled fury in Nyx's voice pinned me to my seat. She was raw as an open wound, bleeding to incriminate the one who'd struck the blow. An insidious notion began to form in the back of my mind, slow and subtle like a cancer.

"*Sweet young thing, little dumb cunt in a dress. Reduced to cuts and portions by the butcher's greedy eyes. One drink, another, then too many to see straight. Then your sticky hands are on me, crawling fast and foul like flies...like you.*"

The cuss word hit me unawares like a drunken love tap, but it only reinforced my growing certainty that we were building to a revelation. Nyx's song enveloped me like a foreign and fearsome memory, and the experience was deeply evocative, pungent, terrible. I could still see the Steadfast Hotel around me, but the darkening room seemed to empty between blinks, the transfixed crowd flashing in and out of my vision—every time the shadows swelled around me, I was helpless and alone, and I could feel something hot and sour prickling my neck like a stalker's breath. My skin crawled, and my every sense recoiled as if I were being violated in the most insidious way. I was on the verge of realising just what it was that Nyx was trying to say.

The dynamic continued to build, Percy and Royce cranking the tension up with every bar. BJ was lost in the jam, playing a counterpoint line that seemed about to run out from under his fingers and take on a life of its own. Marque had settled for doubling the riff, his eyes darting around the stage as if looking for a way out. Nyx was staring, no, *glaring* across the room, all three eyes no longer fixed on the ceiling but rather on a very specific point behind me. That drawn-on eye looked more furious—more *intense*—than the two below, a burning black hole deep as the universe itself.

*"I fell, and I'm still falling—can't ever get that back! Your hands tore me wide open, reduced me to a crack! I never would have let you, but you took away my choice! Ripped and raped and stolen, now all that's left...IS MY VOICE!"*

Nyx stomped on her distortion pedal and screamed those last three words with a terrifying abandon. I swear I heard distant wooden clatters as spectators flew back off their seats. The volume must have been building steadily throughout the song, for now it was near deafening. Royce flailed at his kit like it had done him a terrible wrong, and all four guitars growled out the riff in savage unison.

I couldn't look away from the stage, the only part of the room free from the gathering darkness. I tried to tell myself that someone had been pulling down the house lights all along...but I knew they hadn't. These shadows were born of the music, and I somehow sensed them shrieking like furious feedback even as they swarmed silently around and through the crowd. A collective shudder convulsed the room, as if we were all touched by a probing *something* in search of a target. Then I felt the raging dark leave me, unsatisfied, passing by and swooping to the back of the room.

Nyx screamed again, a vengeful ghost bearing down on its prey, and I dropped my glass. Startled out of my reverie, I turned to Minnie. She'd shifted in her seat to stare balefully across at the bar, and she wasn't the only one. Alex Palmer shrank from all those accusing gazes, head shaking, guilty eyes gleaming with terrified tears, and I don't think anyone in the room still wondered what had turned bright young Nicky into this blackened Fury.

We watched as Alex quailed under the force of Nyx's deafening rage. He lifted one trembling hand, his lips shaping some desperate justification or apology that was blotted out by volume and ignored. The storm of shadows clustered above him, a roiling black tempest hanging over his head like a Damoclean thundercloud—and then it dashed down fast in a hateful hail, dimming him, negating him. Alex crumpled under the assault, dropping behind the bar with a silent wail as Nyx and the Brown Bottles rammed home the last note of her song like a brutal *coup de grâce*.

The distorted chord rang out and hung there, a storm cloud of boiling frequencies, and the amplifiers started to whine. The front room snapped back to its usual cosy dimness, and we blinked at the abrupt return of even that much light. The band stared at each other, stunned by what they'd just created, but the crowd's eyes were on Nyx as she unslung her Jazzmaster and flung it violently into the house amp. The old Fender fell on its back and let out an ugly bark as the speaker cone burst and the tubes exploded. This violence seemed to startle BJ and Marque into action, and they both silenced their guitars. The room rang with a sudden, hideous hush more painful than any feedback.

Nyx turned to give us a look that managed to be exhausted and victorious and regretful all at once, and the eye drawn on her forehead was closed. Some rational part of me insisted it had been all along, but I didn't listen to that idiot.

No-one in the front bar of the Steadfast spoke as Nyx picked up her battered Jazzmaster, still in one piece after her Cobain-esque final flourish, and gathered her leads and pedal. No-one approached her as she crossed back to her corner and packed, wiping that third eye away with a black cloth. But we all watched as she walked out of that place with guitar case in hand, her head held higher than when she'd entered, and we all knew that at least some of the shadows had lifted from her. Some sac of poison had been drained. The wasp had been stung in return.

As if by unspoken consensus, the rest of us stood and collected our things. The Brown Bottles began packing down their gear, subdued and silent. I reached out to Minnie with hands that made promises—things that I would never do, never allow to happen—and she let them speak for a moment before shaking her head and turning away. She was thinking the same thing I was, that we'd already allowed some of those things by leaving Nicky here drunk and alone, that if we'd just stayed or offered to share a cab or *something—*

Alex's latest and last barmaid stood pale and shaking at the end of the bar. Minnie went to her, soothed the young woman into leaving her post, helped her to lock the place up and leave it all behind. We walked out of the Steadfast's once-welcoming embrace into the bitter winter night, and I would bet good money that not one of us ever returned.

I saw a few Come As You Are regulars around after that, and I know they saw me—this city, like all cities, seems small as a sitcom when you live in it, so many familiar faces among the extras—but we didn't talk. I assume that for them, as for me, that furious final chord was still ringing out through their dreams, weakening the beams that held their lives upright.

Alex Palmer was declared missing. Police viewed the disappearance as suspicious, since the pub's CCTV files seemed to have been corrupted, but this was a case they were never going to close and a body they were never going to find. We'd left the Steadfast empty behind us, but we all knew Alex hadn't walked out of there—Nyx's song had been merciless, a force of such utter annihilation that I was surprised I still remembered he'd ever existed. I'd never know *what* had fallen upon him, or *how*, and that was fine; the *why* was enough. A dark debt had been paid, a savage justice had been served, and that was all that mattered.

Minnie and I never played another open mic, or even jammed together. Her red never ran again after that night, and as she'd feared, her beautiful voice fell silent; I hated to play now, every note sounding facile and forced under my fingers. We never talked about why we quit, but I think we both knew. How could we possibly pretend we played with true feeling after witnessing Nyx's open-wound catharsis? Our pathetic passions paled by comparison, became a cruel joke at our own expense. So She n' Me broke up, and soon after, as if robbed of the bond we'd shared, she and I broke up, too.

That would've just about killed me once upon a time, but I almost welcomed the parting. Our bed had been cold and oppressive for weeks, haunted by thoughts and memories we didn't dare articulate. A new truth had been unveiled, our old gods revealed to be nothing more than crude clay idols unworthy of worship. My every waking moment used to be soundtracked by the greats, but now I worked and rested and slept in silence. I left the Church of Rock 'n' Roll, no longer willing to indulge their glib and libidinous lies.

One night, drunkenly trying to make sense of my new world, I picked up my acoustic guitar and smashed its hollow body open on the corner of my coffee table. I crawled amongst the splinters and let them prick my voiceless fingers until they sang the only song that had any meaning now, until the music ran red and wet down my hands. I lay on my back and begged oblivion to fall on me, and as shadows descended from the corners of the living room to blot out my vision, I thought for a moment that I saw what I'd been looking for. Then it was gone, leaving only a drunken drone to ring in my ears like feedback from a black guitar, along with five words that faded out into the nothingness like the final chorus of a radio-rock anthem: *there will be no encore.*

# A Walking Wound

AS THE REST OF the band ate, Jennifer sat and stared out through the service station window into the night that swallowed up the truck stop beyond. The configuration of the trucks' faces, lit by a lone lean lamppost, made her shutter finger twitch. She was sipping pensively at her iced coffee and framing shots in her mind's eye when Lolly noticed and pinched some of her chips.

"What are you thinking about?"

Jennifer turned to her skinhead drummer with a distracted smile. "Hmm? Oh, hey, can you hop up? I need to go grab my camera."

"Sure." Lolly shifted across the booth's bench seat and stumbled upright; behind the kit she was gracefully brutal, but without sticks in her hands she was a certified klutz. "Just don't shoot me. I'm a wreck."

All four members of p83 were showing signs of wear after two straight weeks on the road—thirteen days spent driving in the van and crashing on the loungeroom floors of accommodating promoters, eating meatless junk instead of decent vegan meals, sweating through shows and showering when they could. Much as Jennifer loved Lolly, she was glad the woman was out of smelling distance for a minute.

"Back in a bit," she said to the others. Careena nodded, munching on a veggie burger that would serve double-duty as breakfast, while Bessie was busy drowning her chips in vinegar. Jennifer slid from the booth and made her way across the mop-moistened dining area; WARNING, a yellow A-frame sign declaimed, and the white polished floor was wet with disinfectant like antiseptic on a wound. Glass doors slid apart to allow her out into the night.

She still had the Tarago keys since she'd driven the last shift. She tied her long red hair back and grabbed her Canon and tripod from the footwell before walking across the forecourt, around to the back of the service station where cement gave way to gravel and that single lamppost cast its lonely eye over the truck stop.

Three semis were parked here, their drivers sleeping within or hitting the servo for a shower and a meal—Jennifer thought the middle-aged man she'd seen inside with more hair on his arms than his head was one, the guy sullenly sawing his steak and glancing their way whenever the girls laughed or swore aloud, since his eyes had the same distant road-dulled look as her bandmates. The trucks waited at the edges of the light, dormant giants sat humped in the darkness, their grilles gleaming like fixed smiles. The moon watched the scene from afar, a pale hole punched in the night sky.

Jennifer unfolded the tripod and set up her camera. She adjusted for a long exposure, shuffled across until she had this mise-en-scène framed just the way she wanted it. The shutter counted off three slow shots.

She was about to pack up when a metallic creak drew her attention to the leftmost and nearest truck. Its passenger door was flung open and Jennifer watched as a young woman dropped to the ground, squatting in the gravel for a moment like an animal poised to spring. She didn't seem to notice she was being observed as she rose to her feet and flexed her long fingers, twitched the front of her denim jacket closer together.

Jennifer returned her eye to the viewfinder. The dim woman added another eerie note to the scene: somewhere between mid-teens and mid-twenties, pale face framed by long black tresses, white camisole top under the denim jacket, short black skirt, bare legs down to red slip-ons. She was tall and lean and her arms, her legs, her fingers looked just that little bit too long, a gangly catwalk model fallen on hard times.

The woman walked to the edge of the light and paused, shoulders slumped as if she were exhausted or deeply sated. Jennifer's finger flexed and captured the moment.

She was using a ten-second exposure, and halfway through, the woman's eyes met those of her observer through the viewfinder. The effect was so startling that Jennifer straightened and blinked at the ground until the shutter clacked to announce the time was up. She bent to the fresh shot for examination and saw everything she'd hoped to see—she'd caught a hot one. When she looked up, the woman was gone.

Jennifer frowned. It barely seemed possible that she could have returned to the truck or hidden behind another without being noticed. Little surprise the woman wouldn't want to be seen, though; her presence and appearance intimated a tawdry business she would scarcely want documented by strangers.

Returning her camera to the Tarago, she mused over the woman's circumstances. Since she'd taken to prowling truck stops, they must have been dire indeed—and here was Jennifer, exploiting this desperate stranger's life for art. Some feminist! But at least it *was* art: the woman's eyes had been deep and dark as gun barrels or unlit tunnels, and for all their on-the-road emptiness that Jennifer recognised from the mirror, they'd been electric with some undefinable energy. Black coal burning without flame, negative twin suns.

She couldn't wait to edit the picture.

* * *

The service station was a few hours out of Bendigo, their previous tour stop. From there, p83 drove to Geelong, where they arrived late and crashed in the local band booker's back room for the night. Up and out early in the morning, they explored local shops and cafés while Bessie conducted phone interviews with community radio stations. She fielded the usual questions—*what's the story behind that band name?*—before they headed to the venue. After accepting a free pub feed, they loaded in their gear and sat around waiting for the support band to arrive with the amps while Lolly assembled her drum kit. Then they waited while the openers soundchecked, waited for the doors to open, waited for the first band to get on and get off.

Four hours later, they hit the stage and delivered their set with punky elan. The crowd was small but enthusiastic, and Careena cadged free shots out of the bar staff to celebrate. When midnight had passed and Lolly, the evening's designated driver, had driven the Tarago back to the promoter's house, the women settled down in the back room to relax. Jennifer was finally able to curl up in a corner and upload photos to her laptop.

She smiled at the truck stop pictures, pleased at the way they'd come out, and clicked past them before realising she'd missed that arresting image of the young woman. Navigating back, Jennifer found four pictures almost identical in their composition—including their complete lack of human life.

"What the fuck...?" she muttered. Bessie, changing out of her gig clothes nearby, peered over through the cat eye spectacles that lent her the look of a younger, hotter Shirley Jackson.

"What's the matter?"

"A picture I took at the servo last night...it mustn't have come out. It's not here."

Bessie yawned and shrugged on her bedtime top. "There are always more pics, Jen."

*That's not the point*, Jennifer wanted to say, but remembered once consoling Bessie after a disastrous performance when her voice had blown out: *there's always the next gig, honey.* She shrugged, wrote the shot off as a missed opportunity...and then remembered checking it in the viewfinder last night, remembered how pleased she'd been to nail the scene. It *had* been captured, so where the hell was it?

Jennifer checked her SD card again, found nothing. Clicking back through the truck stop photos as they shifted in place like a flick-book image, she realised the last of them was different. Fourth time around, the leftmost truck's passenger door was hanging open.

She'd captured that last image after all, but the woman who'd dropped out of the semi like a feral cat was nowhere to be seen. How was that even possible? She hadn't been swallowed by the shadows—there was nothing at all where the woman had been standing, no distortion of the image, and she'd been perfectly visible in the vision Jennifer had seen in the viewfinder.

Enough—midnight was two hours past, her eyes heavy with fatigue. Jennifer closed the laptop, cleaned her teeth, curled up beneath a blanket as Careena turned out the lights. She hoped to fall asleep before Lolly started up with her buzzsaw snore, and tonight, her wish was granted. The drummer let loose a single fart in the darkness, a joke worn thin through repetition, and the next sound any of them heard was Bessie's phone alarm at eight o'clock in the morning.

\* \* \*

After a luxurious five-minute shower, Jennifer climbed back into the Tarago for the next drive. Thankfully, it was a short trip to Melbourne and they'd pre-booked at a cheap hotel near the venue, so they had a place to chill for the afternoon. While Lolly collected everyone's clothes and did a much-needed laundry run, Jennifer returned to her laptop.

That final truck stop shot remained stubbornly stranger-free. Jennifer chalked it up to a technical fault—had to be that, or else she was already losing her mind like Nanna—and scrolled back further. Here were the p83 girls horsing around backstage at the Bendigo gig. Here was Careena flirting with the cute barman who'd failed to lure her back to his house. Here was the traditional crowd shot Jennifer had taken from the stage near the end of their set—

Her fingers curled into fists and her head darted closer to the screen. Most of the rockers in the half-full room had flocked toward the stage, leaving a few less enthusiastic individuals to hang back by the bar. One of those was a young woman with long black hair and burning, half-seen eyes.

Jennifer zoomed in. Denim jacket, white camisole top, short black skirt, red slip-ons. As if the outfit needed to be verified; those remarkable eyes were proof enough.

It was *her*.

Okay, so: by coincidence, the woman must have hooked a ride from Bendigo the next day and wound up at that service station the same time as p83. While the band was sitting down to feed, she must've been out in that truck paying off her debt to the driver, a thought that made Jennifer queasy. If they'd known how desperate she was, maybe they could have given her a lift. The middle of the back seat was occupied by a box of their seven-inch singles, the rear of the vehicle stuffed with guitars, drums, and merch, but p83 would have happily squeezed in one more woman somehow if her only other option was wrapping her lips around the cock of some sweaty truckie.

But the more Jennifer thought about things, the less sense they made. The crowd had been small enough that she should've recalled seeing the woman there at some point, and this strange synchronicity didn't explain why she'd disappeared from the truck stop photograph. Bewildered, she called out to Careena and Bessie.

"You guys remember this woman?"

They wandered over half-dressed, looked and shook their heads. "What's so special about her?" Bessie asked.

"Well, nothing. But I thought—I *know* I saw her at a service station night before last, climbing out of a truckie's cab. I snapped her, but look at *this*...there's no-one there. I checked that picture after I took it, and I swear she was in it then. It's all just a bit...*weird*, you know?"

"You're fixating on some truck stop hooker now?" Careena pulled a poor-baby face and patted Jennifer's head. "Either you're learning something about yourself, babe, or it's been way too long since you had a dick in you."

"Wow, thanks. If you were any more patronising, I'd check to see if *you* had a penis."

Careena pulled out the front of her knickers and peered inside. "Nope. But if it helps..."

She picked up an empty water bottle and tucked it between her bare thighs, wiggled it at her bandmates. Bessie laughed and slapped it away. Careena stood with hands on hips, bottle jutting proud, thrusting her plastic phallus in Jennifer's direction.

"Looking for a ride, little girl?"

"Fucking grow up!" Jennifer snapped, seeing only a pot-bellied truckie with his shorts down and a nameless, powerless young woman left with no choice but to allow him into her body. Careena flinched and immediately discarded the bottle.

"Sorry, Jen. All this time hanging around male musos must be taking its toll on me."

Jennifer forced a smile. "And here I was thinking you were a feminist."

"Whoa, whoa. Women are allowed to *think* now?"

Bessie laughed and kicked the offending bottle across the room. "Take *that*, patriarchy!"

Jennifer turned back to her laptop and stared at the crowd shot, at the gangly young woman whose presence had passed unnoticed. She wasn't drinking or dancing or smiling. She simply stood with her shoulders slumped and her black hair hanging down like some *onryō* from a Japanese horror flick, transfixing the lens with that million-mile stare.

"Enough of you," she said, and opened the second truck stop image in Photoshop. By the time Lolly returned to dole out freshly washed clothes, the picture was edited and watermarked and ready for posting—but something kept Jennifer from doing so. Maybe she still hoped she could find the fourth photo the way she remembered shooting it, or maybe the scene reminded her too much of that squalid spectre even without her presence. Either way, Instagram went without a post from Jennifer that day. She got ready and followed the girls down to the Tarago, flexing her fingers in anticipation of the upcoming show.

p83 rocked Melbourne's tits off that night, and Jennifer had no cause to think about the strange woman until she picked up her Canon to take her customary crowd shot. She looked around for a denim jacket and long black hair, but while a few rockers met those criteria, none of them were *her*. As she followed Lolly's cue into "Venerate the Generator", the single they were promoting on this tour, she kept her eyes roving through the sweaty mass, picking angrily at her bass as she dared the woman to show herself.

She did not—not then and not after the show as p83 downed free drinks with the support band, and Jennifer told herself Careena was right, she *was* fixating on this one odd detail of the tour, and she flirted with a dude as if her guitarist's opinion about lacking action was also true, but when the evening was over she left him disappointed and returned to the hotel with her band, and the gangly stranger only crossed her mind again just before sleep gathered her up and took her down.

* * *

Checkout the next morning was followed by a six-hour drive to Canberra, and Jennifer took the first shift, chasing her yawns away with iced coffee. At the midpoint, Bessie commandeered the wheel and Jennifer retired to the back seat with Careena, who had lost herself in a paperback to distract from her mild hangover. With nothing else to demand her attention, her mind backtracked to the disturbing woman in her photographs.

First, she checked her camera to make sure she hadn't captured the stranger in any of last night's pictures. Satisfied she had not, she opened her laptop. The truck stop photos were still devoid of any living presence, though she couldn't shake the thought that the closest semi's dark windscreen was hiding sordid acts from her lens— thick, trembling fingers wrapped in long black hair, wet lips and dead eyes, a selfish satiety. She navigated back to the Bendigo crowd shot and zoomed in to get another look—

And the woman wasn't there.

Jennifer's stomach, near empty, curdled with unease. She'd taken just one shot from the stage in Bendigo, same as everywhere else. There was no chance she'd selected the wrong photograph.

Trying not to panic—*Nanna in the nursing home, looking right at her and demanding to see her granddaughter*—she nudged Careena and tilted the laptop screen her way.

"Remember I asked you about the woman in this picture, the one I saw at the truck stop?"

"Oh, your hooker crush. Yes, Jen."

"Can you point her out now?"

Careena extended one short-nailed finger to point at the spot where the woman had been standing, then hesitated and let it rove around the screen before giving up. "I don't know. Look, I'm tired, hon. I need something to eat and a nap."

"The perils of rock 'n' roll decadence," Jennifer sighed, but she was relieved. Her friends had seen the strange woman in this image and now they could not, just like her. This was really happening. She was absolutely *not* losing her mind.

She scrolled back through the rest of the tour photos, closely scrutinising each one. The stranger did not appear in any of them. There was bound to be some simple explanation eventually, so she could stop worrying about this now, right? Push it into the folder within her brain where she kept everything that made no sense or no longer bore examination: her ex blandly denying he'd been unfaithful when he *knew* she'd read his sexts; the queasy feeling she'd had around her uncle ever since she'd hopped into his lap at twelve and heard a sharp intake of breath that was more than surprise; the way Nanna looked at her like she was a stranger instead of the beloved granddaughter she'd once spoiled with toffee apples and shiny new two-dollar coins. Slam that folder closed, ignore the way it bulged and strained, and just walk away.

But even though it felt like walking a tightrope over a massive unseen maw, Jennifer opened more folders. Everything she'd snapped this year on her phone or her Canon, everything she'd downloaded from Facebook or Messenger—every p83 gig for which she or others had taken photos—the personal history she'd collated from various sources to keep track of her life these past few years. She skimmed the pictures, looked closer when crowds were present, kept her eyes peeled for a certain face, a certain outfit. And with every minute that passed without finding them, she felt the weight of her bizarre plight easing a little more.

As the Tarago entered the Canberra city limits, Jennifer found herself viewing the first ever p83 photo shoot, three years gone. They'd headed to her local library with a lesbian punk photographer who Careena claimed would lend them street cred and came away with three decent promo shots. They were pretty good, even if Jennifer thought they'd have looked better had she shot them herself.

The best picture caught them standing before a bookshelf, and though it was the plainest of the three, it evoked their personalities so well. Jennifer stood to the left in a thrift-shop flower-print dress, purple tights, and badge-adorned camouflage jacket, her red hair long and wild, an anonymous paperback held against her leg with one finger marking her place at page 83—the very source of their band name, though the book's identity was top secret. Careena played up her sultry side, one spaghetti strap hanging off her shoulder, the button of her jean shorts suggestively undone, a message written across her knuckles in black marker: *NOT4 YOU!* Lolly slouched against the bookshelf with arms folded, her distant look, leather jacket, and shaved head giving the impression she'd rather be defying authority and oppression at a rally somewhere. Bessie's mouth gaped open as if she were screaming at the photographer the way she did at a mic, her fists bunched against the front of her Queens of the Stone Age t-shirt like she was about to rip her guts out and let them slop down her tartan skirt and fishnetted legs.

The woman from the truck stop was standing at the end of the bookcase just a few feet from Jennifer, a half-seen slash of wrongness between the shelves and the edge of the shot, one dark eye burning out of the picture like someone was pushing a lit cigarette through it from the other side.

Jennifer jerked back in her seat. She was as familiar with this photograph as any she'd taken herself and would swear on her life it had only ever shown the four of them. She reached out to shake Careena's arm, paused when she saw her friend was serene in sleep. Left alone with this revelation, she stared at the picture as if she expected it to move at any moment—and she *did*, that was the crazy thing, but how could it be crazy if this stranger *was* darting from photograph to photograph?

A thought struck her, and she took a screengrab for future reference. This way, she might have some proof to back her story—

and she was going to need it if she reached out to her friends for support.

The other members of p83 knew Jennifer's family history, knew how deeply she feared succumbing to dementia herself. After all, the lyrics to "Peeling Paint", the B-side of their current seven-inch, had been penned by her about just such concerns; even her song "Cannibal Cat Ladies of the Apocalypse", from their first EP, was an exaggerated exploration of decaying sanity. The girls might see any attempt to explain what was going on here as a paranoid assumption of declining mental health—or worse, proof that she'd been right all along and the rot was already setting in. Regardless, the way her sisters looked at her, talked to her, would change. A divide would yawn open between them, and the pity in their eyes would be unbearable.

Like all good punk bands, p83 had some heartfelt points they wanted to get across, and one of those was *believe women's stories*. Now their bassist was petrified of sharing hers with the band in case they didn't. Jennifer could've laughed, perhaps screamed at this hideous irony, but a taut jaw kept her lips locked.

She said nothing to the others as they arrived at a cheap motel near Canberra's CBD, piled their bags into the room, and divvied up the beds—Bessie and Careena got the singles, Jennifer would share the double with Lolly. She slipped into autopilot mode as they ate a cheap chip dinner and headed to the venue to load in. But it would be two hours before the first band took the stage, at least four before p83 could tear into their set, and the wait stretching out before Jennifer seemed intolerable—all that time trying to ignore the elephant in the room, wondering what it was doing behind her back. She told the girls she needed to rest, acquired the Tarago keys, and fled back to the motel.

She opened her laptop and headed straight for the library shot. Jennifer, Careena, Lolly, Bessie, and no-one else—the stranger was gone. Expecting this, she let out a sick whimper of a laugh as she pulled up local news. It didn't take long to find the article she was dreading.

Somewhere outside Bendigo, a long-distance trucker had been found dead in his vehicle. No further details were given. Police were pursuing inquiries.

Jennifer's stomach revolted and she bolted to the bathroom. Flushing her half-digested dinner, she explored further folders. Back before p83 she went, flicking through party scenes and university events and her first band's poor attempts at co-opting the identity of their influences.

Eventually Jennifer came to a photo of her at fifteen, taken on a crappy digital camera her mother had bought. She and her former best friend Ollie were posing in her bedroom, all black jeans and bullet belts, emo fringes and eyeliner, as Mum tried to take the shot without shaking with laughter at the sheer *teenageness* of it all. The picture brought Ollie bursting back out of the don't-think-about-it folder where she'd consigned him ever since he'd admitted to fingering her while she was passed out drunk in his bed, but that wasn't the worst of it.

Standing in the corner of the bedroom, staring out of the photograph with eyes like deep wounds that never healed, fingers curled into claws: the stranger from the truck stop. The young woman that Jennifer could no longer believe was a woman at all.

"How can you *do* that?" she whimpered, pulling hard on a hank of red hair. "How can you *be* there?"

She didn't ask the next question aloud, afraid it might somehow inspire her stalker to answer.

*And what are you going to do when you get wherever it is you're going?*

\* \* \*

Jennifer returned to the venue in time to warm up her fingers and voice, faked excitement with her friends as she strapped on her bass, and got through the show like it was any other gig. She took a photo from the stage, even though her trusted camera now felt like a traitor for somehow allowing that haunted creature into her world. She made conversation with punters and signed records and pretended all was as it should be.

She didn't let her guard down until p83 retired to their motel room and she was able to close herself off in the bathroom. Jennifer sobbed softly in the shower, her tears lost in the downpour, miserable with a terror she could neither explain nor outrun. Changing into bedclothes, she slipped into the double alongside Lolly, who was scrolling through her Facebook feed. Noting that Careena and Bessie were already asleep in their beds, she reached for her laptop with heavy heart and leaden hands.

The stranger no longer stood in the corner of her teenage bedroom, where she and her future abuser smiled and threw shapes like no later taint would ever stain this moment. Jennifer had expected this, and now she roved further back in time.

These photos had been shot on film, the prints scanned and digitised years later. Here was Jennifer pre-teen and pre-emo, before make-up and punk rock and boys; here was the little girl who thought she might one day be an FBI agent like Dana Scully, or perhaps a fashion photographer; here she was at the age of five, her bedroom wallpapered with posters of *Matilda* and *Scooby-Doo* rather than The Used and Rise Against, her red hair in high pigtails and her teeth bared in a playfully ferocious grin.

And here was the stranger, no longer standing in the corner but looming mere feet from the child's back, fingers spidering out toward her unsuspecting host. Her terrible eyes were clearer than Jennifer had ever seen them and still she couldn't make out what lay at the bottom of those cold-coal pits. But what burned out of them was an undeniable *hunger*. The woman was a walking wound that would never close, an appetite that could never be appeased.

She snapped the laptop shut and tossed it onto her bag, hands flying to a trembling mouth. She chewed her fingers in stress, remembered she'd regurgitated her dinner, and her belly rang hollow with want. The room was black now that her screen was no longer lit, Lolly having joined Bessie and Careena in slumber, and Jennifer wanted nothing more than to escape into the bliss of oblivion—but she shuddered to think what moves might be made while she slept.

Desperate and terrified, she slid over and cuddled into Lolly's back. The drummer grunted and stirred in the dark.

"You okay?"

"I'm scared," Jennifer whispered.

"Why?"

She didn't answer, and Lolly didn't push her. She let Jennifer spoon her and held her hand, silently supportive, until she fell asleep. Jennifer thought she might never follow, frightened awake by black eyes burning inside her brain, but she couldn't keep her guard up forever. Somewhere during that dead stretch between midnight and dawn, the shadows slipped inside her, and she fell deep into the drowning dark.

\* \* \*

Jennifer woke to the feel of warm flesh against hers, the beat of a foreign heart and the song of another's blood ringing in her ears.

The woman—Lolly—was cosy, and she could have stayed there for hours. But she was hungry, ravenous even, and Lolly's warmth only reminded her of appetites that had been suppressed too long. Jennifer pulled gently away and rolled out of bed in the dim, one bare foot falling on the cool lid of her laptop. She silently opened her bag, fetched some clothes, carried them into the motel bathroom. It wouldn't do to wake the others. Too many questions.

She dressed in the cold dark, her eyes and hair colourless in the mirror. When she was ready, she slipped back into the room. Lolly was emitting a thin snore; the others were cocooned in their beds, faceless, silent.

On her way to the door, Jennifer paused by the splayed square petals of an open cardboard box. She reached in for a "Venerate the Generator" single, flipped it over to see the band shot on the reverse sleeve. There was Lolly, gurning like a comedian; Careena, pouting in a borrowed feather boa; Bessie, winding her long blonde hair around her throat like a noose; and Jennifer, deep unlit-tunnel eyes inscrutable behind curtains of black hair, long-fingered hands plucking at the open front of her denim jacket.

Outside, the predawn darkness lay thick upon the city like chilly tar, hushed and heavily pregnant with the tension of a jungle sensing a predator. The streets were almost empty, but there would be weary taxi drivers, early joggers, shivering indigents; wherever game gathered, there were always strays—the desperate, the lonely, the lost. Her belly ached like an old wound. How long since she had properly fed? She would find something, someone, and soon.

Licking her teeth in anticipation, Jennifer smiled at the shadows and stalked into the dark heart of the city.

# The Haunted Heart of Ebon Eidolon

THE PLASTERED CAST CLOSED its doors to the public at eleven o'clock on Sunday nights, but a few select patrons were invited to stay on for lock-ins on special occasions, and the memorial for Ebon Eidolon was certainly one of those. Once the crowd had been pared down to those who'd known Ebon best and longest, Mitch volunteered to head down and close up, and Ricky, busy fetching drinks for the remaining mourners, tipped him a grateful nod.

There hadn't been a big turnout, Mitch noted as he locked the front door against further custom, but that had kept things suitably intimate—and besides, this was to be expected in these trying times. The streets outside were unusually barren even for a Sunday; all across the city, other doors were being barred against a pandemic of unprecedented proportions. Though local businesses were about to take a palpable hit—Ricky's bar included—Mitch found the advent of COVID-19 to be fitting in its way. A good man was gone, and a plague had fallen amongst those left behind. It was as if the earth itself mourned the loss of Ebon Eidolon, and few people were more deserving of such a momentous send-off.

Mitch leaned the A-frame street sign against the wall of the Plastered Cast's narrow passage and turned to regard the stairs. His friend's bar was situated on the second floor above a Vietnamese bakery, and the entrance hall was a sliver of its size, its red walls so close together that entering it felt like squeezing into a vein that would lead to the pumping heart above. The hall ended in a staircase narrow enough to ensure single-file and steep enough to make reaching the bar feel like an achievement to be celebrated with a drink. As his feet thumped up the carpeted wood steps, Mitch thought of a heartbeat and remembered that one special organ had now fallen silent forever.

When he returned to his position at the bar, Mitch counted a grand total of seven people remaining to raise a glass to the memory of Ebon Eidolon. *That feels right,* he noted, saluting Ricky as the barman pushed a fresh pint across the counter. *Seven always was his favourite number.*

"It's on your tab," said Ricky. The Plastered Cast's proprietor was a tall man in his mid-forties, the phallic suggestion of his smoothly bald, egg-shaped head only emphasised by his preference for black roll-necked sweaters. Despite his active involvement in the local art scene, Ricky professed to have no creative abilities himself, claiming that creating a safe space for them was contribution enough.

Prior to his untimely death, the Plastered Cast had been one of Ebon's favourite places to hang out. Coming off the stairs, visitors entered the rectangular main room at its south-eastern corner and could walk directly ahead to the bar, which ate up half the west wall. The vertical surfaces of the bar had been decorated with an intricate collage of influential icons: Siouxsie Sioux and Suzi Q; a smattering of Smiths including Robert, Kevin, and Morrissey's mob; a winning hand of Prince, Queen, King Diamond, Ace Frehley, and Jack Nicholson's Joker. The walls were hung with framed posters for multigenerational movie classics like *Pink Flamingos, The Evil Dead, The Hunt for Candy Parker, Hedwig and the Angry Inch,* and *The Crow.* Funko Pops on top of the premix fridge included Lemmy, Stephen King, and the Thirteenth Doctor, and the ends of the bar were usually littered with flyers for local gigs, exhibitions, and screenings. PA speakers hung from the northern corners of the room and Ricky ran his Spotify playlists through them via laptop; currently he was airing a special mix curated in memory of Ebon, and mournful Celtic folk gave way to HIM's "Join Me in Death".

Mitch carried his beer to the seating area opposite the bar, where three small tables were attended by funky vinyl couches pushed back against the east wall. On one of these sat Sinead, resplendent in tight leather pants and a silver lamé top. At fifty, she was Ebon's junior by five years and had known him for three decades; he had been a rock for her as she'd dealt with the complications of transition. As always, her tasteful grace made Mitch feel like a scruffy bum in his frayed jeans and Trasharama t-shirt, though she'd never mean him or anyone else to do so. As he approached, she flicked back raven-black hair with hot pink nails and flashed him a warm, sad smile.

"I've been thinking about the clown," she was saying to her companion. "The way his routines were choreographed, it should've been funny, but he *terrified* me when he played that role. Almost like it wasn't Ebon under the paint at all."

"Oh, *that* guy? Yeah, don't get me started on him. I never liked who Ebon became when he was made up as the clown."

Sinead's companion was Jasonn Carmenn, a highly regarded alternative dance performer who had worked with Ebon both on regular drag shows and darker, more debauched delights. Mitch fondly remembered their double act as an outrageous pair of goth bridge trolls with prosthetic beak-like noses and prosthetic beak-like cocks, so it was strange to see Jasonn looking so sedate. Dressed down in basic blacks, his long honey-blonde hair tied back, he looked younger than his thirty-five years and much more modest than his onstage personas would suggest.

"What was it called?" Mitch asked them. "The clown, I mean. Since Ebon liked to name his stage characters."

"I asked him once," Jasonn admitted, not enjoying the memory. "He was already made up and in that awful headspace. He looked at me like I was an idiot and said, *evil doesn't have a name.*"

"Ebon was a sweetheart, but he was complicated." Sinead stared into her blood-dark wine. "There were deep shadows in his heart, and I think his struggles with them were what made him so kind."

The love in her voice thickened Mitch's throat. He didn't trust himself to speak without choking up, so he excused himself as soon as Jasonn started talking and walked away to regain his composure. He'd told himself *no more tears*, but tonight he drank in remembrance rather than celebration, and with each beer the shade of sorrow threatened to overwhelm him afresh.

The wall at the north end of the room, between the L-shape of seats on the left and the deserted DJ nook to the right, was tonight the canvas for a projected slideshow of snapshots from Ebon's life: scanned-in photographs of childhood moments, Polaroid scenes of youthful debauchery, digital displays of dangerous drag. Mitch kept his eyes on the screen for a minute and watched these pictures describe the unlikely evolution of Evan Kincaid to Ebon Eidolon. A cherubic country boy whose delicate features were at odds with the football guernsey he wore; a slender, Egyptian-eyed young man finding true expression in the glitter-spangled corners of the big city; and finally, the venerable black angel of the queer arts scene who had left so much grief in the wake of his passing. Ebon's eyes burned out of each shot as if he were very much alive and present—he'd been the softest soul one could imagine, but his drag personas were demons who channelled the fury and malice he otherwise refused to express. It seemed very right to have Ebon's gaze on this little gathering tonight, as if he were passing on his blessing from beyond.

Wrestling his emotions under control, Mitch crossed a tiny dance floor that could accommodate perhaps half a dozen people and approached the north-west corner, where a motley selection of seats copied the right angle of the wall. Here the youngest and eldest mourners sat like opposing extremes, dark and light, battle-scarred youth and hard-won wisdom side by side: Scarla and Marigold.

Scarla was staring into the depths of a wineglass, her generous figure packed into a crimson and black corset and stacked atop thigh-high boots with three-inch heels. Twenty-seven now, she'd been taken under Ebon's wing a decade before, the latest in a long line of protégées who'd bloomed in the light of his black sun. Mitch felt a burst of pride for his absent friend when he remembered how close young Meera had been to self-obliteration before gentle guidance had shown her how to become the Scarla she'd always wanted to be. Her lipstick was as black as her long skirt, a few shades darker than her skin, and her eyes were bright with tears.

"I've had a few fathers," she said, turning to include Mitch as he approached, "but I don't think I'll miss any of them as much as Ebon. Without him, I wouldn't have had the courage to be who I am. He truly was one of a kind."

Marigold nodded and touched her wineglass to the one in Scarla's hands. "So full of darkness, but he used it to bring light and love into the world. Oh, sweet boy—you will be missed. To Double E."

She swigged her wine like it was water, and if boozing had kept her looking this good for almost sixty years, then Mitch approved where even he might otherwise be inclined to recommend moderation. The closest thing Ebon had had to a big sister, Marigold had lived enough lives in her time to fill a must-read scandalous autobiography: teen runaway, sex worker, model, junkie, counsellor, and lately, a kind of woozy wise woman and drunken den mother. Among other things, she claimed to have shot up with Nick Cave and gone down on Michael Hutchence, though her recollections were damaged enough that she sometimes admitted it might have been the other way around. She made herself up like everyone's favourite Hollywood grandmother and wore her scars and wrinkles well.

"To Ebon," Mitch agreed, and let that stand as his eulogy. He'd never been as demonstrative as other gays and felt sometimes as though this set him apart from them as much as his queerness did from normative society. When mates or lovers turned to him for solace, he felt awkward and ineffective, his compassion dammed up behind a clumsy tongue. He'd turned out more like his stoic father than he would have liked, a point driven home by the fact that he was now in his early fifties, the age his old man had been when he died. He sipped from his pint, ran a hand over his cropped scalp, anything to avoid opening his mouth and failing to provide the sympathetic wisdom that had flowed so easily from Ebon's lips.

Mitch soon felt like a loose end and left Marigold and Scarla to their reminiscences. He looked at the projection wall as he moved on and saw Ebon smiling imperiously over the room, a vampiric statesman with his widow's peak and deep dark eyes, just a year from death but looking set to outsit eternity. In this photo, he was standing beside a grinning black man in a leather jacket and *They Live* t-shirt: Wolfgänger, a young synthwave musician who had commissioned Ebon to paint the covers for a triptych of EPs. His sinister synthesiser sound had brought out a playful element in Ebon's work, the images as turbulent as ever but incorporating waves of uncharacteristic pink, yellow, and blue that hinted at the music's Eighties aesthetic.

*Just goes to show there's always so much more to people than you can imagine,* Mitch thought, *and Ebon was a perfect example.*

In the centre of the east wall, just up from Sinead and Jasonn, was an open sliding door that led into the Cast's second room, a modest performance space with a small stage at one end and a litter of old school chairs and theatre seats at the other. Staring at the stage as if imagining himself performing on it, or perhaps recalling one of the many shows Ebon had thrown here and elsewhere, was Carlton Beck. A long-term friend and former lover of the dearly departed, Carlton was rail-thin in his sixties, but his eyes gleamed with the indomitable spirit of someone who'd seen his people suffer through AIDS, discrimination, and prosecution only to rise to ever higher prominence and acceptance. Dressed up to the nines in a mauve suit and black fedora, a silver half-moon dangling from one earlobe, he looked dapper as hell—but his long face was too wistful for Mitch to handle right now, loaded with memories sweet and sad, so he left the man to his ruminations.

As he turned away, his eyes fell again on the projection wall, and though he'd seen this new image before, it still gave him a small start to see it without warning. It was a live shot from a Halloween show at the Mars Bar: Ebon made up as the unsavoury goth clown Sinead had mentioned earlier, his black-lined eyes blank and yet somehow malicious, his cave-dark mouth gaping wide as if to catch not thrown balls but errant souls. Mitch could see why Jasonn had disliked working with Ebon in this guise, why Sinead had found it terrifying to watch—it was the very antithesis of the joyful flamboyance offered by most drag performers. Whatever feelings their friend had been channelling with this character were vile and vicious, and if this clown took amusement in anything at all, it was its own savage antics and the unease they evoked in the captive audience.

The sound of a lighter tapped against glass brought his attention back to the bar. Ricky had lined up seven empty shots and was beckoning the mourners over. Time for an official toast, then. Fine, as long as Mitch didn't have to give a heartfelt speech or anything. He crossed the room as HIM gave way to one of Wolfgänger's spooky synthwave cuts and saw that his earlier headcount had been a little off.

A young man sat on one of the vinyl couches recently abandoned by Sinead and Jasonn, a delicate waif with his big eyes cast down and his slender wrists turned inward. Mitch didn't recall seeing this guy during the memorial proper, but then, he'd been focused on his friends and his drinking in equal measure. The kid certainly had the look of someone Ebon would know, a hollow-boned vulnerability that cried out to the world and invited cuddles from the compassionate or kicks from the callous.

Eight, then, remained to remember.

"This round is on the house," Ricky said, toting a bottle of fine whisky as his guests lined up along the bar. "A toast—and not to dear old Ebon, but to *us*. To all of you, for everything you did for him and everything you've shared tonight. To you, Marigold, for passing on Ebon's lost works to us. Rest assured that mine will hang in a place of pride right here in the PC."

"It didn't seem right that those pieces just rot away in the dark," Marigold said, settling on her stool. "I know Ebon mustn't have thought much of them, and he wouldn't like the idea of them being passed around, but his catalogued pieces were all sold or assigned to private collections by his will. At least this way some of his nearest and dearest will have something tangible to remember him by."

Mitch glanced over at the DJ nook, where seven cloth-wrapped rectangles sat stacked atop one another. As Ebon's oldest friend, Marigold had taken it upon herself to organise his posthumous affairs, to find new homes for his belongings, his pets, and even his lost art. This was her bequest to those present tonight, seven long-neglected paintings she'd discovered buried deep in a spare closet. She had handed out them out just minutes ago, before Mitch had locked them all in, and now they waited in a convenient pile to be taken to their new abodes.

These works were gifts from the grave, and Mitch knew he ought to have been grateful he'd been considered worthy of one—but the paintings had not been included in Ebon's meticulous catalogue, had in fact been wrapped in dirty old cloths and marked *DON'T LOOK JUST BURN*. This boon had been presented without Ebon's foresight or permission, and Mitch didn't like that his friend's careful arrangements had been flaunted, even if it was done with the best of intentions. As well as being excluded from Ebon's personal records, these works had not even been named, but that omission seemed curiously appropriate—these paintings were dark and furious and almost indecipherable, slabs of black slashed through with swirls and stabs of virulent colour. They didn't need anything as restrictive or definitive as names.

"Did anyone want to say a few words?" Ricky asked. Sinead raised one hand, then tapped her pink nails on the bar for a moment as she gathered her thoughts.

"I knew Ebon longer than most of you—except Marigold, of course—and I wish I had gifts for you too, something of his to share. But all I can give is what we all have to remember him by: stories. And right now, I'd like to tell you about the time Ebon helped to save my life."

"Go on, love," Marigold said, and Mitch made noises of encouragement with the others.

"It was nearly thirty years ago now. I was starting reassignment surgery and Ebon insisted I stay with him so he could look after me. I thought I'd be fine, but he was so right. When I was half done, I'd never felt more...*unmoored* in all my life. I was a step closer to being my real self, and that was exhilarating, but I'd burned my bridges back to the me I was used to, that everyone else knew. I felt like an entirely new thing, all raw and dripping. What I'd done was immutable, and now I was even more separated from a reality that didn't seem to have any room for people like me.

"It was a difficult time, but Ebon made it so much more bearable. He brought me soup and wine and hugs and kind words. His love and support were totally unconditional—he told me he'd lost people before and he wasn't going to let that happen again. I thought he was overreacting, but there were moments along the way when I felt so...*alien*, I guess—no longer the wrong fit, but not yet the real me—and in those moments, that difference cut me so deep I just couldn't stand it. I'd always felt trapped between two poles, but never more so than that time.

"Coming out the other side was a dream come true and the best thing that ever happened to me, but the journey was sometimes hard. And I'm honestly not sure I'd be here to tell you this tonight if not for my dear friend. I love you, Double E."

Sinead wiped away a tear and sat down to a round of supportive applause. As if listening and reacting, the slideshow projected onto the north wall changed to a photo of Ebon with his arms wrapped around a younger, beaming Sinead. He was in one of his less frightening drag get-ups and they looked like inseparable sisters.

"Thank you, Sinead." Marigold stood with one small hand braced against the bar to keep her steady. "You're right, we're all stories when we're gone. We're blessed to have so many about Ebon, and by revisiting them, sharing them, we help to keep some part of him alive. I've probably forgotten more moments with him than I still remember, but even when he was alive and apart from me, I felt like he was never more than a heartbeat away."

*Oh, fuck*, Mitch thought. Were they all expected to stand up and tell a tale? He, too, had many a fond reminiscence, but he felt uncomfortable with the idea of performing them even before friends. It wasn't that they were too personal—Mitch and Ebon had never been lovers—but rather that he didn't trust his ability to articulate those memories to others, to get across the magic of those mundane moments.

"And you're right, Sinead," Marigold continued. "Ebon had lost people close to him. Not long after we met—way back in the mid-Eighties—his first love killed himself.

"Kenner was just seventeen, and his family situation was...intense. He was very sensitive, and I don't have to tell you how hard it is for someone like that at the best of times, let alone a gay boy in the macho Aussie Eighties. Ebon loved him hard but, in the end, nothing was enough to keep poor Kenner here. I saw what that did to my friend, and I helped him survive it—just as he helped me so many times.

"You knew Ebon as a wise man—complicated, sometimes troubled, but someone to look up to and rely upon. But back then he was little more than a kid, still finding himself, trying to deal with a disapproving father and all the other issues that coming out brings. Kenner's suicide cut him very deeply, and I honestly think he never really got over it—he was the one who found the body, and I think that scene was forever burned into his brain. In the dark times, I worried that he might end up going the same way. But he survived, and better than that, he thrived. I watched him grow from Evan, a talented boy, into Ebon, the strong, supportive, and loving man. I watched him become the artist I always knew he could be, and I was so...fucking...*proud*."

Marigold collapsed back onto her stool and immediately reached for her glass of wine. Carlton whistled as if she'd just accepted a long-deserved award, and Scarla rested a compassionate hand on her shoulder.

"Do we all have to take a turn at this?" Jasonn asked, expressing Mitch's own unease. "I've been telling stories about Ebon all night, and I'd hate to bore anyone by repeating myself."

"I'm just worried I don't have enough to tell," Ricky admitted. "I didn't know him as long or as well as the rest of you. I feel a bit like a fraud by comparison."

"No," Sinead said, her voice firm. "You were his friend, too. Doesn't matter how long for. We don't have a fucking hierarchy here, honey."

"Amen to that." Scarla hefted her glass. "We're all equals, tonight and always. That's what Ebon believed about the world, and I guarantee it's what he believed about the seven of us."

"*Eight* of us," Carlton said.

"Hey?" Scarla spun on her stool, glancing from one end of the room to the other. "Oh, right. Yes, eight."

Ricky frowned and poured an extra shot, pushed it toward Mitch. "Sorry, I didn't see them before. Could you pass one that one on for us, mate?"

"No worries."

Mitch carried the shot across to the seating area by the eastern wall and carefully placed it on a table before the morose young man.

"Here you go, fella. Have one with us."

The kid didn't look up or show any sign he was aware of the gift. Mitch turned to walk back to the bar, stopping in his tracks when he saw the way everyone was staring at him.

"What's the matter?"

"What are you doing, man?" Jasonn asked, one eyebrow arched.

"Giving our quiet mate a shot for the toast, like Ricky asked. Maybe it's eyeglasses you need, not shot glasses."

It wasn't his best quip and it crashed and burned. Jasonn exchanged a wry glance with Sinead and said, "I think it's you who needs his eyes tested, Mitch."

"Oh? Why's that?"

"Dude," Ricky said. "There's no-one there."

Mitch blinked.

"Uh, yes, there is," he said, as if to a thick child. But the look on his friends' faces rocked him in his skin—like he'd just claimed the Earth was flat or the Holocaust a lie, confusion mixed with a dash of pity. Frowning, he glanced back over his shoulder. The young man on the vinyl lounge hadn't moved, apparently blind to the free whisky and deaf to the conversation.

"You're not funny, guys," Mitch complained. "Come on. I haven't had *that* much to drunk. I mean, drink. I'm not *drunk*."

"If you're going to play silly buggers, I'll do the honours." Jasonn slipped off his stool and crossed to the seating area, picked up the shot, carried it over to a taller table that guarded the entrance to the performance room. He dusted his hands with a smug grin as he came back to the bar, but it slipped off his lips when everyone turned their questioning eyes to *him*.

"Jasonn." Sinead slapped his arm, softly scolding him.

"What?" He looked back at the table to reassure himself, then sat on his stool. "We can quit the games now. Are we making this toast or what?"

"We will when everyone has their shots." Ricky clapped his hands in the air and gestured to the unattended glass, his eyes fixed on a spot at the north end of the room. "Don't listen to these daft sods, love. That one's for you."

Mitch followed Ricky's gaze to the empty seats against the far wall and folded his arms. Sinead tapped her pink nails against the bar, frowning.

"I'm not sure I understand what's going on here," Carlton said.

"Me either." Scarla's fingers anxiously flexed around her vape pen. "I feel like I'm being left out of the joke."

"No more funny business," Mitch declared. He crossed the room and returned the shot glass to its place before the morose young man. "Let's stop pissing about and do this."

"Mitch," said Sinead, her voice low.

"Hang on, hang on, hang on." Marigold tottered to her feet and raised her hands, drawing everyone's eyes to her. "Let's get this straight. Mitch, you say someone is sitting there on that lounge?"

He checked again; the kid was right there in full-colour 3D. "Of course there is!"

"And Jasonn, you say someone is standing over by that table?"

"Yes!"

"Ricky?"

"I didn't see her come in, but she's in the red seat up against the wall," the barman said, pointing at the north-west end of the room. "Next to where you were sitting a minute ago."

Marigold exchanged a worried look with Scarla. "I'm sorry, gents, but no-one is in any of those places."

Mitch spluttered, looking at Jasonn and seeing his confusion mirrored on his friend's face. "Well, where is he, then?"

Scarla brushed aside her long black hair and pointed toward the exit. "He's leaning against the wall by the door."

Carlton grimaced. "I hate to tell you, but you're wrong. You're *all* wrong."

Sinead shot to her feet.

*"Everyone be quiet!"*

They all turned their eyes to her, taken aback by her outburst. She was staring down the room wide-eyed like she'd only just spotted her own anomaly.

"Look, something weird is going on here. Let's all be cool and go over this one at a time. Mitch, you first. Describe the eighth person *you* see in the room."

Mitch swallowed, starting to feel distinctly uneasy. He turned around and stared at the kid, who still hadn't raised his head or shown any sign that he understood he was being discussed. This apparent apathy had ceased to confuse and now began to disturb.

"He's young, maybe a teenager. Blonde. Skinny jeans, black nail polish, red t-shirt with a goth Dame Edna screen-printed on it."

Marigold's hand shook so much she had to place her wineglass back on the bar. "Christ. Mitch, *please* tell me you're full of shit."

"Oh, I'm not," he insisted. "Hey, mate, you want to set my friends straight?"

The blond boy said nothing, moved not an inch.

"Now you, Jase," said Sinead, fingers spasming anxiously against her leather pants. "Tell us who you see."

Jasonn frowned and looked at the table near the performance space's sliding door. "A man in his forties or fifties, a real country bloke—a farmer, maybe? Flanny shirt, beer gut, Ivan Milat moustache. He's not looking at us, but he seems pretty pissed off."

Marigold dropped her head into her hands. Scarla swigged wine like she hadn't tasted any in years. Sinead closed her eyes and said, "Ricky?"

"Middle-aged woman in horrible garish clothes and chunky bracelets, hair dyed bright red, gimlet eyes—I always wanted to say someone had gimlet eyes. Would anyone like a gimlet? I haven't made one in years—she looks like a teacher or something. The horrible kind you suspect only took the job so she could punish children with impunity."

Before Sinead could say anything, Scarla jumped in. "I see a guy with a shaved head who thinks he's a hard bastard, but he's young, he might even still be in school. I had to deal with bullies like him when I was growing up. He's the kind of ignorant prick who harasses anyone different or sensitive, thinks his opinions are valid because they make other idiots laugh, and ends up working a shit job and having kids as fucked as he is, posting racist memes on a Facebook page called Ned Kelly's Aussie Army or some shit."

"Carlton?" Sinead pressed.

"There's a guy sitting through there in the performance room. Funny, I didn't see him when I was in there before. He looks...*dissolute* would be a good word. A wasted bohemian type—a junkie poet or strung-out singer, perhaps. He's good-looking in that cruel kind of way and you can tell he knows it, uses it. Oh, and he's missing the pinky finger on his right hand."

Sinead leaned on the bar, staring at or through it. "Well, I see a young woman standing beside the projector screen. A goth princess who's so full of herself she thinks she's being charmingly cruel when she's really just a selfish cunt. I know exactly who she is, and I know something weird is going on because there's no way she would be here tonight. Marigold?"

The older woman lifted her head with a woozy jerk like the booze had abruptly caught up with her. "I believe you all. But, guys... I don't see anyone. Just you."

Ebon's friends stared at each other, at the spots where their respective visions were said to be, as The Sisters of Mercy took over the PA. For a few seconds, no-one seemed to know quite what to say. Mitch cleared his throat.

"So...except for Marigold, we all see someone that no-one else can see. Fuck." He glanced at the morose kid—increasingly sure he knew who the boy was but not wanting to say it aloud—and fidgeted with his ear stud. "But, guys...do they see *us*?"

The others shook their heads. "You'd think he would have heard what we're saying about him—about *them*," said Jasonn, "but he's acting like we're not even here."

"Maybe we aren't, then," Carlton murmured.

"What, you think this is some *Twilight Zone* shit?" Ricky asked him. "We're all dead or something?"

"Well, no, but..."

Carlton raised his hands and let them drop, at a loss. Ricky tossed back his whisky. Mitch returned to his seat and picked up his glass, feeling uneasy with his back turned to these silent interlopers. After downing his shot, he kept the kid in the corner of his eye.

"Does anyone recognise their...the person they see?"

Marigold said, "I recognise some of the ones *you* see. Mitch, I know who you're talking about."

He couldn't avoid it any longer. "It's Kenner, isn't it?"

"Yes. And Jasonn, from what you said, you're seeing Ebon's father. They were not on good terms and that fractured relationship was a deep black hole in Ebon's heart.

"Scarla...I think your one is a kid who used to harass Ebon at school. I can't remember his name now. He used to bash Double E behind the bike sheds, and I bet he got off on it, too. You're right—he was *absolutely* the kind of dick who would get a Southern Cross tattoo and record rants in his car about vaccination conspiracies and the liberal agenda.

"And Ricky, yours sounds like Mrs Dance, the drama teacher from Ebon's high school. She told Ebon he'd never make it anywhere doing the kind of things he wanted to do, gave him shit grades for his projects, did everything she could to persuade him that what he was doing was sick and wrong. In a way, his entire art career was his way of chucking that bitch a browneye. He said to me once, *Maz, the only dance she wanted me to do was at the end of a rope. And that feeling is forever mutual.*"

"I know who some of them are, too," said Sinead. "Carlton—yours is Edgar Shimmer. He was Toxic City—all the worst ex-boyfriends in the world rolled into one. A thief, a liar, a junkie, a user and abuser. He left Ebon with all kinds of scars, physical and otherwise."

Carlton scowled. "That's *him*? Oh, I heard about that bitch. If we'd ever met, I'd have turned him into a ghost myself."

"What about yours, Sinead?" asked Mitch. "You said you knew her?"

She sighed. "Yeah. It's Terema."

The name rang a bell, but he couldn't put a face to it. "Who?"

"One of Ebon's protégées, a baby bat searching for someone to take her under their wing. But one who didn't turn out as well as Scarla here, I'm afraid. Ebon chose poorly that time—she was a real piece of work, that Terema. A liar, a gossip, a fraud. He saw something beautiful underneath all that chaos, but it was buried too deep to reach. She turned on him, and things got nasty. She ended up in a bad place and abused Ebon when he tried to reach out. She stole from him, spread malicious lies, you name it. Her betrayal broke his heart."

"What happened to her?" Carlton asked.

"She's dead. Ice or meth or whatever. And—I'm sorry—good riddance to bad rubbish."

Mitch's hand flew to his mouth as a notion occurred to him.

"Hang on, hang on. Are they *all* dead?"

Silence fell as they mulled that over.

"They might be," Marigold said. "Kenner and Terema, yes. Ebon's dad, yes. Mrs Dance might still be clinging to life somewhere, if her black heart hasn't given out yet. Edgar should have died years ago, the way he lived. And the bully, well, who knows?"

"That's at least three of them who have carked it," Ricky pointed out. "That kind of tells us everything we need to know, right?"

"Not everything," said Carlton. "Why doesn't Marigold see anyone?"

"You're right, that makes no sense," Sinead agreed. "Maz, you were Ebon's oldest friend. If anyone's going to see ghosts from his past, it should be you."

"Thanks, dear," Marigold said, her voice desert-dry.

"You know what I mean. Of us all, you can claim to be the closest to him. So why can't you see anyone?"

Mitch cleared his throat. "Maybe a better question would be, why can the rest of us see someone? Maybe it's because we're here tonight, but why didn't this happen sooner?"

A small tremor ran through his leg as he realised where his train of thought was destined to arrive.

"Maybe there's something else that sets us apart. Something to do with Ebon that involves only us...?"

He turned and looked down at the far end of the room. Sinead gasped as she caught on.

"The paintings!"

"Yeah. We've only been seeing Ebon's ghosts since we were given them."

"Oh, fuck me," Marigold moaned. "What have I *done*?"

"You said these works weren't listed in his personal catalogue," Mitch pointed out, "but Ebon kept meticulous records about his art. So why were these left off?"

"And why were they stuffed in his wardrobe where no-one would find them?" Jasonn's eyes were wide and wet. "They were marked *DON'T LOOK JUST BURN*. Why would any artist want that? And why wouldn't he just torch them himself if he hated them so much?"

"I think you're on to something there, Mitch." Sinead slipped off her barstool. "We need to take a closer look at those paintings."

Mitch accompanied her to the corner nook where the seven pieces were stacked for safekeeping. The top one was his, so he put that aside and helped Sinead sort through the others and pass them on to their new owners. Ebon's friends laid their gifts on the bar before them, unwound the dirty cloth that had bound these works for years, stared down at the paintings Ebon had seen fit to consign to utter obscurity.

Unframed paintings on reused A2 MDF boards, these works were dark and angry and inscrutable, impressionistic portraits torn screaming from a fevered, nightmare-haunted mind—but as he looked down at his and then over at Kenner, Mitch found he could now see the connection. Was it just confirmation bias, or was he right in guessing that each of Ebon's friends owned paintings of the people only they could see? He stared down at the canvas and understood that the splotch of red in the centre was both Kenner's shirt and the blood he had spilled, realised that the gold feathering atop it was meant to represent the boy's blonde hair. As for the furious darkness that ate up much of the work, that might have been many things—the appetite of Kenner's suicidal thoughts, the fury of Ebon's grief and loss, the night that had swallowed them both and only spat one back.

"I'm right, aren't I?" Mitch mumbled, barely audible over the speakers as they farewelled the Sisters and introduced VAST's "Pretty When You Cry."

"You are," Scarla moaned. "I can see it now. I can *feel* it. I can feel the ugly violence and blind hatred, Ebon's shame and helpless rage—it's all here in this painting. Like it's trapped under glass."

Carlton just nodded. The haunted look in Sinead's eyes said everything.

"What's yours then, Marigold?" Mitch left his painting lying atop the bar and stood at her shoulder. "If it isn't someone who stirred up intense hurt and rage in Ebon, what is it?"

Marigold tentatively touched the thick swirls of black paint with one trembling finger and held it there for a few seconds. Then she whipped it away, shaking.

"Honey?" Sinead asked, her voice thin.

"I don't think it's a person at all," said Marigold, reaching for her wineglass. Her rings tapped a jerky beat on its stem in time with her hand's tremors. "Oh, *fuck* no. Not this."

Mitch placed a gentle hand on Marigold's delicate shoulder. He could make out no coherent details in her painting except gaping black-on-black holes that suggested staring eyes, an open mouth. "What is it?"

"Double E told me...when he was just a little boy, there was this book his parents had given him, a picture book, story book—he couldn't remember what it was, even what it was called. All he remembered was one picture from it: a creepy sideshow clown. Scared the hell out of him, that picture. He used to lie awake in bed for hours, too scared to sleep. With his head on the pillow, he could hear his heart beating loud in his ears, but for years he used to imagine it was footsteps—something coming up the stairs to his room. He was terrified it was the clown from that picture book, coming to swallow him up with its gaping mouth.

"He knew that was silly—his father told him sideshow clowns didn't have feet, and besides, there were only seventeen steps on the stairs to his room and yet the beat went on and on for hours. But with his eyes squeezed shut in the darkness—you know how you can see weird shapes and colours that way—he was sure the clown was just a face for something terrible that was coming from so far away...across the stars and the space between them, maybe, or some other inconceivable distance that no-one could put into words...coming all that way just for *him*. But hey, we all have weird ideas when we're kids, right?"

No-one agreed. They all waited for the rest.

"Thing is, Ebon didn't grow out of that fantasy—he just buried it. He told me that, even as an adult, sometimes he'd lie awake in his bed and hear the sound he *knew* was his heartbeat but still *believed* was something impossible and indescribable, coming ever closer. Something that wore his worst childhood fear as a mask to hide a truth that was even worse. He even wore it as a mask himself, made it one of his characters to try and control it or understand it—but I don't think that helped at all. That silly clown picture and the unknown thing it represented—they terrified him just as much as a man as they had when he was a boy."

No-one spoke for a few seconds after Marigold's tale. Mitch pictured the imagined terror that had kept Ebon awake long into the night, and even though he knew he should roll his eyes at its childish nature, he still shuddered at its primal intensity.

"And you think this is it?" Jasonn asked, pointing to Marigold's picture. "You think he tried to paint it away like the people who hurt him?"

"I can't think of anything else it *could* be. If it were a person, surely I'd be seeing them like you see the others."

"And you don't see anything because, unlike the people in the other paintings, the clown isn't real." Scarla's relief was as raw as a fresh wound.

"I really hope so." Marigold's haunted expression hung heavy on her face, and Mitch was reminded of something a maudlin Ebon had once said when in his cups: *hope is just the smoke from a pipe dream.* "It was always real to Ebon, woven from vivid dreams and a powerful imagination. Who's to say it didn't become as real as anything else?"

Carlton stared down at his own painting—Mitch noted that its centrepiece was a set of four fingerprints, one low and three high, a right hand's thumb to ring—and rubbed his dangling earring like a good luck charm as he asked, "Did Ebon have a name for this...thing?"

"No. He told me there was no point, because evil didn't *have* a name."

Jasonn swore under his breath. The group sat and stared at their paintings, sometimes turning to look at the spectres only they could see.

"So, what have we done here?" Mitch wanted to know. "By taking these paintings, have we inherited Ebon's ghosts?"

"It would seem so," Sinead mused. "Only, calling them ghosts feels wrong. I don't think these people *literally* haunted Ebon."

"Maybe he painted them and hid them away so they couldn't have any power over him," suggested Jasonn. "Does that sound crazy to you? Because it does to me, but it makes sense, too. What we have here is Ebon's catharsis. The scabs from his deepest wounds."

"So why didn't he just burn the paintings when they were done?" Ricky wanted to know. "And if they're connected to the—well, the *ghosts*—then why don't *we* do it?"

"Maybe that would've just released their essences again? I don't know. Maybe this way, all the trauma and the bad shit is caught like an insect in amber—harmless."

Carlton snorted. "Not so harmless if these folks are going to start following us around. Personally speaking, this Shimmer prick is going to be a real crimp on my style."

"Could be worse," Jasonn said. "At least they're ignoring us."

"No, they're not," said Scarla, and her voice was that of a lost child.

Mitch turned to glance at Kenner's shade and flinched in his skin. The boy was looking back at him.

The others all looked to their own ghosts and gasped, finding their gazes returned at last.

"What does this mean?" Scarla moaned. "What are they *doing*?"

"Everyone just stay calm," Sinead urged, sounding far from it herself. "Don't panic."

Mitch was finding it difficult to heed that last piece of advice. Kenner's eyes held no malice, no threat or judgement, but they were the eyes of a dead boy nonetheless.

"What do you want, Kenner? *What?*"

The kid said nothing, reacted not at all, simply kept his level gaze fixed on Mitch. Apart from this small change, none of the visitants gave any indication of their intentions toward the living gathered in the Plastered Cast.

"I'm thinking maybe I should close up," Ricky said. "If we all leave, do you think they'll follow us? Shit, what if they don't? I don't want them staying here forever."

"One way to find out." Jasonn rubbed his face in a vain attempt to hide his swelling terror. "The dead have kind of ruined the vibe of the evening anyway. What do you think, guys?"

"Let's call it a night," Carlton agreed, and that seemed to be the consensus. Mitch wasn't so sure. He imagined himself walking the empty city streets alone, turning to see Kenner standing in the shadow of a shop door—catching the last tram, spotting the boy sitting in the back of the carriage—hurrying through his front door to find sanctuary in his flat at last, only to find Ebon's dead lover sat in the corner of his lounge, waiting, his dead eyes cold and blank, his lips twisting up into a—

Mitch turned to reassure himself and felt as though someone had reached out to punch him in the heart.

Kenner was smiling at him, his lips a cold, cruel curve.

And then, with all the abruptness of an unexpected blow, the lights shut off.

The music died too, and the sudden silent darkness was met with gasps, curses, and moans from the friends gathered at the bar. With the electrics out, the Plastered Cast was a closed box lit only by moonlight streaming in through narrow windows high in the west wall, its occupants reduced to barely defined shadows within the deeper dark.

Mitch felt a sudden dread pickling his stomach. At any other time, a power failure would have been a mere annoyance. Tonight, it was a portent that augured ill for them all.

*Kenner's lips curled into a terrible grin—*

"Did anyone see that?" he asked.

"We can't fuckin' see anything!" Ricky retorted. He fumbled under the bar for some tealight candles to place along the bar top, a cigarette lighter to ignite their wicks. By the tiny shivering flames, Mitch saw the faces of his friends drawn dim and despairing.

"I'm trying really hard not to take this as a bad sign," Carlton muttered.

"The ghosts," Sinead gasped. "What are they doing?"

"Mine was *smiling*," Mitch told her, and hers wasn't the only sudden intake of breath in response. He and Jasonn pulled out their phones and activated the screen lights. Pointing his at the couches opposite the bar, he gingerly edged forward until the illumination touched the table curves and seat backs.

Kenner was nowhere to be seen. Mitch checked the immediate area, half-expecting the kid to spring out of the shadows like a spook in a horror flick with his grinning mouth open wide, but there was no sign of him.

"Mine's gone!" Relief tweaked his voice higher like a tiny huff of helium. "Jase?"

"Yep, mine too. Can anyone else see theirs?"

Mitch and Jasonn patrolled the room to make sure, but it quickly became clear that none of the six spectres remained to be seen by the living. They returned to the bar and the solace of company.

"They're gone!" Marigold crowed, close to hysteria. "Oh, Christ. They're gone!"

"Please tell me it's over now," Scarla said, one hand over her racing heart. "Ricky, where's your fuse box?"

"In the foyer. Hopefully it's just us and not the whole block." Ricky came out from behind the bar and started toward the room's single exit. "Give me a minute and we'll be right as rain."

He'd made it halfway to the foyer when he paused, his back snapping rigid. The chatter amongst the rest of the group ceased at once. Everyone had heard it.

A heavy thump from downstairs.

Ricky forced a laugh. "Someone wants in. Too late now."

Those words settled in Mitch's mind and took on a new nefarious meaning. But before he could say anything, a square of light appeared at the other end of the room and sat waiting for them like a doorway out of the darkness.

Despite the loss of power, the dead glass eye of the projector had flared to life and was casting a new picture against the north wall.

Mitch had never seen this image before, but he recognised it at once, as if he, too, had owned the storybook whose pages it haunted.

A fairground carriage in muted tones, captured late at night when the carnival was deserted and lifeless, and peering through the window cut-outs from its podium beyond—

A sideshow clown, ghost-pale face beaming through the shadows all around, its painted-on eyes empty and yet somehow full of unspoken promise, its round mouth gaping wide to reveal a depthless hungry void.

"No," Marigold whimpered. "*Please.*"

The projector cut out again and the image disappeared, its retinal echo lingering as if burned onto the black. Once more the group was stranded in the dark, deeper now for the sudden intrusion and withdrawal of light. Mitch heard someone sobbing quietly in abject despair, and that sexless sound could have been any one of them. He only knew it wasn't him because his throat was locked too tightly to admit the faintest whimper.

That sound from downstairs came again, and again, and this time it was unmistakable: the thump of weight upon carpeted wood.

Footsteps, coming up the stairs.

Mitch knew no-one had come through the front door—he recalled the *clack* of the lock snapping to just a quarter-hour before. No, he understood full well what this portended, and all the liquor behind Ricky's bar couldn't have dulled the keen edge of his terror.

The footsteps continued, slow but steady. They pushed the air from everyone's lungs, left them breathless and silent as a terrified boy huddled under his bedsheets. Mitch remembered that though there were only seventeen steps leading up to Ebon's childhood bedroom, his imagined pursuer had seemed to keep approaching without ever arriving...but with each step, the heavy tread upon the stairs of the Plastered Cast was growing louder, closer.

Tonight, whatever was coming would finally reach its destination.

He looked past the half-seen shapes of his friends to the blank, black canvas of the north wall, where images of their dear friend had overseen the memorial. But Ebon Eidolon was no longer watching over them—that kind soul had moved on to whatever came next, be it paradise, purgatory, or simply oblivion. Mitch wondered which was waiting for him on the other side of this oncoming revelation.

Then the coronary thump of the approaching footsteps came to an end, the climb complete, and the foyer was swallowed by a deeper darkness that crept into the bar and snuffed out the flickering tealights with one silent breath.

Mitch thought of his dead friend, of the light he had brought into the world, and knew that for each beacon that burned there was an equal and opposite shadow—and with Ebon's glow extinguished, his warnings ignored, there was nothing to hold back the fall of this unnatural night. He closed his eyes and imagined the glow of Ebon's loving soul, a candle to warm a heart by. He held on to cherished thoughts and pretended he was huddled under the sheets in the depths of an endless eve, praying this nameless terror would walk on and leave him shivering but untouched.

When a clammy chill swallowed the room and stole away the warmth of their desperate breath, he gave in to the inevitable and opened his eyes to see.

# The Ballad of Elvis O'Malley

WE CALLED HIM ELVIS, because of course we did. As teenagers in the first decade of the twenty-first century, we had no better context for a 1950s throwback like Johnny O'Malley. The kid slicked his black hair up into a pompadour, always wore a white tee with blue jeans and the inevitable leather jacket, and jammed old-school rock 'n' roll—the only other points of reference were James Dean and Danny Zuko, but although they were technically more appropriate, they weren't as universally obvious. And so, Elvis it was.

I can see now how condescending we were, but back then, the present was the only thing that mattered to us, and like every generation that had come before, we were certain that our own cool cultural traits would define the future. After all, it wasn't like MySpace and *My Super Sweet 16* and My Chemical Romance were going away any time soon. So we laughed at Elvis O'Malley and pigeonholed him, dismissed him, telling ourselves that we were giving him the story he wanted—because in the face of our mockery, he got to be the rebel without a cause. The outsider. The underdog.

I feel bad about it looking back, as any woman will wince at her callow teenage memories, but at the time I just went along with the pack. I've tried to believe since then that there was no real spite or bite to our jokes—we weren't *total* arseholes, and Elvis was a nice enough dude. Maybe I need to believe that I meant no harm because I feel like I knew him better than my friends, was closer to him. That last part was literally true: for five years, Elvis O'Malley was my next-door neighbour.

Every weekend, he'd be out in the driveway of the run-down house he shared with his run-down granddad, working on the wreck of an old Cadillac convertible he'd picked up somewhere, radio tuned to some insect-in-amber rock 'n' roll station. Often as not, he'd be sucking on a cigarette from a soft pack he kept rolled up in his shirt sleeve, because he really ran with that whole '50s deal from go to

whoa. My girlfriends and I would snicker at this display, though we'd fall into a pensive silence whenever he leaned over the bonnet and those blue jeans stretched tight across his butt. Elvis was kind of hot for a weirdo. I mean, *maybe* if he'd had that convertible all tricked out like something off *Pimp My Ride*, one of us might have ended up at Passion Point getting a better view of the back seat...but while it was a work in progress, Elvis would've had to bring girls back to his place. And one glimpse of his grandfather was enough to put the skids on that.

Pops looked like our Elvis fifty years on—same pomp but in a dirty shade of silver, same greaser fashion sense, same perennial ciggie glued to one nicotine-browned lip. He had a gimpy leg and a bottle of whisky always to hand, two things which I figured may have been related in either direction. They had a genial relationship, though I'd often catch Pops watching his grandson with a strange expression somewhere between wistfulness and dread. Maybe he was thinking back to when he'd been that age in the *actual* '50s, recalling the bobby-soxed baby doll who would one day become Johnny's grandmother; maybe he saw himself reflected in his grandson, and missed his long-gone rebellious youth. In any case, going home with a guy who lived with *that*? Pops's mug was not one you wanted to see when you were creeping back from the toilet after midnight in a strange house with that sex stank on you—a greasy smile spreading across his face like spilled oil as his eyes make the most of your bare legs. Ack! No thanks.

Poor Elvis. He didn't jibe with the sensibility of the new millennium, and I couldn't help feeling an insidious stab of pity when I saw him grinding away at a life he couldn't possibly make work. Johnny O'Malley was a kid born out of his time, stranded amongst dyed-pink fringes and pink sunglasses and Pink herself topping the charts, decades away from his true people. Back then, maybe he could've made something of himself, could've lived fast and died young and become a local legend—but here and now, all he could do was age and wither and turn into his Pops.

Props to the boy, though: he gave it a red-hot go. Over the course of our final year at high school, Elvis plugged away at his dreams until fate started to tease him with hints that they could actually come true. The convertible was starting to look less like a piece of rusty old crap and more like something that any of us girls would've been happy to take a spin in—a spin only, mind, but a spin nonetheless. It seemed Elvis might get the one thing he could hope for in life, because if he was going to be forever out of sync with the times and take a few licks for it, he could at least do so in a slick ride. Even if he was doomed to ride alone.

Enter Billie-Jo Brown.

Oh, she'd been there all along, of course. Nothing much to look at if I'm honest, a mousy and pudgy girl who took the occasional desperate stab at being fashionable but always lagged months behind the hottest trends—chunky specs shielding the dull eyes of a dog who's learned to expect a daily kicking, unremarkable hair to match her unremarkable surname, clothes that didn't so much flatter her figure as make fun of it behind her back. Like Elvis, BJ was actually quite nice when you took the time to talk to her, but she just didn't fit—just wasn't *cool*. Some of the dudes at school called her Blow Job Brown and claimed that she made up for her plain looks by being quite agreeable to oral favours, a trial she tolerated with as much grace as someone so inherently graceless could summon. You just knew that she was going to graduate into a boring job, marry the first boring dude with early male-pattern baldness who put it to her, pop out a couple smart but dorky kids, and end up looking like a blancmange poured into a pantsuit. For fuck's sake, she liked Kelly Clarkson and Avril Lavigne, *unironically*.

I have to admit that we sniggered amongst ourselves when she started spending time with Elvis O'Malley, smug little self-involved shits that we were, but that derision didn't last long. You see, like the convertible, BJ began to change for the better under his patient touch. She found a way forward by looking back, stopped chasing trends we'd already abandoned, adopted a style that weaponised everything that had made her a misfit.

Billie-Jo Brown pulled this whole ugly-duckling-goes-full-swan deal on us—baby doll dresses that looked even cooler now than they had fifty years before, newly black hair arranged into a Bettie Page fringe and curled under at the ends, unremarkable specs traded in for jazzy red frames—and she pulled the whole thing off with motherfucking *aplomb*. The newly rebranded Bee-Jay Brown even seemed thinner, though a closer look revealed that she hadn't lost any weight—she just carried it, and herself, with a newfound confidence. Her eyes were alight and alive now, and though her rock 'n' roll Romeo still acted cool in a very Fonzy way, there was a gleam in his gaze that matched hers. Elvis had fallen as hard for Bee-Jay as she had for him, and now he had his doll and she had her rocker. Some kids laughed, but not me, not this time. I was happy to see these square pegs find holes that fit them in this round-arse world.

Now that he had the girl, I figured Elvis wouldn't have time for the car. I couldn't have been more wrong. He redoubled his efforts in the driveway alongside mine, his radio blaring doo-wop ballads and twangy rockers all afternoon and night, Bee-Jay keeping him company as he worked. The two of them laughed and smoked like chimneys and kissed like honeymooners as Elvis brought his ride closer and closer to completion, and all the while, Pops kept watch from behind the screen door. My friends and I had figured him for a dirty old man who'd take an active interest in his grandson's love life in all the wrong ways, but while he eyed Bee-Jay as closely as he did Elvis, I saw no hint of anything skeezy in his supervision. He'd just stand there and watch them work with that same weird expression, like he was happy to see youth in full bloom but couldn't help thinking it was all doomed in the end.

That look made a lot more sense when Dad told me Pops's story over dinner one night. He'd heard it from his own parents, who were the same age as our distinguished neighbour and had also once been, as Dad put it, "bodgies and widgies".

Passion Point is our local make-out spot, a lookout up in the hills that oversees the town and has provided a picturesque backdrop to car-based fornication for generations. On the way up to it, the amorous must navigate a treacherous turn known as the Devil's Hairpin, a spot so notorious for accidents that some believe it's haunted. Turns out that Pops had almost lost his leg after wiping out there on prom night in 1957 with Elvis's grandmother-to-be in the passenger seat. They'd both survived, but now I saw in Pops's eyes a resignation to the inevitable, like he just *knew* it was going to happen all over again. He might as well have been watching old home movies of Elvis and Bee-Jay long after their deaths, and I found that kind of disturbing when I wasn't distracted by another string of texts or a reality TV show or even, sometimes, homework.

One night, Kayleigh and I bumped into Bee-Jay outside Julio's Pizza on a rare occasion when she wasn't glued to Elvis's side, and we chatted a while as we waited for our dinners. I could sense the smirk lurking beneath my bestie's smile, knew that she considered this conversation a joke we could laugh over later, but I was totally sincere—like I said, Bee-Jay had always been nice, and now that she'd acquired style and confidence, she'd become interesting, too. The chat turned toward physical matters, as girl talk often does, and I gave her a friendly nudge as I asked if she and Elvis were doing the deed yet. For the first time, Bee-Jay blushed and looked a little like the awkward Billie-Jo of old as she shook her head and looked down at the footpath.

"Things get pretty hot and heavy," she admitted, ashing her cigarette with a sultry flick that should've looked contrived but came as second nature to her now. "We're real gone, you know? But we're waiting just a little longer. We've got it all planned out—it's going to happen on the biggest night of our lives. The one everyone will remember us for."

"Sounds exciting," Kayleigh said, the flat note in her voice begging to differ.

Bee-Jay nodded. "Yeah. And *terrifying*. But everything has to be just right. Maybe you'll see, one day."

With that, she ditched her smoke, picked up her pizza with a parting wave, and ditched us. Kayleigh pulled a crazy face at me, like we shouldn't have expected any more from a weirdo. "What does she mean, we'll see one day? Does she think we're *all* virgins around here?"

At the time, I just thought it was nice that she had something to look forward to. In our final year of high school, the future loomed unseen and intimidating behind a wall of fog that separated us from the responsibilities and fears of the adult world, and for all that we'd long since begun to participate in some of its rituals—such as sex, for example—its breadth and weight was dreadful to contemplate. Some of us might not even make it there, might aspirate our own vomit or die in a car crash or expire beneath an attacker's assault, and it was sometimes hard not to believe that those might just be the lucky ones. At least they could avoid the tripwires and landmines of adult life, could retain their youth and edge forever, become legends whose lights would never fade even as age slowly dimmed our own soul's glowing on the long journey into the dark.

Toward the end of the year, just when Elvis's Caddy seemed to be approaching a roadworthy condition, it disappeared from his driveway. My first thought was that it'd been ganked, and I felt a little sick at the idea of such cruelty—but if that were the case, he would've been heartbroken, and he was not. This was part of his plan, then, so I assumed he'd rolled it into his little shed to apply the finishing touches. My mind moved on to other matters: our school prom was just two weeks away, and my crush Chad Goodwin had finally taken the hint and asked me to go with him. In my Cinderella fantasies, I made a grand entrance and the whole room turned to stare, blown away by my beauty—that night was going to live on in legend long after I died. I found the perfect dress and everything. This was *going to happen.*

And...nope.

Sure, I dolled up pretty nice that night, but every girl there could say the same, and it's hard for a single rose to stand out in a rose garden. On top of that, after we'd all made our fashionably late entrances, someone hurried in to tell us we needed to *come outside*, we needed to *see this*, so we left the dance mix behind to go see what the fuss was about. The first thing I saw was a dozen of my classmates milling around with their digital cameras out, snapping away like junior paparazzi. When I pushed through the throng, the objects of their attention came into view...and I almost dropped my corsage.

Elvis O'Malley was dressed up to the nines, his jeans traded in for black slacks, his tee for a vintage cream ruffle shirt and bow tie, his jacket for a white sports coat with a crimson carnation—a classic look that he pulled off with panache. Bee-Jay was rocking a sleeveless black tutu dress spotted with roses the colour of her date's carnation, her long hair styled into a cascade of curls like some immaculate wave caught at the peak of its beauty. Both were perched like movie stars on the bonnet of Elvis's Cadillac, finally restored to its original glory—and how!

The Caddy gleamed under the parking lot lights, its bodywork pristine, the fresh paint job a breathtaking shade of lipstick red. Its whitewall tires shone, two-tone perfection, and every inch of bare steel on that ride glowed as if polished a second ago. *Damn*, that car was dope! Every drop of elbow grease that Elvis had poured into it showed in the end result and declared itself well-spent. The three of them were a page ripped out of some 1950s magazine, picture-perfect, classic.

I was so jealous I literally almost puked, but at the same time I was so happy—I didn't know whether to congratulate them, or be inspired by their pure class, or just go home and never try anything ever again. In the end, I took a couple of pictures and went back inside, like everyone else.

But that wasn't the end of it. Oh, no.

The school dance committee always crowned one happy couple as Prom King and Queen, and you can guess who they chose for that honour in 2006. Hint: it wasn't me and Chad Goodwin, the kind of dude who popped his collar even in an expensive tux. No, it was Elvis and Bee-Jay who were elevated to high school royalty that night, fitted with crowns and sashes as the rest of us pretended that our blood was not boiling with ungracious envy. The principal tried to be hip by calling them "Daddy-O'Malley and Baby Doll Brown", and the King and Queen deigned to give a very brief speech.

"This is just the most," Bee-Jay mumbled, her recent confidence daunted by the act of public speaking. Her face was flushed with joy, but her mouth carried a moue of anxiety, as if this appointment to nobility brought with it a weighty responsibility. "Thank you very much."

Elvis shared a long, loving look with his doll before he stepped up to the mic.

"We've been working up to this for a long time," he said, and due to my girl chat with Bee-Jay, I thought I knew exactly what he meant by that. "And it's been a real gas...but now, the wait is over. Tonight, we go down in history!"

They stepped down to a deafening cheer, most of it sincere, and then it was time for their victory dance. The DJ threw on the closest thing he could find to rock 'n' roll—Pearl Jam's cover of "Last Kiss"—and Elvis took Bee-Jay onto the dancefloor for a twirl. They'd clearly been practicing, because they really cut a rug out there. I mean, they were on some serious *Strictly Come Dancing* shit, their rock routines making everyone else look like bumbling amateurs—even the principal himself, who looked old enough to have jitterbugged and twisted way back when and couldn't resist breaking out the old moves to a mix of jeers and cheers.

I swallowed my sour grapes and tried to enjoy the spectacle, even if a few of my peers didn't manage to do the same. But no amount of grumbling and griping could change the fact that this night belonged to Elvis and Bee-Jay, and even after they ducked out early and took off, we were still buzzing about them. Maybe movies had bred in us a disposition toward narrative forms, but this happy ending for the underdogs made total sense.

This was the stuff of which old rock 'n' roll songs were made. This was "The Ballad of Elvis O'Malley".

I don't know much about old music, but I do know that those songs often ended in tragedy—star-crossed lovers burning bright, then flaming out before their time. I remember that thought crossing my mind at one point, somewhere between watching Elvis dip Bee-Jay on the dancefloor and letting Chad Goodwin dip me in the back of his Lexus because it was prom night and I'd just been reminded that you couldn't beat the classics. And it was a thought I had good reason to recall the next day, when Kayleigh texted me the news.

If this is indeed "The Ballad of Elvis O'Malley", then we've done the first three verses. Verse one is the poor but good boy Johnny working on his dream ride; verse two, he finds his dream girl; verse three, their crowning glory at the school dance. Maybe you can guess how the last stanza pans out.

It goes a little something like this: our Prom King and Queen are on their way down from Passion Point, no doubt glowing from the long-awaited consummation of their love, when they hit the Devil's Hairpin and Elvis loses control of the Caddy. Tires screech. Metal crumples. No-one walks away.

Repeat chorus. Fade out. The end.

I don't think I've ever felt as guilty as I did that day. Much as I'd always liked Johnny and Billie-Jo, I'd mocked them too, and the taste of my smug condescension repeated on me like a servo hot dog. Hadn't we forced this fate upon our classmates, when you got right down to it? Sure, we didn't do anything to cause that crash at the Devil's Hairpin, but we knew stories...so all along, we scorned them and set them up as underdogs, knowing that underdogs always came back in the last reel. We'd basically been on some *Carrie* shit, hadn't we? No bucket of pig's blood this time—we were more sophisticated than that. Every town needs a legend, and in Elvis, Bee-Jay, and the Cadillac, we found our own tragic local myth. They *had* to die, because they were perfect. They were the past; they were timeless. Do you think they'd have passed into urban legend if they'd been Elijah and Braxton, wasted on alcopops and singing along to The Black Eyed Peas as they wiped out in a fucking Honda Jazz?

Like I said: you can't beat the classics.

A couple of weeks after the tragedy, I was in the lounge texting Kayleigh when I heard Pops going off in the yard next door. The poor bastard had lost all he had left, and now we often heard him crying and cursing and stumbling around the front yard, ripe as hell and a dozen sheets to the wind. But there was an unseasonal rainstorm tonight, and when I parted the curtains for a peek, Pops was down in the mud, struggling against both his drunkenness and his gammy leg to get back up as he ranted at the uncaring sky. I was reluctant to get involved, but felt I owed something to the memory of Elvis, so I grabbed an umbrella and headed outside.

Pops was wailing as I approached, but his words didn't become legible until he realised I was there and allowed me to brace his weight so he could get both legs beneath him again. Sheltered by the umbrella, leaning heavily on my arm, he unloaded his grief on me as I helped him across the wet grass to his front door. I let him ramble for a while, then hushed him and hoped he'd go easy on himself—after all, none of what happened had been his fault. But after I'd gotten him into his threadbare lounge and dumped him gently on the couch, where an overflowing ashtray and dirty glass awaited his attention, he looked me dead in the eye for the first time. A certain lucidity came over him then, and he told me something that echoed in my mind as I went home to shower away the mud and chilly summer rain—something that kept looping in the back of my head over the next few days, no matter what I was doing, until I decided I had to look into his story.

I did some research online, then went to the local library and looked through their microfiche copies of old newspapers like I was the main character in some dumb horror movie. And what do you know: there was something to what Pops had said, after all.

This one article was published in a Halloween edition of the local paper from 1993, garnished with stupid cartoon pumpkins and shit, and it was about the scant handful of hauntings reported in our boring little town over the years. And there was the bombshell, right below the paragraph about the headless woman who is rumoured to float across the council duck pond on the anniversary of her death.

*Between town and the lookout known as Passion Point is a sharp bend colloquially known as the Devil's Hairpin, which has long been regarded as haunted. Going back as far as the late 1950s, there have been reports of a red Cadillac sweeping wildly around the bend and causing near-misses or full-blown accidents—a Cadillac piloted by two rockabilly kids that always disappears seconds after appearing. And yet, there exists no record of any such car ever crashing at the Devil's Hairpin...*

Well, shit.

Elvis and Bee-Jay hadn't just become an urban legend—they'd already been one for *fifty years*.

It all made a strange kind of sense now. Maybe if I hadn't been so self-absorbed, if I'd paid more attention to the history of my town, I'd have seen this coming—although, to be fair, it's not the kind of thing anyone could be expected to believe.

As Pops had slumped on his couch and reached for the bottle, he'd told me what happened on prom night in 1957.

"Me and Molly are cruising up to the Point, mad in love and keen to get back to it. We hit the Devil's Hairpin, and suddenly, outta nowhere, there's this car screaming around the bend at us. Even past the headlights, I can see two kids in the front, rockers like us but no-one we ever seen before, and the fools are *kissing*, and their Caddy's coming out of their lane into mine. I wrench the wheel away, and those kids look up at us—and their faces stayed with me, 'cause they didn't even look *surprised*. And then they're just gone like they was never there, and we're bouncing off the guardrail and everything goes crazy and I don't remember the next bit so well—just the screaming and the pain.

"We was lucky to survive that crash, but my leg was screwed. Didn't matter, though, 'cause we had each other, and soon we had a family. Years went by, and I lost my Molly to that bastard cancer—then my little girl and her husband, too. All I had left was Johnny, and what a fuckup of a Pops I was for him, never getting over my own grief enough to show him how a man should be. I watched him grow up, looking more and more like me every year, and figured it would all work out...and then he got that wreck of a Caddy dumped in the driveway.

"The first day I saw him working on that car, it hit me like a ton of bricks—he looked *just like* that kid who ran me off the road in '57. I shrugged it off, 'cause that was plain nuts, right? And then Bee-Jay came along, and still I told myself it was okay, 'cause she was no baby doll like I seen in that Caddy...but when she changed her style, I couldn't deny it no more. Somehow, it had been *them* that night.

"I told Johnny never to go up the Point, tried to scare him off that Hairpin—shit, one drunk day I even told him why, told him the whole damn story of what I saw when me and Molly wiped out and I almost lost my leg. He got this weird look, even smiled like something made sense to him now, but he promised me he wouldn't go. He *swore*.

"But all along, I knew he would. Because he *had* to. Poor sonofabitch never had no choice."

Pops started crying again then, and you know what? I did, too.

So that's when it all began, right there at the end—two beautiful misfits trying to escape to an era that would accept them and succeeding in a way no-one could ever have imagined. Elvis spent his final year building up to that one night, crafting his own death with his bare hands without even knowing it...at first. He must've already heard about the ghostly Caddy that haunted the Devil's Hairpin, but he wouldn't have understood his role in the tale until Pops told him what had really happened in 1957. After that, he'd been as resigned to fate as his grandfather, had felt as helpless to change it—and maybe he hadn't even wanted to.

Elvis O'Malley and Bee-Jay Brown were always destined to take that final ride, to go down backwards in history...and not only had they had known that, they'd *accepted* it—embraced it, even, as the perfect ending. Theirs was a tragic tale, but it had a grace that most lives would never know. They'd never grow old, get fat, get divorced, get sick and die alone in a bed somewhere. Their love would never end, its intensity would never fade, and their tale would never be forgotten. The details might grow muddied over the years, but their final ride would live on in legend as long as lovers made their pilgrimages to Passion Point.

Small towns need their stories. The loop closed, and we got one for the ages. Our very own timeless tragedy, our urban myth—"The Ballad of Elvis O'Malley."

I've said it twice already, but hell, one more time for the road: you can't beat the classics.

# I Do Thee Woe

BLACK BLINDS FLAPPED UP like opening eyelids, allowing the pupils in the classroom to look out upon the bright world once more, and Dragan flinched at the incursion of reality. Watching a film, even in a group, had always felt like an escape into a better place, and there were few things he dreaded more than the credit roll. For him, that meant the dream was over, and his life had always been a poor substitute.

With reality restored, Peter Lamb stopped the movie and stood in its place, framed by the large TV screen as he invited his class to discuss what they'd seen. They'd just watched Tarantino's *Pulp Fiction*, and today's subject was the magpie tendencies of directors and the relative worth of what they liked to call *hommage*. Dragan would have loved to sink his teeth into meatier examples of that subject—the debt De Palma and Argento owed to Hitchcock, for example, or the way Italian directors such as Margheriti and Cozzi had blatantly riffed on whatever Hollywood film had made money that year—but it was clear no-one else in the class was steeped as deeply in film lore as he. His fellow adult students ranged from enthusiastic school-leavers used to viewing hyper-cut movies on portable devices to loose-end retirees who thought true quality in film had gone out when digital came in.

And somewhere in the middle, adrift on a tepid sea, was Dragan.

His eyes drifted from their lecturer to the white screen behind him, a blank sheet of paper that only reminded him of the scripts he wasn't writing. Dragan's dearest dream was to make his own film, and while he had no idea how he might achieve such a thing, this course was his first step toward that ultimate end. He'd thought he might meet like-minded people here, hardcore movie geeks with whom he might form a collective and set about the serious business of birthing an independent feature, but once again he found himself slipping through the cracks thanks to his niche tastes and social incompatibility. It was like his time at Magellan Video all over again.

At three o'clock, Peter Lamb wrapped up the discussion and announced the end of class, leaning back against his desk with arms folded as his students stuffed books and laptops into bags and shuffled their chairs back. Dragan looked across the room to where Chloe kept her habitual seat, and as always, she was packed and heading for the door before anyone else had even risen to their feet. She seemed to enjoy the lessons, so why was she in such a hurry to leave? Maybe she had another class, a part-time job, a demanding boyfriend. Dragan sighed at yet another missed opportunity to walk her out. With her sea-green eyes and chocolate curls, she reminded him of the Final Girl from a slasher film, the shy straight-arrow who contained enough inner strength to survive the bloody cull.

Chloe was long gone by the time Dragan left the transportable that housed his screen and media course. Along with other adult education classes, it was held on the premises of a high school, which had always made him a little uncomfortable—not least because it recalled his own awkward and miserable teenage experience. And there were other reasons, as he was reminded when his path crossed that of a trio of uniformed girls.

He paid as little attention to these young women as possible lest they suspect he was harbouring inappropriate thoughts, or worse, in case he began to do so—some of the seniors were far too developed to be seen as children. Take the one closest to him now: no more than seventeen, yet she carried herself like a fully-fledged woman, sultry and jaded and wise to the ways of the world. Her eyes flicked to him briefly as they passed in the yard, her full lips wrapped around the striped paper straw of a takeaway juice, and Dragan felt the less mature of the two even though he had more than ten years on her. She'd be familiar with the foibles of boys and men both, had no doubt experienced more attention and attraction than he—a very low bar, to be certain, but still. The world was at her feet. The unspoken promise of those lips, those curves, those eyes would be enough to get her anything, anyone she wanted. How wonderful that must be.

Her gaze held his for only a second, empty of any interest—she might as well have been looking at a lamppost. Then her friend cried "Layla!" and those eyes slid away, and as the girls walked on, Dragan heard them laughing at some private joke. He tried to believe it wasn't him, and that was probably true, but the response had long been ingrained.

He walked to the bus stop surrounded by a dozen high schoolers who ignored him as they exchanged slang-warped banter he found harder to understand every year. He found himself glad to be beneath their notice; if their attention should be called to him, it would be only to jeer and mock. And even he could understand that, because when he looked in a mirror, he saw the same thing as they: not so much a man as an inflated boy, incapable of cultivating more than a thin pubertal wisp of a moustache, his lumpy figure thrown out of proportion by broad hips. Add his flabby chest to the equation and he cut more of a womanly figure than many of the stripling girls around him at the bus stop, not to mention less of a manly one than the strapping boys who already looked like they needed to shave every morning.

*You inherited your mother's hips*, his father had said, more than once, with the unspoken implication that Dragan had taken on other characteristics deemed unsuitable for a man. He'd always been clumsy and uncoordinated, bad at sports, soft-spoken and insular. Little wonder *tata* had long since stopped asking when he was going to bring a girl home. On the few occasions Dragan had done just that, inviting Bessie or Alita from work over in the days when he'd still lived with his family, his father hadn't bothered with the conspiratorial winks he parcelled out to his other sons. He'd been convinced that nothing more than talk and movie-watching was going to happen behind that closed bedroom door—and what really burned was that he'd been right, every single time.

Dragan boarded the bus and slipped in a pair of earbuds like at least half the high schoolers around him, though he chose to listen to synth-heavy horror soundtracks rather than blandly lascivious modern R&B. He disembarked at the shopping centre near his flat and trudged inside, too much time on his hands and too little inspiration to use it well. He wandered the modest mall for as long as he could, lingering in an entertainment outlet and flicking through movies he couldn't afford, and then he sat alone in the food court and picked at some noodles like an alternate-universe George Lucas who'd never struck upon the idea that would carve his name into history.

Dusk was shading into night when he left the mall. He passed a graffiti-scarred video kiosk and paused before it, wondering how a world of Blockbusters had ever come to this. Once rental stores had graced every major road, and now they'd been replaced by vending machines that stocked only the most popular new releases as if they were cans of soft drink—and for all their bubbly insipidity and lack of substance, they might as well have been.

He was reminded of his years at Magellan Video, a perfect job that had come to an end when declining business had seen its owners lay off most of their staff. He'd hoped that seniority and loyalty might preserve his position, but even there, where his knowledge and experience should have counted for something, he'd been regarded as dispensable. Worse, the job had shown him how little the general populace cared for innovation or engagement in movies—he'd had to bite his tongue every time he'd checked out another boneheaded dudebro comedy or homogenous PG-13 horror, and that was precisely the kind of dreck kept in these kiosks. Why didn't the general public want more from their films? A life so artless and prosaic scarcely seemed worth living.

Dragan turned away from the treasonous kiosk and spotted a pale face and hands hovering in the shadows nearby. He assumed it was an advertisement hung in a darkened window, then started as he realised its true dimensions—a young woman, wrapped in a black kaftan that matched her hair so perfectly she seemed to disappear into the fabric just as her clothing bled into the shadows around it. She might have been dressed in the sleek fur of a panther, camouflaged by the falling night as she waited for prey. Her face was a beautiful mask, achingly familiar and completely foreign at the same time. Her long fingers clutched a thin stack of flyers.

Dragan hoped the woman would speak to him, but his heart sank a little at the thought of what she might say. Her unusual dress and fistful of propaganda led him to assume her purpose was religious in nature, and such people always seemed to zero in on him as if sensing a soul susceptible to their dogma. Sure enough, a smile broke across her face like she'd recognised a perfect mark as she glided out of the deeper shade and extended a flyer toward him.

He took it out of weary obligation; at least a woman was showing him some little attention, no matter the reason. Expecting cult mysticism or fringe politics, Dragan was pleasantly surprised to find that the flyer advertised an arthouse film called *I Do Thee Woe*, and that it doubled as a free pass for the following evening's screening at the Viceroy.

Despite his love of cinema, theatrical excursions were a rare and expensive indulgence for Dragan, and he missed the experience. Going out to catch a movie was what regular people did of a night, instead of praying for oblivion to bring back the dawn or just swallow them entirely. And they took dates.

A reckless notion occurred to him then, and he grabbed at this rare chance to be bold.

"Could I have two? I might bring someone along."

The young woman smiled again—had he really not seen her somewhere before?—and he told himself there hadn't been a condescending edge to it. She handed him another flyer in any case, her cool fingertip touching his for one long second, and then nodded in encouragement before slipping away as if a long day's work was finally done. Dragan idly imagined she'd been waiting there in the shadows just for him, then dismissed the fancy with a shiver. No-one would linger for him, not for any reason that bade well.

He wondered if the flyer lady would be there at the screening tomorrow night, if she'd smile at him again, and thought the odds of both were quite good. It hardly mattered, though, since he'd set himself on a separate and equally hapless course by asking for a second ticket. He wasn't sure what kind of movies Chloe liked, but it was a stretch to hope she'd be into something as obscure as this, a further stretch to assume there was any chance she'd agree to accompany him. Still, he didn't have to actually *ask* her. He'd been bold enough to obtain two passes and give himself the option, and to his way of thinking, that was bravery enough for one day.

Dragan walked home and let himself into the drab flat he'd tried to lighten with framed posters of *Zombie Flesh Eaters* and *It Follows* and *The Hunt for Candy Parker*. He grabbed a two-litre Coke from the fridge and sat down to start an essay on the scripts of Pegg and Wright that Peter Lamb wanted to see Monday next week. But beyond that distraction, the evening stretched out before him like an endless empty shadow, and those dark hours hung around him and rotted. He watched a Flanagan film; he opened the IDEAS folder on his laptop and wracked his brain in vain before closing it an hour later; he watched another Flanagan film. He was glad when sleep beckoned him to bed, closing the curtains on another lacklustre day.

Dragan regarded dream sequences as a bit of a cheat, as movie dreams were usually too linear and plot-relevant to be believable and were often used merely as an excuse to cram in a cheap jump scare.

Real life wasn't so neatly plotted; his own dreams were nonsensical, impenetrable, unspectacular. Tonight's mental movie, then, was remarkable for its thematic consistency.

He was sitting in a cinema auditorium, somewhere toward the middle, and the rest of the seats were packed with people he knew and people he didn't—a full house tonight. The lights dimmed to darkness, and the curtain flapped up like a black blind to reveal a blank white screen that faded to its opposing shade. One line of credits came up in a sober font: *A Film by Dragan Stojanović*.

He settled back in his seat, surprised and pleased. Finally! He wasn't a failure anymore. He'd made it. He'd made *this*.

The black screen cut to a plain and shabby bathroom—grubby mirror, dirty tiles, very much like the one in his flat. The shot was uninspired and poorly set up, angled at an accidental Dutch tilt, and Dragan wriggled uncomfortably in his seat. A simple pseudo-spooky synth score kicked in, sounding less like John Carpenter than a ham-fisted child hammering away at a cheap Casio. The audience was dead silent as the bathroom door opened and an actor edged into the fringe of the shot. He stepped to his mark in the middle of the room, glancing briefly at the camera like the rankest of amateurs. The actor was Dragan himself.

A couple of pre-emptory titters could be heard rising from the audience, and he came to a dreadful understanding: this was not a triumphant dream of self-realisation but an excruciating nightmare just beginning to unfold. He wanted to leave before things got any worse, but the crowd hemmed him into his narrow seat. He could do nothing but watch as the screen-Dragan took off his shirt and dropped it to one side in a poor attempt at casual sultriness.

A laugh rang out from the row behind him, female and raucous. He sank into his seat in horror as his doppelgänger then stepped out of his pants and stood there on the screen completely naked, running his hands through his hair in a self-conscious attempt to seduce the camera. The clumsy angle made his dimensions look even worse than a mirror did, emphasising the bulge of his broad hips and the sag of his breasts whilst diminishing his genitalia to proportions usually associated with Michelangelo's *David*.

The crowd erupted into gales of laughter. They hooted like mocking monkeys. They threw handfuls of popcorn at the screen as if its occupant deserved to be stoned. Dragan looked away, excoriated by his own work, and saw that the young girl in the seat beside him was Layla. She watched the film with a cruel grin, her full wet lips teasing the tip of a striped paper straw, dressed in a tube top and jean shorts so skimpy that she showed almost as much skin as the hapless actor up on the screen. She seemed to feel his eyes upon her and turned, her vicious grin growing wider as she recognised him.

*He's here!* she cried, and of course, her voice somehow cut through the pandemonium all around them. She pointed at Dragan and laughed, laughed. *It's HIM! He's HERE!*

Everyone turned to look. Everyone pointed. Everyone laughed. Dragan tried to stand and push his way along the aisle, but Chloe was sitting on the other side of him and she pushed him back into his seat, snapped handcuffs closed around his wrist to secure him to the armrest. She sneered at his pleas for release, her usual modest blouse and jeans swapped for a revealing Stars and Stripes bikini, and one hand was reaching into the seat next to her to pleasure a grinning Peter Lamb while the other held up an ancient film camera to record Dragan's humiliation, and somewhere behind the jeering crowd stood a woman in a black kaftan who smiled and licked her lips and brought curtains of deep pitch down over the whole wretched scene.

Dragan burst back into consciousness, inexplicably aroused and utterly mortified. He tried to take revenge on dream-Chloe by thinking of her figure in that scanty bikini as he attempted to relieve himself, but in the end, her mocking eyes and cruel laugh drove his readiness away. A half-hour passed before he managed to return to sleep, and if he dreamed anything else that night, he chose not to remember it.

\* \* \*

When three o'clock came around the next day and brought film class to an end, Dragan was already packed up and ready to go. He was second to leave after Chloe, and as he followed her out onto the asphalt, he summoned every reserve of courage he could muster. *Be bold and breathe fire, Dragan*, he told himself, though it didn't help that he knew his name had nothing to do with dragons and in fact meant *beloved*. Well, he'd never end up that way unless he did something about it.

"Hey, Chloe."

She turned and shifted her bag on her shoulder, flicking brown curls out of her face with a toss of her head. Her sea-green eyes showed no particular interest, but at least no boredom or contempt either. Here in daylit consciousness, he found it hard to imagine her ever being so cruel or blatantly sexual as she had been in his dream, and he cringed at the humiliated arousal that vision had provoked in him.

"Hey, Dragan."

"Did you like the film?" They'd just sat through another of Peter Lamb's keynote movies, a Jarmusch flick that Dragan had drifted in and out of as he'd prepared for this moment. "I mean, are you into arty stuff like that?"

She shrugged. "It was okay. I'm into all sorts, really. What about you?"

"It was all right. I like a lot of things too. Arthouse stuff can be pretty cool."

"Yeah."

He was never going to become a screenwriter if he produced dialogue as flat as this. Listening to himself force out these clumsy words was almost as excruciating as his dream from the night before. Dragan paused a moment, hoping his classmates would disperse quickly and give them privacy but knowing he couldn't wait any longer.

"So, I hope this doesn't sound weird or anything, but I got given a couple of free passes to a film tonight." He could already see the shutters coming down behind her eyes as she realised where he was headed, but he flailed on regardless. "Did you have any plans? I mean, would you be interested in going?"

"Yeah, I've got things to be doing. Sorry."

"No problem. Have a nice night."

Chloe flexed her lips into a polite parting smile and then she was off, head down and moving fast. Dragan told himself she wasn't walking any more swiftly than usual, that he hadn't just embarrassed them both. Well, at least he'd tried—even that poor effort had to be worth celebrating.

His father wouldn't have said so. Letting out a breath redolent with the rotting remnants of his anxiety, Dragan took his usual path toward the street and the bus stop. On the way, he saw a schoolgirl sitting alone on a bench attached to another transportable and slowed for a moment. It was Layla.

She didn't look anywhere near as salacious as she had in his dream, nor as womanly as she had yesterday afternoon. She was staring glumly down at her phone, feet crossed and swaying absently beneath her, and she looked more like a lost child than a confident young adult. Dragan felt a pang of guilt for subconsciously sexualising her, for assuming she had it so much easier than him. Sure, young women seemed like they had the world at their feet, but often that world was snapping at their toes. Layla could look forward to being marginalised, manipulated, objectified, hated merely for being who and what she was. Some people—men like *him*, whether he intended it or not—saw her only as a thing to be equally craved and feared, coveted and loathed. She might strive and succeed or fail and fall by her own standards, but as far as the world was concerned, she was just more meat for the machine.

For a moment, Dragan considered offering her the spare movie ticket as a peace offering and nothing more, a consolation for the contempt she had already faced and would go on enduring the rest of her life. But he knew how *that* would look, and he was bitterly amused as he imagined her response. If asking Chloe out had been a bad idea, this fleeting one—no matter how well-intentioned—was so much worse.

Dragan found he couldn't face his flat today; the last thing he needed was to be alone in that rancid cell. Since he had plans for the evening, he avoided his usual stop and headed down the road to catch a different bus. This one took him to a mall he'd never visited before, where he browsed Blu-ray re-releases of classic horror films that his student's income would not stretch to afford. How lucky he was that tonight's entertainment had been offered *gratis*.

*I Do Thee Woe* was about as obscure a film as he'd ever come across. It was not listed on IMDb or Wikipedia, and any references were limited to reproductions of the flyer on indie websites that hadn't seen the flick themselves and could offer no other details about it. He couldn't tell if it was supposed to be horror, arthouse, or both. An enigma, then, and hopefully, a pleasant surprise.

He loitered around the mall until it was time for dinner, then bought something cheap and packed with carbohydrates that would do his figure no favours at all. But what did it matter, in the end? He was born to this body and it would never bend to his will, so he might as well get used to it. He looked up the Viceroy's location and caught the bus he needed to get him in the general vicinity. By the time he had disembarked and walked the rest of the way to the cinema, the free film's eight o'clock start was just a quarter-hour off.

The Viceroy was an old Art Deco theatre tucked away down a side street in a quiet suburb, its former grandeur much reduced by its long-standing state of disrepair. The fading posters that sagged behind its smeared windows advertised the kind of mild melodramas he assumed only pensioners would want to watch, and its cream façade was chipped and shabby from lack of care. Still, Dragan found it a thing of beauty, and was glad for this shake-up of his routine as he pushed through its glass doors and stepped into the foyer.

The paisley-patterned carpet retained too much colour to be the original, and modern soft-drink signage marred the bar's old-school charm, but otherwise the place was a time capsule. A central pillar dominated the room, girt by a ring of cushioned seating; neon tube lighting above the auditorium declared *IN SESSION* but was currently dull and lifeless. One wall was affixed with old photographs of the Viceroy in better days, of its sister theatre the Black Regent before its decline into dereliction, and another held a period-accurate ticket booth that was closed for the night. There was little need of it, as the Viceroy appeared to be empty of any other custom. He thought that was a shame for the clearly ailing cinema, but it suited his mood just fine.

Dragan crossed to the mirror-backed bar and bought a large cup of Coke, savouring the wonderful scent of hot popcorn but skipping snacks for reasons both nutritional and financial. The man who served him was a skeletal relic in a burgundy vest who might well have worked here his whole life, who might have died years before but carried on in his role regardless for all the animation and vigour he displayed, and Dragan amused himself by imagining the man collecting dust and cobwebs in a broom closet between shifts. Refreshment procured, he walked over to the black velvet curtains that marked the entrance to the theatre proper, and the drapes parted to reveal the young woman who'd given him his free pass.

She was wearing the same kaftan from the day before and it shaded into the darkness beyond her, leaving her foreign/familiar face and pale hands to hover in the air like a puppeteer's tools. Again her finger touched his when he handed the flyer back to her, and she smiled as if his presence was in response to a personal invitation and very welcome. He thought he knew why when she gestured down the aisle, for he wandered in to find the auditorium almost empty.

Of the red vinyl seats that sloped down toward the veiled screen in twenty rows, only two were occupied. The first filmgoer was a tubby young fellow in a *Call of Duty* t-shirt who was already halfway through a tub of popcorn and wiping greasy fingers on his sweatpants like someone who had long given up on the attention of others, and the second was twice Dragan's age, grey hair straggling from a high forehead down onto the shoulders of his battered leather jacket. Dragan chose a spot near the centre of the auditorium and made himself comfortable, gazing up at the Art Deco rosettes around each embedded ceiling light and listening to the quiet piano music that filtered in through hidden speakers.

Shoes trod the carpeted aisle behind him, and he turned in his seat to see a bespectacled woman whose psychedelic tie-dye shirt might have been intended to distract from her drab face and flyaway hair. She took a seat on the other side of the aisle, a few rows back from him. Four patrons—hardly a bumper turnout. No wonder the woman in black had been so glad to see him.

At eight o'clock, the lights grew dim and winked out as drapes squeaked apart on their tracks to reveal the glowing screen. Dragan looked back and glimpsed the hovering face of the flyer lady before she closed the foyer curtain and the auditorium fell into darkness. Thankfully, the feature was not preceded with adverts and previews and admonitions to turn off one's phone. The projector cast its storied beam upon the screen, and the movie began at once.

As the flyer had led him to believe, the film was in black and white. He didn't mind that, but the first shot dragged on for at least a minute, and the ones that followed were scarcely shorter. Combined with the camera's focus on a young woman drifting through desolate cityscapes, this put him in mind of Amirpour's *A Girl Walks Home Alone at Night*, which he'd liked but thought could do with a judicious trim. A man appeared, exuding ennui as he gazed profoundly into the empty distance, and eventually his path crossed with that of the mysterious woman. What happened next was not clear, but the man was no longer to be seen and the woman returned to her aimless wandering.

Dragan heard someone entering through the foyer curtain and shuffling along the seats a few rows back—a late arrival. By their position, they must have been joining the tubby young man, who muttered something and then fell silent. Good; Dragan hated chatter during films. But soon he heard worse: soft, wet sounds came from the couple, the dude's dubious hygiene apparently no barrier to public affection. The intimacy only reminded him of everything he was missing in life—all the things he had always gone without and was terrified to think he would never know.

Onscreen, another lonely man travelled a hollow world. Dragan might have thought his solitary despondence a suitable reflection of the people in the meagre audience tonight, but despite their apparent diffidence, it seemed they were better off than he. The discreet sounds behind him carried on unabated, and Dragan turned in his seat to glare back at the offending couple. The young man had been joined by a woman made anonymous by the shadows and they were sitting close, their faces pushed together as if feeding on each other. His greasy hands were wrapped in her dark hair, and as Dragan watched, the man's neglected popcorn tumbled to the floor unnoticed.

He faced front, determined to enjoy his free film. If the couple was going to make out the whole time and miss it, that was their call, and he couldn't let it distract him. He slurped his Coke and lost himself in the long, drawn-out scenes projected before him.

Perhaps ten minutes later, he allowed himself a sigh of relief as the intimate sounds ended and one of the pair—the woman, he assumed—slipped back along the row to the aisle. Had she really come in here only to swap spit with that dude? The guy hardly seemed to give off the magnetism required for such devotion. Dragan imagined for a moment that his companion had been the strangely familiar beauty from the foyer, but the notion was ridiculous. The flash of a face he'd seen in the screen's light hadn't been enough to confirm or deny it, but the flyer lady was well out of the young man's league—or, indeed, his own lowly reach.

Another sad-eyed loner encountered the enigmatic woman on the screen, another wordless confrontation ended with him disappearing from the narrative and her drifting on through windswept streets. Was she preying on these men? Perhaps this was a subtle vampire flick that ignored all the standard tropes of such, or maybe it was something like Glazer's *Under the Skin*, a movie whose celebrity nudity had garnered more attention than the truly disturbing fates met by its male characters. Whatever the case, the other filmgoers must have had more on their minds than what was occurring onscreen, for now Dragan heard another couple making out across the aisle.

The sounds were coming from behind him, back where the old dude in the leather jacket had been sitting. Jesus, even *he* was getting more play than Dragan? The world must be as cruel as his dreams sometimes made it out to be. Dragan tried to console himself by imagining the superannuated rocker's partner was just as old and liver-spotted, but it didn't help. After all, they'd probably been together for decades and notched up thousands of experiences together, and now here they were necking in a movie theatre like a couple of excitable teenagers while Dragan sat alone as he had ever been, untouched, unwanted.

He told himself he wasn't going to look. When he did, he saw very little across the dim auditorium—just two dark shapes with their pale faces pressed together. The bespectacled woman in the tie-dye shirt was sitting three rows ahead of the couple, her brow furrowed in annoyance as she slurped her soft drink, as put out by these public displays of affection as Dragan. For a moment he entertained the notion of crossing the aisle to sit alongside her, to reach out and share the connection everyone else seemed to be flaunting tonight—but that was laughable. Plain as she was, she probably felt she could do better than him, or maybe she had a partner at home. She would be insulted and reject him out of hand, and rightfully so. Feeling a little sick, he turned back to the screen.

Soon the old rocker and his partner must have bored of their fun, for Dragan heard one of them swishing along their row toward the aisle. Did everyone here have a lover to sneak in and suck their face? Perhaps so, for now someone made their way down the centre of the auditorium and slipped into a seat alongside the bespectacled woman. Dragan told himself it was a friend, another arthouse nerd who was running late, but it wasn't long before the wet smacking sounds began again. He twisted around in disbelief and saw the woman's bright shirt obscured by the darker shade of her partner's clothing. She must have been too lost in the clinch to notice that her hand was squeezing the soft drink cup, crushing it until ice cubes spilled into her lap.

Dragan folded his arms, glaring at the screen, and listened as the world drove its merciless point home once again. He'd been born an outsider, foreign to his family, misshapen and maladjusted. He was a man of almost thirty whose body was ill-made for love, whose womanly hips and chest inspired laughter rather than lust, whose intelligence and enthusiasm counted for nothing. He had no skills, no features that would redeem him in the eyes of the world at large. His mother was the only woman who'd ever seen him naked, and that was out of parental obligation—no-one had ever *chosen* to see him, touch him, know him.

He was barely paying attention to the film now. What solace could it be when his life was such a farce? No woman was going to sneak in here and make out with *him*. He thought bitterly of such a thing happening, imagined the woman in the black kaftan slipping into the seat alongside his and raising her lips to his. He imagined that it had been her sitting alongside the other three, a promiscuous film freak or a professional lover working a specialised pitch, moving from one patron to the next when she'd had her fill. He opened his mouth to laugh and found he could not. That line of thought led him to finally understand what he'd been hearing and seeing tonight.

Twisting around, Dragan looked for the tubby young man and saw that his seat was empty. He stared across the aisle to see that the old rocker was also gone—and yet he'd only heard one person leaving their places after each make-out session. Looking to where the current necking couple sat, Dragan could no longer see the lighter shades of the woman's tie-dye shirt. Her dark companion was facing away from him, hunched over the seat where the woman had been as if looking for something, but still the wet sounds continued.

No latecomers had been admitted to share their affections. None of his fellow filmgoers had struck it lucky tonight. With a belated chill, Dragan understood that even someone as inexperienced as he should have known the difference between the sounds of kissing and those of eating.

He faced front again, his mouth dry. Onscreen, that mysterious woman was wandering off into the sunrise with a sated smile, the streets empty of life around her. Maybe if he'd paid more attention to the film, he'd have understood what was going on around him. Even the title was a warning.

The wet sounds across the aisle abated, and now the only noise above the film's soundtrack came from his heaving lungs. Dragan made a cursory attempt to stand up, but his hips had wedged themselves into the armrests, his feet were tired of carrying his dead weight around, his heart was heavy and sick and sore. He was a coward, but that could be a good thing. All he had to do now was give up and let it happen.

The credits had started rolling, each name and role a nonsensical string of random letters, when the flyer lady slipped into the seat alongside him. Her hand rested atop his, and by its touch he understood that she was not wearing a kaftan after all. His earlier idle impression had been correct: her face and hands were the costume. The black matter he had assumed to be her hair and kaftan was the truth of her, and now strands of it slipped swift and soft around his wrist to lash it to the armrest. Her deep eyes ate him up, hypnotic screens reflecting his final scene, and he realised why she looked familiar to him and how that served her purpose: she roughly resembled Chloe, if his classmate had lingered in dark depths all her life, and she looked a little like Layla, too, if that schoolgirl had been swollen with sated appetites and yet still yearned for more. He wondered how she'd appeared to the other filmgoers tonight, if they'd seen unrequited crushes or former lovers or dead wives, but that didn't matter now. Nothing did. His tale had reached its final-act twist and now that sorry story was over. It had not been a success, and there would be no sequel.

The credits ended and the screen cut to black, but the theatre lights did not come on. Dragan sat in the darkness and let it happen, watching on like an impartial camera as she leaned her face into his, her mouth opening impossibly wide to deliver his first and final kiss.

# Pilgrimage

BY THE TIME SELINA arrived in Fortitude Valley, Saturday night was declining into Sunday morning. Bright smears of colour surrounded and swallowed her, ringing with the joyful cacophony of a city well into its cups. She huddled into her black denim jacket and watched her battered boots mark off the steps, wondering how many she'd taken since the beginning. Her body rang hollow, bone-weary, but that fatigue was as nothing beside the sickening surety that she had missed the moment. She'd come all this way, given up everything she had, and for nothing.

Raucous laughter erupted nearby as a group of young men spilled out of a nightclub. Selina swerved across the footpath and paused by a lamppost, letting it carve the wave of exuberant flesh into two rivers of sweat and beer that tumbled by on either side. She kept her head down, but no-one in the boisterous party bothered to look at her. When they'd crossed the street, she got moving again.

So close now. And yet, too late.

Seven days and seven hundred kilometres ago, this had seemed like the best idea Mikki ever had. When she'd unveiled her plan—dark eyes alight with excitement, fidgeting fingers brushing back black bangs—Selina had agreed straight away. Why not? Their lives were already teetering on the brink of oblivion, and they had so little left to lose. They were unemployed, crashing on a succession of couches, burning the bridge they were trapped on with no way to pay the toll.

"Fuck it!" Mikki had laughed, a desperate edge to her voice. "It's like a movie—two girls hit the road, finding adventure along the way. Classic!"

A practical voice in the back of Selina's head nagged—*yes, and what after that?*—but she'd ignored it and grabbed Mikki's hands, dancing around a borrowed room to their favourite metal album, drinking the last of their cheap cask wine. Then, riding the high of the sour grape, they'd pooled their dwindling funds and bought two tickets to see Brutal Future at the Black Cave. In Brisbane—seven days and seven hundred kilometres away. Selina hadn't been sure they'd be able to pull it off. And now that she almost had, her biggest regret was that Mikki hadn't made it to the end with her.

She spotted metalheads in Brutal Future tour shirts vaping and laughing nearby, and knew she'd missed it. Selina faltered to a halt outside a tattoo parlour, her head hanging heavy, each breath coming hard and slow. She must have been the very image of despair, but the clubbers who walked by didn't even spare her a glance. She wondered, not for the first time, if she'd faded into a ghost who walked and walked forever, never to be seen again.

"Ay, miss!"

Selina twitched, turned. A man in mismatched fingerless gloves sat on flattened cardboard behind a beanie that glimmered with the silver and gold of passing charity, staring at her.

"Me?"

"Any change, love?"

She could have burst into bitter laughter. He had more money in his hat than she'd seen for days, more of a home than she'd known for months.

"I've got nothing," she admitted. "Sorry."

"Yeah," he said, his eyes already cutting away, and Selina bailed. Mikki would have set the guy straight, maybe talked him into sharing his loot, but Mikki wasn't here.

Three days in, after four hitched rides and a shitload of walking, they'd cadged a lift with two guys who mentioned a party at a nearby warehouse. Of course they'd gone, and it must've been a wild night, because the next morning Selina's head was hazy and she could remember almost nothing. Worse, when she'd tried to drag Mikki out of there, her friend had refused to budge. She was done running, done trying, and none of Selina's entreaties could change that. Hurt and confused, she'd left everything behind and gone back to the road.

Cars never stopped after that, and Selina spent the next few days on foot. She walked by light and by night, lying down in ditches when the dark grew deep and she could push herself no further. She missed Mikki mightily and cried herself into oblivion, waking to an emptiness that was more than mere hunger. She'd eventually slunk aboard a passing bus and waited for the inevitable discovery, but the driver didn't realise she was a stowaway and the other passengers didn't dob her in, though they avoided looking at her like that was the only favour she could expect. She'd gotten into Brisbane earlier tonight, her time almost up, and kept on walking.

And now, she'd missed it. Here was the Black Cave, doors closed, no bass-heavy heart pumping within. Midnight had come and gone, and so had the show. What to do, now that her quest had failed? Did she just keep trudging on, see where her deadened feet led her?

The Black Cave's doors cracked open, and a pair of longhairs crept out to smoke. Both bore backstage laminates and British accents—a sure sign that Brutal Future's road crew was still on site. Might the band also be lingering after the gig? She wandered closer, waited for her moment. Shortly, a crew of crow-black goth girls swept past, and the roadies turned to watch them. Selina slipped by shadow-fast and made for the doors. One of the goth babes tipped her a conspiratorial grin, which Selina faintly returned as she stepped into the Black Cave.

Broad steps led her down into the dim cavern of the venue, where the PA pumped low-volume rock as the road crew packed down the stage. A group stood by the bar, swilling beer; with a twitch of long-dormant excitement, Selina recognised Gavin Breakstone, Brutal Future's drummer. She considered an approach, but was painfully aware of her interloper status. Maybe it would be enough just to watch, to stand this close and be the smallest part of the aftermath. She crossed the room, her mouth dry at the thought of a cold beer, but she had no money and not enough of Mikki's gall to sweet-talk a drink out of the staff. The barman's eyes slid right off her, seeing nothing out of the ordinary.

Booths lined the back wall, their empty leather seats stretched out like black tongues, and Selina made for them. She noted that one was occupied, then did a double take. The long-haired fellow in the end booth, scratching away at a journal with three Jack and Cokes lined up before him, was Brutal Future frontman Yorick Underhill.

Selina froze, mere metres from a legend. She couldn't reconcile the sight of him here and now with the towering god she knew from photographs and live videos—felt like she'd strolled into a film clip, a fantasy. She and Mikki had discussed wild plots to get backstage, but she'd never imagined her quest would end like this.

Hope and longing overcame the inertia of fear and carried her over to stand at the edge of his table. Yorick continued to write as if she weren't there, and she didn't know which would be worse—if she was truly invisible now, or if one of her idols was ignoring her. She should just walk away and save herself the humiliation, but she'd travelled so far to see this man, losing everything along the way, and that desperation demanded a result.

Yorick swapped his pen for a glass and glanced up, seeing her at last.

"'Ello," rumbled that long-loved voice, and Selina couldn't help but bark out a sob. She slapped one hand to her mouth, mortified.

"Hey, you all right?" The concern in her hero's eyes almost reduced her to a single blink of happy light. "Come on, have a seat, love. I can't stand to see a lady cry."

Selina sat across the booth from him, trembling at his proximity and the weight she'd borne this far. Yorick squinted as if trying to place her, then slugged his Jack.

"Enjoy the show?"

"No," she confessed. "I mean—I'm sure it was awesome, but—I didn't make it in time."

"Pity. It was a cracker, if I do say so meself."

"My friend and I, we left a week ago. We hitched, slept rough, begged for food. It didn't matter, all we cared about was getting here and seeing you. But Mikki...she stayed behind at this warehouse along the way, and I've been all alone, and it's been so *hard*...sorry. Ignore me. I'm a mess." She gave a forlorn laugh. "It's a pleasure to meet you, Yorick."

He listened, the ghost of a smile on his lips, but his eyes seemed to grow dark as she spoke. Had she offended him somehow? He downed the second Jack in a single swig, then stared at the empty glass as if in mourning.

"I wish I could say it was a pleasure to meet you, Selina."

The breath caught in her throat.

Yorick put the glass gently down, and now he met her gaze. His bourbon-brown eyes were so deep—so *sad*.

"Don't get me wrong—you're a sweetheart, I can see that. I'm *honoured* that you came all this way for me. But it breaks my heart to have to do this."

Selina trembled. "Do what?"

Yorick reached into a knapsack, produced a newspaper, dropped it on the table. She saw it was folded over to display a certain page.

"I thought you looked familiar. Yeah, I know you, and Mikki, too." He paused, stroked his long moustache. "I'm so sorry, love."

The photo in that newspaper was achingly familiar—two grinning girls in Brutal Future t-shirts. She and Mikki had always thought it the perfect summation of their friendship. But how...?

Confusion turned to chill stone in her heart when she read the words beneath.

"No-one should have to go through what you girls did."

Selina closed her eyes, her soul frayed down to the last strand, and the only thing that kept her from imploding was the kindness in Yorick's voice.

"Some people can see the lost ones, whether they know what you are or not. I've seen ones who act like nothing's wrong, ones who wear this terrible look like they've forgotten how the world works and nothing makes sense anymore. But you're the first who's come to me, and you walked a long, hard road to get here. So, I feel a certain responsibility."

Selina swallowed, and it felt like consuming herself.

"Let me help you, love. Tell me what you can about the scum who did this to you, and I'll pass it on to the fuzz. *No-one* fucks with our fans."

It was all there in her mind now, details ripping through the fog like knives through denim. Tall, bespectacled, nervous—worked in IT for a water company—Tim. Bearded, sweaty, grinning—had a brother in a Metallica tribute band—Brice.

Yorick noted those details in his journal, his face sad and serious.

"I don't know how these things work, but maybe now you've done what you stuck around to do. You can let go, love. Follow Mikki to wherever we end up after all this sound and fury."

She felt herself dwindling, a candle guttering in the breeze. "Thank you."

"Pleasure's mine. See? It *was* a pleasure meeting you after all." Yorick shifted over, held his arm wide. "Come here, love. Give us a hug and be on your way. Know that you're remembered, and well."

Selina slipped out of her seat, sank into Yorick's gentle clasp. She felt his warmth encompass and embrace her, knew a final moment's peace before the light went out and her pilgrimage ended at last.

Yorick sighed, dropping his empty arm. His tour manager was approaching, looking puzzled, and before the questions started—*were you just talking to yourself?*—he raised his third bourbon in a silent toast.

*To Selina and Mikki, wherever you are.*
*Rock on, girls.*


*For Lemmy*

# Heritage Hill

AS MIDNIGHT FELL FURTHER behind and left us to the tender mercies of that long stretch of quiet darkness before dawn, we stood at the end of the disused railway platform and each came up with a spooky story about the unnamed hill that rose from the shadows before us.

*"Back in the old days, this is where they used to hang witches. They built gallows up on the hill so everyone could see them swing. But it meant that as the witches choked and kicked and died, they could cast their final curses over the whole town."*

That was Tabby, starting things off on a suitably morbid note that impressed me as much as the insolent flick of her Zippo when lighting a cigarette or the way her black work slacks clung tight to her shapely legs.

*"Decades ago, this guy robbed a bank during a big storm, thinking it would be great cover. He parked here to wait it out, but the storm grew so bad that it whipped up all the dirt and covered his car completely, burying him alive. No-one discovered it, and over time, it grew into this hill. If you dig to the centre, you'll find his car, and inside, his mummified body, still screaming his final scream and clutching the cash he stole...and if you try to take it, he will stop you."*

A typically colourful story from me, overthought and overwrought, but it kept Tabby's eye on me the whole time and brought a smile to her lips, so I considered it a success.

*"It's like a giant dinosaur egg, right, and one day it'll hatch, and this massive T-Rex will stomp all over the town."*

And that was Brandon taking the challenge none too seriously, to no-one's surprise.

Of the four of us, it was Tunde who came closest to guessing the truth of that nameless hill—not that we'll ever know for sure. But for what it's worth, I think my best friend touched upon something real that summer's night as she stared at the shadowy bulk and conjectured aloud as to its true nature. She always was the smartest person I knew, and I was low-key jealous of that intelligence as well as deeply proud of it. But we haven't spoken in a long time now.

Not since that night.

\* \* \*

We made for a strange pair, Tunde and me. She was your typical Anglo Aussie chick—mayonnaise-pale and blonde, straight and sporty—while I was the weird, queer African-Australian girl. We used to joke that we should swap names so that I was Tunde and she Azalea, that I needed her by my side to balance out the diversity quotient. But in all seriousness, our bonds were sister-strong and long-lasting, and we'd been inseparable for ten years. She always had my back, and she'd go along with whatever daft plan I came up with, if for no other reason than to make sure things didn't run completely off the rails.

My mission on this summer's eve was a simple one: drop past the service station on the main road as the midnight hour approached, chat to the hottie on shift, and see if I could convince her to hang out with us when she knocked off.

Tabby Jamieson had been number one on my hitlist for weeks now. Something about her just drove me wild on the inside, sparked all sorts of fantasies in my fervent teenage brain. Well, a number of somethings: the way she poked the tip of her tongue between her teeth when she smiled, a quirk I found desperately erotic; her casual attitude to the job at hand, as if she'd humour this social contract just enough to fund her own pursuits and no further; the tattoos that spotted her pale skin wherever it wasn't covered by her uniform of black slacks and polo shirt. In fact, it was her body art that made me think I might be in with a shot. As an outsider in pretty much any way you care to name, I could relate to the semi-colon inked behind her left ear because sometimes I was amazed to still be here after all the shit I'd been through, and the rainbow tattoo on the inside of her left wrist made me wonder if she was proudly declaring her own preferences to the world. Maybe she was just an ally or maybe she was like me, and after many a night tussling with her in my imagination, I just *had* to know.

Tunde harboured reservations about my plan—between us, we owned neither a car nor a licence to drive, and even if my scheme went off without a hitch, she would be stuck with the thankless role of third wheel—but she agreed to back my play. I appreciated it all the more because her right foot was still encased in a moon boot from where she'd badly sprained her ankle at football practice three weeks ago. I worried that walking around town might impede her recovery, but she insisted she'd be fine so long as no running or climbing was involved.

"Better hope we don't have to flee a pack of rapists, then," I quipped before we left, and she rolled her eyes behind the spectacles she preferred to contacts. "But seriously, thank you."

"Where else are you going to find a wingwoman who'll put up with you?" She sighed in mock resignation and squeezed my hand. "The things I do for you, Azalea."

That evening didn't find us sweltering under the traditional dry heat of an Australian summer as we walked; the air was balmy and heavy with the promise of rain, so at least I hadn't sweated through my top by the time we hit the servo. Traffic was minimal at eleven thirty on a Tuesday night, so we had Tabby mostly to ourselves. Tunde distracted herself by alternately browsing the chocolates and her phone, leaving me to carry the weight of the conversation. I knew that Tabby liked the same kind of horror movies as me, so I started on safe ground before digging my way deeper. She was two or three years older than my nineteen, so I let her regale me with anecdotes and second-hand wisdom like I wanted to learn from her. And yeah, I did, but most of the knowledge I hoped to gain was of an intimate nature.

I was out and proud, but my experiences with other girls were limited—drunkenly pashing curious classmates who wanted to tease the boys, holding hands with our school's other open lesbian until we realised we just didn't fancy one another, that exhilarating night Hailey Brooke let me finger her in Sam Fontis's bathroom. I had a lot to learn about sex, and porn could only show me so much. Tabby Jamieson was just the kind of hands-on teacher I desired, but I couldn't tell if that was even remotely an option.

She leaned her elbows on the counter as we spoke, her wry eyes on my face the whole time. I wondered if she'd clocked me as a lesbian yet, and if so, if she thought about me the way I did her. When

I complimented her rainbow tattoo, hoping for some context, she merely grinned and told me how much it had hurt.

Once Tabby's colleague pulled up outside at a quarter to twelve, preparing to take over the graveyard shift, I bit the bullet and asked if she wanted to hang out with us for a while.

"Sure, why not? Thing is, my stepbrother's coming to pick me up. Do you know Brandon? He might want to hang for a while, too."

I glanced at Tunde, who had made some complimentary noises about Brandon's arse, and she flicked me a nervous grimace that I chose to ignore. "I'm sure that'll be fine."

So that's how the four of us ended up sitting in Brandon Jamieson's VZ Commodore at five minutes after midnight, wondering where to go and what to do.

"Want to chuck some laps of the mainy? There's bugger-all else going on."

Tabby's older brother by marriage, Brandon shared with her an air of freewheeling charm, but the two looked nothing alike. His indigenous blood lent him deep brown eyes and rich dark skin that were a photo-negative opposite of her blue and white, and his black hair hadn't come out of a bottle. He was a friendly sort who grinned often and his body was wiry, capable—Tunde appreciated a sporty fella, and I could kind of see why she found him attractive, even if he was genetically predisposed to being not at all my type.

"Dude, this car absolutely *reeks* of pot," said Tabby, something Tunde and I had been too polite to mention. We'd been inside the VZ for less than a minute and were already exchanging looks to gauge whether we were getting a contact high. "Have you been dutching it out?"

"Nah. I've got a bag in the glovebox to drop off at Pauly's."

Tunde shot me a glance across the back seat: *so, this cute guy is a drug dealer.* I shrugged and flexed my face: *it's a bag of weed, big deal, relax.*

"It worries me, driving around at this hour with that dank shit on us. The cops will smell it a mile off."

Brandon sneered. "Fuck the cops."

"If you get pulled over and they find that, maybe they'll bung you in a cell, and then you can fuck the cops all you like."

Tabby made a circle out of her left thumb and index finger, then pushed her fisted right hand through it. The action gave me impure thoughts but brought a sour scowl to Brandon's face. This was clearly a sore spot for him, and I thought I could understand why. Historically speaking, we darker folks have had a somewhat conflicted relationship with the police. They have a habit of leaning harder on us than is necessary, and we have a habit of not surviving the experience.

"Any pig touches me, Tabs, I'll smash the cunt. They've done nothing but fuck with us blackfellas from the start. Like Ice-T said: *fuck the po-lice.*"

"That was N.W.A," said Tunde, the whitest girl alive, and the car fell silent. I could almost hear her toes curling in embarrassment.

"Let's go for a walk instead," said Tabby, and the momentary awkwardness dissipated. "We used to roam the streets all the time when we were in high school. I kind of miss it."

"Stuff that," Brandon scoffed. "Looks like there's a storm coming."

"Oh, noes! Raindrops!" Tabby's face stretched into a silent scream, then relaxed back into her habitual knowing smirk. "Geez, Bran. If it starts getting too wet, we'll just come back to the car."

"Fine," he grumbled. "Are you going to be okay with that foot?"

Tunde nodded in her seat behind him, then blushed and answered aloud. "I'll be cool."

She glanced down at her moon boot, and I could almost hear what she was thinking: *how am I supposed to be cool in this fucking thing, lumbering around like Frankenstein's monster?* I knew this not only because I was her best friend and fine-tuned into her wavelength, but because she had said it aloud more than once in the past three weeks.

We left the VZ parked alongside the servo and headed across the road on foot. The community centre car park was empty of all life, the odd lamppost beaming a bright cone of light down onto bare bitumen, and we passed on by. Few cars traversed the town's streets this late, but I couldn't stop picturing a cop cruiser pulling up alongside us. I imagined them asking what we were doing, Brandon smarting off, the cops getting physical and bundling us all down the station to be sorted out—at which point his car would be searched, the cannabis found, and the whole situation would become a clusterfuck for everyone.

No doubt this seemed more likely and more ominous to me because I'm black. Sure, things are much better now than they used to be, but experience proves it's always prudent to be on guard. Even a small town like this had grown away from the intolerance of past generations to the point where I felt safe coming out and expected no more persecution than the occasional muttered insult or bullshit rumour, but nowhere and no-one was perfect. On the face of it, the mostly white population was friendly and respectful...but nevertheless, I sensed something strange here that I'd never picked up on in the city where I'd spent the first nine years of my life. Perhaps I just wasn't attuned to it at such a young age, but it seemed more than that to me. My current home felt charged with some invisible tension, a kind of background radiation left behind by the toxic racism that had once been openly espoused and accepted here. People were nice to me but sometimes seemed a little awkward and didn't even appear to know why, like some unseen ghost of the past was whispering slurs in their ear just below the threshold of comprehension. I usually put it down to them trying a little too hard, worrying about being thought racist and gently overcompensating instead—but sometimes I wondered.

We passed the community centre and the library was next, its wide glass eyes blank and dark. Once it had been the town's train station, but the building had long since been renovated and repurposed. It still sat on the end of the railway platform, though, and apart from one carriage that had been turned into a vegan café, the rest of the operation had been left to rust for decades. The platform itself sheltered beneath a long iron roof that was home to a flock of pigeons, its bitumen skin spattered by the birds' copious evacuations, and that roof led to two brick buildings once used for ticket booths and storage and such; their cream colouring had curdled to a jaundice-yellow, some of their rooms converted into dingy band rehearsal spaces and model train clubrooms, and those left empty bore signs that read *WARNING: ASBESTOS* and *DANGER: FRAGILE ROOFING.* To our right as we walked along the platform, a long stretch of road ribboned along with the sun-faded plains of the soccer fields on the other side; to our left, the disused tracks and then a chain-link fence that did little to separate them from the waste beyond, a mini-hinterland between the remnants of the old town and the central business district of the new one.

The roof came to an end after the second building, and we were left traversing the remainder of the platform with no shield from the sparkling eyes in the night sky above us. Its bitumen was cracked with age and wear, sprouting tufts of grass and prickles, and every so often a headless steel post rose up from the centre of the walkway to loom over us, a parade of thin towers stripped of their lights that stretched out for perhaps a hundred metres. I wondered how long they'd stood there and how long they'd continue to do so, pictured them against a barren wasteland and a purple sky like some prog-rock album cover.

At one point, Tabby dropped off the platform to walk along the old weed-choked tracks and I joined her there, eager for rapport. She pointed out splashes of graffiti on the chest-high wall of the platform, lovers' initials and heavy metal lyrics and the ubiquitous crude penii, but I was more interested in the posts that broke up the stretches of chain-link fencing to our left. Each had been topped with a unique arrangement of bolts and iron scraps welded into strange, almost cosmically suggestive sculptures, and the rust that coated everything gave them a sense of inscrutable age and meaning, as though they were representative tributes to older, odder gods than the one worshipped in our town's plain little churches. I resolved to return in daylight to photograph them.

At the end of the platform, a few steps led down to the dirt. From here, nature took over for a hundred metres, whereupon one would hit the netball courts and then a crossroads; the disused railway tracks snaked east toward the gaping mouth of an overpass and, after that, out to the highway. Amongst the eucalyptus trees ahead of us, a vast hump rose into the night sky.

"What is that?" Tunde asked, squinting through her glasses. "I've seen it driving past, but never up close."

Brandon shrugged. "Just a heap of dirt, I guess. Nothing special."

"But why here? Is it run-off from work they were doing on the line or something? It's been sitting here untouched for a long time." She was right; the hill, perhaps twenty feet high with sharp slopes all around leading to a flat peak, had grown patches of vegetation and even a few trees over the years. "Are we sure it's not a lookout or something?"

"Doesn't seem high enough for that," Tabby said. "Maybe it's here for no real reason. Hey! We should *give* it a reason. Let's see who can make up the best story about it."

"What do you mean?" Brandon asked. He was a good-looking dude, but during the walk, his conversation had been less than scintillating. Even Tunde had seemed to lose interest in any part of him that he didn't sit on.

"I thought it was obvious," Tabby sighed, "but to give you an idea, I'll go first."

She sat on the edge of the platform and lit a smoke, thought for a few seconds, then regaled us with her fantasy about the hill being used as a hanging-place for local witches. Few—if any—women would ever have been hanged for witchcraft in Australia, but I appreciated her dark turn of mind.

"You next, Azalea." I thrilled to the sound of my name in her mouth. "I reckon you'd have an interesting take on this."

I thought about it for a moment, then spouted the first thing that came to mind—my story about a bank robber being buried in his car, along with the loot, by a wild sandstorm. Tabby nodded and sent me her maddening grin, the one that trapped the tip of her tongue between her teeth. Maybe I was barking up the wrong tree, but in any case, I was making a good impression.

"Nice one! Okay, Bran—you get the idea now?"

He did, but his story was as mundane as it was brief and misinformed. I'd thought it common knowledge that *Tyrannosaurus rex* had never roamed the ancient plains of Australia, but historical accuracy mattered little to Brandon. He laughed off our derision and turned to Tunde, passing the challenge on to her. She sat on the edge of the platform, gently tapping her moon boot against it, staring absently at the crown of the hill.

"It's always been here," she said, "and it's always been a bad place. The earth is...corrupt. It's *sick*. It's never been used for anything, or even named. The only reason it's still here is that everyone just wants to ignore it and hope it goes away. But it won't. It'll stand here for centuries to come, an incurable cancer on the skin of the world."

Tabby clapped and nodded Tunde's way in appreciation, which caused my heart to throb in ugly jealousy. I even saw white for a moment, which left me reeling at its intensity until I realised everyone else had seen it, too.

"Whoa, cool!" Tabby hopped down from her seat on the edge of the platform and stared over my head. "I *love* lightning. Encore!"

"I told you a storm was coming," Brandon said. "We should head back to the car now. I've got to drop that bag off to Pauly soon, anyhow."

"No way! You know what we should do? Climb the hill and watch the lightning from up there!"

Brandon blew air through his lips like a frustrated horse, dismissing the idea. Tunde shook her head and glanced down at her moon boot. No way she'd be able to make the climb without flexing her sprained ankle—the hill's slopes ran upward at forty-five degrees.

"What about you, Azalea?" Tabby flicked away her cigarette and nodded toward the hill. "You're up for a quick adventure, right?"

Oh, was I! I smiled and nodded my assent. Tunde flashed her eyes my way for a moment—*you're going to leave me down here with this dude?*—but it was too late to back down now. Besides, she'd come out tonight to support me in my erotic ambitions, so she knew what to expect.

"Right, that's settled, then. We'll pop up there for a few minutes and scope it out, you two wait here. Bran, can we trust you not to mack on Tunde while we're gone?"

Her brother held his hands out to her, a what-the-fuck expression on his face, and Tunde grimaced at the ground—both looking like kids being pushed together by playful parents. The sky went white again as if this awkward moment had been captured by a colossal camera.

"Come on, we don't want to miss it."

Tabby nudged me with her elbow—our first instance of physical contact!—and led me to the foot of the hill, placing one shoe on it to gauge its firmness. The dirt seemed willing to bear our weight, and the occasional small tree sprouted from its hide in case we needed handholds. Tabby began striding up the slope without a look back, which was convenient as she couldn't see me watching her climb, savouring the way her black work slacks stretched tighter against her rump.

I followed her arse like a donkey follows a carrot on a stick, wondering if it might be my prize for accompanying her on this adventure. Surely I was registering on her gaydar by now—was she just being friendly, or was she looking forward to getting me alone up there for a quick pash and fondle while we were out of sight? My excitement dwindled when I wondered if Brandon was thinking similar things, left alone with a cute young woman who was in no position to run off. I reminded myself that he wasn't a creep, that Tunde could look after herself if it came to that, and I'd be well within summoning distance should help be required.

Tabby reached the peak of the hill and dusted off her hands before turning to offer me one. As I reached out, the sky flashed white with lightning again, and I barely recognised her in that strange stark glow. Then I was jerked up onto the hilltop, and I let myself stumble into Tabby's arms. She staggered but held her balance, and I clutched at her waist to steady myself. For a second or two, we were in a loose and clumsy embrace, my breasts pressed to hers, her throat just inches from my lips. Her scent of perfume and nicotine was thick in my nostrils, and her breath tickled my cheek. My heart kicked out so hard I was scared she could feel it pounding against her chest.

"Whoa, you okay there?" she asked, but there was no hint of chiding to her question, only concern. She stepped back and broke contact. Below us, I heard Tunde quietly clear her throat: *dial it back a bit, Azalea.*

"I'm fine," I said, less to Tabby than to my friend below, and she turned away to pace across the flat surface of the hill. I remembered Tunde suggesting in her story that it had no name and no known purpose; I assumed she was right on the first count but perhaps not on the second, for someone had planted a ten-foot steel pole in the centre of the hilltop. I couldn't see any footprints that would indicate regular usage, but a few pieces of rubbish were caught in the weeds and grasses—a plastic soft drink bottle, a McDonald's wrapper, the usual thoughtless human detritus.

"Hell of a view, isn't it?"

I crossed to stand beside Tabby at the western edge. From here, we could see the soccer fields opposite us stretching out to the streets beyond, could see where the road below wound to a roundabout at either end. This part of town lay before us like a scale model, bracketed by the grain silos on the docks beyond the community centre and the ostentatious shopping mall past the netball courts. The sky spread wide and open above us, and even when it was cluttered with clouds like tonight, there always seemed to be more stars visible here than there had been in Sydney; they clustered above this country town as if swarming to feed. The lightning flashed again, and I counted to five before I heard a distant grumble of thunder, a massive beast slouching by the outskirts on its way to a bigger feast.

"Wish we were higher. Feels good to be above all this, doesn't it?"

I agreed, though it felt better to be standing within the subtle electrical field of her being. For a moment I pictured us caught in the inevitable summer rain, kissing in the gentle downpour, and cursed my romantic imagination. Down below, a phone pinged as if to remind us of more prosaic concerns.

"That's Pauly!" Brandon called out. "I'm going to have to go in a minute."

"You should come up here first!" Tabby replied, and I felt a pinch of jealousy at having to share her with anyone else. "You too, Tunde. Are you sure you can't make the climb?"

I walked to the northern edge and looked over. My best friend was testing her moon-booted foot on the slope of the hill. She saw me peering down and shook her head.

"Any other time, you'd be running up and down this thing for the fun of it," I said.

"Right now, I can't even kick a footy, let alone get up there without mangling my ankle all over again."

"At least you and me get to see this." Tabby stretched her arms wide to encompass the breadth of the town below, reminding me of the brief seconds I'd spent in that embrace myself. "Not that there's much to see, except the lightning. Ooh, there it goes again."

"What do you suppose this is for?" I asked, walking over to the pole thrust into the centre of the hilltop. Its hide was spotted with rust, and it ended in an empty open mouth that might have longed to funnel the sky down into the guts of the hill.

"No idea." Tabby crossed over to slap the post with an open palm, and we listened to its hollow ring sing of the impact. "It's not a flagpole or a sign."

"Tabs!" Brandon called. "I've really got to go."

"Whatever!" his stepsister replied.

"Message me if you need a lift, okay?"

"Sure!"

I frowned as something occurred to me. "Should we really be standing up here next to a metal post in the middle of a storm?"

"Good point! We should be fine, though. It isn't right above us or anything."

As if to repudiate Tabby's words, lightning flashed again, and this time the thunder lagged by three seconds.

"It's moving in," I said. "Maybe we should go with Brandon now. Otherwise we'll end up getting all wet."

"I don't mind," she said, turning back to the view below, and I scanned those words for any hint of flirtation. Uncertain, I stood alongside her and stared out over the town that had been my home for a decade.

"Where are you from, before this?" Tabby asked.

"Sydney. My dad got transferred here for work."

She turned to me, looking less than self-assured for the first time. "I'm sorry, I meant—I don't want to sound weird, or rude—"

"It's cool," I told her, and it was—I'd gotten used to that question over the years. "I was born here. My parents came over from Sierra Leone in the Nineties. I've only been to Freetown once, though, when I was a kid."

"Awesome. Me, I'm from a long line of locals. I'm boring."

"You're really not, though," I said.

"Aw, thanks."

I could have said more—*you're pretty interesting, actually, and you're totally hot, and are you into girls and if so would you please please please take me to bed sometime?*—and I wanted to, but prudence kept my lips sealed against such clumsy words. Lightning split the sky, casting its weird glow over us, and for a moment Tabby again looked like a total stranger, someone I could never and would never know. Thunder crashed in agreement above us, a second behind the strike.

"You're pretty cool, Azalea. I'm glad we came out tonight. If we hadn't, I would never have been able to do *this*."

Tabby spun away from me and skipped around the pole, arms in the air, singing to herself like a solo dancer at a silent rave.

"You're going the wrong way," I pointed out, laughing as I moved closer. "Witches do it widdershins."

"That should be a bumper sticker," Tabby said, reversing her routine and dancing anti-clockwise. She came to a halt before me. "Hey, speaking of witches—you and me should hang sometime."

I smiled and opened my mouth to agree. Then the air flared white around us brighter than ever, incandescent and so close, so thick with ozone and electricity that every hair on my body stood on end, and a deafening clap struck all sense from my head. For a long second, it felt like the ground had dropped away and left me hanging in mid-air. Then the earth hit the soles of our feet as if we'd dropped onto it from a great height, and we both crashed to the dirt.

"What the *fuck*?" Tabby crawled onto all fours. "Are you okay? What *was* that?"

I was too dazed to respond, staring through retinal echoes at the vision before me. She followed my eyes to the steel pole, which was glowing from root to tip with a sickly white light and singing a long, trembling, hollow note. The light seemed to be pulsing up and down its length at the same time, and I couldn't be sure that wasn't just a trick of the eye.

"Lightning!" she breathed, scrambling to her feet. "We could've been killed!"

"Don't touch it!" I gasped.

"Pretty low on my to-do list, actually. *Wow.* This shit is *intense.*"

I got on my feet and pulled Tabby away from the pole. She shook free of my grip, stared a few seconds longer, then turned and locked eyes with me. We had no words for what was happening until the light faded around us like the moon had ducked behind a heavy cloudbank, dimming the world to shadows. Then we had plenty of words. They were short and desperate. And the last of them, cried out by Tabby, was "Look!"

In this fresh darkness, the soccer field had grown out to encompass the whole town. No, that wasn't right—it was as though the field, the streets, the homes had never been there at all. The earth lay pristine and ancient before us, a plain that stretched from the nearby hills to the shore of the sea, with no sign that humans had ever lived here. No platform, no cars, no people. No Tunde and no Brandon.

I turned to look at Tabby, who was staring at her feet. She glanced up and grabbed my arm, her eyes wide and intense, and then she said the three most irresistible words in the English language.

"Don't look down."

What else could I do? I looked down, and the hill we'd climbed was no longer there. The pole was still behind us, glowing and humming to itself, but it was planted in mid-air. We were standing on nothing at all.

I gasped and Tabby squeezed my arm hard enough to hurt and I gasped again.

"Don't move. We're okay. We're okay."

I nodded, still staring down at the twenty-foot gap between the soles of my sneakers and the ground below. My mind insisted I was going to drop at any moment, which caused my legs to twitch in anticipation of an impact that did not come. The earth directly beneath us was darker than the shadows of night, a black-stained patch like an ink spill, and to my dizzy mind it seemed like the worst place anyone could land—but somehow, we didn't fall.

"What the fuck is going on?" I whimpered. Tabby opened her mouth, closed it again, and just shook her head.

And then the sun came up.

This was nowhere near as bright as the lightning—we might've been looking through a dark photo filter. But yes, the sun rose and arced across the sky and set, followed by scudding clouds and the pale face of the moon. And then again, and again, and again.

This, at least, was a spectacle we could somewhat understand—something we'd seen before. We were watching life in fast-forward, a time-lapse record of the land that would one day become our home. Flashes of light and colour flickered across the scene—animals, birds, there and gone in a split-second. I caught glimpses of astonishing megafauna that no human had ever laid eyes upon, as ancient as Brandon's T-Rex but less familiar. Trees rose from infancy to stand tall and then fell back into the earth. Fires flashed across the plain and razed green to grey. The land shook off its coat of ash and bloomed again.

Tabby's fingers let go of my arm and slid down to clutch at my hand. I squeezed back as we watched history unfold, our hearts in our mouths.

Black bipedal figures appeared in flashes across the land. They grouped together and clustered at certain points, building fires that cycled light to dark and settling camps that expanded and retracted before moving on. Humans had arrived, so this surreal display had reached the edge of the last fifty millennia or so.

"It's slowing down," Tabby muttered, and I saw she was right. The clouds cycled less quickly, and the images of people and animals took a little longer to flicker from sight. Some of the country's first settlers appeared and disappeared very close by, at the edges of the dark patch below our feet—I thought I saw some lying supine on the blackness, bleeding—and due to their fleeting presence, I couldn't be sure they weren't staring up at us in fear. As they flashed beneath us and away, across the plains and back again, I noted something else happening down there, and when Tabby's fingers tightened in mine, I knew she'd seen it too.

The corrupted soil beneath us was slowly rising like a cake in an oven, the earth growing up to meet our feet. It had a long way to go at this stage, but I could see the hill we'd been standing on in our time expanding into being. The vibrating pole planted in the air behind us hummed and sang in encouragement.

The landscape before us changed little over the thousands of years that passed before our eyes. Trees fell and were replaced or not, fires pulsed in and out, wurlies were erected and removed, but the country remained almost untouched.

Until the white men came.

At first, they dotted the plains like their indigenous predecessors had, taking in the lay of the land. Sometimes groups of them clashed with the Aborigines, smoke-puffing muskets against hand-carved spears, and blood was spilled on both sides. Soon we could no longer see the black figures *en masse*—the tribes had moved on, and now single dark faces flashed in and out amongst the pale settlers, surely trackers or bearers or prisoners. Then the trees began to disappear, and a dirty scar was carved into the ground—the first road. Areas cleared, and the skeletons of buildings rose from the sod to grow skins of wood and cement. As we watched, the town began to take shape before us.

And the budding hill beneath us continued to grow—faster now, as if excited by these new developments. More figures flashed in and out of being around it, sometimes white, sometimes black, often dead. The hill rose until the soles of our shoes hung only a few feet above it.

The main road bloomed into a business district and streets grew out of it like aorta from a heart, branching off into more roads lined with homes, churches, gardens. Camera-flash horses pulled carts along thoroughfares that turned from dirt to tar. The long steel railway sutured the earth alongside us as the platform grew at its side, and passengers flickered in and out of the carriages that shot back and forth faster than the eye could follow.

This time, I was first to notice it.

"It's slowing again."

The closer this condensed history came to the present, the clearer the passage of time became, because the years flew past with less urgency. Whatever was running this picture show wanted us to see something, or else was putting off the end of the display.

We flinched as a group of people appeared around us, flickering and dancing on the hilltop just a couple of feet below. They were all indigenous and held clutches of burning leaves that puffed smoke out all around us. High school Australian Studies lessons came back to me then, and I realised they were enacting a smoking ceremony—they must have cottoned on to the nature of the hill, because these rituals were intended to cleanse places and people of evil. The fast-forwarded clouds of smoke meant that I couldn't be sure these newcomers from our past weren't looking at *us*.

Then brighter light burst atop the hill, burning away the darkness, and a group of white men appeared on the peak. Their illumination came from lanterns and flaming torches, and their spare hands held clubs, hammers, rifles. High-speed violence erupted in a ring around Tabby and I and we watched in shock as the townsmen beat the Aborigines to a pulp, stamped their smoking fires out, dragged them back down the hill.

Unused to seeing such brutality, I shuddered and leaned into Tabby's shoulder. She reflexively shrugged me off, sending me a look that had far too much in common with the hateful sneers of the men we'd just seen, and I realised I couldn't rely on this stranger for help. She came from the same stock as *them*—shit, one of them might well have been her ancestor. And we've all seen how hatred slides down the family tree like shit down a greased pipe, smearing itself over everyone below—it's basic physics, genetic gravity. I couldn't trust this white bitch as far as I could throw her, because behind whatever liberal façade she'd thrown up lurked the stupid snarl of a tribe that had spent thousands of years killing its rivals to ensure its inheritance. She could never be my lover. She could never be my friend. Millennia of spilled blood and race memory ensured that, from the moment of her birth, Tabby Jamieson was my mortal fucking enemy.

She might have seen some of this sudden animosity on my face, for the familiar spite that flashed through her vanished at once. She turned and held both my hands now, shaking her head. This pale slut had the audacity to try and play nice when she had everything that had ever been denied me and mine! I wanted to spit in her face, knock her down, roll her off my hill. Fuck her? I couldn't stand the sight of her.

Her eyes flicked over my shoulder and widened. She squeezed my hands so hard I thought for a moment she was attacking me, and I tensed to strike back. But she let me go and pushed one shoulder so that I turned and saw what had so appalled her.

The platform we'd walked down to get here had been in place for a long time, and whatever year we were watching now—at least a century before our time, I hadn't seen any cars yet—it was well after the railway and its attendant facilities had been established. Below us, stretching out to the station itself and the buildings that would one day house crappy teen cover bands and model train clubs, the platform ran in a perfectly straight line as if to defy nature, and each of those light posts we'd passed was already in place. Each one still had its head, from which a reassuring glow would be emitted to ward off the night when trains were running, but they were dead now.

And from each of the nearest dozen posts dangled a dark and helpless figure, kicking and twitching and finally growing still at the end of a rope as shadows watched and jeered from the edges of the platform, their pale faces warped by flickering flames.

The sick spite within me surged for a second at this sight, and then it was purged from my heart by a rush of horror. This atrocity was beyond the scope of my vilest thoughts, and I was disgusted that I had been manipulated, if only for seconds, into swallowing the same racist rhetoric that had gouged wounds in the world since time immemorial. Now I was shown the result of believing those lies, and it sucked the wind right out of me. These men had made their home here by displacing the original caretakers, and they had risen a town from the soil that had once nourished only trees, and the dark fruit I now saw hanging from these iron branches grew from the rot in their hateful hearts.

"Motherfuckers," Tabby hissed. She was shaking with horror and disgust and sorrow—and yet for a long paranoid moment, I had thought her my enemy.

Unable to watch as the lynch mob plucked their harvest from the poles and threw it in a wagon to be taken away, I looked down at my sneakers and tried not to throw up on them. The peak of the hill was now just inches below my feet, and I imagined it swelling with malicious pride at the act it had encouraged, throbbing like a stimulated sexual organ. Because I understood now that Tunde had been right, this *was* a bad place, a cancer in the heart of our town, and I knew it had played some part in the unconscionable act we'd witnessed. I'd have run off its edge into the night if I hadn't thought I might be trapped in 1890 or 1910 or whenever the hell we were right now.

I realised Tabby had come to the same conclusion when she spat at the ground and said, "Fuck you. You *made* them do that, didn't you? *Bastard.* I'm going to hire a bulldozer and *fuck* your shit *up.*"

"I doubt it had to push very hard," I said, expecting an argument, but her eyes were wet with guilt and slipped from mine after only a second.

We both understood that this hill exerted a malign influence on its surroundings, but we'd heard too many tales from our colonial past to believe it was that simple. If this place could force someone to do ill, Tabby and I would've been rolling around in the dirt with our hands on each other's throats. Instead, it placed a gentle and insidious pressure upon certain points that were already inflamed. It was the mate in the pub who said *you're not going to let them get away with that, are you?* It was the whisper in an ear when the lights had gone out that insisted *you always knew you weren't good enough, she's going behind your back, and if she's not she will soon enough, cheating lying fucking whore.* It was the wordless call to the ape we'd once been, that snarl of primal, territorial rage insisting all unlike must die because that was survival and that was the way it had always been and always would.

But to blame it entirely for what we'd just seen was letting those murderers off the hook. The hill might have whispered in their ear, but only to reaffirm their poisonous prejudices. Those men, whose descendants no doubt walked the streets of this town today and had little or no clue that their inheritance had been needlessly protected with such spite, those vicious men—they'd been murderers all along, and if they hadn't killed before that savage night, they'd been building up to it for a long time. And since I'd never heard anything about such an atrocity taking place here, I could only assume they'd gotten away with it. Their friends, their peers, their bosses and wives had turned a blind eye to the carnage, or had actively helped clean up the mess so that these fine, upstanding citizens could carry on free of guilt or blame, leaving a trail of bloody footprints to lead innocence astray so that one day their children might feel entitled to do the same.

Sickness ate at my very soul, and I knew what I had to do. If I ever escaped this nightmare, I was going to hunt down the truth and dig up the muck and fling it in the faces of everyone who had a vested interest in keeping it hidden. The murderers and their conspirators were long dead, and I had no desire to hurt innocent families who would be horrified by their ancestral connection to slaughter...but *fuck* this town for ever having the gall to bury the truth and carry on as if evil had never found a happy home here.

All trace of the lynching was gone now, and time sprinted on to bring us up to speed. Power and telephone poles grew abundant, their dark lines stretching across the town like filthy spiderwebs; silos rose from the ground like slow-motion missiles, blocking the sea from our sight. And hatred continued to blossom across our town's history. A group of young men clashed on the footpath nearby, Greeks and Caucasians going at it with drunken fists, and then police cars arrived and the cops waded in to subdue both sides. Before the melee flashed away into the past, at least three combatants were left curled on the ground, their lives changed forever. And as the sun and moon swapped shifts like flick-book caricatures and the town grew larger still, we were presented with another slowing of time as a young woman was chased to the foot of the hill by two men, their faces as dark as hers was pale. They pinned her to the northern slope and I looked away, unable to witness what was coming next. Tabby watched for a few seconds longer, her fists clenching in fury, before joining me in ignorance.

There must have been so much bad shit going on out of sight, behind closed doors and curtained windows, but at least no more horrific visions presented themselves before us. Time spun on until we began to recognise modern makes of car blinking on the roads like fresh lives in a video game, and the crown of the hill had now reached the bottom of our feet, which left me wondering if we were standing on it or still supported by the invisible force that had suspended us here. Finally, the slide show came to an end and left us with a single static image: the view that Tabby and I had surveyed upon first climbing the hill.

"Is it over?" I asked.

This vision grew dimmer and dimmer until the landscape was blacked out almost entirely. Maybe the light was being swallowed by the steel pole planted in the centre of the hill's peak, for it now glowed twice as fiercely until I could see almost nothing else. Flickers of matching incandescence sometimes scarred the corners of my vision like retinal echoes, if they weren't just that. The hollow song of the pole had swollen in volume, ringing in my ears like a scream.

I turned to Tabby and saw her face washed out by the intense glare, her eyes and mouth wide. She might have been yelling, but it was impossible to make out any sound other than the pole's feedback. The light, the sound became my everything, and I was beginning to feel detached from my body altogether. For all I knew, it had been devoured by the white and left my soul stranded in this screaming, blinding hell, and maybe the hill would absorb us into its sick heart for sustenance or maybe this was it, this was the eternal end, all we would know now and forevermore.

A large flicker streaked between us like a lightning strike and dashed into the pole as if drawn by magnetic force. When it made contact, everything cut to pitch black and true gravity reasserted itself. I began to drop into the endless well of nothing, but before I could begin to understand what was happening or brace myself, I crashed hard to the earth once more.

Gasping at the impact, I realised my fingers were gritting in dirt. Looking up, I saw that I was back on the hilltop, spreadeagled as the warm summer rain dashed itself against my face. The moon hung off to one side in the night sky, apparently motionless, as if it weren't plummeting through space around us at over three thousand kilometres per hour. Then I realised what I was looking at: my own sweet here and now.

I scrambled to my feet, woozy from all I'd seen and felt. Tabby was groaning and trying to get her feet beneath her. I helped her rise and then, struck by the same thought, we turned to look at the pole. It was lifeless, lightless, nothing more than a simple shaft of steel.

The true nature of the hill throbbed in my mind like an infected tooth in a sore jaw, and I couldn't stand to be there a second longer. Holding on to each other for balance, Tabby and I stumbled to the northern edge of the hilltop and half-slid, half-fell down the slope until our feet were planted firmly on level ground once more. Casting an anxious glance behind to make sure the hill wasn't reaching out to draw us back and absorb us, we staggered over to the end of the railway platform and leaned against the cement, our minds reeling at what we had experienced.

Tabby lit a cigarette with shaking hands, the everyday clink and rasp of her Zippo such a welcome sound. I glanced over my shoulder at the row of posts that ran down the platform, remembering to what dire use they had once been put, and wondered if I would ever be comfortable in my own skin again. The rain came down, too gentle to wash away anything I felt or thought.

"What the fuck *was* that?" Tabby murmured. I hoped she didn't expect an answer, because I had nothing to give in return. "Oh, man. This place is *sick*. This whole town—all because of *that*. People are bad enough, but *that* makes everything worse. Like it feeds on our hatred...and *grows*."

"We should never have come here," I said. "And I'm never—"

Tabby shot around to face me, galvanised. *"We!"*

I knew at once what she meant. "Where are the others?"

We pushed ourselves away from the cement edge and scanned the area around the hill, peered out across the road, stared down the straight spine of the platform. Rain dashed the air like static but hid nothing—no sign anywhere of Tunde or Brandon. I pulled out my phone, only to find it was dead. I'd charged it before coming out tonight, but either the battery was drained or the lightning strike had fried its innards.

My curses led Tabby to try her phone, with the same result. "Damn it! How could that happen? We weren't up there long, right?"

I gave her a look, and she got the message. We'd watched millions of years unspooling before us—how could we judge the passing of time outside that reverie? After witnessing such a dark wonder, our phones not working was hardly much of a mystery.

Tabby looked up at the moon. "It's lower than before. We must have been up there for at least an hour! They must have gotten sick of waiting for us."

"Brandon was already leaving, remember?"

"True. Maybe Tunde got a ride with him?"

"No. She would've waited for me. Unless she wanted to give us some privacy."

Tabby tilted her head. "Privacy?"

I barrelled on, trying to bury that word and its implication. "I mean, maybe if she waited and called out, and we didn't answer...if she tried to ring me, but my phone was dead...she couldn't have climbed up there, so maybe she got the shits when it started raining and walked home alone. Or maybe you're right—maybe Brandon came back for us and ended up giving her a lift."

"I'm sure it's something like that," Tabby said, but she didn't look at me.

"Shit, and I can't even call her! She should be all right, but I worry about her walking on that ankle. And alone."

Just like that, I realised my best friend was also my greatest responsibility, because this was part of the unspoken pact we'd made—and I'd neglected that duty, haring off in pursuit of pussy instead of making sure my injured mate was safe.

"I'd better go. I'll walk the route she would have taken, see if I can find her on the way."

"Yeah, yeah. Which way you going?"

It turned out that Tunde and I lived in one direction, Tabby in another. We'd have to part ways now.

"Can we talk about this later?" I asked as I squeezed her goodbye, the contact reassuring but not promising. She nodded when she stepped out of my embrace and folded her arms, looking away as if she didn't want to watch me leave. I walked to the road and turned left, glancing back to make sure Tabby wasn't planning to stay by the hill and possibly do something dumb. She was already up on the platform, stalking away with another cigarette in her mouth and the Zippo striking its distant, distinctive sound. She didn't look up at the headless posts or across at me, and the rain washed her away into the night.

I followed the trail that Tunde and I had blazed many times in the past, hoping to see her limping along somewhere up ahead, and I ended up walking all the way to her yard. I didn't see her along the way and her bedroom light wasn't on. I hoped she was tucked up in bed, grumbling to herself about how selfish I was and how she was going to kick my arse tomorrow, and told myself that *had* to be true. The alternatives were beyond my willingness to entertain.

I walked home in the gentle shower and put my phone on charge, relieved to see it still worked. Tunde had tried to call me six times between one and one-thirty, and it was almost three now. I messaged her and apologised, hoped she was okay, told her I had something weird to tell her tomorrow—well, later today. Then I dried off and went to bed and stared at the ceiling until the sun came up, when fatigue finally overruled my buzzing brain and shut the system down for a few blessed hours. The whole time, my body was keyed to react to the ping of my phone, but Tunde didn't message me before I fell asleep.

Or during my slumber. Or after I woke.

Or indeed, ever again.

\* \* \*

Tunde didn't make it home that night.

I woke to the ringing of my phone and clutched at it in search of relief, but it was her mother calling. That was a conversation I wouldn't have relished at the best of times, let alone before fully waking, since I had to admit that I'd lost her and had no idea where she'd ended up. It didn't go down well, and fair enough, too. I hated myself for ever letting her out of my sight.

Tabby and I had been too shell-shocked to exchange numbers, so I found her on Facebook and sent her a friend request, a message. Both were ignored for the rest of the day, but I was too busy most of the time to notice, since I was with Tunde's family and then the police.

How could I explain what had truly happened? I knew they wouldn't buy it, so I lied, feeling like the biggest piece of shit the world had ever seen. I told them that Tabby and I had just lost track of time up on the hill, a flimsy excuse that was immediately contested—not only was it awfully convenient that both our phones had gone flat at the same time, but how could I not have heard Tunde calling to me? The police suspected we'd been doing more on the hilltop than I was willing to admit, an irony that would have been hilarious under other circumstances. Tabby came in separately and gave a statement that was basically the same as mine; apparently, when it was suggested that she and I had been distracted by a prolonged moment of intimacy, she was so surprised that she laughed. So much for all my efforts, then. But I had bigger things to worry about now.

It turned out that Brandon had taken his bag of pot to Pauly's house and dropped it off as planned, mentioning to his friend that he was waiting on a message from Tabby. The pair of them had then proceeded to get stoned for the next two hours before Brandon left and returned home without hearing from his stepsister. Tabby had spoken to him the next day and he told her all this, protesting his innocent ignorance of anything else. The police, less willing to take him at face value and given nothing to work with by Tabby and myself, went to his house the next night and braced him about Tunde's whereabouts.

Now, Brandon had seemed pretty chill to me, but it was clear that he'd harboured some resentment toward cops. Just how much is difficult to ascertain, but according to the police, he took drastic exception to their presence at his house and quickly turned hostile. He accused them of scapegoating him because of his race, refused to allow them inside, and became verbally abusive.

What happened next is unclear due to conflicting accounts, but the officers did gain admittance to his home, because that was where one of them decided Brandon was a physical threat and hit him with a Taser. Fifty thousand volts is enough to ruin anyone's day...but a witness who was present inside the house claimed the cop zapped Brandon two more times while he was down. The police disputed this testimony, but the result was the same either way. The system shock brought on a severe seizure, and Brandon Jamieson died there on the floor of his own front hall.

I only saw Tabby once after that. She hadn't replied to my friend request or any of my messages, but I figured we needed to talk about everything that had happened, so I dropped into the service station when she was on shift. From her expression when she set eyes on me, it was clear I was the last person she wanted to see. Our conversation was short, stiff, and painful.

"I know it's not your fault," she said after a man paid for his petrol and left. "Or Tunde's. But I wish we'd never gone for that walk. If you hadn't come here to chat me up, Brandon would still be alive—and Tunde, too, if she's... I mean..."

"But—the things we saw. The things we know!" I was desperate to get through to her, grasping at straws. "You said you were going to get a bulldozer—"

"No. I'm never going near that fucking place again, and that's the end of it. I'm sorry, Azalea...but you remind me of everything that happened and everything we saw, and I just, I just can't...please don't talk to me again, okay?"

So, not only did I lose my best friend that night, but also the chance of another connection—if not a lover, at least a mate. And that hurts, but I can't blame Tabby for how she feels about me now. After all, she's right. My selfish lust started a bewildering chain of events that led to us witnessing old hate crimes—and then, to her losing her stepbrother to what may have been a new one.

Given the track record of this town and the presence of that cursed hill, there may well have been more to Brandon's death than simple misfortune. Perhaps a voice had whispered in the corner of that cop's mind, placing further pressure on their trigger finger—*go on, zap the son of a bitch again, you know what these black bastards are like, no-one will punish you if you juice that prick some more.* In any case, the police decided that no disciplinary action was required, and Brandon's name went down on that grand roster of civilians who had tragically died in the process of being apprehended—another black death to be tagged and protested, another black mark on the history of this town to be brushed under the rug and forgotten, if not outright justified. *Well, he was a drug dealer anyway, and he had a record, you know what they're like, it was just a matter of time.*

At least the police didn't try to put Brandon in the frame for Tunde's disappearance. According to the witness who saw that fatal confrontation, the officers had seemed convinced of his guilt at the time, but the authorities found no evidence in his car or home. Pauly's testimony checked out, as did phone tracking—so an innocent man died that night, another pointless tragedy. Two in as many days.

And I know what lies at the heart of both.

I've spent a lot of hours imagining Tunde in the grip of a faceless kidnapper, the horrible things they might have done to her. But I don't believe that's where she ended up, because there's something else I can't seem to shake.

Just before Tabby and I were returned to the world, a flicker had shot between us, and its contact with the pole might well have been what saved us from an unknown but terrible fate. That flash of—*something*—had been too fast to make out any detail, but it was about the same size as us, and that detail led to an appalling suspicion. It grew so strong that I made myself return to the hill, during the day this time, and when I'd gotten as close to it as I could bear, I noted a trail of broken dirt that ran up the slope to the top. It might have been made by anyone, perhaps even investigating officers. Anyone could have forced their way up if they were clumsy enough, or desperate enough, so anyone could have gouged that groove in the side of the hill. It needn't have indicated they were wearing something heavy and awkward on their foot.

I can't know for sure, so it's just one more oddity to ponder—even though I know I'll never have closure on any of them. There had to be *something* I could do, though, and I remembered the resolution I'd made whilst standing up on that hill.

This town had been denying its crimes for over a century, and its rug was lumpen with sins swept aside. It was time these atrocities were exposed to the light, for what good is a future whose success is greased with secrets? All we know is built on the bloody bones of the past, true, but we need to be better than the architects who chose these designs for us. Call it what you like—progress, colonisation—but our beloved country exists as it is today because it was once invaded and captured, its first peoples raped, enslaved, and murdered. We need to accept that, be ashamed, and pledge to do better, even if it's not our fault, because even those of us born so distant from such abominations are tainted by the stain of association...and lest we forget, the trickle-down effect from those crimes means this shit is still happening on *our* watch. Atrocity walks in our shadow every day, and it's only ever a whisper of suggestion away. Ask Kumanjayi Walker, or Rebecca Lyn Maher, or Wayne Fella Morrison, or Joyce Clark, or Tanya Day, or Ms Dhu. Or Brandon Jamieson.

Hatred is our heritage. Some people have a vested interest in reminding us of that...and some places, too. They're out there, swollen and greedy. And growing—the one time I returned to the hill, I was certain it stood just a little higher than before. Growing like cancers on the skin of our country, just like Tunde said.

I miss my friend so much that sometimes I wonder: if I were to climb that hill at just the right time—say, when the night is thunderous and full of electricity—would I be party to such visions again? And after I'd been shown a repeat of the sordid history of this town, would I finally see what happened to Tunde?

I think so. But would the journey be worth such a risk, considering Tabby and I might have been saved last time only by the intervention of another? It's one thing to know, another to have that knowledge destroy you. I love Tunde and always will, but I don't need to follow her into the shadows. I know that's the last thing she'd want for me. So I hold off, and I do my research in the hope that it may shine a light into the darkest corners of this town, and I wait for the pieces to fall together.

And on stormy nights, I lie in bed and stare up at the lightning-lashed sky, counting off the seconds as the thunder moves closer and closer, and the ringing in my ears is the echo of a haunting hollow song.

# Our Tragic Heroine

QUARTER OF AN HOUR after walking off stage, alone in his dressing room, Narcisse leans on his tattooed hands and stares into the bulb-framed mirror. A mild tremor galvanises his body, and it's not from the adrenaline release of rocking out to ten thousand people. His phone lies on the counter before him, its face turned away as if ashamed.

When he can pull his wet eyes free from their doubles in the mirror, he sees his figure framed by the ephemeral opulence of the room behind him. Lilies sprawl from glass vases, funereal white and raw-flesh pink, virulent yellow and ominous black; their heady fragrance is underpinned by notes of cinnamon from the incense that burns in three brass holders, sending curls of smoke dancing through the leaves, and an acoustic guitar sits upon its stand like an upstart prince on his throne, awaiting the caress of restless fingers. Everything is just the way he wants it, a life-long dream come true— but now, at the height of Our Tragic Heroine's burgeoning career, Narcisse has good cause to question the cost of such dreams.

The man standing before the mirror is known to friends and family as Jason Partridge, but long has he sought to leave that persona behind. Staring back at him is the star he always knew he could be: a lean, sculpted torso beautified by scrolls and loops of black ink, pink feather boa draped around hard shoulders and reaching down to brush at the waist of leather trousers, stylish bottle-black hair dripping a fringe over kohl-rimmed azure eyes and a sensuous yoni-split of lips. Jason has often gazed into mirrors and marvelled at Narcisse staring back at him, but tonight that wonder has taken on a sharp and melancholy edge. The eyeliner, having survived seventy-five minutes of stage-born sweat, is now running down shapely cheeks to the corners of his mouth, and salt tangs his tongue as if he'd licked his own pungent skin.

Tonight's gig was their biggest yet, the first date of Our Tragic Heroine's national tour in support of their wildly successful debut album—the kind of show he's been dreaming of since he turned thirteen and formed his first triumphant E-major chord on a second-hand Yamaha guitar. He and his best friends have worked so hard to reach this pinnacle, spent countless hours in rehearsal rooms and studios plotting their ascent toward this lofty goal. And now that the rush is wearing off, he's wondering: *was it all worth it?*

The dressing room door cracks open, and the near-telepathy he's developed with his band tells him the identity of his visitor even before Simon Khachaturian—known to the world at large as Sigh—slips into the corner of his eye and closes the door behind him. Narcisse watches as his singer's reflection enters the frame of the mirror and leans against the back of a chair, black lilies draping their heads at his shoulder like mourners seeking consolation. Our Tragic Heroine's vocalist fits neatly into the décor of the room, his rangy figure wrapped in a deep burgundy velvet suit over a paisley waistcoat, his narrow face—equally expressive as his four-octave voice—half-hidden behind long, sweat-dampened locks as dark as Narcisse's own. He stares at the floor as if waiting for his cue, then lets out a melancholy breath that echoes his stage name.

"You got the message, too."

Not a question; Sigh needed only a single look to confirm it.

"What have we done?" Narcisse asks quietly, either of his friend behind or the rock star crying in the mirror before him.

"Us?" Sigh looks confounded by the question. "What *could* we have done?"

Does he not understand? Narcisse closes his eyes for a moment, blocking out his desperate reflection, and now all he can see is the screen of his phone—the terrible message it had been waiting to share with him since he and his brothers led the crowd through a rousing rendition of their debut album's acoustic finale.

*Guys, I'm so sorry.* Narcisse had wondered what Patrice could possibly be apologising for, even as his eyes had taken in the answer. *It's fucked up, I can't even find the words—but you need to know—*

"This was a long time coming, man," Sigh says, cutting into his thoughts. "Decadence always brings a reckoning. We *all* knew that. And we did what we could to stave it off—we helped in every way we knew. But some things are just…inevitable."

Narcisse wonders if his singer understands the ambiguous nature of his words. He must do; the man's a brilliant lyricist, erudite and eloquent and *knowing*. Every line he commits to the page, to the stage, is layered with subtle strata of meaning. He must realise, then, that the reckoning of which he speaks has come not only for another, but for them, too.

"We need to talk about this," he says, and right on cue—as if kicking in on the first beat of a verse after a guitar and vocal intro—the rhythm section enters.

Ansh is still shirtless, because he likes the freedom it allows him when attacking his drum kit and because he's proud of his stringy brown body, but the stick-twirling exuberance he displays whilst playing is nowhere to be seen now. His eyes are huge, disbelieving, and Narcisse can tell that Ansh Kapoor—known to the fans and the media as The Captain—has yet to shed a tear, still struggling to comprehend what has happened. His wiry arms hang lifeless like the long black hair that reaches down to them, and it's a sure sign of shock that his fingers aren't tapping out restless rhythms against the thighs of his red tartan punk trousers.

He's been guided into the room by the sure hands of their bassist, who looks less stunned and more resigned to their mutual revelation. Pickman—legally known as Paul O'Donnelly—is the only member of the band not to have black hair due to dye or ancestry, his rust-red locks tamed into a severe and stylish short cut that accentuates the androgyny of his fine-boned face, and he, too, is yet to change out of his stage gear: a long black skirt over heavy goth boots and a purple t-shirt that bears the glitter-speckled words *NOBLE HERO*, the name of the fictional band from their album's conceptual storyline. He wears as much make-up as Narcisse, but it has not run, because Pickman is also yet to weep over the terrible news.

The Captain lingers near the door, lost in his numb and unexpressed grief, as Pickman crosses to the table near Sigh and prepares himself a glass of the absinthe Narcisse had requested as part of their rider. The guitarist's thoughts flash to the group photo from the centrefold of their album sleeve, where they sit like Wildean decadents in a gothic Victorian parlour around a silver service dominated by a bottle of the green stuff, and again wonders at how far they've come since their days in the run-down Jacoby Apartments, where weeknights would often find the four of them gathered at a card table with one wonky leg as they passed around bottles of cheap red and plotted their eventual rise to stardom.

*The* five *of us*, Narcisse thinks as he turns away from the mirror, remembering that they'd used to share intoxicants more dangerous than mere wine, and sees another kind of red blossoming in the plastic barrel of a syringe.

"I can't believe it," The Captain mutters, his head twitching in denial. "Not now. Nah, man. No way. Not like this."

"I was just telling Narcisse that this was always going to happen," Sigh says. "It's awful, I know. It's so fucking tragic. But for all that, we can't honestly say it comes as a surprise."

"*Some* of it did," Pickman murmurs, throwing a glance at his guitarist, and Narcisse *knows*—he saw it, too. "And that makes me wonder how much of it is ours to own."

"None of it!" Sigh holds out his hands, beseeching. "I know what you're thinking—that we took advantage of a bad situation, that we wouldn't be here right now if we hadn't. But remember, what we did, we did out of love, with blessing and support. We weren't the only ones who wanted this success."

"Bit of a double-edged sword, that, isn't it?" Pickman takes a seat and sips at his absinthe. "We were blessed, yes—but at what cost?"

"All swords are double-edged," Sigh points out, and then the dressing room door bursts open for the third time in as many minutes. But this time, the entrance is as loud and happy as it is unwelcome.

"There you are!" cries Rhiannon Lloyd, toting a popped bottle of champagne in one hand. She's still wearing her stage costume, too, though hers, as befits a dancer, leaves a lot more leg and cleavage on display. "What a fuckin' show! You were great, the fans were great—*I* was great! Who's having a drink with me?"

She glances around, her ebullience undented by their morose silence. Looking at her silver hair and dark-rimmed eyes, the sepia and black dimity outfit that makes her look like a sexy goth moth, Narcisse can't help but feel irritation—it's not her fault, she's playing the role they made for her, but she's inauthentic in a way that reveals the artifice of everything surrounding their heartfelt songs. Rhiannon's just starting to cotton on to the mood of the room when he lifts one hand to her and says, "Get out, please."

She looks cut by his words, his low and defeated tone, and the champagne wavers in her grip. Sigh is quick to cross the room and place a conciliatory hand on her shoulder.

"Sorry, Rhi, no offence. Look, we've just had some really bad news, and we need a little time together to process it, okay?"

The dancer stares at him, at all of them, belatedly taking in the shattered expression they share. "Oh. Shit. Um, I'm sorry, guys."

"It's okay," Narcisse says, and throws her a tired smile to show there are no hard feelings—she's blameless in this, after all. "We'll join you for a drink later."

"Sure." Rhiannon sends each of them a look that vacillates between confused and sympathetic, allows Sigh to direct her back out the door. When she's gone, the rest of the band can hear him calling to Nudge, their amiable but very capable security guy. Pickman reaches out with one hand and plucks anxiously at the low E string of Narcisse's backstage acoustic; The Captain finally moves his fingers, using them to grasp the soft petals of a nearby lily as if only now realising how fragile beauty can be; Narcisse turns back to the mirror and stares at himself, blames himself, trying to ignore the black rectangle of his phone like that could repudiate the news it bears.

Sigh is soon back, closing the door. "I've asked Nudge to keep everyone away from the room for a while. There won't be any more interruptions."

"Something's been interrupted, all right," Pickman says, "and permanently. So, what are we going to do about it?"

"What *can* we do?"

"We can start by actually saying her name," The Captain snaps, and all eyes flick to him. "All this pussyfooting around, and for what? She's dead, man. Dimity's *dead*."

And there it is, out in the air at last.

*Guys, I'm so sorry.* Patrice's message, still ringing through their minds like a brutal blow to the head. *It's fucked up, I can't even find the words—but you need to know. Dimity died tonight. The centre just called. She's gone. Twenty minutes ago, just like that. I'm so sorry.*

"We wouldn't be here if it wasn't for her, and we all know it." Pickman drains his drink and returns to the table, lines up another three glasses. "We just finished celebrating her life, or a version thereof. Now we need to celebrate her memory. Come on."

Our Tragic Heroine gathers around the table as Pickman prepares them each a glass of absinthe, melting in sugar cubes with spring water through a slotted spoon; Narcisse is sure he's not the only one thinking of their album shoot, the parlour, the creation of an image they strive to uphold even now when there is no-one around to see.

The Captain sniffs back impending tears, and Sigh drapes a comforting arm around his shoulders, gives him a comradely squeeze. Then Pickman is passing the glasses around, and together they raise them, looking as always to Sigh to be their voice.

"To Dimity Hardacre," the singer declares, closing his eyes. "Our beloved muse, our dearest friend—our tragic heroine."

They sip at their absinthe, pensive, and Narcisse thinks back to the lounge of that dingy Jacoby apartment where it had all come together, the four of them swilling cheap red wine as they sat around the card table and told Dimity the name they'd decided on for their band.

"You're calling it *what*?" she asked, pausing in her preparations, holding the rubber tubing taut around her arm. Her eyes probed each of them, but it wasn't long before they dropped back to the table and the loaded needle waiting to get her off. "Bit close to the bone, don't you think?"

"It's honest, and it's evocative, and in a way, it's a tribute," Simon said, his gaze flicking away from her as she lined the needle up with a raw hole in the crook of her elbow. "You brought us together, Dim. We would never have all met if it wasn't for you. You lent your hands to fate, guided the four of us to where we needed to be."

"And your tribute is to tell the whole world that I'm a fucking wretch?"

Dimity ignored any answers that may have been forthcoming and sank the plunger down. Her eyelids fluttered and she slumped in her seat, sighing as though she'd just relieved herself of some painful wind. A loop of purple hair caught in the corner of her lax lips, but she didn't seem to notice; beside her, Ansh reached up and gently untucked the errant strand. The four of them watched her, waiting for their friend to surface from her momentary rapture—a shared ritual common in its observation. She only roused when Jason leaned over the table to cook up his own tar-brown shot, and she assumed control of the process with well-practiced hands that, as always, bore traces of paint around the chewed-down nails. He let her fix him up, and in that moment, he was as close to her as he could ever be, closer than if they'd been lovers. They shared the needle, shared their blood. The act was sacred, a pact sealed with trust.

"Like Pick pointed out, the blessing was a mixed one," Narcisse says now. "Dim was flattered to be our muse, but it forced her to see herself in a different light. She saw herself through our eyes—the ugly weakness of her condition and the fucked-up romance we saw in it. We glamorised her suffering, and she didn't feel comfortable with that."

"But what we did was truthful," Sigh argues. "I certainly didn't make her problems sound *desirable*. The album is a paean to the beauty of her soul, and yeah, I can see how it romanticises trouble and addiction, but it's also a clear warning about the consequences. If anyone ends up shooting smack because of it, they've not paid any attention to what I'm saying."

"Fair call," Pickman concedes, "but that's not what I meant. True, we're not responsible for our audience in that way—just *her*."

"But like you said, she saw herself anew because of us, and she changed for the better," Sigh argues. "She got off the horse. She would've been out of that place in another week, home and sober. Patrice didn't say, but I'd bet anything she didn't die from an overdose."

"She was clean, man." The Captain nods, fervent. The youngest of the group, he's always looked up to Dimity like a big sister, always been the quickest to believe both her earnest truths and her junkie lies. "I know it."

"I believe that, too." Narcisse finishes his absinthe, realising that none of them could know for sure—what with rehearsals and press commitments and everything that came along with playing in a professional band on the rise, they hadn't seen Dimity in months. They'd relied on her cousin Patrice to keep them updated on her progress in rehab, to pass on news of their own, always thinking that soon there would be time enough to see their old neighbour and good friend. They'd regarded it as a break while she got better and they got famous, but was that the truth? Now, he can't help but feel that they'd abandoned her when she needed them most.

"There's another thing," he says. "The moment she died. You can work it out closely enough from what Patrice said, from when he sent that text. I think it was while we were on stage, playing our last song."

Pickman nods, getting it. "Oh, yes. Of all our songs, it would have to be *that* one that sees her off."

Sigh frowns, not liking where that train of thought is headed. The last number they're playing at these big theatre gigs is also the last track on their debut record—the record that wouldn't exist if it wasn't for Dimity. It's a showstopping acoustic ballad that may well, in time, prove to be their signature song: "Dorian's Last Dance".

Narcisse remembers Dimity's face as they played her that song for the first time in the lounge of her shabby apartment, sitting on the floor amongst Indian cushions and curls of cinnamon incense smoke like a troupe of derelict hippies: he and Paul strumming acoustic guitars, Ansh rapping his sticks on a pizza box, Simon too nervous to pull his eyes from the lyrics penned in the exercise book before him. Dimity looked like she was watching as all her secrets and shames were pulled out and paraded before her, each one buffed to a melodic shine that made them seem almost beautiful. Oh, none of the lyrics were directly about anything she'd done, and no-one outside their inner circle of friends would ever know that Dimity was the inspiration—but *she* knew, and couldn't decide whether to be flattered, appalled, or both.

"What do you think?" Simon asked her, finally able to meet her eyes, biting his lip at the ambivalence he saw there.

Dimity shook her head as if rousing from a nod-off, but she couldn't help a smile from touching her lips. "If that song was about anyone else, I'd think it was the best fucking thing I'd ever heard."

Ansh frowned, desperate as ever for her approval. "You don't like it, Dim?"

"Oh, I do!" she assured him. "It's an amazing song, it really is. But...knowing it's *me* in those lyrics...it's like you're celebrating everything about me that I hate."

Simon grimaced. "Oh, man. I'm sorry, Dim. It's... I'm not trying to be funny here, you know, but it's supposed to be a love song."

"I know, sweetheart." She leaned forward to touch one paint-flecked hand to the back of his. "And I love that you guys made the gesture. But it makes me wonder...is this how the world sees me? Is this all I'm good for—a song that will make total strangers feel *sorry* for me? I mean, I know I'm just another dumb junkie loser with aspirations to Great Art, but...I want to *make* that art. I don't want it to be made *of* me."

"And you will," Jason said, "we're going places, I just know it. And you're coming with us, Dim. We love you and we love your work. We were thinking that, you know, you could help us out with the visuals. Design gig posters, t-shirts. Maybe paint the album cover."

Dimity stared at each of them, and they didn't understand at the time. They didn't realise that, to her, it seemed like she was being asked to become complicit in her own backhanded apotheosis—to aid and abet their characterisation of her as a damaged angel with track marks on her broken wings.

"We'll see," is all she said then. "I wish you all the luck in the world, boys, and no-one wants to see you succeed more than me. But do you really need to go picking through my poor bones for inspiration? I mean, *fuck*. What's the album cover going to be, a pair of my dirty undies?"

The image on the front of their first record is of Rhiannon-as-Dorian, with streams of stars pouring from her kohl-lined eyes as void-black darkness yawns open behind her, a ravenous gulf whose unending appetite will not be denied. The album is called *To Dorian, with Love.*

"What are you telling me here?" Sigh wants to know now, fingers clenched tight around his glass of absinthe. "That you think our song somehow killed her?"

"No, of course not," Pickman murmurs. "But the timing..."

"Come on. That track's a *celebration*, man."

"Sorry, but no, it's not. Call it what it is, my brother. It's a requiem."

Sigh's mouth drops open to frame a retort, then snaps shut again. He labours over his lyrics and concepts, every word and image chosen with precision, so he looks utterly thrown to realise he's missed such an obvious distinction. Pickman nods sadly, then turns to Narcisse.

"You saw it too, didn't you?"

Oh, he had.

The final song brought the four of them to the front of the stage, as close as they can get to the clutching hands of ardent fans, lined up on chairs of rich wood and crimson velvet—Narcisse and Pickman toting acoustic guitars, The Captain manipulating mellow beats from a Kaoss Pad, Sigh crooning some of his best and most heartfelt lyrics. Rhiannon performed an emotive dance behind the band, acting out Dorian's swansong, and warm lights fanned out across the crowd as glittering tinsel confetti streamed down from overhead like silver rain. The large video screen above the abandoned drum kit would now play a short film wherein Rhiannon performed the same dance as seen below, intercut with poignant scenes of Dorian accepting her destiny and giving way to an encroaching darkness that would flare, so bright and possibly hopeful, to a brilliant sepia corona over the last chord.

Halfway through the second verse, Narcisse leaned back, exulting in the ceremonial symbiosis of audience and band, and spun halfway around on his chair to watch the screen. What he saw was almost enough to throw him off the beat. Only muscle memory and musician's instinct kept his hands moving through the simple chords.

He'd watched the film that was to accompany "Dorian's Last Dance", and this was not it. Not at all. What he saw instead was a procession of clips that seemed to have been shot in the familiar saturated tones of a Super-8 camera, and the woman dancing and smiling and shooting up and crying and staring intently out of the screen was not Rhiannon Lloyd. It was Dimity, of course, horsing around in the small yard of the Jacoby in a summer dress as the sun flared and washed out a dreamy afternoon—dragging broken nails down the inside of her forearm to open up the syringe-stab scabs as she sprawled naked and bruised on the dirty tiles of her bathroom—gazing solemnly into the lens with her eyes full of sorrow and love and condemnation.

Narcisse stared at this vision for the rest of the verse, only turning when the professional voice in the back of his mind prodded him to face the crowd for the big chorus. He tried to put the film from his mind, to focus on the peak of this amazing show, and he just about managed it. The professional voice assured him that someone had lined up the wrong video, that someone was pranking them with the reality behind their sheen of drama. But there was another voice singing back-up inside his skull, and it told him that such clips could not possibly exist. *Look closer*, it seemed to croon, and when he focused on the masses of people clapping and chanting along before him, he understood why.

Spotted throughout the crowd were hundreds of fans wearing tour t-shirts emblazoned with the album cover, hundreds of chests bearing the image of Dorian weeping stars before the widening abyss...but now that stylised image had been replaced by the earthly one that inspired it. Dimity stared back at him hundreds of times over from within the audience, one face replicated time and time again amongst the infinite variations of diversity around it, and the effect was delirious, maddening. Narcisse blinked and blurred the crowd, stared down at his fretboard, and by the time he stood to take a bow along with his brothers, those shirts showed only the familiar design he loved enough to have had it tattooed on his bicep.

He leaves that surreal detail untold for the moment and explains what he saw on the video screen to Sigh and The Captain, who turn to Pickman for corroboration. The bassist gives a grave nod, and The Captain immediately produces his phone to search through fan-shot footage of the show that's already been posted online. Clips of "Dorian's Last Dance" confirm that what his brothers say is true.

"How the hell could this happen?" Sigh wants to know, bewildered. Narcisse doesn't have an answer for that, so he shrugs—but he knows it was no simple substitution by a mutual friend, jealous of their first true moment in the sun. They'd have known about any such film had it been shot—hell, they'd have been in it, cavorting with her—and besides, no-one could have gotten into the theatre and fiddled with the video projector without the crew knowing.

"She wanted to tell the truth," The Captain says. "We turned her life into a lie, didn't we? All this time, we thought we were doing her a favour—but Dim never wanted to be put up on a pedestal. She was a simple soul. She just wanted to be accepted for who she was."

They fall silent, thinking of their friend. Narcisse is remembering a hundred mental snapshots of Dimity Hardacre, and they all reflect what his drummer has just said. Dimity was always about careless fun, uncomplicated enjoyment—he's always thought of her as a young soul, wide-eyed and open to the world. Perhaps that's why none of the band ever tried to sleep with her, youthful and horny as they were then and now; despite her vices, she'd always somehow come across as an innocent, sensual rather than sexual, sisterly rather than seductive. They'd all kissed her from time to time, a playful dance of lips and tongue, but that had felt more like a drunken act of sharing, of trust and friendship, than a prelude to anything carnal.

"I really thought we'd done a good thing," Sigh says eventually, his eyes haunted, and then quotes from Gilbert & Sullivan: "*Pray observe the magnanimity we display to lace and dimity.*"

"We all did," Narcisse says. "But for all that we tried to help her with toxic exes and fair-weather friends, with her dramas and her addiction...how are we any better? We begged her to get clean, but then we'd shoot up with her sometimes anyway, like we were *encouraging* her to keep fucking up. And it was easy for us to drop that shit, since we were just experimenting—we weren't going to get hooked, because we had the perfect cautionary example of where that would lead sitting right there in front of us.

"We've always called Dimity our muse, but that's being too generous—to *us*. She's our fucking meal ticket, isn't she? We observed her life from the outside and then we *stole* it right in front of her, and we turned it into a fantasy, and we built our name on her misery."

"We *used* her," The Captain whispers, and bursts into tears at last. Pickman draws him into a hug, his own eyes finally unleashing the flood he's been holding back ever since the news came in. Narcisse remembers Simon once telling them all that Dimity means *twice-warped* in Ancient Greek, and now he sees the truth of it—warped once by fate and circumstance into a perpetual victim and hopeless addict, and again by her best friends into an insidious icon for troubled teenagers the world over.

"Did we ever really see her at all," Sigh muses, his voice thin with sorrow, "or did we just see what we *wanted* to see?"

Then, sudden and unwelcome—a series of four knocks on the dressing room door.

Unless some emergency has come up, Nudge has failed in his duty. A rush of irritation overtakes Narcisse, for this grief and guilt is private.

"Go away!" he barks.

The only response is another four knocks—one for each of them, he thinks, before anger takes over. He glances at himself in the mirror and sees furious sparks in those electric blue eyes. Reaching the door in a half-dozen quick strides, he pulls it open to confront the interloper.

"Rhiannon? I told you—"

The words die in his mouth. His hand falls from the door handle and slaps loosely against the thigh of his leather pants. His abrupt change in mood is noted by the rest of the band, and he can distantly hear them rallying behind him.

She stands in the doorway, dressed in that stage outfit, swaying gently on the spot; no champagne bottle dangles from her limp hand, but for a moment, Narcisse thinks her drunk. She's staring at him with wide, intense eyes, and as soon as he thinks of the way Dimity had gazed out of the video screen during "Dorian's Last Dance", he understands what he's seeing. He hears The Captain gasp at his shoulder and knows he's not alone in this strange revelation.

Sour sores open in the pale bare flesh of her forearms, and streaks of tainted blood run down to her wrists. Bruises appear on her legs and throat like faces on photographic paper dipped in developing fluid, shit-brown and piss-yellow, and the Dorian costume fades away in just the same manner. The stage make-up disappears from her face as those features become sallow, sunken-eyed, so familiar—as those long silver locks darken to a tumble of messy purple—as firm feminine curves soften and grow less defined, professional pulchritude turning to everyday eroticism. In moments, Dorian is gone and Rhiannon is gone and *she* stands before them, naked in every way, detailed in every last particular, unvarnished and unveiled. She's beautiful and plain and deep and disastrous, her ragged lips trembling with curses even as her wet eyes widen with love.

And then she seems to blur as if draped in gauze, reduced to basic expressions of her complex self. The intense reality of her, every pore of her skin and every strand of violet hair reproduced in absolute clarity, is swiftly replaced by an abstracted representation—the woman before them is now rendered in strokes of paint, her outline marked in thin slashes of black and her pale skin stippled with brush marks, her nipples dabs of darker pink and her belly button a single stab of sable, and the style is instantly recognisable to all four men because they've seen dozens of canvases by this same hand.

"Dim," The Captain whimpers, and as if she takes this as a request, she begins to fade away right there in the doorway, the white wall of the theatre corridor appearing through the rough but knowing strokes of paint that comprise this impossible self-portrait. But before the vision vanishes completely, Narcisse sees her brush-struck mouth move five times. A blown kiss, and four syllables. And somehow, he understands them perfectly.

*Now you see me.*

Then she is gone, and the corridor itself now begins to dissolve as Jason's tears return, hotter and harder than before. Behind him, he hears Ansh's anguish deepen, and Paul utters a low bark of agony, and now Simon, too, succumbs to the sorrow. He turns and embraces his brothers, and together they cry for their lost friend, their manipulated muse. They weep in regret and guilt, in loss and love. And when Rhiannon Lloyd ventures back down the corridor, drawn by all this noise and still clutching champagne to her chest, she's as disturbed as she is pleased to find herself pulled into the group hug and greeted like a long-lost sister.

"Oof! Are you guys okay?" she asks with a hesitant smile, remembering how they'd sent her packing just minutes before.

"I think we will be," Sigh says through swallowed tears, speaking as always for all of them. "But we need to make a change to the show. Just a little one, but it's very important."

Narcisse slaps his back in support, their band-born telepathy ensuring he already knows what his singer is saying. "That wasn't your video for 'Dorian's Last Dance' that played tonight. It was a...a tribute to our dear friend. We owe her so much, and we want the world to know that. So if we can, we're going to show that tribute at every gig from now on."

"Oh, but I put so much work into my video!" Rhiannon protests, before softening at the tears she sees shimmering in the band's eyes. "Still, never mind. You've got to remember what's most important. And it's your story in the end, so you're forgiven."

Narcisse stares at her as if she's said something quite profound, then lifts his lips in a sad smile and plants an affectionate kiss on her forehead.

"That's what we're hoping."

# Thee Most Exalted Potentate of Love

AS I FOLLOW THE crimson-carpeted stairs down into the dim cave known as the Burly Baby Bar, it occurs to me that this is the first time I've been in a burlesque joint since my short-lived stint as a dancer three years ago. Back then, I would have killed to get on the bill in a place like this. Tonight, I'd kill to get out of it.

My resentment has nothing to do with the Burly itself, though, because it's amazing. The walls of the basement club are a deep, rich red that reminds me of an exposed heart, and flying buttresses hold the roof up against the weight of the world above. The mirror-walled bar is stocked with anything your liver could possibly desire, and the way the corseted table-service dames smile and sashay between booths, you'll happily spend more than you can afford. The stage is big enough to fit a dozen high-kicking showgirls and the music makes me want to jump back up there myself.

Instead of a DJ, the Burly Baby Bar employs a band: a tattooed rockabilly babe picking on a Gretsch guitar half her size, a beanpole stand-up bassist, a clock-tight drummer, and a mad-professor keyboardist. They're jamming out a half-time hip-hop version of a Cramps classic as a dancer twirls and slinks across the boards, owning the stage like someone handed her the deeds, and a hundred memories flash across my mind—good, bad, great, and totally fucked. This joint should be my regular hang, but right now, it's the last place in the world I want to be.

My companion is less conflicted, his eyes flicking to a buxom serving girl in a whalebone Union Jack corset before turning back to me. Blythe is my minder tonight, ensuring I carry out my last-minute obligation. He's the only guy affiliated with the Grinners I respect at all, so I've decided not to kill him if I can possibly avoid it.

"Ten minutes until the handover," he imparts in a discreet yell as the dancer flounces off through purple velvet drapes and the small crowd roars their approval. "Let's grab a drink and get a good seat."

"I'm gonna hit the Ladies first."

Blythe squints, hesitant to let me out of his sight, and I give him an oh-come-on-now look. He admits a terse nod and brushes past a group of drunken university boys on his way to the bar. I scan the Burly from wall to wall, noting too many familiar faces hovering over tables and booths, until I locate the toilets. One door is emblazoned with a cartoon goth sporting big horns and bigger cans, and it's labelled *BAD GIRLS*.

The bathroom is kitted out with brushed-steel fixtures and rad burlesque caricatures on the cubicle doors, its purple paint job enhanced by the *Dia de los Muertos* skeletons dancing across the walls. I check for a window that might provide an escape route, but no dice—we're in a basement, after all. I hit a stall and change my tampon, dumping the old one into the receptacle like a bullet-riddled body...and I fully expect to see a few of those before this night is through.

I really don't appreciate being called in on this job, but it's hard to say no when three guns are pointed at your head—and that was the way King Grin phrased his "request" when he and his goons braced me in a car park this afternoon. So tonight, I'm working for the Grinners like a good little girl...and maybe some other night, someone royal gets iced like a sore muscle when I happen to have a solid alibi. We'll see.

Stepping out of the cubicle, I wash my hands and exchange dour looks with the woman in the mirror. Her pitch-black hair shines in the dim light, tied back in practical French braids with a red rose bobby-pinned over one ear; she's wearing crimson-framed glasses because I didn't bother to put my contacts in this morning. Her full-sleeve tattoos are hidden by my favourite maroon leather jacket, as is Pickles in his holster beneath; the black tank top she's wearing emphasises my inked collarbone and the tempting curves of my favourite weapons. Her tight black pencil skirt isn't my idea of working apparel, but the Grinners caught me out shopping, so I'll have to go with it; it accentuates her broad hips and flatters a behind that men have literally died for. You can't see it, but she's wearing my favourite scarlet peep-toe pumps, which sucks, because if I need to make a run for it, I'll have to leave them behind...and if that happens, you better believe King Grin is going to wake up one of these mornings with a tiny but important piece of himself shoved into his creepy mouth.

I stalk out of the toilets to find Blythe in a vermilion-vinyl booth near the bar, angled to give us a good view of the club floor with a column at our backs. I slide in across from him to find a glass waiting: vodka with a slice of lime. Nice of him to remember.

A bequiffed announcer in a sparkly jacket strides on with an old-fashioned radio microphone and introduces She-Ra Na Gig to the stage. The band kicks into a slinky version of The Cure's "10:15 Saturday Night", and I check the time on my phone: quarter past ten on the dot. Damn, these guys are *good*.

"You spot Greening yet?" Blythe asks, and though I've never seen the guy before, it only takes me a couple of seconds to make him.

"Back corner," I say, sipping my vodka as I eye the guy. He's grungy from his messy hair down to his Converse-clad feet, wearing a stylishly faded Mudhoney tee and ragged jeans, sunk into his shadowy seat with a retro-style record bag clutched tight to his lap like it's giving him the best head he's ever known. "Nervous—he's new. What's in the bag?"

Blythe looks like a mellow metropolitan dude to the casual observer, his thick beard and lumberjack *chic* as carefully contrived as that of any urban hipster trying to convey a rough-and-tumble sensitivity, but that's merely camouflage—and the sliver of cold steel in his voice is a welcome reminder of his lethality.

"Don't ask. You see what's inside, I whack you. Boss's orders."

I brush off his warning like cat hairs on a costly jacket. "Marlowe is making the trade in person?"

Marlowe runs the Icemen, a rival mob with even fewer redeeming qualities than the Grinners. But at least he doesn't wear blue suits and pepper his speech with cold-related puns.

"He'll be here any minute. He's already got four people keeping watch."

Casual as you like, I count them off on my fingers. "The two Nigerians pretending to be drunk by the bar, the kid in the sideways baseball cap, and the serving girl in the Union Jack corset."

If I'm hoping to surprise Blythe with my sharp eye, I'm left disappointed. He nods in a matter-of-fact manner, not even asking how I know the fake drunks are Nigerian. A cool customer, this one.

"But that's not all. This deal must be the worst-kept secret in town. There are more players in here tonight than the Crown Casino."

Since the Burly is tucked down a side street in the middle of a city full of distractions on a Saturday evening, there are maybe forty people in the room. It's a crime, really—this joint should be jumping seven nights a week—but since we're talking crime, it's a good thing they're quiet. I spy at least half a dozen paid killers in this room, flirting with table-service girls they'd murder in a heartbeat for cigarette money. It's no scene for civilians, and I'm dreading the likelihood of them getting in the way.

Blythe speaks my thoughts aloud. "I'm afraid this is going to get a bit messy."

"No shit, Sherlock. Thanks for the invite, by the way."

"Not my doing, Jamie."

I narrow my eyes. "It's Miss Rosethorne to you."

"Well, Miss Rosethorne, you can thank Sardonicus for your mandatory employment." That's another name King Grin likes to go by—pretentious as shit and overly obvious to boot, but it fits. "Seems he's a little cross you whacked his favourite mistress."

I shrug and sip my drink. "Bitch tried to slip a pigsticker between my ribs. I discouraged her."

"Oh? And why was she naked in the back of your car in the first place?"

Trust Blythe to know all the sordid details. "Orders from Sardonicus, I guess. Either it was a sloppy attempt at a hit, or it was a stitch-up so he could pull me into *this* clusterfuck. Clearly, he doesn't want to risk anyone he finds valuable."

"Clever girl."

"Which rather begs the question: what are *you* doing here, Blythe?"

"I'm getting the job done like I'm paid to. The whys and wherefores can wait."

Bullshit. Blythe's too canny to take this at face value. I respect him because he's sharper than a Japanese chef's knife—if I were starting my own crew, he'd be the first person I'd tap. Maybe *that's* why he's here. Maybe King Grin thinks he's a little too smart for his own good.

"Look, Jamie—Miss Rosethorne—there's something else you should know. Might be bullshit, but nonetheless." Blythe leans forward as if to impart an embarrassing confession. "I caught a whisper says the Souljacker's gonna be here tonight."

I arch an eyebrow and reconsider my opinion on his mental acuity. "*Jesus*, dude. You believe in fairy tales now?"

"This is on the level. Don't ask how I know, but the Souljacker's for real."

Yeah, right. I've heard that name too, usually from lips scarred by ice pipe burns.

"It won't matter even if he is. There are enough guns in here tonight to give Charlton Heston's corpse a hard-on."

Blythe glances away—there's something he's not telling me. I watch the stage and wait, clapping heartily as She-Ra Na Gig exits with pasties swishing.

"We've got guys outside," Blythe says. "Anyone but us makes it out with that bag, they won't get any further."

"But the Icemen will have cover too, and then there's the freelancers. This deal could turn into the biggest bloodbath of the decade."

"Just make sure we get that bag, and everything will be fine."

Yeah, right. When I hand the prize over to King Grin, I'm sure he'll just shake my hand and forget he has a dozen reasons to kill me deader than yellow jeggings. I'm annoyed that I woke up bleeding and the day has only gotten worse from there, so the vodka goes down quick.

"You want another?"

"On a job? Of course. A girl's not a camel, you know."

Blythe grins and stands up, turns toward the bar. Then he sits down again so fast it's like he never moved in the first place.

"Shit," he hisses, low and desperate, as if someone's tapped him on the shoulder and he's turned to see the bony jaws of Death leering back at him.

I recline in the booth and get a good look at the entrance, where two rather conspicuous motherfuckers have just sauntered down the steps. One's wearing dark sunglasses despite the late hour, dressed in an ankle-length black coat over black leather pants and a half-buttoned black silk shirt, chiaroscuro contrast provided by long, snowy white rock-star hair and skin pale as milk. The other's fat and shaved bald in a spike-studded collar and massive shitkicker boots, mummy-wrapped in leather straps adorned with silver pentacles, his eyes completely red without any hint of an iris. As they survey the terrain, a slender young woman in a white evening dress slips by behind them and looks around as if in need of help. They pay her no attention, more important things on their minds—a mysterious record bag, perhaps.

Somewhat ominously, the rockabilly guitarist starts picking out the intro to Portishead's "Over", those stark notes hanging over the club like Morricone teasing the start of a Sergio Leone gunfight.

"The Souljacker," Blythe whispers. "Do. *Not*. Look."

I shift forward in my seat, trying not to laugh. "Seriously? I expected more. Which one is he, then? Albino Lestat or FetLife Fester?"

He stares grimly at me as the pair strolls by us to take a booth at the back of the room. "Not them. The woman. It's *her*."

Startled, I glance over at the dame in white again. I'm getting nothing off her says she's connected—no hustle, no killer vibe, not even a suggestion she likes a bit of rough. You could walk down any street and see a dozen women just the same, like they're an off-the-rack fashion—gorgeously commonplace, matter-of-factly sexy. They're running offices and raising kids and it's all James Blunt singalongs and vanilla sex and maybe a vaguely naughty night out with the girls every other month. She's looking around the room like she's expecting to see her boyfriend here snorting coke off stripper tits, and then her eyes are flicking toward me.

"Jamie!"

I snap my head back to Blythe. "I told you, it's—"

"Shut up. Whatever you do, don't look in her eyes."

I narrow mine, remembering what I did to the last man who dared tell me to shut up. "You scared we'll turn to stone or some shit?"

"Just trust me, okay? I swear on my blackened heart, this is legit. Don't look and don't go near her."

"That's going to be tricky," I tell him, as white grows in my peripheral vision. "She's coming over."

"Oh, bollocks. *Don't look at her eyes.*"

Suddenly Blythe's hand is covering mine, and the tremor in his fingers tells me he's absolutely terrified. *Blythe*, of all people, shitting himself over a slip of a girl—and that's so strange it makes my mind up.

Blythe and I stare into each other's eyes like we're having a very important and very private conversation, and then I sense another presence at the table. In the corner of my eye, I can see the white of her dress—a regular Jane who's wandered into an alien world. But it's odd, because up close, she just doesn't *feel* right.

"Hey, guys. You got a light?"

There's no authority or threat in her voice. She sounds sincere, naïve, a victim waiting to happen. I should be laughing at Blythe for making me think this dip is a danger. But for some reason, I'm not.

"Don't smoke," Blythe mutters, without tearing his eyes from mine, and I wonder if the woman can smell the lingering scent of his cherry roll-ups as well as I can.

"Okay," says the woman. "Catch you later."

She wanders off in the direction of the next table. Blythe pulls his hand from mine before I can flick it off and immediately grabs his beer. I watch the woman repeat her question at the nearest table, where Konz, a Thai thug who collects thumbs for shits and giggles, goggles at her like a starstruck schoolboy and can't offer his lighter fast enough. She fishes a cigarette out of her handbag and sparks it as Konz and his associate A-wut look on, enraptured. Everyone sees, but strangely, no-one comes over to request that she put it out. I see the stage manager frown and make a move in her direction, but after the woman glances his way, he seems to forget what he was doing and returns to his spot.

"There's something *off* about her," I muse.

"No shit," Blythe says, his glass empty. "She's a walking nightmare. Gets inside your head, jacks your soul and works it like a puppet. Look too deep in her eyes and you're hers forever."

I watch Konz and A-wut laugh like loons at something the woman says. "Same thing could be said of many women. Admit it, you've been my bitch ever since we met."

He manages a shadow of a laugh. "You don't understand. She's not just hot and charismatic. She didn't just do a hypnosis course or something. She's... Jesus, I don't think she's even *human*."

"Oh, fuck off." I can't believe what I'm hearing. "Blythe, I don't know what the hell's gotten into you, but come *on*, man."

"I'm dead serious." Blythe can't bring himself to look her way, like she's the worst of all psycho exes. "I'm telling you—if shit kicks off and she gets her hands on that bag, put a bullet in my leg and then do the same to yourself. Let the guys outside try to deal with her. Trust me, it's the easy way out."

I'm surprised my eyebrows don't shoot straight off my face.

"Who the fuck you think you're talking to here? She gets the bag, I'll murk the bitch in a heartbeat. Now, where's my drink, Blythe?"

He sighs and checks that the woman is out of his path before heading to the bar. I mull things over and come to a decision:

whatever this chick's deal, I'll keep from making eye contact with her. Weird as he's acting tonight, Blythe is neither a fool nor a coward, and he wouldn't be this scared of anything less than an actual demon.

I watch the woman wander away from Konz and A-wut's table, followed by their worshipful stares, and drift up to the front of the stage. She ignores the dancer and smiles at the band, and one by one, they make eye contact with her. Nothing changes in their demeanour, but she nods in satisfaction before turning away, and I watch her closely as she crosses the floor. She's got a delicious figure beneath that dress, too slim for burlesque but hot enough to give any of these girls a run for their money. I find myself hoping that Blythe's wrong, that she's just a regular skirt—that this deal goes down nice and smooth so I can work my magic on her after, maybe take her home to trade licks for the night.

But...deep down, I know that's not right. *She's* not right. Much as it pains me to consider it, perhaps there's something to this Souljacker shit after all.

As Blythe returns with hands full of booze, I see the woman approach Greening in his corner booth. He looks suspicious for a second, then beams at her like the one who got away has finally come around to his way of thinking.

"She's made Greening," I mutter as Blythe sits. "If she's as bad as you say, shouldn't we be stopping her?"

"Go ahead. Make a move and see what happens."

He's got a point. The atmosphere's so tense that a sudden fart could spark an instant firefight and kill us all. I sip my vodka as the band signs off with one last repeat of the haunting guitar riff and the current dancer exits to a chorus of whoops.

"Ah. Drink up, Miss Rosethorne. I think the *real* show is about to commence."

Blythe tips a glance toward the door. A devil-bearded man in a black Nehru suit has entered the club, trailed by a hulking Rondo Hatton lookalike with massive skull-crusher hands. The first guy looks so much like a Bond villain that he just *has* to be Marlowe, head of the Icemen. The deal's about to go down.

The pair run their eyes over the room as they walk in, and though no-one returns their gaze, you can bet there's not one player here who's unaware of their presence. Marlowe spots Greening and his cruel lips purse into an imperious smile. He mutters to Rondo, who glares around at us in alert antipathy as he follows his boss toward the corner table. They walk like men who get whatever they want, like they could swagger right through a wall if they chose, and as they approach Greening, I see the woman in white stepping back into the shadows.

Blythe's hand is in his lap now, surely wrapped around something deadly. I slip itchy fingers under my jacket and touch Pickles, ready to move.

Marlowe speaks to Greening, who gives a cowed nod in return—a mouse playing hardball with lions. The spangled stage announcer introduces the next performer, but half the room is watching Marlowe and Greening converse instead of the dancer who's creeping onto the stage in a fringed cloak. Marlowe's hench-giant pulls out a thick envelope that looks like a postage stamp in his massive hand, drops it on the table with a heavy thud that everyone with a vested interest can hear. The air is thick as honey, ready to explode in a chaos of cordite.

I glance at the woman in white, lurking near the deal like a mere casual observer. She raises one slender hand in the air and clicks her fingers. As if cued, the guitarist kicks in with a three-note rock riff on her Gretsch, and the dancer throws her a confused look. Then the band jumps aboard, and I recognise the song. It's an Eels number: "Souljacker Part 1".

My gut groans in warning.

Greening looks down at the bag in his lap, then glances over at the woman. Most of her face is wreathed in shadow and smoke, including her eyes, but I see her mouth crease into a gentle smile as she shakes her head. Greening looks back to Marlowe, and now he smiles too—wide and wild, like he's trying out for King Grin's crew. He lifts his hand up above the edge of the table, only it's not the record bag he's holding, and then—

I'm already moving by the time Greening's gun barks and spits two rounds into Marlowe's face, already out of the booth and across the floor with my ears pulsing at the volume of the gunfire as the boss man goes down in a rain of blood and brains. Rondo's lurching forward, roaring and reaching out with his steam-shovel hands, but a volley of shots from various points in the room sends him crashing to the floor like a felled tree. I head for a cigarette machine near the bar, and Blythe's making for the bar itself, and everyone's up out of their chairs in a hurry. The screaming starts, but oddly, the music doesn't stop.

I drop to the floor beside the cigarette machine, covered from most angles out on the floor with a short outcrop of wall to keep my back safe. Greening is standing now, still grinning like Sardonicus himself, but only for a second before that kid in the sideways baseball cap leaps up and pops a hot one into his throat. Greening goes down in a geyser of gore, and the room erupts into a flurry of moving bodies as shrieking civilians make for the door in a blind panic.

The dancer throws herself through the drapes, the band playing on in her absence as if somehow unaware of the chaos. The drunken university kids are staring at the spectacle like they went to see *Snow White* and got *A Serbian Film* instead, glasses frozen halfway to their mouths. Konz and A-wut are sliding down behind their chairs, guns in hand, and everyone else is trying to find cover whilst keeping their eye on the prize. The kid in the baseball cap is closing in on the corner table, but the two Nigerians unleash a barrage of thunder in his direction and the cap parts company with his head, taking most of his brains with it.

Now Konz and A-wut are closest, and the former throws some random lead around the room to keep us occupied while the latter makes a play for the briefcase. They both stop dead when they catch sight of the woman stepping out of the shadows, and when they turn back to us, they're smiling like lovesick kids and raining rounds our way in a deafening cacophony. One shot spangs off my cigarette machine, and with my life now possibly measured in heartbeats, I find myself craving a smoke for the first time in months. One more puff, one more drink, one more lay—one more second, one more breath, one more heartbeat.

I can do this.

Life's a bitch, but she's *my* bitch.

I throw a glance backwards and see that those two goth freaks have decided to get involved. Albino Lestat hauls a sawn-off shotgun out of his coat and throws a few booming shells at Konz and A-wut, then goes for the next closest target—me. But I've already pulled my own piece: my M&P 9mm, aka Mustard & Pickles, aka Pickles. I put a shot through each lens of his sunglasses, and he jerks like a body-popping robot as he crashes back against the wall.

FetLife Fester shoots me a ravenous grin that reveals file-sharpened teeth, and his hands move faster than I can see. I flinch down and hear his throwing knife thud into the cigarette machine a couple of inches above my head. Cursing like a blue-balled sailor, I throw myself to one side as the second knife cuts through the air I'd just occupied, executing a clumsy roll and coming up on my knees. The pencil skirt compromises my move and I fall forward onto one hand, aiming Pickles with the other. No more knives come as Fester hasn't got three hands, but when I pull the trigger, he suddenly has three red eyes.

Scuttling across the floor to take cover by the booth I'd been sitting in twenty seconds ago, I see A-wut down and very still, Konz sitting beside him and cursing the ragged hole that's letting his ropy guts slop out onto the carpet. The Nigerians have taken cover behind the bar with Blythe, and the three of them are having a rather vigorous exchange of opinions, letting their bare hands do the talking as the barman runs for the stairs. Two familiar free agents have spread out, one heading straight for the corner table, one making his way around the back of the room. The second one spots me and throws down, but I've got him pegged and a single shot puts his lights out.

The first guy gets to the table, wisely keeping his eyes down and his gun up, and steps over the prone body of the woman in the Union Jack corset. That's when she twists up and is on him, the blade in her hand punching into his groin fast like a snakebite. He drops with a scream and she grabs the record bag, but she makes the mistake of locking eyes with the woman in white. She turns to us with a huge grin and runs the knife through her own throat, spurting freshets of crimson as she collapses over the body of the man she's just killed.

Well, that escalated quickly. In half a minute of carnage, the herd's been thinned down to us, the Nigerians, and the band—everyone else in the room is either dead or cowering under tables. But Blythe is copping a hammering behind the bar, and I need his help. I can't draw a bead on his foes without risking his life too, so I pop Pickles back in my holster and grab the first thing that comes to hand—the glass I'd emptied just a minute before. I line up the Nigerian who has Blythe in a hammerlock and make my pitch. The empty vodka vessel strikes the back of the guy's head, he goes down fast, and now Blythe's got room to twist out of his other opponent's grasp. While they duke it out, I draw Pickles again and make for the table.

The woman in white has tired of watching the show and now she's stepping out of the shadows, flicking away her cigarette as she reaches for the record bag. I draw a bead on her, my finger tightening on the trigger—and then, for some reason I'll never understand, I warn her.

"Freeze, bitch! You move or look at me, I will put you down!"

She pauses, one hand on the bag, and I remind myself she's the most dangerous person in the room. The way the others met her eyes and smiled and let us turn them into tomato paste—*why haven't I shot her yet?*

There's a victorious crash from the bar, and then Blythe yells, "What are you waiting for? Cap her, Jamie! *Now!*"

He's right. He's right.

"Jamie, for fuck's sake, just shoot her!"

I throw him the quickest of glances to tell him *shut up, I've got this*, and when my eyes flick back to the woman—

*Oh.*

She's turned to look me right in the eyes.

I can't explain what I see. I just don't have the words.

For a second, it's nothing—merely a hot fox with amazing eyes, and I've been there often enough. *But*—the next moment, it's so much more. It's like stumbling across the truth of the universe in plain sight, discovering that predetermination is real...learning that everything I'd ever done was bringing me to this point, this one inevitable and immutable communion. The world slides back around the supernova of her stare, and the walls of my mind come crashing down.

Oh god, Blythe was *right*—she's not human, not even something humans could possibly comprehend. Everything's turned a virulent red that's poisoning me, paralysing me, and while I can still see her body, within that form she's expanding and becoming something else—a seething mass of screaming faces, a twisted city hive, a writhing psychedelic galaxy. She's huge, her limbs are spires, the Burly Baby Bar is gone and I'm standing on the surface of an alien planet as infinity rains down in flames around me, and her eyes are suns and there's something dark in the centre of them that's beyond definition, and I'm so far past terror that it feels like love. There's only her and me, and then just her. I'm gone.

Then the insanity snaps back in like a sudden implosion and she looks just like a woman again. She's shaking her head at me, understanding, almost kind, and without a moment's hesitation I spin on my high heel and put a bullet through Blythe's right eye. The mirror behind him shatters as he jerks and falls, and I smile so hard at pleasing my new god that I feel my face might split in half. In fact, maybe it should!

*Yes.*

I put Pickles up to my head, screw the red-hot barrel into my temple without even flinching, and tense my finger.

*For you, my everything. This and anything you ask, so gladly, without question or hesitation. My life for you.*

But again, she shakes her head. A reprieve, a blessing even greater than my death—she has further use for me! Oh, *rapture!* I watch in awe as my everything, my sweet Souljacker, picks up the record bag and walks away, stepping daintily over the corpses in her path and the pools of blood they've spilled into the carpet.

Just before the steps leading up to that tiny, insignificant thing we call a world, she pauses and glances back at me. I figure this is it, the moment she will allow my final fatal offering, and I'm suddenly orgasmic at the thought, gasping in helpless ecstasy as my finger tightens on the trigger.

Instead, she winks, and then—she's gone.

And then my mind comes back to me like a mesmerist has clapped his hands, and reality reasserts itself, and I realise exactly what's just happened.

With a spasm of terror, I let Pickles fall from my temple and look around at the aftermath of tonight's show. Bodies litter the club, either motionless and leaking into the carpet or shivering and moaning under the tables in abject dismay. The floor looks like a Jackson Pollock in shades of blood, brains, and shit. Behind the bar, Blythe is down and he's never getting up, and that's on *me.*

Oh, Jesus titty-fucking *Christ.*

I can't take time to think about this right now. I need to bail on this incredible disaster and lay low, preferably in a different hemisphere—I can't see King Grin letting my failure slide, no matter how extenuating the circumstances may be. I glance over at the stage, realising the music has finally fallen silent; the band is staring out at the room, as freshly woken to reality as me, their mouths almost comically agape. The drummer abruptly throws up onto his snare drum, and the upright bass hits the floor with a discordant crash.

The impact jars me into movement. I hustle past the corpses of men I killed, hurry down the side of the stage. I duck through the velvet drapes, down a hallway, into the change rooms. A hail of screams erupts as I burst in, dancers huddled under make-up tables and staring like I'm the last thing they'll ever see. I tuck Pickles back under my jacket to show them I mean no harm, then push through into their toilets.

My fondest wish comes true—there's a window in the far wall. Unfortunately, it's maybe two feet tall and six feet off the ground.

Pushing open the nearest cubicle, I spy a feminine waste receptacle and drag it beneath the window. With a growl of frustration, I kick off my beloved scarlet peep-toe pumps and tug up my pencil skirt until my legs are free, stepping carefully onto my improvised stool. It wobbles as I unlock the window and slam it aside, and then I'm looking at a gap even that slip of a Souljacker would have found daunting. I poke my head out and see that a disused loading dock runs behind the club, its ramp sloping down below the level of the basement—this toilet window is the only spot in the Burly Baby Bar that opens onto the outside world. Gasping at my luck, I brace myself and go for it.

The window's a tight squeeze, but my arms and head slip through without much hassle. My boobs and broad hips are another matter, and for a few seconds I think I'm going to get stuck half-in and half-out until someone comes along to either arrest or execute me. But I didn't get this far without a goodly reserve of determination, so I wriggle and writhe until my booty painfully pops free, and then I'm falling through the night air.

This horrible sensation lasts only a second before I land awkwardly in a rubbish skip filled with folded cardboard and broken glass, losing my specs for a moment as unseen substances slime my clothes. Peering over the edge, I see no-one approaching down the loading ramp, so I hoist my aching body over the lip of the skip. This time I manage to land with something a little more closely resembling feline grace.

The recessed dock slants upward and opens out onto the main street. There will be eyes on that, but I can't stay here, either. Glancing around, I notice a rusty fire escape fixed to the building opposite, and I hustle barefoot across the alley toward this stairway to heaven.

And then a shadow is rising out of its fellows beside me, and before I can turn, a fist slams into my face. The blow steals my feet from under me and the slick pavement meets my head with an almighty wallop. The stunning impact is followed by a flurry of kicks that blur into one long stab of pain, and that's me gone for the duration.

I don't pass out, not really, but things get kind of hazy for an undetermined period.

By the time reality comes back into a blurry semblance of focus, I'm someplace I don't recognise: a cold, plain cement room, blazing with artificial light, that appears to be completely empty besides my not-so-good self and another woman. I watch her in confusion for perhaps a minute, trying to place her, before I realise I'm looking into a large mirror that has been hung on the wall to show me just how fucked I am.

The blurred woman in the glass is sitting on a steel-framed chair, her hands cuffed behind me and her feet chained; she's been stripped naked, bereft of everything including my glasses. She's sporting a black eye and a bloody face that looks all wrong; with some annoyance, I conclude that my nose has been broken again. The pebbled flesh of her thighs is bare of everything but my familiar tattoos; between them, she's leaving a dark stain as my menses seep unchecked onto the seat.

The bastards are trying to humiliate me. Rage blooms in my battered body, and I strain at the cuffs with a self-righteous fury that almost convinces me I can break them. No dice.

I imagine what I'm going to do to my captors when I get free, and I'm deep in a scenario involving their genitals and a sack of starving rats when I hear footsteps in the corridor outside. I turn my head to glare at the door as a key turns in the lock, and then I see who's responsible for my no-star accommodation.

It's King Grin, of course, with two of his flunkies. He smiles at my bedraggled state, refusing to succumb to my drop-dead stare—but then, of course, he's always smiling.

The story goes that Sardonicus's mother was nine months pregnant when she was attacked by a meth-head psycho dressed as a clown, and that when she gave birth immediately after stabbing the lunatic to death with his own knife, the baby came out with a rictus grin that never went away. The constant smile is unnerving to say the least, especially when coupled with the cold eyes that burn above it. King Grin might look like some cut-rate Joker at first, all spider-thin limbs and wild hair and Hugo Boss suits, but it only takes a few seconds of his attention before you wish he were anything so benign.

"Jamie Rosethorne," he purrs. "Quite the funky handle, that. Did you make it up yourself? Sounds like the heroine from some paranormal romance trash. Bet you wish you had a hunky werewolf boyfriend to come save you now."

Yeah, he's dead creepy, our Sardonicus, but I don't do scared.

"Pardon my French," I say through punch-puffed lips, "but *s'il vous plaît aller coller une bite dans votre oreille.*"

King Grin waves one hand, unfazed by the murder in my eyes. "Charmed, as always. You know, things could be a lot worse. You're lucky I'm a gentleman at heart."

"Oh, I can tell," I mutter, nodding down at my blood puddle.

"You see, I have men upstairs who *hate* you—nasty fellows with no sense of morality, or even hygiene. Can you imagine the sick shit going through their minds right now, knowing you're chained up down here naked and helpless? I could let them in, you know—see what happens."

"Go on," I croak. "I *dare* you."

"But then, we've all heard the story about the last man who tried to take advantage of you when you were naked and handcuffed. I heard it took you twelve hours to fashion a lockpick out of the bone of his pinky finger."

"Ten, but let's not split hairs."

"Fine. How about you tell me why a certain record bag I retained you to acquire is missing, and why we caught you trying to do a runner down the back alley?"

I huff out a kind of laugh. "Don't you know?"

"I'm not in the habit of asking rhetorical questions. So: *where's my fucking bag?*"

"Didn't you see her?"

King Grin licks his teeth in annoyance. "See who?"

"The woman in white. Everyone else killed each other and she walked right out of there with your precious bag in hand. How could you miss her?"

Sardonicus exchanges a look with his goons; on anyone else, it would look like a frown. "My men saw nothing until you tumbled out into the skip."

I let out a guttural laugh. "Oh, they saw her, all right—they just don't remember it."

"I'm afraid you're going to have to explain that."

"Blythe told me, but I didn't believe him. The woman in white is no woman at all. She's the Souljacker."

King Grin narrows his eyes to slits of ice that sit at odds with the wide grin below. "I expect a better standard of lie from you, Miss Rosethorne. Why don't you try a little harder?"

"Oh, I thought it was bullshit too—but she's real, and she's the last person in the world you want to make eyes at. Not that she's a person *per se*, but, whatever."

King Grin looms, piercing me with his dead-soul stare. "So this woman has the bag? Why didn't you stop her?"

As much as it hurts, I can't help but laugh again.

"Oh, I tried! We all did. But everything Blythe said was true. One look in her eyes and she's *got* you. Konz, Greening, even the band—they all looked and became her slaves. I had her dead to rights myself, but as soon as we made eye contact..."

I make my point by hocking up and spitting a gob of semi-congealed blood. Sardonicus leans out of its path, but the closest Grinner isn't so lucky. He splutters and wipes his face, pulling an electric carving knife from his belt, but his boss waves him back.

"What about Blythe?"

"That's what I'm saying. I *liked* Blythe—shit, he was the only one of you bastards worth a damn. But I looked in her eyes and she made me turn and put a bullet in his brain, and I didn't pause for a second."

King Grin's eyes widen a touch. "Someone was going to put him down, and soon. But *you*, Jamie?"

"You don't get it," I gasp. "She made me put the gun to my own head, and I was ready to pull the trigger—I *wanted* to do it, I *came*, I wanted it that bad—but she changed her mind. What do you think that means? She has further use for me—probably to find out where *you* are. She'll be back...and compared to her, everything in your shoddy little empire is a children's tea party. Everyone in this building is dead meat walking—and that means me, too. Do us all a favour. Put one in my head right now, and then run like hell...because if you don't, I guarantee the Souljacker will come, and she will wipe that fucking smile right off your face."

He examines me for long seconds, gauging the truth of my words.

"If the Souljacker exists—if she's such a force of supernature—then why are we having this conversation? With power like that, she could wipe us all out and rule the world! Come on now, Jamie. Tell us the truth, and maybe you *will* get a bullet in the head, nice and quick. Don't make us get *creative* with you."

"I don't know what she is, what she wants," I pant. "Maybe she just gets off on playing with people's minds. But she's stepped up her game now—probably because of whatever's in that bag everyone wants so bad."

King Grin blinks slowly, then turns to his henchmen.

"Find whatever CCTV you can from that street. Find me a woman in white. *Find that fucking bag*. And as for our friend here...she must be getting peckish. Fetch her a can of dog food. Next week."

Sardonicus and his men leave the cell without a backward glance. I'm alone again with my pain and my thoughts, just the way I like it...but I have to wonder how long I'll stay that way.

Not long at all, as it turns out.

It's maybe a half-hour later that I hear the unmistakable thunder of gunfire from upstairs. I wish I'd asked the Grinners for a last cigarette, because I know full well what it means.

Time's up.

The storm doesn't last long. The silence is worse, but I know it's just a precursor to the ultimate horror.

I don't bother to struggle against my cuffs and chains when I hear the steady clock-tick of high heels approaching down the corridor. There's only one defence against what is coming, and it's something I don't need hands to prepare. As the cell door swings wide at her touch, I close my eyes and wonder how long I can last before they're forced open and I'm pushed out into the heaven of her gaze, the hell of her will.

# Nymphaea

AT NINE O'CLOCK ON the Sunday morning when everything started to come undone, Alec Petrovic knocked on the side door of a house in the hills and remembered how unwelcome such a disturbance would have been in his youth, when he'd only have been up at this hour if he were still too high to sleep. But the agony and Ecstasy of those times were gone now, replaced by the constant dull ache of middle age, and he'd become something he wouldn't have thought possible or desirable back then: the kind of man who goes for a walk at nine o'clock on a Sunday morning.

Only that wasn't true today, was it? Today he *was* still up from lack of sleep, and his nerves *were* still jangling from a pill, because last night he'd been given a chance to relive his reckless youth and he'd grabbed it with both hands. This morning he knew again the chemical comedown, and it was worse than it had ever been in his glory days. He felt like an electrified corpse.

The side door opened a cautious crack, then swung wide to reveal Kevin Hendricks's daughter Stephanie. Had she taken after her swarthy father in appearance, she would have been short, curly-haired, and plain—the kind of girl who slides under the eye despite her intelligence and makes up for it with hair dye and anime accessories and fervent feminism, able to find herself as an active and motivated young woman without weathering the weight of constant observation. But tall, auburn Stephanie was the spit of her model-bodied mother, gorgeous in a way that people appreciated a little too much, the kind of girl who would always be assumed superficial and stupid because she was surely too hot to be anything else. Though Alec had little stake in her future, he ached for Stephanie to be appreciated, and that ache was prone to swell up at the least opportune times.

"Hey, Alec. Dad's still getting ready. Come on in."

He closed the door behind him and watched as Stephanie slumped back onto the couch. She lay there on her stomach, one hand holding her phone and one thumb flicking away, coltish legs curving up into the air behind her like the tail of some gamine mermaid. Even this early on a Sunday morning, dressed in a baggy old t-shirt and tight cotton shorts, she was a vision of health and beauty—and no doubt she knew it, too. How strange to be a teenage girl: widely derided for assuming the eyes of the world were on you at all times, and yet forever being proven right.

Alec looked away and examined the titles on Jessie Hendricks's bookshelf, blinking away the blurs his fried brain added to their edges, until Kev came bustling down the hallway in his hiking boots and the same ratty jeans he wore every Sunday.

"Okay, morning. Let's be having you." Six inches shorter than Alec and dark where he was pale, curly where he was straight, Kev had the innate ability to look like a scruffy tradesman no matter how he dressed, and his down-to-earth manner quickly put people at their ease. "How are you, mate?"

"I'm good," Alec recited, watching as Kev grabbed a water bottle from the fridge and an apple from the bowl on the counter. "What's the plan?"

"Nothing fancy. We'll take the usual trail around the reservoir and be back in time for lunch. Speaking of—oi, Epiphany."

His daughter, who had spent a month wanting to be known by that name five years ago, turned to throw him a withering stare just in time to spot the apple hurtling her way. She yelped and flipped over, catching the fruit more by luck than skill.

"Eat that, it'll do you some good." Kev fetched himself another apple and grinned at Alec. "These days, it's all energy drinks and fast food with her lot. Snapchat and crap rappers with face tatts."

"That's not bad—*Snapchat and crap rappers with face tatts.*" Alec spat the bar like an MC half his age and Kev immediately began beatboxing, much to his daughter's disgust.

"You guys are such dags! Go for your walk already before you embarrass me to death."

"How's the gratitude? You're lucky you didn't make the same mistake I did, mate—and no, Steph, you weren't a mistake. We worked hard to make you, your mum and me. We were at it like rabbits, day and night."

"Oh my god, stop it!" Stephanie dropped her phone and covered her ears. "I'm in my happy place, I'm in my happy place..."

Kev laughed and led Alec outside. The wooden decking they stood upon turned a right angle and cut across the back of the house, breaking into a short set of steps at the other side that led to the lawn; the yard then sloped gently downward for the length of a tennis court and was interrupted by a local creek that ran through the property, a metre deep this time of year, before rising again into a thicket of trees that lined the back fence. It was a beauty of a scene, backdropped as it was by the hills looming beyond, and just one reason why Alec couldn't help but envy his friend's good fortune.

Alec had met Kev three years ago when he started work at a car rental outlet, and they'd hit it off at once, which was rare for the former and commonplace for the latter. They'd gone bushwalking each Sunday for almost as long, weather, commitments, and hangovers permitting. Even slogging up steep tracks or sweating in the summer heat, it was a pleasant way to pass a few hours, and their bonding sessions had the knock-on effect of melting an inch or two from Alec's burgeoning belly. Stella had approved of that, if little else in the end.

They caught up on workplace gossip as they left Kevin's cul-de-sac and followed the main road around a few curves, then cut off onto a dirt track that led through the trees and down into a nearby basin. Kev led the way along a winding path, their eyes sweeping up at the eucalyptus trunks towering over them on either side and down at the ground to watch for snakes. Alec let the scents of the bush rush through him like they could spring-clean his innards and flush the nicotine tar from his lungs, the fatty tissue from his ventricles, the throbbing chemical hangover from his tired brain. The sky above was a raw, vicious blue dashed with hints of cloudy white like a vast cataracted eye, and the ambience of insect calls and birdsong reminded him that a man out of his element was never truly alone and unobserved.

Down in the belly of the basin, mundane conversation exhausted itself, and Kev ventured into pastures personal.

"So, you really are doing okay, mate? You look a little rough around the edges this morning."

"Big night. I went out with some younger lads from my old job and overdid it a bit. I'll walk it off."

"Oh, okay. I thought you might've been going through some shit. You know, with Stella and all."

"Nah. I'm coping."

Six weeks and two days had passed since Alec had been forcibly returned to his natural state of solitude. Stella Rafanelli had been very good to him, but it haunted him to understand he hadn't returned the favour anywhere near as much as he should; their year-long relationship had been characterised by clashes between her compulsive competence and his apparent inability to get his shit together, not to mention other issues that he dearly hoped she had kept to herself. Stella was a long-term friend of Kev's wife Jessie, and he shuddered to think of the damage she could do if she chose to air some of her more personal grievances.

"You don't have your eye on anyone else?"

"No, man. Too soon." Had that question been ever so slightly more pointed than it needed to be? But he hadn't been looking, was very discreet even when he did. "What about Stella? Has she said anything to Jess about, you know—"

"No, no. Stella's not the type to jump in the sack with someone else so soon."

"I know. I just thought—never mind."

Kev ran one hand through his mop of dark curls, threw him a sympathetic look. "I get the feeling...not that I know anything much, you understand...but maybe you guys could still fix things. You know, if you wanted to. If you put the work in."

Alec would have liked that, but there was just so much baggage to sort through, and at the age of forty-one, he felt incapable of changing enough to salvage the relationship. It wasn't only about being more responsible, more committed—there were deeper issues that had torn holes in their hull, sent them sinking to the bottom. The kind of thing he really, really hoped she hadn't shared with Jessie.

For example, there was that time near the end when she'd gone through his phone history and confronted him with the list of videos he'd watched on Pornhub, every title featuring some iteration of *barely legal* or *sweet 18* or *teen slut*. He'd argued that most porn actresses were on the young side, such was the nature of the game, but that had cut zero ice with Stella—who, at thirty-five, had already been prone to making younger-woman jokes and now found it humiliating to consider that perhaps she wasn't young *enough*. Imagine if she happened to mention *that* to Jessie, whose daughter was almost *sweet 18* herself! Not that Alec thought of Steph that way, of course. She did draw the eye from time to time, but he couldn't help that. And it didn't *mean* anything.

Soon they were walking along the floor of the basin and slivers of the reservoir were now and again visible through the trees to their left. They reached a point where the trail branched off, and Kev called a halt.

"I need a piss. Back in a tick."

He disappeared into the trees off the right-hand side of the track, leaving Alec to check his phone and stretch his legs. That put him in mind of Stephanie sprawled on the couch, her lissom limbs as tender and flexible as any he'd ever seen—but he didn't want to think about that now. Bad enough that once or twice, he'd allowed himself to—

*What do you think this says about you, Alec?*

Stella's voice. He pushed it back into the busy buzz of his fried mind. Not today, thanks.

Alec winced at a pressure down below, realising he, too, needed to relieve himself—he'd put so much booze and water into his body over the last twelve hours that he'd been hitting the toilet almost constantly. He turned to the left, heading toward the reservoir, and found a suitable tree halfway down the slope. He unzipped and pissed, soothed by the relief into a kind of torpor, and found himself staring through the bush at the slice of reservoir's edge he could see from here. Sunlight danced on gentle ripples and the world around receded to a dim remembrance. The vision was framed by two tall trees that leaned over to lock their arms together, forming an archway to the water. The longer he looked, the more it resembled a portal into another plane, idyllic and ineffable.

Alec's head spun and he clutched at a nearby branch to steady himself. When was the last time he'd felt this woozy, detached from the world he'd always known? Oh, it was half a lifetime ago, when he'd gone out to a rave with his mates and copped a pill much heavier than he'd been expecting. He'd wandered through the rooms in a reverie, the pounding two-step and drum n' bass receding to a featureless din like he was lost in a melting dream, and all around him beautiful young faces and pneumatic young bodies heaved and thrust to the endless rhythm, trim lips wet with spit and booze, and a figure had emerged from the seething mass of hot flesh, had come right at him with the unerring accuracy of a nightmare nemesis and opened her mouth wide and out of it had come—

A laugh.

Not in his memory of a munted night out. Here and now.

Nearby.

Alec looked around and found Kev nowhere in sight, though it couldn't have been him. That laugh was octaves higher than he could have managed—the playful titter of a young woman.

There! Again, and his head swivelled back to look through the pair of embracing trees he'd imagined as an archway. The sound had come from farther on, down at the reservoir. This time he was sure he heard at least two voices, raised in amusement. A shiver shuddered his spine, but the laughs didn't seem to be directed at him. They sounded carefree, the kind of good humour expressed by people who believe themselves to be alone and unheard—it might have come from a couple of girls splashing each other in a pool.

Alec blinked at the hyper-real world blazing around him, heightened by the fading influence of last night's pill and the increasing effects of no sleep, and stumbled down the slope. The bush ended perhaps twenty metres on, where those two trees twisted over to clutch each other with thin, twisted arms. Alec walked beneath them and felt a fleeting lick of change, as if he'd crossed over, and now he found himself standing near the edge of the reservoir, a body of water perhaps two hundred metres across in either direction. He'd seen it dozens of times before and had never taken much interest in its rippled green plain; it was always empty, besides the occasional duck cruising by at the head of a V-shaped wake.

It was not empty today.

The young women in the water all wore long auburn hair and the same body shape—small breasts and flat bellies and slim limbs, thin wrists he could have encircled with a thumb and forefinger—and they were all naked. They tittered amongst each other and glided through the waist-deep water by the edge of the reservoir as if it were a secluded pool in some fantasy forest, unselfconscious and unconcerned with the outer world. Alec stood a few metres away and watched, stunned, until one of the girls noticed him and alerted the others so that he found himself fixed with seven pairs of eager eyes.

The women—girls, really—didn't scream in outrage or duck down to hide in the water. Seven smiles spread across seven faces, slow and sweet, as though they'd seen a lovely bird perched on a nearby branch. Their eyes were wide, round, dominated by dark, dilated pupils that lent their beauty a disturbing edge. Maybe they were party

Matthew R. Davis

girls still rocking on from the night before, tripping hard and skinny-dipping.

But Alec knew better than that. He knew they couldn't really be here, because he *knew* them. He *recognised* this scene.

The nearest girl waded to the edge of the reservoir, the water parting smoothly around her narrow ribs, and Alec stumbled closer even as he told himself it was a stupid idea. Gentle laughter emitted from the others, overlapping echoes, their voices so near to identical as to make no difference. And the resemblance didn't end there; the young women shared a face with minimal alterations, seven sisters surely born of the same mother, and there couldn't be more than five years between the youngest and the eldest, who would be *barely legal* at best. He smiled sickly as he stepped to the edge of the reservoir, knowing this to be some joke his mind was playing on him—it was funny, true, but it cut a little too close to the bone for his liking.

The lead girl, the apparent eldest, extended one slender arm toward him. Alec tore his gaze from her mesmeric, too-wide eyes, only for it to fall on a body as eloquently constructed as any classical poem or song. Her breasts were capped with pale nipples almost indiscernible from the flesh around them, and her belly came unencumbered with any navel that he could see. He swallowed hard and his eyes flinched away as he tried not to let his gaze settle on any one of them, on any part of them.

"You aren't really here," he said, and the girls laughed as if this statement was patently ridiculous. "You *can't* be. You're hanging on my wall."

His loungeroom wall, in fact, was where this scene was to be found: a print of *Hylas and the Nymphs* by John William Waterhouse, a painting that had courted controversy both from visitors to the Manchester Art Gallery where the original was displayed and from one particular visitor to the flat where his own copy was hung. Stella had appreciated the artistry of the print, but not the implications of its presence in her boyfriend's home. He'd owned it for many years and argued no salacious intent, but there it was in pride of place, a portrait of seven naked and uncomfortably young women, and it had only added to the suspicions that led Stella to check his phone history. In the end, she'd felt justified as well as disgusted, and Alec had just felt...empty.

The lead naiad tittered at his remark. Her laughter was a soft song as hypnotic as her eyes, and her waiting hand was an invitation that her sisters keenly backed. They nodded and smiled and one, the youngest, dropped her gaze and shyly traced circles in the water with her finger. She looked to be barely high school age. Alec flinched away, confused and entranced and disgusted.

"I don't know what you want," he said, "but I remember what happened to Hylas."

The naiads exchanged amused glances amongst themselves: *Who?*

"I always kind of thought the girls in that painting were standing on a carpet of bones. The remains of any guy foolish enough to fall for their charms."

The lead girl raised one hand to her mouth in polite shock, though her smile remained.

"This is insane! I'm still tripping balls. Hallucinating from lack of sleep. You aren't here, and I need to *go.*"

The lead naiad kept her hand extended, inviting him to fill it. Another girl ran a primitive comb through her long locks; one touched a breast with a curious finger as if only now discovering its existence; yet another met his eyes and kissed her fingertips with gentle lips. None of them came across as carnal, but their innocent sensuality was overpowering.

He could do it, Alec knew. He could wade in and let their hands stroke him, pull him away to wherever it was they called home. But he knew it would end badly—just *knew* they wanted to strip the flesh from his bones with hidden razor teeth and fill their little bellies with another man too swollen with disgraceful lust to think straight. And if they weren't actually here at all, which had to be the truth of it, well...perhaps Kev would come looking and find him frolicking in the reservoir, pretending that slick weeds were soft hair and hands—or worse, floating face-down like a discarded fast-food wrapper.

The nymphs reached for him, devastating in their apparent youthful naivete and naked splendour, and Alec turned away, laughing a cracked laugh. He staggered back to the trees, and behind him, the girls voiced a sighing chorus of disappointment. He wouldn't fall for it—they were probably hiding gills on their pale swan-necks under that russet hair, serrated shark teeth behind their smiling lips.

*Oh, man. I need some fucking sleep.*

What the hell was in Ecstasy these days, anyway? Or was his system just so unused to chemical abuse these days that it was fracturing under the strain? Alec imagined himself being offered the pill again—"They're Red Lilies," his mate had urged, which meant nothing to him—and politely turning it down. That would have been the wiser course...but since when he had he trod such avenues? *Wise* was not a word his friends would be bandying about at his funeral, was it? *Fuckwit* might be more like it.

When he returned to the path, eyes heavy with dim awareness and legs leaden with fatigue, Kev looked up from his phone and frowned.

"You all right, mate?"

"Uh...yeah?"

"You look a bit peaky. Did you just have a quiet chuck? That's what you get for trying to keep up with the younger lads." Kev grinned, remembering long-gone days and hazy nights. "No fool like an old fool. Let's keep trucking."

They resumed their trek along the thready track. Before the curve of the hill hid this portion of the trail from sight, Alec looked back. It was an instinctive, insecure move, like Orpheus on his way out of the underworld, and he half-expected the repercussions to be equally dire. But he saw nothing out of the ordinary as the trees closed in on the trail, heard no songs wafting to him on the gentle breeze. Reality had been restored, his grip on it again tight and familiar.

Nevertheless, he decided that when he got home, he'd finally do something right by Stella and take that bloody Waterhouse print off his wall.

\* \* \*

That afternoon, Alec stood in his lounge and stared at *Hylas and the Nymphs*. So weird—that scene at the reservoir today could have been this painting come to life, simply shifted from a lily-laden pond to a larger body of water. And those *eyes*...they reminded him of something, but what?

Oh, of course—he'd already flashed on it earlier today. That night at the rave almost two decades ago, tripping the high fantastic on that hardcore pill, wandering around like a lunatic in an urban hellscape until that girl came at him out of the crowd, lips wet and eyes dilated from Ecstasy. For some reason she'd picked him to be her new wasted buddy, and they'd headed outside where conversation was at least technically possible, and she'd clung tight to his arm like a lover as their mouths ran on and on like broken taps. The high embraced them warmly, and they couldn't keep from touching each other on the hands, the face, the hair.

Gemma, her name was, and a bright gem of a girl she was, too—blonde and buxom and just begging to be asked for ID she looked so young, her apparent innocence at odds with her club-wise behaviour. They'd clung together until Alec's mates had started mellowing out and decided to head home, and Gemma came with them. He took her into his room as the sun came up, and she lay there passive but agreeable, and he knew this was it. She smiled and returned his kisses, obligingly lifted and shifted as he undressed her, and when he was inside her, she closed her eyes as though concentrating on her own private place. The pill heightened every detail, lent it a universal significance: the impressions left on her pale skin by a tight brassiere, the panting parting of her plump lips, the smell of sweat both stale and fresh at her armpits and hairline. His first time with a woman, somewhat late at the age of twenty-three but so very welcome.

They woke groggily to each other the next afternoon and their sex then was dry and functional, almost obligatory, without the drug-infused intimacy they'd shared the first time. In his more honest moments—and there had been more and more of them lately—Alec allowed himself to consider the uncomfortable possibility that she'd gone along only because it was expected, a toll paid to allow this foolish youth safe passage out of an awkward situation. When it was over, they sat wordless on his couch like the strangers they were and chain-smoked until he felt safe enough to drive her home. Her little brother was playing in the front yard, and *damn*, the kid looked about ten. Gemma recited her phone number and he watched her shuffle inside like a regretful penitent, head down, until her brother's keenly curious gaze drove him away.

He texted her a couple of times, received no reply, got the hint and moved on. She sometimes sprawled beneath him in his mind on lonely, single nights, but he didn't see her again until two years had passed. He was idling at some traffic lights in town when a gaggle of schoolgirls swept across before the hood of his car, and when one half-turned, laughing as long blonde hair blew out of her face, he recognised her at once: Gemma, a little older, a little less full in the face. He was stunned, half-hoping she'd see him and half-hoping she would not, dreading the thought of her turning away in shame. The girls were wearing their high school senior jumpers, each with their nickname in bold at the bottom of the class list, and of course hers was GEM. Two years since he'd brought her home from the rave, and now she was *perhaps* eighteen. Fucking hell.

Guilt snaked into his fantasies after that and watched his exploits with queasy eyes. She was occasionally supplanted by short-term girlfriends—Tracy, nineteen to his twenty-eight, fast to love and faster to flirt; Rosalie, twenty-one to his thirty-five and too acutely aware of that fact around his friends and family—but Gemma crept back when the nights were cold and the bed empty, still high and wet and welcoming, her eyes wide and round and so dilated the pupils threatened to swallow the sclera altogether, and sometimes in dreams he fell into that darkness himself and knew this was his punishment for tasting fruit that had scarcely begun to ripen.

Well, he could at least rid himself of the reminder. Alec lifted *Hylas and the Nymphs* from its hook and took the print into his spare room, slotted it in the storage space at the top of the wardrobe. The wall looked naked without it and that blankness was a constant reminder of the painting's absence—his eyes kept returning to it as his tongue had once used to probe the raw sockets where milk teeth had fallen out. Even now, the scene was too close for comfort; he felt about as safe as he might have done had he taken a live grenade off his mantel and put it in a kitchen drawer. When Alec went to bed early that night, his numb mind screaming for sleep, he could feel the physical presence of the Waterhouse in the next room as keenly as seven actual people—could see those wide round eyes so clearly that he might have been looking right through the wall, and the nymphs looking right back through him.

* * *

The next morning he fell into his routines and responsibilities, allowing commercial radio and jocular conversation with colleagues to push the previous day from his mind. It came rushing back every time he saw Kev, however, and he decided to learn if his experience had any basis in objective reality.

"When we were out walking yesterday," he said at lunchtime as Kev chowed down on a sandwich and Alec settled for a warm-ish pie from the food truck, "did you see or hear anything?"

"Trees, and lots of 'em. More specifically?"

"Like...other people. I thought I heard something while we were taking a piss break. Young women, laughing."

Kev pulled a dubious face. "I didn't hear nothing. There might've been hikers on the far side of the reservoir."

Inconclusive, but he wasn't going to think any more about it— he'd obviously had a delusional episode in the aftermath of extreme intoxication, and that was that. The vision lingered, though—it didn't blur and drift apart like smoke, like dreams, but sat on his mind as firmly as any other memory from yesterday, clear as Kev's bright eyes as he questioned Alec about Stella, as the subtle sheen of Stephanie's smoothly shaved legs.

Worse, it followed him when he left work and lay in wait where he least expected to find it.

On the way home, Alec stopped off at a supermarket to grab a few things. A young woman was directing customers through the self-serve checkouts, her face dotted with acne scars beneath heavy foundation, her body carrying a little puppy fat beneath the red polo shirt and black slacks that announced her authority. He was passing by to a free till when the girl turned his way and waved him through, half-seen in the corner of his vision for a split second, and—had her eyes been round and wide and dominated by dark pupils, like the nymphs in the reservoir?

*You're just freaking out,* he insisted as he scanned his items, *that pill is still messing with your perceptions.* He stole glances at the girl, but now her face was turned away as she spoke to a co-worker. Was the second young woman looking over, recognising him? He couldn't see her eyes as the shop lights reflected in her glasses, but she was equally youthful as her colleague, and they seemed amused by something. He packed up his groceries and left with his head down, feeling mocked by their mirth. *Were* they laughing at him? Could they be—

Oh, he was just being silly now. Both the young women had been blonde, and the idea of water nymphs wearing disguises to work a day job at Coles was fucking ridiculous. Besides, the naiads had all looked alike, and these two had not even come close to their paint-worthy beauty. His mind was still jarred by that disturbing vision, that was all, and maybe it thought he would be less disturbed by the hallucination of the nymphs if he experienced it again, tried to fold it into his own reality. But didn't that imply his truth was more malleable than expected? And if he could create his own illusions in such convincing detail, how could he ever know what to believe?

That was too terrifying for words, so much so that the alternative—an exterior haunting of some kind—was almost attractive by comparison. It was far less plausible, but Alec decided it was worth a look, if only to dismiss the possibility. He couldn't bear to bring his framed print back out, though, and kept a safe distance by conducting his research online. He remembered that Waterhouse had painted witches and mediaeval *femme fatales*, so was there some occult angle that might help explain his predicament? He looked, denying that he was in denial and insisting he was just doing his due diligence. Did it mean anything that many of Waterhouse's women, including the naiads, were modelled on a real lady, one Muriel Foster? Could there be significance in his depiction of the creatures in *Ulysses and the Sirens* as avian harpies instead of the beautiful temptresses of legend, as if revealing an unpleasant truth—or that they not only all bore that same familiar face, but also numbered seven like the nymphs? Ultimately, the only fact he uncovered that rang with truth was the entomological meaning of the word *nymph*: an immature form of an insect that does not significantly change as it grows. *The real nymph was inside me all along*, he thought, and snapped his phone cover closed with a bitter laugh.

He imagined Stella looking over his shoulder, watching as he browsed more of the painted girls that she'd come to see as a red flag, and reopened his phone to gaze upon her instead. Here was one of his favourite pictures, taken six months ago, before she'd turned over the stolid rock of his psyche and seen what squirmed in the dark beneath. Stella sat in the sun with a glass of white wine in one hand, stylish shades pushed up on her head like an Alice band to keep her long, honey-brown locks out of her face, smiling right through the lens for him and him alone. He remembered her simple satisfaction with the day, whiling away a pleasant weekend afternoon in her back yard with her man; he remembered how he'd grown bored with the idyllic indolence and moaned until she finally agreed to go inside with him and watch a film she didn't care about instead. So many of his memories of their relationship were like this now: she trying her best to be happy with him, he proving himself unworthy of her efforts. What had she ever seen in him? It was a wonder they'd lasted a whole year.

*What do you think this says about you, Alec? And how am I supposed to believe that I'm what you really want?*

He pushed Stella away for the evening, just as he'd done so many times before—but she returned to him that night in bed, summoned by thoughts of some saucy snaps of her he'd found on his phone. Younger, trimmer bodies tried to replace hers in his imagination, bleeding through from dark, humid places, and the warmth in her eyes faded until they were as cold and judgemental as they'd been during those final, arduous arguments. Finally, he pushed her away and rolled over to sleep, thankful only that her pupils hadn't expanded to fill the whites of her eyes like spilled ink spreading across virgin paper. But that thought followed him down into the deep, and when he woke an hour before his alarm was due to go off, he was sure he'd spent the night adrift in an endless pool of chilly black, a reservoir with no shore, just waiting for pale hands to drag him into the bleaker fathoms below.

\* \* \*

Wednesday was merely another middling day, like all the other Wednesdays before it throughout his history. The only thing that gave Alec pause was the party he'd been invited to this weekend: Jessie Hendricks's 40<sup>th</sup> was to be held at her home in the hills, just a couple of kilometres from the spot where Alec had, it seemed, briefly lost his mind.

After work, he headed to the nearest shopping centre, wondering what to buy a woman for such a milestone. He'd always known which video game or dark rum or club scarf his male mates would appreciate most, but when it came to women, he just gave up. He knew he'd make a hash of things if he tried to buy his partners perfume, underwear, flowers—Stella, for example, would surely have found the first ill-matched to her other scents, the second either wishfully too small or insultingly too big, the last unsuited to her allergies. In the end he plumped for a decent bottle of champagne, and when he walked out of the shop, he passed a gaggle of schoolgirls in fawn skirts and jumpers who laughed riotously at something he hadn't heard, and as he passed, they all seemed to glance at him with wide, round, dark eyes.

Alec lurched to a halt, determined not to look. He ignored the way their laughter darted up into the domed ceiling of the shopping centre and danced about like birds among hilltop trees, told himself their eyes had been normal. After all, the implications if otherwise were beyond preposterous. It was the pill, then—*still.* How long did these fucking things take to wear off nowadays? What if this last dose, so long after any relevant precedents, had permanently altered his brain chemistry? Was this the beginning of a long, steadily accelerating slide into dementia?

*Relax. It's just the drugs. You'll be fine.*

He chided himself for his choice of illusion on the way back to his car. Sure, the drugs, whatever—but why had his mind decided on *this* vision? Was it trying to tell him something he'd been keeping from himself? He'd always considered himself a normal, borderline boring person—deep down, he'd expected Stella to find him dull and be driven away by *that*, not by a growing suspicion that his erotic preferences were outside the norm. His imagination barely stretched to some fairly vanilla sexual fantasies, the occasional guilty taboo aside, and he hadn't been a regular reader since outgrowing his fascination with Greek mythology in early high school. This kind of hallucination should have been well beyond his basic capabilities.

And yet his dream that night might have been plucked from the mind of a mediaeval playwright, set as it was in that soft-edged reservoir bower and populated by those seven young women he dreaded as much as his own desire, and the words that flowed from the previously mute mouth of the lead naiad were so foreign to him that this might somehow have been the case. Again he spurned their outheld hands, noting that some of those Foster faces had changed into more familiar ones—Gemma, inevitably; Stephanie, treacherously—and before the edges of the dream folded over him, the head girl spoke...and when he woke, he was startled to find her words ringing in his mind, as crisp and well-remembered as if he'd written them himself.

"This song is yours to own and cannot be unsung. We are idle as the ripples and insistent as the waves, patient as time and tide alike. We can wait for you, good sir. And we will."

\* \* \*

The party was in full swing when Alec walked in the open side door of the Hendricks house on Saturday night, a playlist of Jessie's '90s faves cranking on the lounge stereo system, a raucous group of her friends milling about inside and another on the deck out back. He presented the champagne to Jessie with a hug, shook Kev's hand, and retreated to the kitchen to pour himself a whisky. Stephanie drifted through the lounge with a coterie of her female friends, a half-dozen tender teens packed into tight tops with laughter spilling freely from moist mouths. He looked away from them and spotted Stella on one of the lounges, fiddling with the stem of her wineglass. She shrugged her lips upward at him and he tipped her a nod before slipping out of the kitchen to lose himself in the party. Just one more thing he felt the need to escape.

He was a couple of whiskies in when Kev collared him for a conversation.

"Hey, I heard something weird the other day. My neighbour Poz, he told me a body turned up in the reservoir a few years back. So maybe you *did* hear something. Maybe it was a ghost, calling out to you!"

Kev pulled a silly face and waved woo-woo hands. Alec tried to hide his serious interest in this new information.

"Yeah? For real?"

"Yep. I mean, just about any sizable body of water is going to have drowned someone at some point, but still. Apparently, this guy wasn't much missed. He was a paedo or something. Guilt must've gotten too much." Kev shook his head, his dark eyes shading darker still. "Mate, if some dirty old prick put his hands on Steph, that's where *he'd* wind up."

Alec nodded to show his support but felt like a fraud. He'd never touch Stephanie, that was certain, but that didn't mean he couldn't think about it once or twice. And he hadn't even wanted to do *that*, felt like a traitor for ever going there, but maybe it was beyond his control. Maybe he was just made that way—maybe most men were, and never brought it up for fear of censure. Or perhaps he'd just been shaped by his first experience, Gemma setting a standard he couldn't shake and didn't want—but the fact remained that part of him *did* want it, the part of him that had been tempted to join the nymphs in their play even though conventional wisdom told him it was wrong, wrong, wrong.

He didn't know if Kev's gossip, vague as it was, should comfort or further disturb him. If the report was right, perhaps that body in the reservoir had been a victim of the nymphs and their carnivorous wiles. Which would mean he wasn't alone—wasn't going crazy.

*I thought we'd decided that was just an hallucination.*

Of course, that explanation would also bring with it many deeply disturbing implications, but this was a party, and there was no need to think about any of that shit right now. Alec slurped whisky and talked and smiled and showed the world everything was fine, just fine. After a while, he headed into the kitchen to top up his drink, bopping his head along to Korn's "A.D.I.D.A.S." and smiling vaguely at the chorus. As if taking this as some unwholesome cue, Stephanie sprang into his path, her eyes bright with curiosity.

"Hey, Alec, can I ask you a question?" she asked, and her junior coven formed a loose circle around him as though he were a spirit to be banished or commanded.

"Sure, Steph. What's up?"

"Well, it's a bit weird, but we're mates, right? You can tell me."

Mates. Peers, even—maybe they had a few things in common. Would Stephanie think him cool for still popping pills, pulling all-nighters? She was about the age where he'd started down that track.

"Fire away."

"Is it true that guys watch porn, like, all the time?"

Acutely aware that he was standing in a ring of grinning young women quizzing him about masturbation, Alec tried to laugh. He noted that two of Steph's friends had auburn hair like hers; one, her bestie Kiersten, was a natural blonde and had now dyed it darker, as if the look was contagious. This parallel with the nymphs discomfited him even further.

"Um...what?"

"It's just that guys at school talk like they watch it every day and shit. Is that normal? Is it like checking Facebook for dudes or something, you got to pop on every few hours and see what's new?"

"Uh...it's matter of preference, I guess. We didn't have easy access to internet porn when we were that age, so it wasn't like that for us."

"But you totally would have been smashing it all the time, right? I mean, guys are guys. You can't help it."

Was this a kind of flirtation, or just genuine if somewhat inappropriate curiosity? Maybe he was the cute older guy, the cool one Steph had told her mates about, and she was now gauging his sexual knowledge for future reference...or maybe he was just a hopeless idiot who needed his ego stroked by the intimation of acceptance by people less than half his age. He was well aware which possibility was the better bet.

"You probably don't want to be having this conversation with me," he said.

"Ah, it's cool, dude! We're all adults here—well, *almost*. We all do it, you know? And you're probably the master of your domain lately, since you broke up with Stella."

"Oh my *god*, Steph!" Kiersten gasped, drowning in laughter. "You're terrible!"

The girls pulled her away and left Alec bemused, carrying thoughts he'd rather not entertain in public, or at all, even if he already suspected he would be doing so later in forensic detail. He carried his fresh drink across the party and nibbled at the edges of conversations, feeling too old to relate to Stephanie and her friends yet too young or immature at heart to be at ease with his peers. After a while he headed outside for a cigarette, and he had just cashed the butt when he spotted Stella weaving through partygoers toward him. Her approach had all the implacable inevitability of fate, and he experienced the odd sensation of his stomach sinking and his heart lifting at the same time.

"Can we talk?" she asked.

*I don't know. Can we?*

Alec wasn't even sure if he could form words, so he simply nodded—after all, he'd denied her too much in the past. She led him down onto the back lawn for privacy, and they sat on the grass about halfway down to the creek. The starlight flattered Stella, made invisible the tiny lines starting to creep in at the corners of her eyes and mouth, smoothed away any resemblance to her beloved *nonna*. It made her look younger, but he told himself what he liked most was that softening of the family likeness; the Rafanellis had tolerated him as a dubious short-term prospect at best, and Stella's mother and grandmother especially had been given to mentioning her upwardly mobile ex-boyfriend Mario at any given opportunity. They seemed to miss him more than she, the perfect partner she'd let slip away and could never replace with such dregs of manhood as Alec.

"How've you been?" she asked, staring down at the creek.

He just breathed out, but it sounded a lot like a sorry sigh.

"Yeah, me too. Look, I know we had our problems," Stella began. "And you probably think I'm totally over you. But I can't just drop everything we had, everything we were. It's frustrating—thinking that we almost had it but didn't quite get there."

"I'm sorry, Stel," he said. "I know I've been a stupid, thoughtless man—"

"I'm not after an apology, Alec. I just needed...*need* to know what you really want. Maybe there's still a way to bridge the gap between us, you know? But I can't build that bridge alone, and that's what it felt like I was doing. If I knew you wanted to help—to work on things properly..."

She let the sentence hang, its unspoken implications heavy in the air, and Alec felt crushed to a pea within the weight of his own worthlessness.

"I did want to sort things out. I still do. I just...don't know how to grow. I'm scared that I'll never be able to work it out, and I'll just keep letting people down. Letting *you* down."

Stella let her hand fall on his forearm for a moment, an echo of all the times she'd reached out to him. "Wanting to grow is the first step. We all live the way we want to, babe. Sometimes that's because it's comfortable, and after years of inertia, that's hard to shake off. But if we have a good enough reason, we can become better people. I want to be better than I was before. Don't you?"

Alec opened his mouth to agree, and then a shriek dashed the words from his lips. Figures pounded through the grass to his right, and he turned to see Stephanie and a couple of her friends dancing around each other as if in some strange courting ritual, laughing as they lunged at each other. One of the girls slapped Stephanie on the rump of her tiny shorts and she gave an outraged giggle, trying to return the favour and land her open palm on her attacker's butt. Kiersten dived in while she was distracted and tackled her, and with a whoop of surprise the two of them tangled in each other's supple limbs, fell to the grass in a writhing puzzle of moonlit skin, lay laughing at each other through lips so close a slipped tongue could have crossed the distance between them.

"Clearly not," Stella said, her voice flat and hard as a pebble from a creek bed, and Alec turned to see her rising to her feet. "I guess I know what you want, Alec, and you can't get it from me."

"Hey, no—"

"Have fun with your teenage fantasies. Maybe one day you'll grow up and act your age, but I won't be waiting around until you do."

"But that's not— I mean, come on!"

"Don't. Okay? Just—*don't*. I won't bother you again. I'm going back to the party to hang out with the other old crones."

"Stella—"

Too late. She was stalking back across the grass to the deck, and Alec knew he'd fumbled his last chance with her. Stupid man. Stupid little *boy*. He didn't deserve her consideration, her patience. Alone again, and well suited to it. *Idiot.*

Alec sat there between the chirp of cricket-song from the trees ahead and that of No Doubt's "Just A Girl" from the house behind, his face fallen into one hand. Why couldn't he ever get anything *right*? After all these years he was still just a dumb kid, clumsy and hopeless, breaking things left, right, and centre with no clue how he could prevent it. Little wonder no woman was game to trust him for long with anything so delicate as her heart. Sometimes he believed he'd ill-served every woman who'd ever given him more than the time of day, all the way back to Gemma.

With the emergence of the #MeToo movement and subsequent outing of numerous sex offenders, many men had looked inward to see if they had anything to answer for, and Alec was no exception. Perhaps the ensuing guilt was excessive—he knew he was no predator, had never done anything out of malice or manipulation—but maybe he needed it to sharpen his insights. Think about it: the first girl he'd ever slept with had been just that, a *girl*—and for all that he'd not known her true age, hadn't he chosen not to even ask her? Sure, it obviously hadn't been Gemma's first rave that night, nor her first sexual encounter, but she had been intoxicated, vulnerable—and hadn't he taken advantage of that fact? He told himself she'd been willing, and yes, she had reciprocated, and yes, if she'd spoken a single word of demurral at any stage, he would've complied. But he couldn't help thinking that maybe she'd decided it was easier to go along with what he wanted rather than speak up and risk an angry response. Alone and exposed in an unfamiliar place with her thoughts muddled by drugs, her companion a stranger who might turn violent if she defied him—what else could she have done? The possibility that she had felt unsafe with him, had compromised her own choices to placate him, left Alec horrified. He'd never meant anyone any harm. Had he dealt it nonetheless?

Alec planted his glass in the lawn, as empty as he felt. *You bring all this on yourself,* he thought, *you just let it happen,* and then: *this song is yours to own and cannot be unsung.* Great, he was quoting his own dreams now. That was not a good sign. Anything generated by his mind was surely not to be trusted.

Rising to his feet, Alec cast a glance back at the house. The party heaved on without him, not missing him for a beat, and Stella had disappeared into it to drown her frustration and hurt in wine. He imagined her venting to Jessie, perhaps mentioning what she thought of Alec's predilections and in which direction they tended to skew—maybe even accusing him of a specific impropriety, when all he'd done was look when startled by a sudden sound—and could see the eyes of his friends turning to him, smaller and brighter and harder than those of the illusory naiads, judging him as unhealthy and unwelcome. Best if he stayed out here in the cold, in the dark, stranded in the endless waters of night.

*What do you think this says about you, Alec? And how am I supposed to believe that I'm what you really want? I mean, you've owned exactly ONE painting your whole life—so why is it of a bunch of naked teenage girls?*

That was a question he'd never thought to ask himself until then, and he'd failed to provide Stella with a cogent answer. Thinking of it now, he wondered if he'd set these ruinous events in motion all those years ago when he'd bought the Waterhouse print, or if he'd always been destined to fall under its apparently corrosive influence. That notion robbed him of any agency and hence, one could argue, responsibility, and as depressing as that was, some comfort could be found in the thought that he wasn't to blame for his failures. But this song was his to own, after all, and it was time he accepted that—even if he'd always been fated to meet temptation at the water's edge.

Upon that thought, he rose and traversed the gentle slope of the back lawn toward the creek. The moon looked down, disinterested in his movements, and so unjudged, he reached the bottom of the lawn. He stood at the edge of the swathe cut into the earth by the shallow creek, perhaps a metre deep, and watched the surface rill lazily in the lunar light.

And then, inevitably, he heard quiet laughter dancing through the air from somewhere nearby. The melody of a girl—no, two, or more.

He'd been too focused on Stella's departure to note whether Steph and her friends had returned inside. Maybe they'd gone for a walk along the creek to sneak in a quick toke or some space for girl talk, and if he couldn't relate to the adults in his life, maybe he could find a sympathetic ear from those on the cusp. Or perhaps it wasn't them he could hear at all—but did that even matter anymore? He might deserve to be alone, but that didn't mean he *wanted* to be.

Alec turned to the right and walked slowly along the edge of the creek, toward the source of the laughter. He imagined what he might find ahead, but he didn't have to fear his worst thoughts. He could be safe, a friend. Appropriate.

*Stop it. You're a vain, pathetic little man. Don't humiliate yourself any further.*

Alec sucked in a deep breath. This was sure to be another terrible idea. He should turn back to the house, be the man Stella wanted him to be even if he couldn't do so at her side. He kept walking.

The trees cut him off from the view of the house, and ahead he could see where the creek flowed beneath the Hendricks's fence and on into the neighbouring yard, which was empty of light and life. Between that border and he, a smudge of paleness danced in the water.

So she hadn't returned to the party. She was waiting for him, bare as the bones beneath his flesh would one day be; he couldn't see the expression on her face, but she was watching his approach. She stood in the centre of the narrow stream and waited for him, covered to the waist by water, one hand gently waving him on.

Alec paused at the edge of the bank, wisdom fighting instinct. He saw she wasn't alone in the creek—her friends cruised through the water to join her, all six of them bare and beckoning. He raced through a series of possibilities—live-streamed prank to shame him, deepest fantasy come true, validation of all his illusions—then decided it didn't really matter anymore. Some things were too weighted with inevitability to bother fighting back. He stepped into the stream, shuddering at the chilly caress of the water.

Back at the house, he heard an explosion of sound over the music pounding from the party, young voices shrieking freedom and joy into the evening sky. He recognised Stephanie's distant laugh and understood something crucial. But it made no difference now, not really. He waded deeper into the creek and the girls slid through the black water toward him, their auburn hair shaded dark by the night and their eyes even darker. They weren't smiling and laughing now, their faces as drawn and solemn as Gemma's had been that dry, awkward morning, and like hers as she'd advanced on him from the flickering shadows at the rave, their pupils were wide and round as black suns, as deep and mindless as hunger.

# The Black Regent

JOSIE HAD HEARD ABOUT the Black Regent, of course. An old Art Deco theatre that had sat disused and derelict for decades without being touched by the spate of urban remodelling going on all around it, the Regent was the kind of place that bred eerie rumours amongst the local kids, the kind that doomed teenagers would flock to in the slasher flicks Josie loved. So when Warren approached her in the Horror aisle of Magellan Video and asked her to come to the Black Regent after he closed up shop for the night, she didn't brush him off straight away.

"Man, I *love* this shit," he said by way of introduction, running a fingernail along the DVDs from H to J, each movie another vertebra in a long and colourful spine. This much had already been made clear by conversations he and Josie had shared at school or parties—his lack of self-assurance was less obvious when discussing his favourite films, his voice louder, his eyes and hands alive with passion. "Argento, Carpenter, Nakata, Flanagan—they're like my saints. But amazing as their movies are, they're just...*ideas*. Fake fantasies—a passive experience, you know? But the real stuff's out there. You just have to know where to look."

At first, Josie only wanted him to make his point and go away. Her homework had taken hours to kill, and all the while she'd been looking forward to devouring a slab of chocolate as she watched bloody deaths on a thirty-six-inch screen—any more obstacles between her and those things, and she might just turn to murder herself. But here was something new: Warren was wearing a confident smile that flattered his narrow face, unfazed by her lack of enthusiasm. His eyes held hers without dropping or cutting away, and he didn't fidget with his phone or his floppy hair.

"I know a place, Josie, and it's the scariest thing I ever saw. You want to come take a look with me?"

"Huh?" Josie's eyebrows shot up of their own accord—was shy Warren suddenly asking her out, and in public, no less? "Be kind and rewind, dude. *What* did you just ask me?"

"I know it sounds weird, but it's legit, I promise. I found something incredible, and I've been wondering who the hell I could ever share it with—but you'd be *perfect*, Josie. You're not like everyone else. You'd *get* it."

A little disturbed by the new intensity in Warren's eyes, Josie glanced around the ailing video store, the last of its kind in the area. A half-dozen people were wandering the aisles or placidly watching looped previews of new-release pablum on wall-mounted screens, and none of them looked anything like her; here as much as anywhere, she felt like a black rose planted in a garish plastic bucket. She needed more from life than these drones—demanded diversions and adventures, and the more reckless and ill-advised, the better. Maybe that was why she didn't dismiss Warren's weird overture out of hand, was why she could already feel her apathy giving way to genuine interest.

"You know how amazing this scary thing of yours would have to be for me to even *think* about going off into the night with a guy I hardly know?"

His eyes lit up as if he'd caught a faint hint of consent. "Oh, believe me—this is *the* shit. Josie, trust me on this. I swear you won't regret it. Will you come?"

"I don't know. When were you thinking?"

"Why not tonight? It's like ten past ten now—I finish my shift and close up in twenty minutes. What do you say?"

Josie and Warren saw each other at school all the time, exchanged words probably every week, and so far, no red flags had popped up to warn her away from him. He seemed mellow, vaguely cool, but appearances could be deceiving; Josie was barely eighteen, but many years had passed since she'd decided all humans were just slime moulds with pretensions to civilisation. So, what was the worst this one could do? Frames of carnage from her favourite films flashed across the silver screen in the back of her mind, but she dismissed these possibilities in a heartbeat. Her gut feeling was that Warren was harmless, and if her anatomy was mistaken...well, he wouldn't be the first guy to regret crossing her.

"What is it, then, this terrifying place of yours?" she asked, and Warren told her, smiling as if he'd been rolling those three words around in his mouth with relish. Josie felt a chilly tingle of curiosity in the back of her head and knew that this was where anyone with common sense would politely decline.

"Okay," she said.

* * *

Josie hung around until Warren closed Magellan Video and then followed his motorbike across the eastern suburbs to the Black Regent. She parked her Laser GL in a quiet cul-de-sac behind his Honda and joined him on the footpath, where he stood staring across the road like a tourist returning to his favourite monument. Her eyes were drawn to the dark bulk that loomed on the other side of the street, and a tickle of morbid fascination goosed her heartbeat. She had to admit that Warren was right—this was totally the sort of thing she vibed on.

"Well, Miss Hughes. Ready for the thrill of a lifetime?"

"I'm warning you now," she said, lighting a cigarette. "You try and pull something funny on me, you'll regret it."

Warren raised his hands in supplication. "Nothing creepy, I promise. Well, it's gonna be *creepy*, but not in that way."

"Fine, let's go," she prompted. "It's getting late, and I want to watch my movie before I crash out."

"Ah, yes, *In the Mouth of Madness*. Girl's got taste."

The tall fence keeping the Regent closed off from the footpath wore drapes of morning glory vines as if to discourage the curious, and the one gate she could see was pointedly chained shut. Josie hoped Warren didn't expect her to clamber over it, but instead, he pulled at a clump of leaves and lifted it like a flap of ragged flesh. A gaping maw interrupted the diamond pattern of fence wire beneath, and he beckoned Josie through before closing the gap behind them.

Straightening, Josie saw they were now standing in a disused drive that ran down the side of the old two-storey theatre. The Regent loomed over them like a black ship on the night tide, and she felt a delicious twinge of apprehension.

"So where do we get in?"

"Around the back," Warren murmured. "And you might want to keep your voice down. We are trespassing, after all."

"Oh, great. You might have mentioned that we'd be breaking the law."

"Where's your sense of adventure? Come on, this way."

Josie shadowed him as he crept around the nearest corner of the building, his head turning from side to side as he went. Surely no-one was watching, and yet she couldn't help but feel like they'd walked onto the set of a play such as the Regent had seen hundreds of times over—the theatre a one-sided shell, the moon a pale disc pinned to a black drape of sky above. Warren moved past a loading dock, where a heavy door sat stolid and impassable in the wall four feet off the ground, to a busted window at the back of the building.

"Here."

Josie looked around the deserted, rubbish-strewn car park behind them. All was cloaked in shadow, so anything could have been lurking back there and watching, licking its lips in anticipation of following them in. When she turned back to Warren, he was disappearing through the window into darkness. A flap of cardboard dangled after him from one taped corner, the glass broken and cleared away long ago.

"Your turn." A pale claw pushed out through the cardboard. "Here, take my hand."

"Keep it. You may need it."

"Ha ha."

His fingers remained outstretched, and Josie began reaching for them. A sudden vision burst like a flare inside her skull: *Warren pulls her through the window, throws her to the floor inside the pitch-black theatre, springs onto her quick and savage. An hour later, he leaves. Alone.*

She shrugged. Let him try and see how far he got. She tossed her cigarette into a rusted barrel, then reached for his hand. With Warren's help, she clambered awkwardly through the window and dropped to the floor inside. When she was standing steady, he let go and stepped away from her.

*Good boy.*

By the moonlight creeping in through their point of entry, Josie could see that this room was full of broken junk. It smelled of mildew and must, of rust and neglect. Warren was barely visible, and only now did she realise he had pulled a black sweater on over his work shirt to blend in with the dark. She supposed he would have just as much difficulty seeing her—her wardrobe came in all colours as long as they were black, and her rust-red hair faded into the night like bloodstains on a funeral dress. All anyone else would see of them was ghostly faces and pairs of equally pale hands floating along beneath them.

*But there's no-one else here, right?*

"Well, we're in. Now what?"

Warren's teeth gleamed in the moonlight. "Now I fill in the back story. There's a terrible tale to tell, and when I'm done, you can either hop back outside or continue the tour."

"Oh, I'm sure you'll scare my socks off. Come on, then."

Josie heard Warren rubbing his hands together in the dark. "Okay. So, the Black Regent is one of two Art Deco theatres around these parts, the other one being the Viceroy. They were built by the same man in 1934, but my tale doesn't truly begin until 1972."

"So instead of spirits in period dress, we're talking ghosts in high-waisted flares."

A snort of amusement from Warren. "No."

Josie's mouth ran away from her, as if trying to hold back the heavy atmosphere with the reassuring sound of snark. "Oh, I know! There was a murder spree, and the killer comes back on every anniversary to bump off horny teenagers...and it's *tonight*."

Warren sighed. "Do you mind not interrupting my monologue?"

"Sorry. Go on."

"Thank you. Now, the owner of the Black Regent in 1972 was Joseph Buller, who'd made his name on the stages of London's West End. When he retired, he moved to Australia to enjoy his twilight years—but an artist never really retires, does he? Buller ended up buying the Regent cheap and installing a projection booth so he could screen films, which was how he kept the place afloat, and he scratched his dramatic itch by directing a local acting troupe."

"Someone's been doing their research."

"You'll see why. One of the actors was a woman called Margaret Bachelor. I've seen some pics, and she was a total hottie—but by all accounts, a dreadful actress. Despite this, Buller gave her the female lead in his last play, *Thumbs Dug Deep*."

"He was probably shagging her."

"I think our mate Joe was one of those old theatrical queens, but who knows? Apparently, he liked his murder thrillers—*Thumbs Dug Deep* was about a strangler stalking young women on a cruise ship."

Josie gave a low whistle of appreciation. "Tonight's feature presentation: *Titanic*, starring Leonardo DeSalvo."

Warren snorted out a laugh, then covered his mouth as if embarrassed—or as if he didn't want to be heard.

"In the second-to-last scene, Margaret's character discovers the captain guiding the ship off course, and he strangles her to death. After that, the other survivors realise he's the killer, he gets shot by a vacationing cop, and he falls over the side. Sharks have been following the ship because of the bodies he's been dumping, and they eat him."

Josie grinned. "Wow, morbid. I'm *so* gonna Google this later."

"Max Kellum, the guy playing the captain, was a renowned method actor whose career was going off the rails—emotional issues, erratic behaviour, basically an alcoholic by this stage. Buller gave him the role as a favour, hoping he'd pull his head in. Margaret had a bad feeling about their showcase scene, but Buller swore to her that everything would be fine."

"Ominous much?"

"Oh, yeah. Come opening night, the play runs like clockwork, right until the big reveal. Margaret walks in and sees what Captain Max is doing, so he chokes the life out of her. The curtain goes down for scene change, and the audience is left buzzing about the unexpected twist, the shockingly intense strangling...and the fact that Ms. Bachelor has finally delivered a convincing performance."

Josie nodded, knowing exactly where this was going.

"Unfortunately, that's all they ever got to see of *Thumbs Dug Deep*. As you can guess, Margaret was playing dead far too well to be acting. Everyone knew that Max was going through a nasty separation from his wife, but no-one realised the depth of his depression or the amount of drugs he was taking to deal with it."

"Actors on drugs? The mind boggles."

"During the trial, Kellum admitted to being off his face on a cocktail of narcotics, said that once he got Margaret's throat in his hands, all he could see was his wife, and it made him so angry that he just...*squeezed*."

"Lovely."

"Buller took it hard, blamed himself. He was wracked with intense guilt and grief, spent his days wandering the halls of this very theatre like a lost man. Eventually, his friends got worried and checked him into the hospital."

"A mental hospital?"

"Nope. No-one thought Buller was crazy until the next day, when the nurse came in and found something...horrible."

Silence followed this proclamation, until Josie realised he was waiting for her to ask. "Okay—what did he do?"

"He'd bitten off his own tongue, chewed it, and swallowed it."

"Ouch!" Josie sucked in a pained breath. "Really? Is that even possible?"

"Apparently. They decided to pack Buller off to the loony bin after all. But as he was being transported there, he got out of his restraints, bit a nurse on the face, and made a break for it. They never caught him. Joseph Buller disappeared into the shadows of history."

Josie waited for the next delicious detail, then realised he'd reached the end of his spiel. "Oh. And that's all, is it?"

Warren smiled. "No way. So, shall we begin the midnight tour?"

"Hang on!" Josie protested. "What's all that got to do with tonight? Does Buller *live* here or something?"

"No-one is living in this building, Josie. What's your decision? Will you go, or will you stay?"

She took a deep breath—not to fight fear, but rather her irritation with Warren's mysterious manner. Or perhaps she was just nettled by the way he'd hooked her so easily with that story.

"I wouldn't give you the satisfaction of watching me back down."

"Excellent!" Warren rubbed his hands together again, pleased. "Let's move on, then, shall we? The door is right here."

Something rattled and scraped at Warren's side. Peering through the dim, Josie saw him sliding a moth-eaten curtain along its rail, revealing a decrepit-looking door. With a jolt of unease, she saw a line of pale, jaundiced light along the bottom edge.

"Is someone else here?" she asked, sharp as a blade.

"Ssshh!" Warren turned to her fast, finger at his lips. "From here on in, be very quiet. If you absolutely *must* say something, whisper it."

Josie felt the first pangs of anxiety. Up to this point, she'd been vaguely concerned about cops or security catching them in here—but now they were about to head out into a lit corridor inside a derelict building, whispering to each other to avoid detection.

*Detection by what?*

Probably a couple of Warren's friends, lurking in wait to lurch out and frighten her. Then she'd realise the scam and yell at Warren, who'd offer her a drink to calm her down...and that was where she said yes and they hung out and got tipsy and then she let him kiss her, right? She'd noticed the way he sometimes looked at her from across a room—his keen eyes undercut by the wrought line of his mouth, like he wanted to speak bold truths to her but didn't dare.

*He's certainly dared tonight, and I've gone along with it—so what else might he now be brave enough to try?*

"After you," she said.

There came a portentous creak from aged hinges as Warren eased the door open, and Josie heard a sharp intake of breath. Either he was a good actor, or he really didn't want to be heard in here.

The hallway was only dimly lit, but the fact that anything could be seen at all this late at night was alarming. Josie peered down the corridor and saw why: here and there, someone had screwed old candles into disused lamp casings—and lit them.

"Warren," she whispered. "Did you do this?"

He grinned and shook his head.

"Then who's here? Tell me!"

He winked, then pointed to the right and started creeping in that direction. With an uneasy mixer of curiosity and dread washing around in her gut, Josie followed as quietly as she could, which wasn't as quietly as she'd have liked. The carpet had been torn up, and the old wooden floor puffed dust from creaky lips. Chunks of debris lay wherever they had fallen, unnoticed, and the discoloured walls ran up to a high ceiling that was lost in shadow. Every one of those candles was a risk, Josie realised—this place was an inferno waiting to happen.

The long hallway curved all the way around into a once-grand foyer. Josie saw a couple of illegible tags spray-painted on the aged wood, so they weren't the first to visit this place in its phase of dereliction, but she was surprised the graffiti was so minimal; it wasn't human nature to trash one area when there was a whole building just begging for it. The walls had suffered some damage, though—they were scuffed all along at shoulder height, and here and there, gashes and scratches defaced the panelling in close-knit groups. Near the front of the theatre, they passed a flight of stairs accompanied by a grand banister, and Josie guessed these led up to a mezzanine level, perhaps even balconies. The steps looked firm, but she felt disinclined to trust them under her boots after forty-odd years of neglect.

As they walked, Josie pondered the passing of time and the inevitable shift of paradigms. This theatre had offered stage shows and then films, until both had been surpassed in popular taste by home entertainments; the young man walking beside her worked in a store that had helped push the Regent into its grave, providing videotapes and laser discs and then DVDs and Blu-rays, but now that, too, was receding into redundancy thanks to online streaming services. Sure, there would always be an audience for stage and screen, just as some people would always prefer physical media, but some things would inevitably be lost in the shuffle—including institutions like the Black Regent. Looking around her now, Josie couldn't quite bring herself to regret the loss. In its decay, the old theatre offered a different type of entertainment, delights that she could never find in any brightly lit and well-maintained venue or on such a small canvas as a thirty-six-inch screen.

They came into the foyer together. More candles—a dozen points of light flickered gently in subtle draughts that found their way in from outside. Looking about, Josie could see paler patches on the walls where paintings had been hung, and the shell of a deserted cafeteria off to one side.

"Cool, isn't it?" whispered Warren. That cocky gleam was back in his eye, his anxiety hidden away—and yet the fact that he knew this place well, had been here before and was *still* nervous, kept Josie on edge.

"It has a certain ramshackle charm," she admitted, strolling toward the dust-choked cafeteria. "But I assume it's not the décor that's giving you the willies."

"What? No way. I'm the one who gives the willies, baby."

Warren was cracking wise to show he was unafraid, but the joke fell flat, its lewdness unconvincing in the oppressive atmosphere. Josie peered into the dim cavity where people had once sat and picked at meals, quaffed wine, tried to seduce each other. If that last was what she'd believed Warren's intention to be, then no longer; the hollow ring to his humour had put paid to that.

"Very nice," she murmured. "What's with all the candles?"

"There's a storeroom full of them backstage. I guess they were used as props, or stockpiled in case of a blackout or something."

"So, who's been lighting them?"

"If we're lucky, you'll see soon enough."

Josie sighed and dropped that line of questioning for now. "Fine, be all mysterious, then. Is it okay if I take some photos?"

Warren shrugged, so she slipped her phone out and took some quick and grainy snaps of the darkened foyer. She imagined the kind of creatures her favourite movies would have lurking in these surrounds and looked forward to dreaming of them later. Josie was the kind of girl who kept a journal about her nightmares, who turned them into abstract poems and wondered if this was the voice by which the world would come to know her. She had to do *something*, right? Half her classmates were already grinding away behind supermarket checkouts or fast-food counters in preparation for their future labours, and still she searched for a better option. University, perhaps—but then what?

She shook such thoughts away for now. In this place, her mind should be on the shadows of the past, not the mists of the future.

"Right, done. So, what's the next stop on the tour?"

Warren bowed and gestured with one arm to a set of double doors that gave way to the auditorium.

"Josie Hughes, tonight's the night you make your grand debut on the stage of the Black Regent."

\* \* \*

Standing on the stage where a woman had been strangled was bad enough—but staring out at rows upon rows of empty seats made Josie feel even more anxious, as if an invisible audience was waiting to watch it happen again. None of those disquieting candles burned in the auditorium, and she could see no farther than the first row of dilapidated seats; beyond that, the cavernous chamber stretched out beneath a cloak of darkness, and every sound she made sent back a mocking echo. She wanted to pull out her phone and dispel the febrile shadows with sterile digital light, but Warren had insisted she not, whilst still refusing to give a reason.

A series of wooden creaks approached her across the stage. *Warren's treading the boards*, she thought, and could easily imagine him coming out of his shell in the glow of the footlights, twirling a pantomime villain's moustache and chewing the scenery with relish.

"It's so creepy up here," he whispered when he reached her side, and then he startled her by articulating her own thoughts. "Knowing that a murder was committed right at our feet...and feeling like the crowd is still here in the darkness, waiting for an encore."

"For sure," she agreed. "I think I've had enough adulation for one night. Where now?"

"We exit at stage left and go to the dressing rooms."

The impression of being watched abated once they were backstage, but only until Josie realised that the dilapidated hallway was aglow with flickering light, more candle stubs crammed into rusted sconces and ignited to show the way. The ability to see again was a comfort, but then, *someone* had been here tonight to light these wicks. The thought didn't sit well with her, especially when Warren muttered, "We've got to be careful now."

"Why?"

"We're close."

"To what?"

He shook his head, unwilling to surrender his secret just yet. Instead, he pointed at the nearest wall, where three rusty lengths of rebar leaned against the sour, peeling plaster.

"They're still here. That's good. Grab one."

Josie's stomach pickled. "You expecting a fight?"

"It pays to be careful."

*Fantastic*, she thought, and wrapped her hand around one of the rods. She imagined what it would do when laid across someone's head at full force and felt just that little bit safer. Warren hefted one of the other makeshift clubs, remembering the weight.

"Let's move on, but keep it quiet," he whispered. "Tell me if you see anything strange."

"Like what?"

He let out a quiet, cracked laugh. "You'll know it when you see it."

Josie swallowed a lump of nerves. "Warren, you've got me seriously spooked now. If some of your mates are back here in monster masks waiting to jump out at me, you better say so now. You win, okay? I'm freaking."

His response—a squeeze of her free hand and a wan grin—wasn't quite as reassuring as she'd hoped. "If anything happens, just make sure you stick with me. I know this place inside out."

The two of them crept along the hall, wincing every time a creak called out through the silence to give them away. Josie flexed edgy fingers around the rebar, ready to lash out at a moment's notice. She was tempted to belt Warren for bringing her here and getting her so worked up, but why? He'd only made the suggestion; it was she who'd said yes. Once again, her impetuous nature had dumped her into a dubious situation and left her more circumspect side to pick up the tab.

Not one of the dressing room doors was closed. They gaped like lazy mouths, or else lay flat on the floor, asleep at their posts. Josie peered into each one on the way past, half-expecting to see corpses sitting before the dull-eyed mirrors, applying flaking make-up to skinless faces...but the rooms seemed empty of anything bar dust, broken light bulbs, and mouse turds.

As they passed the fourth door, Josie saw a faded, five-spoked shape on the wood where a star must once have hung. She looked in, immediately noticing that this room's dusty floor had been marked by passing feet—and now, glancing back along the corridor, she finally saw that the same disturbances ranged all along its length. She hadn't spotted them before because she'd been walking straight up the middle of the hall. Whoever else had been here liked to move close to the walls.

"Look!" she blurted, and then flinched as one of the wardrobes in the fourth dressing room burst open. Josie sucked in a shocked breath that froze in her throat.

It came out of the wardrobe with arms outstretched, its fingers distorted into claws, its jaw working fast and loose around choking gasps of need. The sheer horror of it shattered Josie's reason at once, reduced her to shivering, mindless prey. She squealed like a burned baby and back-pedalled into the corridor, her heartbeat a hammer in her head.

"Run!" Warren yelled, high and thin, as he pushed her along the hall.

Josie threw a frenzied glance over her shoulder as they pelted away, and there was nothing to be seen—almost as if there never had been. As they ran, she tried to convince herself that she'd imagined it, or that one of Warren's friends was back there in the dressing room shaking with laughter beneath clever prosthetics, but she couldn't believe those deadly delusions for a second.

She looked back again, and this time it was shockingly *there*, out in the hall and shambling swiftly along the wall toward them. Its clothes had rotted away to rags, revealing a hide that had mummified in a most bizarre way, but it was the face that convinced Josie of its awful authenticity—that, and the soft clicking sounds spitting from its horrible maw.

She wanted to scream but she could barely breathe, her lungs frozen in terror. Her head spun from the lack of air and her boots collided with each other, bringing her crashing down to the groaning floor. Warren grabbed her with a shout, but she was already lurching to her feet, sucking in a long moaning breath that almost drowned out the wretched gasps of the thing at her heels. Sensing those gnarled nails reaching for her streaming hair, Josie ran faster than she'd ever believed herself capable.

Trapped in that one moment, teetering on the cusp of capture, she had no idea how long they sprinted down that long and winding corridor, her perception of time and distance swamped by the cold ecstasy of terror. Her sweaty fingers clutched at the useless rebar as if letting it slip and fall would bring her the same fate, and she dared not look back to see how closely death shadowed her.

Warren snapped her back into focus by pulling her sideways onto a set of dusty wooden stairs that disappeared up into a candle-free darkness.

"Up here!"

Josie flung a desperate look back, saw the nightmare had receded far enough to give her a dash of hope and reason. "Where are we going?"

"Projection booth."

The steps groaned but held firm under their pounding feet. Josie tripped and stumbled upwards in the dark, panting hard and fast like a stallion, and was relieved to hear a door opening beneath Warren's hand. He shoved it closed after her and then they were sealed in the pitch-black projection room, the only sound that of their ragged breaths.

"What the *fuck* is that?" she gasped.

Warren gave a strangled laugh and said, "I think that's Joseph Buller."

Josie replied with a string of breathless profanities that ended abruptly when Warren put his hand to her mouth.

"Ssshh!"

She almost gave him a thump with the rebar, then subsided against the door and listened, hearing nothing now but the furious kick drum of her heart.

No—wait—

A slithering step. And another.

Warren dropped his hand from her mouth to free her voice, and his own was straining under the pressure of anxiety. "It's coming up."

"Lock the door!"

"There's no lock."

"Then where do we go?"

"There's a fire escape. Come on!"

They hustled across the room, their eyes beginning to adjust to the blackness; Josie barely managed to avoid the looming bulk of an antique film projector, a stream of spoiled film dangling from one reel and brushing her cheek like a spider's web. Then Warren came to an abrupt halt, and Josie ploughed right into him.

"Ouch! What's that?" Josie heard his hand sliding over a rough surface in the dark. "Oh, *shit*. There's something blocking the door!"

"What?"

"I don't know! It wasn't here last time!"

"Hang on!" Josie rummaged in her pocket, caught her phone in a slippery grip and managed to get it right way up, one finger triggering the screen. The sudden brightness stabbed at her eyes in the dark, and she kept them narrowed as she opened her torch app. Warren looked grim in the backwash of light.

"Um, brace yourself."

"Huh?"

Josie's phone glowed twice as bright, showing her the projection room clearly for the first time. The chamber was small and cluttered with dusty junk, and the object blocking the door was a waist-high wooden crate—but her eyes flew straight to the rust-red spray of dried blood on the pale wall behind Warren, and the two semi-devoured corpses slumped at its foot. She shrieked and jerked backwards, her finger reflexively stabbing the screen and killing the light.

"I don't know who they are," she heard Warren say in the fresh darkness as he dragged the crate aside. "Someone else who got curious, I guess. There are a couple more of them around the place."

He stood up straight, his foot striking a loose object that rolled across the invisible floor with the unmistakable metallic rattle of a spray can. Then the other door clicked open, and those choking gasps were mere metres away, and Josie could have sworn they took on a tone of triumph.

She whimpered and jerked toward the fire escape door, stumbling into Warren as he wrestled it open. Behind them, those slithering footsteps closed in. Josie looked back and saw a twisted black-on-black silhouette shambling across the all-too-small projection booth.

A grunt of relief, and suddenly Warren was gone. A gasp of pure terror wrenched itself from her throat, and Josie flung herself out into the night after him. The cool breeze swept across her fevered face as the fire escape clanged beneath her boots, blowing her to the left, toward the steps that led down to safe ground.

And then Warren's arms wrapped themselves tight around her, pinned her to his shaking body. Josie's breath was squeezed from her lungs by the sudden embrace, and the rebar fell from her spasming hand into the darkness.

*NO!*

*It was a trap all along—*

"Look!" Warren gasped into her ear.

Josie stared down at the fire escape gantry and saw her foot dangling over empty air. The rusted steel stairs had broken away from the platform and toppled to the ground thirty feet below, a skeletal spine bracketed by ribs of twisted steel. Her rod clanged against it and skittered away out of sight.

Pulling them both away from the edge, Warren reached back with one hand and shoved the fire escape door shut. No sooner had the old latch clicked into place than they heard those gnarled claws scratching at the other side, a sound of frantic hunger. A thrill of terror shot down Josie's spine, and she flashed on those bodies again, two sexless, limbless lumps of ravaged grue and bone, broken ribs caging nothing, tongueless mouths forever screaming—

"Over there," said Warren. He had one foot planted against the door and was leaning back against the railing to brace himself. Catching Josie's eye, he nodded at the other end of the fire escape. She dropped to all fours, scurried beneath his outstretched leg, and found a knotted rope dangling down from the gantry into the night.

"Ladies first, but *please* make it quick."

For a few seconds that felt so much longer, Josie thought she wasn't going to be able to do it—thought she would hunch here frozen in panic until the door burst open and their death fell spitting and clawing upon them. That got her legs swinging over the edge, her stomach reeling as she tipped forward and the ground loomed up at her. Then she was dropping, and her panicked hands clutched for the nylon rope. She was sure that her sweaty fingers would fumble the grab and leave her plummeting to the ground below, but they were determined, and clutched the rough strand as if it were life itself. Her thighs clamped shut around the rope, and there Josie hung like a spider cursed with vertigo, thirty feet above the unwelcoming earth.

"Hurry!"

Josie let her thighs relax and kicked at the rope until her frantic foot found the nearest knot. With a deep breath and a wish, she began inching her way down, not letting one hold go until she'd found the next. She discovered it was much easier with her eyes closed.

"Move, Josie, *now!*"

She heard feet thumping on the fire escape above, heard Warren's rebar clatter on the old gantry, and then the rope swayed roughly to one side as he grabbed hold and swung aboard. The fire escape door burst open with a grating screech.

"*Shit!*"

She somehow managed to move even faster, and Warren was so close behind her that he almost kicked her in the head. She looked upwards and waited for his feet to jerk as the thing grabbed him and pulled him back up, but all he did was swear repeatedly under his breath as they descended. Then she saw a silhouette at the railing, moving across the pale face of the moon like some ghastly, choking eclipse—toward the place where the rope was tied.

Josie looked down. Maybe a dozen feet to go.

*Oh, fuck it.*

She dropped, crying out as she fell, then landed hard on both boots and was dashed furiously into the dirt, feeling the breath explode out of her like she'd been gut-punched. She rolled weakly onto her side, gasping for air and choking on dust instead. Curled up and clutching at her numb feet, she heard Warren plummet to the earth beside her. They lay that way for a few seconds, hacking, moaning, sobbing in shock.

When Josie remembered why they'd fallen, she rolled onto her back and stared up through tears at the metal gantry. A dark shape hung over the railing up there, and she couldn't make out any details no matter how fast she blinked away the wet blurs, but she knew it was looking down at her. It didn't move, just loomed over the rail and stared with horrid, sunken eyes that she was so glad she could no longer see. The moment it showed signs of pursuit, she would scramble to her poor feet and fly, but until then she was frozen, locked in a staring match she dared not lose.

After a minute that seemed like an eternity, the shadow finally withdrew. Footsteps shuffled across the fire escape, and the door was dragged shut with a definitive clang.

And then, silence.

More silence.

Then: "Warren?"

A groan. "Yeah?"

Josie sat up, wincing at a half-dozen potential bruises, and stabbed at him with one quivering, accusatory finger.

"*That*...was the fucking scariest thing that's ever happened to me in my entire fucking *life*."

Warren moaned and rolled up onto his butt, a hint of that new confident grin sneaking back onto his dusty face. "Told you so."

Josie fumbled in her coat, found her battered packet of cigarettes. "God *damn*. Want one?"

"Usually, no. Right now? Hell, yes."

They smoked in silence for a while, trying to catch their breath, pin down their equilibrium.

"You think that was him?" Josie asked, when her voice sounded almost normal again. "You really think *that* was Joseph Buller?"

Warren nodded. "Makes sense when you think about it. You hear those sounds it was making? I reckon that's what a person might sound like if they had no tongue."

"But there's no way he's still alive!"

A shrug. "Buller was old when he vanished, and that was over forty years ago. And judging by the way he looks, his *face*...yeah, my money's on dead. He's pretty frisky for a corpse, though, isn't he?"

Josie nailed him with a gaze. "And you asked me to go into that place all unawares, knowing that thing is in there waiting to kill and *eat* us."

Warren grinned. "Hell of a rush, isn't it?"

"I thought I was going to *die!* That was the most intense thing *ever!*"

As one, they both looked up at the empty gantry.

"I'm going in again," Warren said. "Soon."

He dragged on his cigarette, butted it out on the ground that had broken his fall, and turned to Josie. Now she knew why his eyes gleamed with a newfound confidence—death had nipped at his heels, and in that terror, he'd discovered a new perspective on life. How scary could school be, could the rejection of a girl be, when he had *that* experience by which to measure his fears?

"I've done this four times now, and every run is different—that thing is reacting, learning. It's even setting traps for me now! But I love the challenge—running, fighting for your very life, it's so fucking *hardcore*. And as it turns out, it's even more fun with someone else.

"So, Josie Hughes...what have you got planned for the weekend?"

She looked up at the wreck of the Black Regent, then across at his face. He waited for her response, no nerves now, and his smile said he already knew the answer. Josie recalled the rapture of terror she'd known inside the old theatre, the hit of pure adrenaline that had carried her along mere seconds ahead of a hellish end, and felt her own lips curve up to mirror his.

"Nothing I can't cancel," she said.

# Vision Thing

HALLOWEEN AGAIN—MY FAVOURITE day of the year, touching on my deepest interests and my most beloved memories—but night is falling when I finally drag my sorry carcass out of my unmade bed and stumble naked into the kitchen to make myself a coffee, and I've already spooned the brown stuff into my cleanest mug before I notice the girl with the black dog tattoo sitting at my table.

The world has receded to a hazy horizon beyond the fog of depression lately, true, but it's difficult to believe I didn't spot her at once, since she might have been calculated by some invasive algorithm to tick so many boxes on my personal lust list. Raven-black hair trails down over her shoulders, and her breasts rise modest but firm beneath a t-shirt displaying the cover of The Cure's *Disintegration*. Down below, she's wrapped in a schoolgirl-style tartan skirt and her calves are sleek and tight beneath black knee-socks, her feet tucked into sable and crimson saddle shoes.

She looks a little like the first girl I ever had a crush on in primary school, a little like the woman I carved my arms open over in my early twenties, and a lot like Toni. She's got a few tattoos, but the one that catches my eye is under her right sleeve, a hellish black dog staring out of her skin at me like a hungry wolf.

Her own eyes are worse. They're deep and dark and remind me of a shark's pitiless stare, an impression only deepened into unease by the way her lips split into a wide grin that reveals way too much of her teeth.

"So, here we are at last," she says, and her voice is smoke and honey and blood and bass.

I open my mouth to ask the obvious questions, but already I know there's no point. This might be a dream and it might be real, but I instinctively understand this is no ordinary woman, and I don't waste time wondering how she got into my house. I do belatedly remember I'm naked and cross my hands over my crotch. This makes her laugh, and she sounds like someone who very much enjoys her amusements. She sounds like someone who could find the comedy in a war-orphaned child bleeding to death as they're raped by a gang of jeering soldiers.

"Are we going to do the thing?" she asks. "You know—who are you, how did you get in here, what do you want, all that malarkey? No?"

I shake my head, strangely resigned to this weird visitation. "Just tell me if I'm awake or asleep."

"You can work that one out for yourself. Or, hey, here's another question you might want to ponder: are you alive or dead?"

I cast a glance back down the hallway because this seems like a valid concern. Maybe it wasn't my flesh that rose from bed just now.

"That's right. Dead and awake, or alive and asleep, or maybe some other combination? But don't sweat it too much, Wee Willy Winkie. We've got time to kill, places to go."

I have the strangest feeling I don't need to ask where, or why. She grins as though she can read my mind, and for all I know, she can. Or she *is* my mind.

"Good, you're vaguely self-aware. That should make things a little more enjoyable. Now, you might want to throw some clothes on, because we're going out—and if you get arrested for public indecency in the first five minutes, our night will peak way too early."

*Where are we going?* I think, just to test her.

"Don't bore me," she says, "you've already guessed where. But since we're coming up to the end of a scene, I'll lay it on you nice and dramatic to smooth the transition:

"You know what I am, and you know what I want. I'm going to take you out and show you the world, and I'm going to tell you the way I see it and the way it sees you...and at the end of all that, you're going to kill yourself."

She clicks her fingers.

"Next scene."

\* \* \*

I'm dressed now, and we're out on my street. Did I throw on some dirty clothes, brush my hair, shrug on my long coat, and lead her out the door, or did we just jump-cut past all that to this moment? Feels more like the latter, but the weird thing is, I can taste coffee.

"Look at all this, Winkie," says the girl with the black dog tattoo, waving at groups of costumed children with one hand that now has a Satanic stogie burning between its black-nailed fingers. "Halloween used to really *be* something, you know? Bonfires lit in piles of bones, paeans to the dead, offerings of blood and meat—it was a celebration of life as much as death. Now, it's just another excuse for supermarkets to spruik their cheap trinkets to idiots who think the day is about plastic pumpkins and cartoon skulls. I think we need to take Samhain back to the darkest, oldest days. I'd love to see the guts of these kids strewn through the trees like paper streamers, candles lit inside their hollowed-out skulls, their bones drained of marrow and thrown into the fire. What do you think?"

She should know that I'm barely listening. Even such savageries as she's describing seem to pale in comparison to the trials I've suffered this year. Being out on my favourite night just reminds me all the more, because it brings to mind so many precious reveries that drown out the snarl of the stranger at my side.

For example, last year, Toni and I decided to dress up as The Sisters of Mercy circa 1987, me as Andrew Eldritch with a greasy quiff draping over the collar of my leather jacket and my eyes hidden behind mirrored shades, she as Patricia Morrison with her black hair sprayed up and a cheap bass guitar clutched in lace-gloved hands. We were ridiculous and amazing, stupid and beautiful. We were...well, we *were*.

A puff of cigar smoke engulfs my face. I smell sulphur—too obvious, she's trying too hard—but also semen and burning flesh, black roses and flat cola.

"Slow down. We'll get to her in due course, Winkie."

She's really leaning into that joke. Penile insecurity is rife among men no matter what they're packing in their slacks, but it's a cheap gibe. You'd think that whatever she is could do better.

"Oh, give me time, boy. We're just warming up here."

I want to know her limits. "Pretty sure this is just a dream or fugue or something, so go ahead and do your worst."

"If this *is* just a dream or a fugue, then you can do *your* worst," she shoots back. "Why not try it and see? Check out that kid over there with his mummy—bucket in his hand for all the sweets, but he hasn't even bothered to dress up! It's Halloween, for fuck's sake, and he wants sweets for walking up the block in a t-shirt and jeans! Doesn't that just sum up the fucking *zeitgeist* for you, Winkie? This whole era of entitled little shits whining that they deserve the best of everything without lifting a finger to earn any of it? That attitude really grinds your gears, I know it does—so why don't you go over there and pop him one in the kisser? Teach him how the world really works—random violence and pointless spite, get used to it, shithead. Kick his mum's arse while you're at it, because she's the one who raised him this way. You remember how it feels to split a woman's lip, right? This would be even better, because you'd *mean* it."

I glare at her, stung. "Oh, you bitch."

Thing is, yeah, I did split Toni's lip once, but it was an accident and I tell you it was one of the worst moments of my life, one of those horrible seconds when everything lines up perfectly for disaster: I'm a little drunk, grabbing the fridge door and pulling it open, and Toni's standing up fast from where she was squatting to fill Frost's water bowl, and my elbow and her mouth pass through the same space at the same time and *thump*, the sensation's travelling up my arm just as I realise what's happened and I'm turning in shock to see her staring at me and for just a moment I can tell that she thinks it was deliberate, *me* of all people doing this to her after all the promises I made not to be like her bastard ex, and then reason kicks in and she accepts my horrified apologies and wipes the tears from my eyes, but I can still feel the shock of impact and now I know how it feels to strike a woman and the only difference between me and a domestic abuser is the matter of intent, I would *never* choose to lash out like that and yet it doesn't matter because it happened and I felt it and now I *know* and I will carry it with me forever.

"I'm not doing that," I say, "I don't even *want* to hit anyone," and for a moment I see my fist crunching into a man's face, a very specific man's face, and I can tell from her grin that she saw it, too, and I know we'll be coming back to that before the night is through. "This might all be a bizarre dream, but for all I know, you're just some rando who broke into my house and talked me into going for a walk, and if I hurt someone, the consequences will be very real."

She pokes her tongue out at me, and just as I note that it's not forked, the tip splits in two and wags mockingly at me. I've only myself to blame for these clichéd demonic elements she's putting into play, because she's pulling them from my head. Thing is, I'm a total atheist and always have been—so where is all this devil shit coming from?

"Come on, Winkie. You know there are precisely two possibilities: either I'm an imaginary projection of your depression, your rage, grief, and self-hatred, or I'm an external influence that's somehow invaded your mind to push all those same buttons. It's up to you to decide which—but frankly, it doesn't matter, because you'll be dead all the same."

"Why do you *want* me to die? Why is it worth all this effort?"

"Because you don't deserve to live," she says, "and a girl's got to get her kicks somehow."

She ashes her cigar into the hat of a passing prepubescent pirate, who doesn't notice this minor cruelty or its perpetrator. His dog, a cute little beagle, stops for a moment to lick my hand hello and send me a mournful look before running after his captain. Perhaps my cantankerous companion can't be seen, but I can. Noted.

"They say that a man is defined by his work. Let's look at yours, shall we?"

The girl with the black dog tattoo gestures to her right—

\* \* \*

—and we're standing in front of the print shop where I spend forty hours of each week when I'm not taking time off to lie in bed and stare at the ceiling crying at the pointless misery of my ongoing existence. We're in the city proper now, and there are no trick-or-treaters in sight. It would've taken us hours to walk this far, yet the moon is still low in the sky. Maybe this is all just in my head, or maybe she can warp reality as well as read minds.

"You hate your job," she says. "You hate that your boss insists you call every man *sir*, and you cringe inside every time you say it. You hate that you have to toil away and please other people just so you can be allowed to live and do things for yourself. You hate wearing a uniform, as if you are as much the property of the business as any of the stock and hold as little worth. You hate having to wear a Santa hat in the Christmas season just because it's company policy, a lame jollity that loses its point by being strictly enforced. But most of all, you hate that you're a writer who's struggling to get published and noticed, yet you spend all day printing out the work of other people, shitty joke invitations and poorly composed posters and even crappy manuscripts. You hate feeling that you are so much better than all these people when you know deep down that you are really, truly, *nothing*."

She's right on all counts, of course. I've been going through the motions at this place for years, dreaming of something better and shying away from the risk involved in leaving.

I shrug. "It is a truth universally recognised that work sucks. So what?"

"Work reminds you that you're a tool to be used, a flesh asset and nothing more. Yet without a job, you're regarded as lazy scum by everyone from the government downwards, made to feel like a selfish drain on the country's resources. You have no other worth but to work. Essentially, you are a slave, and if you opt out, you'll be replaced and no-one will miss you. You're not needed and you're not appreciated. Your job *hates* you."

Her eyes pin me to the spot as she delivers this sermon, and they're so deep, so dark, so compelling. I can see worlds within worlds in there. Is it my own brain I'm seeing, or is she truly some supernatural entity intent on bringing me undone? And ultimately, does it even matter?

"It does not, and neither do you. But come on, this is Level One stuff. We've only just started."

She grins, and for a moment her jaw is distended too far and her teeth are long, yellow and lupine, and her tongue lashes her chops like that of a starving wolf. Then she looks normal again, or at least as normal as she can, but the dog inked on her arm is now wearing that same savage expression, like it's scented raw meat fresh and bleeding from the kill, and its eyes follow me around like those of an old portrait in a spooky mansion—and shit, a writer should be able to come up with a better analogy than that, even on the fly.

"Damn straight, Winkie. All these years sweating it out over a keyboard, and that's the best you can do? You're pathetic. And no-one knows that better than the ones who brought you kicking and squealing into this wretched world."

She grabs me by the shoulders, spins me around once, and—

\* \* \*

—now we're standing outside a Chinese restaurant on Gouger Street. She points through the golden-lettered window, past a roasted row of headless hanging ducks with whom I feel a sorry kinship, and I see my parents sitting at a table, clinking their glasses with my brother and his husband.

"Dear old Mum and Dad. Think of all they went through to birth and raise you with the highest of hopes, only to watch you wriggle through life like a worm through shit. At your age, they were running a successful business and raising two sons, regarded by their peers as genuinely good and worthwhile people, valid members of the community. What have *you* done, apart from get loaded, get fired, and let down any woman who got close enough to love you? You started bands that went nowhere fast and were forgotten even faster, wrote stories that were used as filler by backroom publishers who stopped caring as soon as their books hit Amazon with their titles in Chiller font on covers full of slapped-together clichés. You've been paid in exposure so much that if you could bank that shit, you'd be rich—but you've got no savings, no assets, no prospects. You want to see your future? Look over there."

She points farther up the footpath, where a scraggly old man in dirty track pants is fishing empty bottles and cans out of a bin and dropping them into a plastic bag. I always find that sight depressing, because I've often thought I could all too easily end up in such a miserable state. One guess where this harpy pulled that notion from.

"Lucky your folks had two kids. Your brother has carved out a place for himself through hard work and a drive to succeed. You think you've had it tough, Winkie? Can you imagine what it was like for *him*, growing up gay in less enlightened times, knowing that every day could bring him verbal abuse, violence, or even death? In other families, *he* might be the one considered a failure, since he'll not be carrying on the bloodline. He was always the quiet one, getting things done without drawing attention to himself, while you flounced around with your dyed hair and your rock star clothes and made out like you were going to be a big deal—and look how *that* panned out. Here he is, happily married and living in his own house, having dinner with your folks while you never even got so much as a text to ask if you were free.

"Mum and Dad have made their choice, pal. They don't waste any more love or time on you than they have to, and why should they? They've bailed you out time and time again, hoping one day you'd get your shit together and grow up—something you have singularly failed to do."

I watch my family for another long moment as they take pleasure in the simple rituals of food and good company, and I can't help but feel a yawning pit inside me that could only ever be filled by their pride. They've always told me they believed in me, loved me and supported whatever I wanted to do, but I've felt like a disappointment to them as far back as I can remember.

"It's Halloween," I mumble. "They know I always have plans for tonight. That's why they didn't ask me out."

"Yeah, keep telling yourself that."

She grabs my upper arm in a vulture-claw grip and pulls me along the footpath to where it opens out into a small alley. On the corner, a ragged man sits on a ragged blanket, and he's sorting through the cigarette butts he's plucked from the gutters, picking out what little tobacco he can find to make a wretched little roll-up. Beside him sits a gaunt hound, a mongrel of a thing as unkempt as her owner, her eyes just as glazed and hopeless.

"Take a good look at *true* despair, you self-indulgent tosser. This is what's waiting for you in the end, because you'll never get your act together enough to avoid it."

The cigar is back between her long fingers, and she sneers as she taps ash into the threadbare cap that this beggar has laid out to catch charity from any passers-by who deign to notice him.

Could she really be a part of me, this contemptuous thing?

I find my wallet and fish out a two-dollar coin to go in the cap along with her invisible gift of scorn. The man barely looks at me as he mumbles his thanks, and the dog raises her head long enough to make up for it by rubbing her cold nose on the backs of my fingers. I scratch her head, and her eyes lose that fog of despair for a moment as they meet mine. I could almost believe she's reaching out to me, relating, attempting to tell me something.

"Too late to start trying to make a difference now, boyo. You've already been judged and found wanting. Speaking of which...where do you suppose we're going next, hmmm?"

"Please don't," I mutter, and wish I hadn't. That's the sound of weakness, the blood in the water that attracts the predators. It's the begging whimper from a harassed and helpless child that lets the bullies know they can carry on and get away with anything they want.

She grins like a shark, makes a production of the coming transition. The black dog tattoo is grinning at me too, its slavering jaws wide, its pitiless eyes cruel.

"Time to really stick it in and break it off, sunshine. Time to show you what you've spent most of the year trying to avoid. Time to check in on the one thing that gave you hope, until you fucked it up like everything else in your lily-livered life.

"Next scene."

\* \* \*

And we're right where I knew we would be, outside the picket fence I had once painted myself, where yellow roses dangle over the wooden spear-tips to attract unwary fingers. Just a few metres away, a home I had entered as often as I had entered its occupant, and with no less pleasure. Oh, the nights I'd spent behind those doors, on those floors, under that shower, in that bed! The very best of times, and I'd never see their like again.

The bedroom light was on. Toni was home. And a strange car was parked deep in her driveway, a snug-fit metaphor for things I couldn't bear to imagine.

"You knew we were coming to this, Winkie. This is the big one. Shit, I don't even need to say anything, do I? Just look. And *know*."

Until earlier this year, Toni had been my sun, my moon, my gravity. I'd known she would always be there, and I'd taken that for granted—taken *her* for granted. She'd brought a million mundane miracles into my life, and I'd only noticed them when it suited me to do so. I loved her, I really did—still do, so much more than is healthy or right—and yet even as I held her close with one hand, I'd been steadily pushing her away with the other, and something fucked in my head had kept me from really noticing it or doing enough to prevent it even when I did. I wanted Toni more than anything I'd ever known, and I'd *had* her, and I'd not done justice to the love she'd offered me. More than anything, this is what was killing me: I had proved that I didn't deserve what I craved the most.

"No shit," says the girl with the black dog tattoo, and she looks more like Toni than ever, right down to the burning resentment in her eyes that I'd glimpsed in our worst arguments. "You had it all, and you didn't live up to your responsibilities, so now it's someone else's turn.

"Think of all the things she used to do for you in that bed, and know that right now, she's probably doing them for *him*. The looks she gave you that spoke of her love, desire, and trust; the special little touches that you thought were just for you; the endearments, the kisses, the thrusts, the intimacies. Now it's *his* Winkie that knows the keen grip of her fingers, the succulent favours of her mouth, the loving depths of her willing flesh. Doesn't it *burn* you, boy, to imagine how she moves beneath him, atop him, the variations of lust they try out together? To know you had all these things offered to you in perpetuity, and the only reason you no longer do is because you let her down harder than any man she's ever known? You used to shit-talk her ex, that misogynist prick whose treatment of her was downright criminal, but guess what? *You're even worse.*"

I close my eyes and grasp a rose stem. The thorns bite deep into my fingers, my palm, and I let the sting distract me from my thoughts. It lasts maybe a nanosecond. No pain could be greater than the one laid out before me—no pleasure greater than the one laid out before *him.*

"And after all the ways she's shown you that you're through, that she can't ever be with you again, you still love her."

I say nothing and tighten my grip on the rose stem until I swear I can feel the tips of its thorns grating against bone.

"*Pathetic.* You never could deal with change, could you? While she's in there working through her fantasies with her new man, you're under that ratty quilt getting yourself off to fading memories that are dead and gone forever. And don't think she doesn't know about that—she just chooses not to think about it. Why should she, when she's got someone else to occupy her time? Not to mention her orifices."

"Stop it," I mutter again, but this time it's not the cowed whine of a victim. It's a threat in and of itself. A hollow one, perhaps, but it's an assertion nonetheless.

"Oh, poor baby, getting all uptight because I'm besmirching the good name of your ex. What's so good about that cunt anyway? What is it you actually *love* about her, Winkie? Is it her eyes, those windows of the soul? They're just little pouches of vitreous jelly full of rods and cones and lenses, sitting in her skull like cheap cameras. The heart she pledged to you, and now to him? Just a lump of meat, an ugly, impartial pump for squeezing blood through transparent tubes. Those tits you lavished so much attention and affection on? Bags of subcutaneous fat, fit only for feeding mewling spawn. The woman you love is nothing more than a collection of grotesque shapes and fluids shoved into a sack of skin. She's shit and sweat and gas and acid, piss and pus and bile and blood, milk and mucus and meat. Everything you know of her, everything that makes her *her*, is just electrical impulses generated by a lump of veiny porridge. Where's the romance in that?"

She doesn't look much like Toni now. My former love once put a picture of me through an app that showed the user how they might look as the opposite sex, and it's pretty much that now glaring back at me throughout this putrid rant. Is this how I truly feel, down in the deepest Tartarus-black pits of my soul? Could I really be so hateful?

I close my eyes, think of Toni, and at first, all I can see is her writhing under the amorous attentions of my replacement, and again I think of smashing his fucking face in, as if it's all his fault and not mine. I push past the bitterness, think of the ways she used to smile at me, how she'd stare into my eyes as though she could read the base code of my very being—the countless little loving things she did for me, the thoughtful gifts, the selfless sacrifices she made just to be my lady.

*No.* She's far, far more than the sum of her parts, and my worst hurts will never be stronger than my love and respect for her. I repudiate all that this vinegar-tongued virago is saying.

"Everything is absurd if you reduce it to base components," I point out. "You're just a bunch of electrical impulses too, you know—and a nasty, pointless bunch at that."

The girl with the black dog tattoo spits a stream of steaming sputum onto Toni's roses. "Oh, but I do have a point, and it's to prove that you don't."

Maybe. I've certainly told myself that a thousand times these past months. I let go of the thorny stem, and the blood welling from my wounds looks almost black under the streetlight.

"If you're so willing to bleed, why don't you go the whole hog? Let it all out, Winkie. Every poisonous pint in your venomous veins. It's no good to you now, and certainly no good to anyone else."

I spy movement, and my heart lurches. The doggy door has flapped open and here comes Frost, the rescue dog we named after one of our favourite comic actors because he's a little pudgy and a lot charming. The dear little Jack Russell must have scented me, and now he's popping his front paws up on the fence, pushing his eager snout carefully through the roses to lick at my hand. There's a melancholy in his eyes as if he's missed me, or maybe he's just disturbed by the taste of blood on my skin. I whisper a greeting to my estranged boy and ruffle his head with my good hand, suddenly blinking away tears. I never thought I'd see him again, thought he'd be better off without my worthless arse intruding on his turf—but here I am and here he is, and he's as affectionate as he ever was. Toni might not be able to forgive my mistakes, but Frost would never doubt my worth for a second.

"My beautiful boy," I whisper, my voice ragged, and I can barely see him for the tears. "You're not a good dog, Frosty Flake. You're the best."

"How touching," sneers my companion, her tattoo snarling at my darling Frost like it wants to leap out of her skin and savage him. "It's just a dumb animal. You bought its loyalty with food and affection, but it'll take to the new guy just as well, and it will forget you. It's a traitor."

"Shut your fucking face," I growl. "And don't you dare call Frost an *it*."

My voice cuts through the silence of the street in a way that hers does not, and all at once I'm aware that it's going to be very awkward if Toni becomes aware of my presence out here. I'll look like a stalker, talking to myself and bleeding on her property, sweet-talking her pet like I'm trying to woo him away. Not good.

"Time to go," I say, ruffling Frost's head one last time.

"That's *my* line. I'm running the tour here, Winkie."

"Then let's go wherever it is you're planning to take me next. It can't be any worse than this."

"Fine. All aboard! Next stop, the end of the line."

\* \* \*

She takes me home, of course.

"Be it ever so humble," she sneers, waving one hand around as she drags me from lounge to hall to bedroom to kitchen. "Shit, *humble* isn't even the word. *Hovel* might be more appropriate. How long has it been since you dusted this place, dragged out the vacuum cleaner, moistened a fucking mop? If those dishes are left any longer, the mould on them will be advanced enough that cleaning it off would be murder. Way to *adult*, Winkie. I thought you were supposed to be a middle-aged man, not a toddler."

"You sound like my mum," I snap, only to see that dear woman all too clearly in this demon's face when it turns to glare at me.

"A home is a reflection of its occupants. What does it say about you that your abode is probably crawling with cockroaches? Apt, don't you think?"

"Oh, because cleaning is the measure of a man's worth," I shoot back. "Keep the lawns edged, the toilet sparkling and the oven immaculate, and you've earned yourself the right to live. *Bullshit.* Cleanliness is a pyrrhic victory, because the war against entropy is one you can never, ever win. I might be a bit of a slob, but that doesn't invalidate my life."

"*Everything about you* is invalid. Why do you exist? What do you bring to the world, that you deserve to consume its oxygen? What happiness, what help?"

"What does anyone? Most people don't cure diseases or invent new ways to see the world."

"*Most* people don't break hearts, waste their potential, and take up space that could have been used by someone more worthy."

"Of *course* they do!" I bark. "We're all fucked up. Every single one of us. So what?"

"Is *that* your argument? That you're no worse than the dregs of society? Come on, Winkie. You could have been so much *more.* You've got brains, much as it pains me to admit it, and you've got talent. But you've spent your whole life pissing your advantages up against a wall. Time for that to end. Here, let me show you how."

The girl with the black dog tattoo pulls me to the door of my bathroom.

"Under the sink, drain cleaner—swallow it. In the shower, a razor—break it open, slit your wrists. Fill the bath, drown yourself. And that's just the start." Back to the kitchen, raving like a madwoman now. "Oven—gas on, head in, game over. Knives in the drawer. Hell, you want to go out like some of your heroes, pour those bottles of wine down your throat as fast as you can and choke on your own puke. Start a fire. Find a live wire. Make a noose from a belt or extension cord and hang yourself—you can even jack off one last time as you go, just to give whoever finds you an image they won't forget in a hurry. This place is chock-full of methods to end your life. You're surrounded by ways out at every turn. *So why don't you just die?*"

She sounds almost desperate now. Could be that Mum was right when she called me the most stubborn person she's ever met.

"What's in it for you, you goddamn psychopath?" I realise I'm on to something here. "If I didn't exist, neither would you. You owe me your life!"

She howls in frustrated laughter. "Assuming I'm just a hallucination, perhaps...but what if I'm not? What if I'm something you can't even begin to understand?"

"Even then, you need me. I'm your prey. Your purpose. Without me, you're nothing."

She claps, her sneer an ugly mask. "Oh, nice try. Your cod philosophy is as trite as your attempts at profundity. That's like saying you owe your existence to pizza, and without it, you'd die."

"That's not what I'm saying, and you know it. It's like—all those TV shows and movies where the bad guys want to wipe out everyone in the universe? I mean, what happens if they win? What do they do *after* that? There'd be no point to their existence!"

"There's no point to what you're saying."

"If all you do is go around killing people, then you *need* people."

She shakes her head, almost sadly, but there's relish in the way both she and the dog tattoo lick their lips. "Thing is, Winkie...there are always *more* people. I can go on doing this for millennia—maybe I already have. Worthless as you are, you idiots just keep breeding. And as disgusting as that is, you're right—it keeps me in a job. So, sure, I need people—but I don't need *you*. And neither does anyone else. So: drain cleaner, razor, gas, alcohol, knives? Take your pick. If it helps, I'll be here with you while you go, and I'll hold your hand so you're not alone. I can look just like Toni while I do it, and I even promise not to gloat until you've shuffled off. Can't say fairer than that."

Did she just admit that she exists separately from me? That she's not some kind of sick construct of my own subconscious?

"What difference does it make? If I *was* you, wouldn't I say that anyway, just so you can believe this trial is something else that's not your fault? So you can blame a Big Bad Wolf for doing this to you and abdicate all personal responsibility? *Again?*"

"You're right," I admit. "It doesn't clear things up at all. But neither does it change anything. Because, believe it or not, *I* make a difference, and that's something you can't take away from me."

"Yes, you add to the amount of effluvium this poor world has to deal with. Good show."

"No, it's more than that. I know I don't amount to much, but I am *not* nothing. And if you want an example of that, all you have to do is look at the dogs."

She narrows her eyes at me.

"That's right. We met three of them tonight, and all of them came to me for a pat. Just that—just a second's solace—but for a moment, I made their lives better. They don't care that I broke my lover's heart and I'm devastated by that fact and can't forgive myself for it. They don't care that I haven't become the golden boy I could've been if I just applied myself better. They sense that they can reach out to me, and they do, and for a second, we connect in the most simple and innocent way. So, even if you want to discount the happiness that I *have* brought to the world—to my family, my lovers, my friends, even to total strangers—well, there's still that.

"Dogs are a good judge of character, and they *like* me, and you know what—I like them, too. To them, I pass muster. I *matter*."

I'm looming over her now, going on the offensive, and she's still sneering, but she seems to be shrinking into her saddle shoes, and the snarling face inked on her arm is just that—an image that can be ignored, a thought that can be dismissed.

"In fact, I should thank you for showing up tonight, because you've helped me to see this. Well done to you, girl with the black dog tattoo! I could even write all this shit down, get a story out of it. So much for convincing me to die—you've done the opposite! *You've failed!* So you can take your stinky cigar and all your rancid rants and you can stick them approximately eighteen kilometres up your possibly imaginary *arse!*"

I rock back on my heels. I'm yelling at my kitchen wall.

She's gone.

And I'm standing here in my house, alone and fully dressed, with the night pressing itself up against my windows to peer curiously in at this weirdo screaming at nothing.

But at least I'm still standing. Sometimes, that's triumph enough.

I don't know what to think about all this—don't know if I travelled across the city in mere minutes or spent the whole trip right here at my home, lost in insidious illusions. My hand is bleeding, yes, but that could be from anything, even the roses in my own yard. I don't know if I just banished my own self-hatred for a spell or if I vanquished something vile from an outer plane, and I don't know if this victory will stand or if I've won just one more battle in a lifelong war. After all, whether she's me or not, the girl with the black dog tattoo feels too familiar to be something new in my life, so maybe I've faced her down before—maybe this is a campaign I've fought each and every night and then forgotten. I don't know what to think. But I know what I can do now.

I walk down my hall, past the bookshelf that holds the trophies of my tiny life—the CDs I made with my bands, the books I've been published in, the framed photos of joyous moments and flawed but wonderful people who helped define my miserable but not unworthy life—and I enter the lounge, where my laptop waits for me to lift its lid. I do so. And I start to write.

# [Afterwords]

THERE IS NO SUCH thing as a born artist. We emerge as blank pages that will become palimpsests over time, written and rewritten to suit the needs of ourselves and others—a human life is a dog-eared exercise book full of sloppy scribbles, furious cross-outs, and prudent self-edits, an ongoing first and (I believe) final draft of a story that no-one else can ever tell quite the same way. But how much impact do those first few pages have upon the story entire? How soon does the tale begin to take shape in ways that will echo throughout the decades of narrative to come? In essence: can a story's outcome be guessed even from the very first line?

I wouldn't have thought so. After all, apart from a hazy recollection of being spoon-fed to the tune of Dad-made aeroplane noises, I can't consciously recall many memories from before the age of three or so. But they still exist, splinters of experience I was too unformed to understand at the time—fragments too minute to grasp with adult fingers or see with adult eyes. Some of them may even date back to my expulsion from the womb, the first true event of anyone's life and one of the most formative and traumatic moments we will ever know. Lately, I'm inclined to believe that this is the case. And here is why.

Here is my first page.

Though I was once presumably quite the spunk, nimble of nucleus and fleet of flagellum, I proved to be a rather diffident foetus. I barely moved or kicked as Mum carried me to term, so indolent that her own mother questioned whether I was even alive in there. I seemed happy to take my time, so Mum was startled when, after eight quiet months, her waters broke and announced my imminent arrival. She duly headed to the hospital, where I continued to confound expectations by refusing to budge for two days. Her waters dried up and I became distressed, so the decision was made to pull me out. The team prepped Mum for the pain to come by giving her a dose of ether.

Deep in the grip of anaesthesia and wracked by the throes of childbirth, Mum was visited by my maternal grandfather. But Poppa Benton hadn't come to hold her hand and help her through the ordeal. Having fought off illness long enough to see his youngest daughter married, he had passed away shortly after my parents' wedding. Now here he was two years later, comforting Mum as she cried—telling her that soon, she would need to be there to help her mother, his widow, my Nanna.

At 7:50pm on Wednesday May 11, yours truly made a typically tardy and dramatic entrance to this world—torn from the womb by forceps as Mum sobbed through a conversation with her dead father. Born almost three weeks premature with a V-shaped impression on my forehead from the forceps that would take a year to fade, I was yellow with jaundice, and after a quick introduction to my parents, I was whisked away to another room to spend the first twenty-four hours of my life alone and blindfolded in an incubator, denied my mother's loving touch.

I know what you're thinking, and it's the same thing that crossed my mind when I finally heard this story not so long ago. Ether is some pretty heavy shit, so is it any surprise that Mum saw someone who couldn't possibly be there? But even I had to check my natural scepticism when I heard the next part of the tale.

A couple of years on from that strange day, I was healthy and developing normally as far as anyone could tell; Mum was five months pregnant with my brother Ethan. On May 11 at around 8pm, her sister Glenys came home from a run and went to bed feeling dazed and sick. Sadly, she never woke up. A cerebral haemorrhage kept her under for a couple of days until the hard choice was made to let her go. And so, just as predicted by my deceased grandfather two years before—to the very day, almost to the very *minute*—Mum had to look after Nanna as she grieved the tragic loss of a child.

Now, my mother has never been prone to flights of fancy. She's always been the pragmatist of our family, keeping three dreamy boys anchored to reality even as she allowed us the room to be whoever we wanted to be. She told me this history as a simple matter of fact, never once veering off into speculation—and I, of course, immediately made plans to write about it.

Because that's who I am and who I feel I've always been, and maybe now you can see the seeds of it right there at the start. I grew up a happy and healthy child, but as they say, Wednesday's child is full of woe: I was also thoughtful and melancholy, overly sensitive and sentimental, given to roaming off to be alone with my thoughts and drawn to the darker side of life. Mum started reading to me at a very early age, filling my head with words and colours and ideas—she introduced me to *story*, and I took to it like a duck to water. From the very first, I was writing tales that involved giant chickens, poop jokes, and decapitation; I loved action films, and that was where I came by much of my interest in gore and spectacle, but the darkness kept creeping in. I swiftly dismissed religion as preposterous but found myself fascinated by fantastical beasts and mythological monsters: ghouls and ghasts, gorgons and ghosts, vampires and werewolves, dragons and demons—even Elizabeth Bathory turned up as the villain in a story I wrote at age ten. When I wasn't working through my early propensity for comedy, I was walking into the shadows to see what I could find there. And the older I grew—the thinner the palimpsest became, written over and over until old fears could no longer be seen, only felt with eyes closed and mind open—the more I discovered. After all, *everything* casts a shadow, and the more I looked, the more I recognised the tell-tale movements within each one. I learned that every inch of the dark is seething and heaving with nightmares, anxieties, guilts, traumas. And the more I saw, the more I wrote.

My beginning makes perfect sense to me now, as I continue to learn more about myself and the weird way my brain works. So, I was born during either a supernatural experience or a drug-induced hallucination? Well, every story in this book features paranormal happenings, and sure, I've done more than my fair share of substances. So, I spent the first day of my life alone, blinded, untouched? Well, for many years I believed I would never know love and intimacy because I felt utterly undeserving of them, and I still struggle with that sense of unworthiness now. You can see how, for me, learning the story of my birth was like hearing a missing puzzle piece snap into place. It doesn't explain everything, but, man...doesn't it just feel *right?* I was born amid ghosts and loneliness, so it seems fitting that I grew into a dreamer who felt everything so deeply it hurt and tried to deal with the confusing complexity of existence by turning it into art. You don't need such shadings to be a writer—I'm sure there are plenty of great, well-adjusted authors who cruised right out of the womb like a kid on a waterslide and never spent so much as a minute hating themselves without understanding why, or feeling guilty because their parents have spent so much love and money on them, or believing everything they ever do is just another clownish fuck-up—but I don't see how they could be of any use to an accountant, you feel me?

Again: there is no such thing as a born artist...but, looking back, I can't see how I could ever have been anything else. And I wouldn't ever *want* to be, because the songs and stories I have created mean the world to me. I've often questioned my personal worth and the validity of my continued existence, but *never* that of my work, and knowing that I can do this one beautiful thing has undoubtedly saved my life. These expressions are, in a sense, the best of me, and I can only hope they mean something to you, too.

Now, let's look at the circumstances of *their* births, eldest to youngest, and see what shaped them into the tales they've come to be.


### "The Black Regent" (August 2000)

I think of my collections much the way I think of albums, which means that sometimes a straight-up banger is required to provide contrast to the deeper, moodier material—enter "The Black Regent". This was written *way* back when I still lived in Port Pirie and initially featured actual VHS tapes at Magellan Video; the store didn't have a name then, but it's popped up in my fiction a couple of times since. The tale's age provides a small tingle of nostalgia now—Adelaide's movie rental stores are almost entirely gone, though permit me to give a quick shout out to the last one standing, Galactic Video, and also to Vicious Video, a local trader that sells cult VHS tapes (and kindly stocks my books). Old stories seldom receive any attention from me in these more exacting times, but this one earned its redemption through periodic rewrites and now stands as a monument to persistence—it took *twenty-one years* to find a home!

Josie Hughes was a rare double-dip character for me at the time, going on to gobble up a supporting role in an unpublished novel called *We'll At Night Play*, a kind of Laymon-does-*Beowulf* story where she was shot by a maniac and her fate left undefined. That manuscript didn't age well, though, so we can ignore it and assume she went on to bigger, if not brighter, things. So long as she kept a few steps ahead of old Buller, that is...

## "Thee Most Exalted Potentate of Love" (May-June 2014)

Originally called "Jamie Rosethorne and the Souljacker Blues" because I couldn't think of anything better, this story ended up sharing a name with the Cramps song that features in it. The unfinished first draft was set in a strip club and featured ladies dancing to Kendrick Lamar, but it just wasn't coming together until I thought of the burlesque posters I'd been putting up for the Adelaide Fringe and the lightbulb went on. The Thai thug Konz was named after my neighbour at the time, who would shout me weed and Heineken and ramble on for hours—a mercurial parolee well-versed in Muay Thai who once almost attacked me with broken beer bottles for mentioning the colour pink and who turned up in another story, "His Favourite Phantom", in a toned-down form that still comes across almost as an insensitive caricature!

I wanted to include this story for its gallery of grotesques, its salty tone, and its unapologetic violence—it can't all be narrative navel-gazing and poetic subtexts about grief and guilt, you know. It's a rare story of mine that features guns, partly because they're not a part of daily life in Australia unless you're a farmer and mostly because *fuck* guns, but let's not dwell on the knotty implications of glamourising them when we just came to the Burly Baby Bar to have a drink and get our freak on. That venue and its house band turn up in another novella, so it seems they survived this catastrophic interlude to entertain another day.

## "Steadfast Shadowsong" (July 2016-January 2017)

I've been involved with Owen Gillett's band icecocoon since the very start—producing some early four-track demos and helping behind the scenes before joining an early incarnation of the group on keyboards. I soon shifted to five-string bass, and over the course of six albums (two unreleased) and many years, the fluctuating line-up has often reduced to just Owen and myself. In 2016, we decided to do something different and play a pair of icecocoon songs as an acoustic two-piece at a couple of open mic nights; I say different because our previous gig had been supporting UK alt-prog outfit Anathema and our next-but-one would be warming up for US concept rockers Queensrÿche. Accompanied by Meg (whom I'd just started seeing) and Amie, Owen's partner at the time, we duly turned up at the Daniel O'Connell and The Grace Emily to perform our drastically stripped-down numbers—and at the latter pub, I got to thinking I'd like to write something using an open mic gig as a setting. An early version set at a seaside pub left me cold, but I started afresh at the end of the year and finished it at Meg's kitchen table while Amie was over, lending a neat circularity to things.

The story took a few drafts and close publication calls before it found its true shape, but I rather like the way it turned out, and I mustn't be the only one. "Steadfast Shadowsong" was one of two 2019 Australasian Shadows Awards winners for me (standalone novelette *Supermassive Black Mass* was the second), and the fact that Kaaron Warren is the only other author to win two in one year is a healthy serve of validation for all the work I've put into my writing. Another came when I met *The Stranger* author Kathryn Hore in 2023 and she remembered me by this story—she'd read it as part of the Shadows judging panel and had never forgotten it.

This story could be seen as a derogatory flex toward musicians who focus their efforts on cover songs and tribute acts, and whilst I have friends who do that...well, *mea culpa*. Sure, I started out on covers as a teen like everyone else—it's a good way to learn song structures, confidence, how to play with others and before a crowd—but I switched to my own compositions as soon as I could and never looked back. Originality is everything to me, and obsequious regurgitation is anathema. I'll never turn into one of those snowy-bearded white men in pork pie hats hacking out blues progressions under the delusion that returning to a simple classicist approach signifies maturity. Fuck that! I love music too dearly to give it anything less than everything, and since every little project I think up seems to swiftly develop into a full-blown opus beyond my increasingly disorganised ability to realise, I think I'd better stick to fiction as my main jam. For instance, I had the mad idea to record a companion album for this book...but time and life got the better of me again.

## "Andromeda Ascends" (February 2018)

A writer comes to know their own stories very well, but this one feels strangely unfamiliar to me, and the circumstances under which I wrote it must account for that. I bashed out the first draft in four days and then managed to strain my back at work, the pain growing steadily worse over a weekend which included a live reading with

Paroxysm Press—and when I went to see a doctor, I tripped on a footpath and only kept myself from faceplanting into the cement by spraining both wrists! Thus, my recollection of this story is the four days I spent curled up delicately on the couch at the house Meg and I had recently moved into, feverishly editing with claw-like hands...and perhaps that explains why this tale feels fresh every time I read it, in a way that others, subject to hours and hours of revision and hence familiar almost to the point of contempt, do not.

The expensive, modernist beachfront house came straight from the Brighton esplanade, where I often strolled by night to take in the sea breeze and mull over story ideas. My first take on this concept bore the working title of "Barron Skye", because the touchstones I had in mind were Laird Barron and Mastodon's *Crack the Skye*; I soon decided it was too exploitative of its inspirations and rebuilt it into the version that went on to be my first nomination for an Aurealis Award. "Andromeda Ascends" was originally published between stories by Brian Lumley and Clive Barker, which made the table of contents a real thrill to read, and it was my first work to appear in another language, translated into Polish by Emilian Wojnowksi for *Nowa Fantastyka* magazine in 2024.

## "The Ballad of Elvis O'Malley" (May 2017-April 2018)

This story was born as I drove around on my postering job, listening to Adelaide rockabilly band The Saucermen. It got me thinking about a young guy back in Port Pirie whom everyone knew as Elvis, who drove an old Caddy and even sang in an old-school rock 'n' roll band, and one of my grandparents' neighbours who became his girlfriend and adopted his retro style. I was curious as to how someone like that would make their way in a modern society, what role they could possibly play so far out of the time in which they clearly wished they could exist. For some reason I decided to make it a pseudo-historical story, addressing the 1950s elements from a 2006 context, all narrated from some nebulous present day.

I didn't know how this story was going to end when I began writing it, so it took a while to find its conclusion; one draft was sent to a magazine looking for Stephen King-inspired stories, so I leaned into the *Carrie* and *Christine* comparisons in that one before easing off again. It ended up in a flash fiction anthology to benefit those affected by the Australian bushfires of 2020...and no, your eyes do not deceive you: "The Ballad of Elvis O'Malley" is not, in fact, flash fiction at all. You may have noticed that I can be a bit *extra* on occasion. (Women wearily nod. Wolves howl. The world spins on.)

## "Pilgrimage" (August 2017-July 2018)

This story is set in Brisbane's Fortitude Valley, which I visited in 2017 when icecocoon flew over to play an industry show headlined by Devin Townsend. (We went out drinking with the Dyssidia boys afterward and I missed my flight home the next morning, needing Meg to bail me out so I could perform a spoken-word gig in Adelaide that night—very rock 'n' roll!) The tale functions as a fond tribute to the legendary Lemmy Kilmister of Motörhead, who passed away at the end of 2015; the rather direct working title reminded me of the Nine Inch Nails song by the same name, which is why I didn't change it to something more typically flowery. This story was shortlisted for a 2019 Aurealis Award alongside *Supermassive Black Mass*.

## "Our Tragic Heroine" (March 2019)

A rather basic genesis here: I sat down with a few Rekorderlig ciders and watched a Blu-ray of Jane's Addiction playing *Ritual de lo Habitual* live, then opened my laptop and began to write this story off the top of my head. I was back in Pirie to do some work with my folks, and so this tale began at their kitchen table, where I had once pecked out my early stories on a manual typewriter and then an electric one. "Our Tragic Heroine" explores the thin line between inspiration and exploitation and examines how good intentions can blind people to the ugly underbelly of their actions—something I'd recently been reminded of in a very personal and painful way.

## "I Do Thee Woe" (August-September 2019)

This tale has its roots in my time at film school—a few small details from my year at MAPS made it into the story, though the characters and situations are cut from whole cloth. The title is a rather poetic translation of Rammstein's "Ich tu dir weh" that I once saw online and that subsequently disappeared from the internet as if it never existed. Cheers, I'm having that!

There are a few connections to my other work in this one. (Let's get ahead of ourselves and call it the Matthewniverse. Badoom-tish!) The Viceroy is the sister theatre to the Black Regent, which has a tale of its own between these very covers, and Dragan used to work at Magellan Video, where Warren is employed (and also the Alita mentioned here, the protagonist of a novella yet to find a home). *The Hunt for Candy Parker* is a 1981 Australian slasher film that I invented for an unpublished novel; the attentive reader will note that a poster appears elsewhere in this book, and both the movie and its lead actress play a larger role in the published but uncollected "His Favourite Phantom."

### "Vision Thing" (November-December 2019)

This story was written specifically for *Black Dogs, Black Tales*, and its working title was "The Girl with the Black Dog Tattoo". The anthology's remit to discuss depression gave me free rein to dig into that subject, and I really opened myself up and bled onto the page for this one—I was separated from Meg and in a wretched emotional place, so a lot of scalding truth and merciless self-examination made its way into the fiction. Such flagellation can make for a real slog of a read, but I hope I managed to evoke the truth of these feelings without wallowing in them—self-loathing can become an oddly masturbatory act if indulged too deeply. (The fact that the story was shortlisted for an Australasian Shadows Award implies that I may have succeeded.) The Sisters of Mercy references, including the title, came about because I had seen them live just a few days before I started writing this.

Though "Vision Thing" expresses a lot of ugly confusion, depression, and pain, it does cling on to a mote of hope, and it's very much worth noting that things did turn out for the best in the end: Meg and I took the time to work on our broken relationship, and we reconciled a few months after this tale first saw print. I should point out, however, that whilst we love dogs—and animals as a general principle—we're cat people at heart.

### "Heritage Hill" (April 2020)

Steve Dillon tapped me to write a story for *Outback Horrors Down Under*, with the only stipulation being that it had to have an

237

Antipodean theme or setting. *What's something that is intrinsically Australian?* I thought to myself. *Oh, I know—institutionalised racism!* And on that merry note, I started laying the tracks for this deeply angry and appalled story.

I don't usually grind my axes so openly in fiction, but the subject of bigotry is one that has long engaged and enraged me. "You can't say that in front of him, he doesn't like racism," my mates would advise newcomers back in the day, like it was some weird fucking quirk of character and not a reasonable response to a deeply ingrained and shameful aspect of our national character. Oh, yes, it is, my friends, and if you don't agree, maybe you're a part of the problem: Australia held a public referendum to decide whether to add our First Nations peoples to the constitution and let them advise on matters that directly impact them, and the majority of our population voted *against* it—in *2023*. Our chequered history and how to deal with it now is a complicated issue, and a lot of folks were confused or misinformed or had concerns about the process, but *for fuck's sake*, people...!

The titular hill is based on a similar one in Port Pirie, and for some time I'd been planning to write a warm, nostalgic piece based on a youthful experience of standing up there at three in the morning, watching the lightning with some friends in the gentle summer rain. With my new and much less cuddly theme in mind, I wanted to avoid making my narrator a right-on white dude or an indigenous Australian (predictable and presumptuous, in that order), so I cast them as an African-Australian. Azalea can relate to the central issues because she's black, but since she's not native to this country, she's still set at a cultural remove—and at another, in some ways, because she's also queer. (That angle was organic, since the original concept had a guy yearning for a girl and she simply stepped into his place.) I enjoy exploring different perspectives, and I hope I do them justice by treating them with the respect and understanding they deserve.

For me, this character work was validated when "Heritage Hill" was shortlisted for a 2020 Shirley Jackson Award. As a fan of Shirley's incisive texts—*The Haunting of Hill House* is my favourite, natch—it's an achievement in which I take a great deal of pride. (The award went to my mate J. Ashley-Smith for his great novella *The Attic Tragedy*, so I honestly didn't much mind losing.) This tale was also shortlisted for the Washington Science Fiction Association Small Press Award, and Steve Dillon read it on Print Radio Tasmania in 2023. I thought this story might be my most contentious, but so far, it's possibly the most prestigious.

## "A Walking Wound" (July 2020)

The seed of this story was planted as I sat and ate chips one night, staring out the window of the Perrys service station at Dublin—not the one in Ireland, sad to say. The protagonist is a redheaded bassist and photographer because I'd been listening to L7, a band I've dug since I was fifteen; Jennifer Finch was the reference point here, and though I find that placeholder names rarely stick, this one did. (The fact that I'm in love with a redheaded bassist and photographer is, for once, purely coincidental.)

I could've delved a lot deeper into life on tour here, and I may well do so in the future. I have such fond memories of being crammed into Tarago vans and hotel rooms with my brothers in Blood Red Renaissance as we touted our musical wares across the country: the camaraderie and the shenanigans, the sweaty catharsis of the shows, the laughter and the drinking, the seemingly endless flatulence. We played to tiny crowds and trashed nary a hotel room, but *damn*, man...I really miss it.

## "The Haunted Heart of Ebon Eidolon" (June-October 2020)

The first weekend of June 2020 was a real rollercoaster.

Friday began with the news that my friend Raven Baylock had passed away, so there were tears before I'd even gotten out of bed. A queer multi-media performance artist who was widely loved for his gentle and supportive nature, Raven entered my orbit many years ago through Emily, who had joined icecocoon as a keyboardist and then became my girlfriend; he provided make-up and gore effects for some Blood Red Renaissance live shows and the photo shoots I directed for the sleeve of our first record, *Champagne Tragedy*. Despite his gentility, he created a performance piece for the album launch that involved him tearing a man's heart out, and he once promised to cut my throat if I ever messed Emily around, so it's safe to say he was a man of many shades! We stayed in vague touch over the years, though, like many, I regretted not trying harder when I learned he'd passed—the last time I saw him was at The Coffee Pot bar in 2016, where he made an instant impression on Meg. She and I were separated when the bad news broke and hadn't seen each other for three months, but she came over to my house that night to check on me, a reconnection that led to us working through our issues and ultimately healing our relationship—in a way, a final loving gift from our dear, departed friend. The next night, I was enjoying the latest Laird Barron novel with a quiet rum or three when I received the news that I'd won two Australasian Shadows Awards. Like I said—rollercoaster!

Owen and I attended a memorial gathering shortly after news got around, and on Halloween of that year, Raven's final, posthumous exhibition was held. At some point between those two nights, I thought about doing something in his memory and figured I could write a story as a tribute to him. I approached the organisers with the suggestion of handing out a free booklet on the night, and they agreed that he would have loved the idea. I wanted to work with Meg, but she was recovering from a bout of pneumonia; I rediscovered a creepy picture of a sideshow clown she'd shot in 2017 and liked it so much that the image then fed back into the story to tie the whole thing together. I printed up thirty-three copies of the booklet under the imprint of idiotsavantgarde, a tinpot record label I created to release BRR's music, and nervously handed them out at the exhibition. I was rather worried that I'd bitten off more than I could chew: here I was, a cishet man writing about queer and trans people in full knowledge that they would comprise most of the work's initial audience! But the feedback I received was warm, and people loved the gesture. I got to hang with some old friends I hadn't seen in years, including Emily, and made some new ones too. Even in his absence, Raven brings people together through respect and love, and that's what I tried to show with this story...even if there's a rather downbeat ending to it all.

The Plastered Cast is a thinly disguised version of the Broadcast Bar (RIP), where I performed at Paroxysm Press shows and launched *If Only Tonight We Could Sleep* with a live reading/acoustic gig that included a cover of the Cure song that lent the book its title. (It's up on YouTube if you're feeling adventurous. Yes, I remember what I wrote about cover bands just a few pages ago! This was a one-off and the rest of the set was comprised of my songs.) I've made a small change to this tale since the booklet version and its reprint in Bards & Sages' *Best Indie Speculative Fiction of the Year IV*: one of the artists initially appearing on the bar's playlist had some shocking charges of abuse levelled at them, and as I no longer felt comfortable seeing their name attached to a loving tribute, I swapped them out for someone less problematic.

Oh, and I strongly recommend you look up Red Wallflower if you like your art dark, beautiful, and original—Meg has done book and magazine covers, album sleeves, urbexing, art shoots, live band photography, and so much more. She's a genuine artist in a way that too few people ever are, and she thoroughly deserved her 2024 Ditmar Award for Best Artwork. You rock, baby.

## "Nymphaea" (August 2020-July 2021)

Given some of its queasier themes, I guess the main thing I want to say about this story is that it's not autobiographical, though certain elements are taken from my life. The Hendricks house is based on the home of my dear friend/BRR guitarist Hutchie and his wife Renee, and he and I sometimes used to go bushwalking of a Sunday morning, and I did attend a few, er, *ecstatic* raves back in the day...and I did have a framed Waterhouse print hanging in my bathroom when I wrote this, but it featured just the one woman, and she was wearing clothes. That said, this story did feel somewhat uncomfortable to write, and that unease was what persuaded me to pursue it—if an idea makes you squirm, you've probably touched on something worth addressing.

It was the conflation of the gorgeous views I saw walking in the Adelaide Hills with possible permutations of *Hylas and the Nymphs* that led to this tale's birth, though it took a while for me to work it out. Even before I started, much of that beautiful scenery was ravaged by bushfires, and as I didn't really know where things were going, the ending had to find itself. Sometimes I just keep on writing until a line announces itself as the last one, and then I know I'm done.

And now for the part everyone loves: lists of other people's names!

Thank you, Scarlett, for taking on another of my books and gently shepherding it to publication.

Thank you, Sean, for your thoughtful editing suggestions.

Thank you, Don, for another fantastic cover.

Thank you, everyone who took the time to read this manuscript and provide some eloquent promotional praise. I love your work and it's honestly an honour to know that you appreciate mine.

Thank you, editors who selected these stories for their first publication—R.E. Sargent & Steven Pajak; Steve Dillon; Eugene Johnson; Chris Mason & Louise Zedda-Sampson; Tee Wood & Cassie Hart; Peter Kirk; Paula Dias Garcia, Sam Agar, Marc Clohessy & Issy Flower; Jarrod Barbee & Patrick C. Harrison III—as well as the sub-editors who proffered advice on how to make them better. Know that when I reject suggestions, it's never done without good reason and I'm very grateful for the ones that stick.

Thank you, Horror Tree, Darknotes (RIP), Authortunities, Duotrope, and various Facebook groups with long names too unwieldy to reproduce here, for spreading the word about open submission calls.

Thank you, Tracy Crisp, for drawing my attention to Barbara Hanrahan's article "Weird Adelaide" as quoted in the epigraph, and for that time we hung out in the Port Pirie library talking about writing.

Thank you, everyone who has ever taken the time to read, review, and/or promote my work—and yes, that very much includes *you*. I'd say I couldn't do it without you, but that would be patently untrue since I'd do it even if no-one cared, so let's say you make it so much more worthwhile, and I deeply appreciate you.

Thank you, fellow writers and workers in the Australia/New Zealand spec-fic community (and abroad, too), for your boundless support, friendship, talent, and kindness. You're my people and I couldn't ask for a lovelier bunch of weirdos with whom to drink booze, share trials, and talk shit.

Thank you, musicians who broadened my mind, opened my heart, educated me about other cultures and lifestyles, and inspired me to speak my own truth. I've namedropped a few herein—as well as a few I don't personally care for that were contextually appropriate—but there could never be enough space to list every artist whose work is a part of my life, nor all the fellow music addicts who have shared a stage or studio with me over the years.

Thank you, everyone who is trying in their own way, big or small, to make the world a kinder and safer place for all people to live a free and genuine life. There's a push for artists to be apolitical lest they alienate potential fans (or income streams), but all art *is* political in what it doesn't say as much as what it does, in what it chooses or refuses to address about the world, and horror even more so—and if you've read this far, you'll know that I stand firmly on the side of compassion, education, and alliance, and the hatemongers twisting this world into a stupider, crueller place can fuck right off.

Thank you, Dad, and Ethan and Nicole, and especially Mum for allowing me to tell your story of my birth. I love you.

And thank you, Meg, for more things than I could possibly enumerate here without boring even you to tears. It's a long, hard road we've walked together, and I'll never truly deserve your grace, but it's a privilege to be your chosen one and I love you madly, for always.

# Publication History

"Andromeda Ascends" first appeared in *Beneath the Waves: Tales from the Deep*, Things in the Well, 2018.

"Steadfast Shadowsong" first appeared in *Dig Two Graves Vol. 1*, Death's Head Press, 2019.

"A Walking Wound" first appeared in *Another Name for Darkness*, Sans PRESS., 2023.

"The Haunted Heart of Ebon Eidolon" first appeared in *The Haunted Heart of Ebon Eidolon: A Dark Tale in Tribute to Raven Baylock*, idiotsavantgarde, 2020.

"The Ballad of Elvis O'Malley" first appeared in *Burning Love and Bleeding Hearts*, Things in the Well, 2020.

"I Do Thee Woe" first appeared in *Screaming in the Night: Sinister Supernatural Stories Vol. 1*, Sinister Smile Press, 2022.

"Pilgrimage" first appeared in *Breach #10*, 2019.

"Heritage Hill" first appeared in *Outback Horrors Down Under: An Anthology of Antipodean Terrors*, Things in the Well, 2020.

"Our Tragic Heroine" first appeared in *Tales of the Lost Volume 2*, Plaid Dragon Publishing/Things in the Well, 2020.

"Thee Most Exalted Potentate of Love" first appeared in *If I Die Before I Wake Vol. 7: Tales of Savagery and Slaughter*, Sinister Smile Press, 2022

Matthew R. Davis

"Nymphaea" is original to this collection.

"The Black Regent" first appeared in *If I Die Before I Wake Vol. 4: Tales of Nightmare Creatures*, Sinister Smile Press, 2021.

"Vision Thing" first appeared in *Black Dogs, Black Tales*, Things in the Well, 2020.

# About the Author

Matthew R. Davis grew up in Port Pirie and has lived in Adelaide (Tarndanya), South Australia, for most of his adult life. He has won two Australasian Shadows Awards and has been shortlisted for a Shirley Jackson Award, a Ditmar Award, a Washington Science Fiction Association Small Press Award, and multiple Shadows and Aurealis Awards. He has published around a hundred short stories and is the author of *Supermassive Black Mass* (2019), *If Only Tonight*

*We Could Sleep* (2020), *Midnight in the Chapel of Love* (2021), *The Dark Matter of Natasha* (2022), *Bites Eyes: 13 Macabre Morsels* (2023), *On Track...The Cure: Every Album, Every Song* (2025), and *Ribspreader: The Novelisation and the Screenplay* (with Dick Dale, 2025). He has been the lead vocalist, bassist, and main songwriter for Blood Red Renaissance and bassist/backing vocalist for icecocoon; he plays multiple instruments, has performed in many bands since the age of eighteen, and has written hundreds of songs. He likes to dabble in other mediums including spoken word, graphic design, poetry, and indie film. He shares his life with the award-winning artist Meg Wright, aka Red Wallflower, and her cats Juniper and Lexi.

www.ingramcontent.com/pod-product-compliance
Lightning Source LLC
Chambersburg PA
CBHW020359030726
47496CB00007B/2210